THE JANUARY HOURS

S.G. Tasz

The Uglycat Press
Las Vegas, NV

Copyright © 2021 by S.G. Tasz

Editing services provided by Chimera Editing.
www.chimeraediting.com

Cover design and character art by Joseph Reedy.

ISBN: 978-1-7340752-6-7

To family near and far, far away.

TABLE OF CONTENTS

Book I

WELCOME TO HALCYON

Chapter One

Charlie slid the mop across the cobblestones, keeping his head down to avoid the grimacing eyes of Atlas looming overhead. It had always creeped him out, that tortured look on the planet-saddled Titan's face, as if the sculptor had captured him in the moment before his strength failed. A spigot on top of the globe sent water cascading into the shallow pool below the statue when the place was open. But it was after midnight now and the fountain, like everything else, stood silent and still.

He splashed the mop into the yellow plastic bucket, letting the water dribble off the soaked yarn a little longer than necessary before slopping it onto the floor. The thick silence once again filled the room like a heavy cotton quilt, constricting his chest and sealing his mouth. Taking a single breath felt like a grave offense.

And yet without that stifled nothingness, he wouldn't have heard the soft scuffle behind him, the subtle *chk-chk-chk* near the entrance of Ripped! Fitness and Nutrition.

He wouldn't have made sure to keep his head down and his shoulders loose to project oblivious calm.

He wouldn't have swerved the mop in such a way that he could pull the six-inch Bowie knife from his belt without breaking his natural movement.

He would not have whipped around to upset the ambush in a perfect fake out.

At least, it would have been perfect—except that there was no one there.

"Hello?" he demanded of the empty hallway, keeping his voice low so as not to ruffle the overly sensitive silence. "Is someone here?"

No answer. No movement. Only the silence, resealing its soft, smothering self around him even thicker than before. He tightened his grip on the knife as his palms started to sweat. He *had* heard something. He was almost certain of it. Then again, dead silence was a tricky thing. You could listen with all your might, and in the end, it would turn out to be nothing. Nothing but your own blood racing through your veins.

Chk-chk-chk.

His ears perked. *That* wasn't nothing. That was the same scuffling sound, behind him again.

No. Not just behind.

You idiot, he thought, rolling his eyes in self-reproach. *You know better than that. You know better than to avoid looking up.*

Flipping his knife so the blade stood upright, he crouched, then sprang, pivoting in the air as he prepared to attack. Another perfectly executed move, save for one thing: the wet, slippery floor. Instead of whirling into a coordinated strike, his ankle wrenched to the right and sent him sprawling into the fountain. He roared as his head smashed into the strongman's knee and his consciousness wavered into blackness.

Chk-chk-chk.

He hit the water face first, and the sting of chlorine in his nostrils and eyes yanked him back to reality. Flailing his arms and legs, he finally managed to roll onto his back. He'd made the mistake of averting his gaze once already, and he'd be damned if he let it happen again.

Which meant he had the perfect view when slumped, salivating thing lurking on top of the world leapt from its perch and dove straight for him. He grunted as it plowed its full weight into his stomach.

And here he'd thought the silence had made it hard to breathe.

The creature grinned at him, it's teeth slick with foul, brown saliva. It had him dead to rights, with the emphasis on "dead." He should have been afraid. Instead, searing anger burned hot and powerful through his shaking limbs.

"Go on then," he snarled up at the hideous face. "Kill me. But you better make it fast. My friends are coming. And when they find you, they are going to rip your fucking head off."

The creature only smiled wider. It raised its gnarled hands. Bony fingers curled into claws, each one ending in a sharp, ragged fingernail.

He screamed, a primal, furious noise right into the hideous face. He would not be intimidated. He would not look away.

It plunged its jagged talons into his cheeks. Blood spurted into his eyes. The roar of anger became a shriek of pain.

After that, he saw nothing at all.

Chapter Two

Cari tipped her nose up to the narrow slit at the top of the Prelude's passenger side window. The frosted January air smelled like dust and gasoline as it brushed her cheeks and rustled the knot of hay-colored hair gathered at the base of her neck. Not exactly fresh, but better than the smell of stale cigarettes baked into the car's interior. Bald tires crunched over the frozen dirt road as they sped through the desert. Out the window was sand, a few scraggly creosote bushes—and nothing else. Only this road, and the gray line of mountains in the distance, and a landscape so hostile and bland it almost made her believe the car was a spaceship, and they were not in Nevada, but on the moon.

"Don't stare like that," Libby grunted from the driver's seat, the slim cigarette bouncing between her lips. "People will think you're on drugs."

Cari snorted at the empty scenery. "What people?"

Her mother's eyes smoldered, but she didn't say anything else. Her caved-in cheeks hollowed even more as she sucked on her cigarette. She was an emaciated woman with hunched shoulders, short wavy hair that was so blond it was almost white, and skin as pale as the winter landscape surrounding them. To the outside world, Libby looked as meek as a nun, and Cari suspected she did everything she could to reinforce that assumption, such as wearing bland, shapeless clothes like today's ankle-length jean dress and white wool sweater, both of which were at least three sizes too big. But Cari knew her mother for real, which meant she was maybe the only person in the world who got to see the person behind the persona.

She snorted again. *Lucky me.*

The dirt road ended in a T-intersection with a paved county highway, where Libby turned right. A mile or so later they passed a pitted green sign. "Welcome to Halcyon. The City of Fortune. Population: 508." Beyond the sign, the empty desert continued, broken only by rotting wooden billboards with faded signs advertising goods and services long gone. Without those, it would be impossible to tell that they had entered a city, let alone what had once been the site of the largest precious metal mine in west-central Nevada.

The road curved to the left, cresting over a hill and diving into a shallow valley. At the bottom, a handful buildings huddled between the left side of the road and the foot of a modest range of red and purple peaks. Buildings littered the slope as well, growing older and more antique the further up one looked, while the structures on the ground were nothing more than dull, gray cubes. Cari noted the familiar storefronts as they trundled by. Bar. Strip club. Another bar. Payday loans. All shuttered and in various states of disrepair. The sight always made her chest ache. Even though she was only sixteen, Cari knew that if places like *that* couldn't suck enough money out of people to make a go of it, things must be worse than bad.

They ran through town in seconds, plunging back into the raw desert as the road morphed from a two-way street into a divided highway. The car's motor coughed and rumbled, struggling to meet the speed demands of its new circumstances. It didn't have to suffer long—the first exit would get them there. Cari could already see the pink and red swirled dome of the Edensgate Shopping Center, shining like an opal on top of the sprawling single-story complex. A little further and she could make out the details of the ecru faux-marble exterior, embellished with Corinthian columns and arches like the Colosseum—or at least like the pictures of the Colosseum she'd seen in her Ancient History textbook. She'd always been fascinated by the design of the mall, mostly because it was so different than anywhere else in town. It was rumored that the architect who'd designed Edensgate had worked on the monolithic Caesar's Palace resort in Las Vegas. Whether that was true or some local BS, the similarities were undeniable. Especially today—the strobing red and blue police lights were as brilliant as any Vegas neon.

"Whoa," Cari said. "That's weird. I wonder—"

Her chest slammed against her seatbelt, knocking the breath out of her lungs as the car screeched to a halt.

"What are you doing?" she wheezed at her mother. "You can't just stop in the middle of the highway!"

Libby ignored her. She sat silent, staring at the police cruiser with perfectly round eyes. Her hands gripped the steering wheel like she was trying to strangle it, and the cigarette trembled in her lips, sprinkling ash all over her lap.

She looks terrified, Cari thought, rubbing the spot on her chest where the seatbelt had assaulted her. But why? It was just a police cruiser. No reason to think the cop would give them a second look.

Unless…

"Mom, have you been drinking again?"

Libby whirled on her daughter, her blue eyes cold and furious. "What did you say to me?"

"Nothing!" Cari shrank back against the door. "I just...you saw the cops and stopped in the middle of the highway and you seem nervous so I was just thinking that maybe one reason would be—"

"Enough!" her mother spat out. "I've had it with your disrespect. You've been acting like a brat all morning, and I'm sick of it." She snatched up the army green backpack at Cari's feet and launched it at her. "Get out of my sight."

Cari gaped at her, clutching her backpack to her chest like a shield. "We're on the highway, Mom. I can't—"

"Out! Get out of my car right *now!*" Libby lunged forward as her left hand pulled back, palm flat and sharp as a blade.

"Okay, I'm going!" Cari fumbled with the handle until it turned, releasing her to onto the thankfully deserted highway. "Sorry."

Libby didn't wait for her to close the door before she hit the gas. Cari jumped back as the car flung itself into the nearest turnaround and fishtailed back down the highway, the door at last swinging closed in response to the vehicle's wide swerves.

"Thanks for the ride," she mumbled at the receding bumper. "Love you too."

She shuffled over to the relative safety of the shoulder, pulling her sweatshirt more tightly around her as a midwinter gale bit through the thin fabric and burrowed into her skin. It was a quarter mile to the exit lane. She'd have to walk fast if she was going to avoid frostbite. At least there wasn't any snow—her sneakers were way too thin to hold up against any kind of drift.

To avoid thinking about the miserable conditions, she focused on the scene that had just taken place, turning it over in her mind to try to figure out what the hell just happened. Libby had been pretty defensive at the accusation that she'd been drinking again. She also hadn't denied it. But Cari checked all the normal hiding places every day before she went to work and after she got home. If Libby had been ferreting booze, she would have found it.

On the other hand, her mother was at home all day, thanks to her disability pay and what was left of Cari's father's meager life insurance policy. Who knows what all she got up to?

Or who got up to it with her.

Cari stumbled as she veered onto the exit ramp, the sense of impending doom compounding the lost feeling in her toes.

Nelson.

The name of filled her with anger almost hot enough to thaw her tingling limbs. Yes, it had to be him. Her mother had thought she'd kept it a secret, explaining the left-behind sweaters and sunglasses by saying that, in his capacity as their neighborhood prayer circle leader, he was providing her individual counseling. It sounded plausible, and Cari had wanted to believe it. Had tried desperately to believe it. Then she'd found a used condom wedged between the couch cushions. That discovery had prompted a sixty-minute shower and the certainty that her mother was lying to her.

And if Libby was lying about having the affair, that would cover any party favors her lover happened to bring along on his little visits, wouldn't it?

Her teeth chattered as she finally reached the bottom of the exit ramp. The turn-in for the mall was still several hundred yards away. Rather than risk additional health hazard, Cari turned off the sidewalk and slid down the shallow embankment into the parking lot. Still cold, but at least she was out of the wind.

Edensgate had four main entrances, each facing a cardinal direction, and each presided over by a carving of the corresponding god in the recessed triangular space above the door. The cruiser idled in front of the east entrance, which featured a winged man sailed above a pasture, vase in hand, pouring water over the fields below. Beneath that, the marble frieze contained a series of deep gashes that looked vaguely like letters, but more like decorative nonsense. And beneath *that* stood a heavy-set officer in the process of ripping down the caution tape that had been strung between the columns on either side of the door. He was middle-aged with a big brown mustache and the lumpy appearance of life-long privilege. His darks eyes tracked her as she approached, narrowing more and more with every step she took. By the time she mounted the sidewalk, he was squinting as her as if he were staring at the sun.

"Help you?" he grumbled.

"Just going to work," she murmured, dropping her eyes submissively. "What happened? Is this a crime scene?"

"Accident. Some janitor fell into the fountain and cut himself up pretty bad. Made one hell of a mess."

"Oh, no." She peered at the tinted sliding doors but couldn't see anything beyond her own reflection. "That's awful."

"Uh-huh" He tossed the ball of plastic ribbon into a nearby trash can. "Shouldn't you be in school?"

Her jaw tightened. Despite the cold, a bead of sweat formed on her neck. She suppressed the urge to slap it away. "It's, uh, still winter break. School doesn't start up again until *next* week."

"Oh…yeah. I suppose your right."

He frowned but stepped out of the way to let her through. She could feel him studying her as she passed, his frown deepening, as if he were trying to remember where he had seen her face before. She ducked her head further and kept moving, happy at last when the dark doors cut through the space between them and severed the look.

Technically, she hadn't lied to him. It *was* winter break, and school *was* closed for the rest of the week. Not that it mattered to her, of course.

But he hadn't asked about that, now had he?

Chapter Three

Even though she'd come through the east entrance a thousand times or more, the sight never failed to take her breath away. A lush hand-painted sky covered the ceiling, illuminated by soft white light and trimmed with gold-leafed cornices. Directly overhead, the golden chariot of Helios burst forth, trailing a blaze of orange and yellow sunbeams while a choir of cherubs looked on in awe. As the corridor stretched away, the colors deepened from sunrise to twilight as the fresco cascaded down the opposite wall a hundred yards away, melding with a giant mosaic of sapphire glass studded with shards of twinkling mirror. The corridor itself looked like an ancient city street: storefronts along both sides, with fake windows and balconies affixed to the walls above them and a floor tiled with fashionably uneven cobblestones. It was all so detailed, so lovely—and so very empty.

The mall had been built in the mid-nineties, back when the town still enjoyed unparalleled wealth courtesy of the Halcyon gold mine that had been basically printing money since the 1800s. That all ended eight years ago, when the mine coughed up the last of its shiny rocks and nearly everyone in town was instantly out of a job. The younger, more capable population left town for greener pastures.

The rest—whether they were old, sick, or simply in denial that the ride was truly over—survived by any means necessary. Some went on welfare. A few took to the streets. One guy went to Vegas and let a German tourist eat his kidney, or so she'd heard. Either way, nobody needed high-end boutiques or fancy restaurants anymore. There had been one renovation attempt shortly after the mine shut down, probably to try and stem the bleeding with tourism, but it hadn't worked. Now all that remained in the once-grand complex were a few low-rent specialty shops, a shabby second-run movie theater that was only open for two matinees a day (if that), and the Suttermill Department Store, the mall's last anchor tenant. Until three 'o'clock this afternoon, that is. Then it too would go the way of The Dinosaur—a kitschy archeology-themed gift shop that had somehow held on until just last summer—and Cari's job would go with it.

Inhaling the sweet, semi-perfumed air, Cari made her way toward the arched window opposite the entrance with the words Guest Relations carved into the faux masonry above it. Why a mall as dead as this one needed a greeter, she had no idea. Not that she was complaining. It was nice to see a friendly face first thing in the morning, to have someone smile at her, wave hello, and at least pretend to be happy to see her. Ordinarily he had a wave and hello locked and loaded before she was even through the door.

But not today. Today, he was too busy trying to see around the corner into the main rotunda to register that she had entered the building. A man in his early 60s, with a round face and curly graying hair, he looked like a slightly younger version of Santa Claus.

She paused next to the window out of his sight, trying to see what he was seeing. Even standing practically at his elbow, it still took him a good thirty seconds to sense that he was not alone.

"Oh!" he shouted as he recoiled back into the window. Clutching his chest, he at last offered her a smile, if a someway embarrassed one. "My apologies. I'm afraid I'm a bit...distracted today."

She smiled back. "I get it. Big events going on I hear."

"Uh, yes. Quite." He dropped his eyes to the desk and what looked like a stack of blank papers. "Have a nice day."

"You too." She continued down the hall toward the wide brick archway leading into the rotunda. The area above the arch opened onto the second-floor observation balcony, giving the impression that one was walking under a bridge. On the other side, the marbled glass dome cast a dusty pink light on the piazza below, most of which was occupied by the one-and-a-half story fountain depicting the Greek god Atlas, genuflecting as the world lay heavy upon his shoulder blades. A pair of idle escalators led up to the balcony and the remains of the food court. Another series of storefronts lined the rotunda's perimeter, all caged and blank except for the Black Lotus Defensive Arts Academy, which was only open three days a month, and Ripped! Fitness and Nutrition, open four hours a day and pulling about as many customers.

Cari shivered. As found as she was of Edensgate, the vibe of the rotunda was undeniably creepy.

The new red tint in the fountain water didn't help either.

"It was this new mopping solution we're using, sir." The words, spoken in a deep, calm voice, echoed in the all-but-empty space. "It's more concentrated than the old stuff. Charlie probably used too much without thinking, and maybe didn't look where he was walking, and...it was an accident."

Peeking around the fountain, Cari spotted a trio of people. One of them she recognized as Sam, the pudgy, middle-aged assistant manager, clad in his typical drab business shirt and khakis. He stood with his hands on his hips, scowling up at the other two, a man and woman whom Cari did not recognize. The man wore a green button-down shirt and black cargo pants. A green baseball cap covered his short blonde hair. He looked a little like a cop, only instead of a badge, a logo of a padlock with wings graced his left breast pocket. The woman's green coveralls had the same logo in the same place. She was slightly shorter than her counterpart, with russet brown skin and curly black hair tied up in a navy-blue bandanna. She stood with her back half-turned on the men, chewing her thumbnail and staring at the floor, as if waiting for the soonest possible chance to flee.

"Don't treat me like an idiot, Cooper," Sam railed. "I know how things are in this town. I know Ray has been letting this place go to hell because that's just what happens around here. But *I'm* not from around here. And I refuse to be sabotaged, not out of resentment and certainly not out of incompetence."

"Yes, Mr. Berger," the guard named Cooper said. "I promise that's not what's happening. Right, Grace?"

The woman shrugged but didn't look up.

"Anyway," he continued, "We've contacted the fountain maintenance company in Carson City, and they said they can be out here to flush the system in a few days."

"*Days?*" Sam screeched. "I've got site visits scheduled. I don't think the Wal-Mart executives are going to react well to a blood fountain."

"You sure about that?" Grace muttered under her breath.

Sam turned on her. "What did you say? Because unless it was some brilliant insight about how to fix this—"

"With all due respect," Grace said, in a tone that contained none, "making you look good for a bunch of...*investors*, is not my job."

He glowered at her. "It is if I say it is."

"We don't work for you."

"But your firm does. What do you suppose your boss will say when I tell him his shift managers aren't acting like team players?"

Her brown eyes flashed with sudden fury. "What do *you* know about being part of a team?"

"Grace—" Cooper began.

"Now you listen to me, little man." She towered over Sam, who did his best not to cower. "What happened to Charlie is horrifying. I'm sick over it. And now you have the nerve to question *my* loyalty? What the hell gives you the right?"

"Okay, okay." Sam held up his hands. "I didn't know you took waste removal so seriously."

She seemed about to say something else when dropped a hand on her shoulder. She blinked at the touch, as if waking up from a trance. After a moment, she allowed him to pull her back in line.

Cari frowned. Something about the way he was looking at Grace seemed...odd. Given the outburst, she would have expected him to be angry or embarrassed. Instead, he looked nervous, like an older sibling who knew they were on the verge of getting away with something but hadn't quite managed it yet. Be cool, it said. A few more minutes and we'll have done it. Just. Be. Cool.

"Okay, fine," Sam huffed, running a hand through his hair. "So, we have a blood fountain for a few days. How can we work with that? Let's brainstorm. Um...we could get some pumpkins and a few of those fake spider webs and arrange them all around the fountain. Tell them we're preparing for a Halloween in spring promotion." He shook his head in disgust. "No, no. That's a terrible idea. Haunted crap only sells in October."

"Yeah," Grace said as Cari shuffled covertly past them. "*That's* why it's a terrible idea."

The metal security gates were still shut when Cari arrived at Suttermill. She would have opened them, but they were so old and stiff in their tracks that it was impossible for one person to slide them more than a few inches without help. As she pried the gates apart wide enough for her to squeeze through, she wondered why anyone still bothered closing them at all. Suttermill had been slowly selling off its inventory for three months. Now, on its last day of existence, there was almost nothing left except for the display tables, mannequins, and a few items too ugly to sell.

Her sneakers squeaked on the linoleum as she walked down the center aisle past the darkened makeup counter, its brilliant white bulbs having cast the last of their judgments on the women of Halcyon long ago. On the other side of the aisle was an army of holiday decorations. Tinsel reindeer, garlanded trees and red ball towers clustered in what had once been the shoe section. At the far end, a rosy-cheeked elf statuette offered up a perfectly wrapped present to passers-by, a sign propped against its feet: "Free If You Can Ho Ho Haul 'Em Away." She bopped the fluffy green and white striped bow as a hollow sadness panged her chest.

Cari had only been working at Suttermill since last June, but nonetheless she had come to think of it as home. Better than home. It was a haven, a place where she could feel halfway normal for a few hours. That had been especially vital since September, when her mother had refused to let her set foot in "that bastion of corruption and immorality," aka Halcyon High School. At first, Cari had dismissed it as another one of her mother's fickle crusades, taken up in a passion and dropped almost as quickly. Instead, it proved to be the one mission Libby decided to see all the way through. She filed the paperwork and made her case to the school board, all the while giving a tour de force performance of a loving, caring mother. And of course, they believed her. Why wouldn't they? She was the picture of parental concern. After that iron curtain had fallen, the Suttermill job had been Cari's only reprieve.

And now it was ending. The trucks were coming later today to pack up everything that hadn't sold. The hideous tablecloths. The chipped coffee cups. The reindeer and the elf. All would go, and it would be over.

What the hell was she going to do tomorrow, when all she had was her mother?

And…Nelson?

She jerked herself away from the thought. Today was still today, and she would enjoy it as best she could, for as long as she could. All. Day. Long.

"You're late," Holly grumbled as Cari arrived at the register, her eyes never leaving her clipboard.

"Sorry. My mom dropped me off at the wrong door," Cari said, hoping her breezy tone would disguise the lie. "How are you?"

"Shitty," Holly snapped. "I had to pull an all-nighter moving stuff onto the loading dock. I only got about twenty minutes of sleep, and that was because I literally passed out at my desk."

She shoved her backpack and sweatshirt into a cubby under the counter, taking a surreptitious look around the store as she did so. For having worked all night, Holly had left a lot of stuff on the floor. In fact, the only thing that backed up Holly's story was Holly herself. Frosty blue eyeshadow caked her sunken eyes, and her wavy blond hair was greasy and mussed. She even wore the same low-cut, shimmery magenta blouse from the day before, though based on the obvious seams and exposed tag, it appeared to be inside out. Not that Cari was going to tell her—she was in a bad enough mood already.

"If you needed help, you could have called me," Cari said, pinning her name tag to her buttoned-up blue shirt. "I wouldn't have minded."

Holly chuckled bitterly and rolled her eyes. "Why? So, the district manager could rip my head off for making a sixteen-year-old load trucks in the middle of the night? You'd love that, wouldn't you?"

Instead of defending herself, Cari stayed silent. This happened sometimes with Holly. She would make weirdly paranoid accusations that seemed to come out of nowhere and would disappear just as quickly. When Best thing to do was just be quiet—and then change the subject.

"So…were you here when that janitor guy fell?"

"No," Holly said around a yawn. "I was probably in the truck bay when it happened."

Cari frowned. "But I heard he was seriously injured. You didn't hear him splashing or screaming, or—"

"I said I didn't see anything, okay?" Holly snapped. "I only found out an hour ago when Sam told me about it."

"Okay. Sorry," Cari said, allowing the outburst to roll off her back once again. In the relatively short time Cari had known her, Holly had never been a particularly sunny person. But that hadn't always been the case. Apparently, she'd been life of the party in high school, at least the way Holly told it. And smart too—she'd been on her way to

Stanford when the mine crapped out and the money dried up. Now here she was, stuck in a town with no prospects and no way out. Sure, she was still a monster bitch. But at least Cari could understand why.

"What is going on with Sam anyway?" Cari pressed the no sale button and the register dinged open. She began counting down the register. "Seems weird that an assistant manager would come all the way from San Francisco when Ray lives a mile down the road."

"Ray's out," Holly said around a yawn. "Heart disease. From what I heard, the corporate owners were thinking about cutting their losses and selling the place when Sam stepped in. I don't know what he said to them, but it must have been pretty convincing because they promoted him on the spot. I guess he thinks he can resurrect this dump somehow." She glared at Cari. "If any new jobs come up for grabs, I call dibs. Got it?"

Cari nodded stiffly. Satisfied, Holly turned her attention back to her clipboard. That's the way it was with adults in this town ever since the mine closed. Looking out for number one came before everything else. Even kids. *Especially* kids. For whatever reason, anyone in their mid-twenties and beyond seemed to have a special iron maiden in their hearts for the children of Halcyon.

Cari slammed the register closed and checked her watch. Eight AM. "Time to open," she muttered in Holly's direction.

"Mm-hmm," Holly murmured dreamily.

Something in Holly's tone sent a shiver up her neck. Despite having acknowledged the statement, Holly still stood with her back to Cari and her head bent down, rigid except for her hand, which jerked and spasmed as it dragged the pen across the clipboard. When Cari peered at what she was writing, the shiver increased. Instead of words or numbers, the page was covered with angular, nonsensical scrawls.

"Holly?" Cari ventured her hand forward to tap Holly on the shoulder.

Holly whipped around, emitting a wheezy gasp. It was as if she had forgotten Cari was there.

"What?" she practically screamed.

For a moment, Cari couldn't answer. She was too distracted by Holly's eyes. The right one was its normal brilliant green, but the other was as dark as coal. And not just the iris either.

Holly's entire left eye had gone completely black.

"*What*, Cari?"

Cari blinked. Holly stood with her hands on her hips, staring at her impatiently with two perfectly normal eyes.

"Uh, I'm s-sorry," Cari spluttered. "It's…it's eight 'o'clock and the doors are still mostly shut, so…"

Holly gazed toward the front of the store, then back at Cari. "Oh. Okay." The half-irritated, half-exhausted tone in her voice was the closest Holly ever came to an apology.

Cari stepped aside to let Holly out from the behind the counter. She watched with a furrowed brow as Holly struggled to pull back the sticky gates. It must have been a trick of the light. Or maybe exhaustion. Maybe she was overtired, and she had seen something that wasn't there. Either way, there was nothing wrong with Holly now.

"Cari! Get your skinny ass up here and help me!"

At least, nothing more than usual.

Chapter Four

It was a long slog until lunchtime. Everything worth buying had been snatched up weeks ago, and the store was open several hours before they had their first customer. Then things picked up. *Way* up. The news of the tragic accident at the Atlas fountain had hit the town and everyone wanted to be the first to see where it happened. Once they'd finished gawking and taking pictures, they were left with the question of what to do next. They had driven all the way out here, after all, and Suttermill *was* closing today. It got so busy that, for the first time in weeks, Holly had to jump on a second register to keep the lines moving. By the time things slowed down, it was half past one.

"Take your lunch," Holly said, bracing herself against the counter with one hand and wiping her forehead with the back of the other. Her sallow cheeks had grown greenish, the dark circles around her bloodshot eyes now a deep midnight purple.

"Are you sure?" Cari asked. It wasn't like Holly to let her take lunch first. "I mean, no offense, but you don't look so good."

"I'm fine!" Holly snapped. "Go."

Cari ducked her head in apology. Operating on no sleep wasn't doing anything to improve Holly's innate surliness, which made Cari even less inclined than usual to contradict her. She grabbed her bag from under the counter and went in search of sustenance.

As she left Suttermill, her eyes meandered across the rotunda to the stilled fountain. An eerie feeling wriggled up her neck as she stared in horrified fascination at the brilliant red puddle lapping at Atlas's feet and the white marble globe stained with rust-colored streaks.

It looked like the world had bled to death.

She tore herself away from the ghoulish scene and darted into the Edensgate Cinema before it could draw her back in. As soon as the smell of burnt popcorn hit her, the eerie feeling dissipated. The small lobby enveloped her, with its dingy purple carpet and overheard lights that always had at least four on the fritz. It didn't look like much, but it was the only place in the mall where she could find something that resembled lunch.

To the uninitiated, the food court would seem a more logical choice, but it was a long walk for a short drink—the vending machines were half-stocked on a good day, and the food always seemed to be on the verge of expiration. As strange as it was, the theater was the safer option.

She bypassed the empty ticket booth and headed straight for the concessions counter. A black-clad figure lay sprawled face down across the glass with his head wrapped in his arms. She grinned at her good fortune. Padding silently across the carpet to stand in front of him, Cari raised her hands high, then slammed them down on the counter near his ears.

He shot upright with such force that he nearly toppled backward into the soda machine. The thick loop of chain connecting his belt to his wallet clattered against the rungs of his stool.

"I wasn't sleeping!" His dark eyes darted back and forth before they landed on her. "Jesus...don't you know you're not supposed to wake a sleeping man? I could have killed you."

She smirked. "Pretty sure the rule is 'Don't wake a sleep*walking* man'. If everyone got murdery because they were awoken unexpectedly, there would be a lot more stabbed alarm clocks."

"I've stabbed, like, a thousand alarm clocks, so..." He yawned and ran a hand through his wavy black hair. "How's it going, Mayhem?"

Cari groaned as she rounded the far end of the counter. "I hate it when you call me that."

His face wrinkled in a hurt-puppy pout. "Why you gotta be so mean to me? It's not my fault that's your name."

"How do you figure that?"

He waggled his eyebrows. "A magician never tells."

"Fine, be that way." She scooped tortilla chips into a partitioned plastic bowl and shellacked them with bright orange goo from the cheese dispenser. "But if you're going to use my dumb nickname, I'm going to use yours, *Rex*."

"If by dumb you mean awesome, then go right ahead."

Cari's exasperated sigh hid her secret relief. At least something about this day felt normal, even if it was simply that Drexel (aka Rex) Ranganathan was still an irritating teenaged boy.

"How's your mom?" Rex asked as she joined him at the counter.

"Don't ask," she said with a snort. "How's this month's family?"

"*Seriously* don't ask." He swiped a chip from her tray. "Seven kids in a two-bedroom house. I had to shove an air mattress into the crawlspace over the garage. I give it a month. Two, tops."

She shook her head in sympathy. Rex had been meandering through the Halcyon foster system since the sixth grade, when he was the new kid at Trilby Middle School. But his orphan adventures started long before that. He had told her everything about his foster families, about his past lives in Reno and Tahoe and even Vegas for a little bit. Different details, but all with the same "return to sender" finish. Behavioral issues, they said, though Cari suspected it had more to do with the color of his skin, his flashy rebellious streak, and the fact that, with a few regional exceptions, Nevada was a fairly homogenous state. No one wanted their neighbors to accuse them of "raising a terrorist."

"I 'spose you heard about the thing that happened last night? The guy and the fountain?" Rex stabbed at the rapidly congealing cheese with a sharp corner of his chip.

Cari nodded, nibbling the edge of her own. "I heard it was an accident."

"That's what they want you to think," he said. "But do the math. Suttermill is going under, morale is low, no one cares what happens to the stock. Thieves probably figure it's an easy target."

"You think it was a robbery gone bad?"

"Maybe. All I'm saying is that I'm glad our last movie starts at four instead of ten, or I'd be sweeping the floor with one hand and carrying a Molotov cocktail in the other. With an *Anarchist's Cookbook* in my pocket, too. Just in case."

He went in for another chip. Cari swatted his hand away. "You do that now. With the Cookbook I mean, not the Molotov cocktail. I hope."

"You can never be too careful." Rex grinned. "Speaking of tactical combat…"

He stooped and rummaged through a low shelf. When he straightened, he held a slim blue clamshell case featuring a muscle-bound figure in full combat gear, sword in one hand and a gaping, disfigured human head in the other.

Cari squealed, her lunch forgotten. "You got *Splatterfield Three*? I thought it didn't come out until next week."

"It doesn't." He winked at her. "But I know a guy."

She smiled indulgently. As a dedicated member of every video game rewards program he could join for free, it was much more likely that he'd been on some high priority wait list. But she would ignore the fib if it meant she could play the latest installment of the best 1-v-1 brawler *ever* before it hit the shelves.

Rex fired up the game console he kept hidden under the counter (the only good birthday present he'd ever gotten from any of his foster dads) while she mashed buttons on the remote for the wall-mounted television channel. A few clicks later, and the showtime display disappeared. The screen lit up with a blood-soaked meadow where a phalanx of cyborgesque commandos squared off against a rush of zombie-like monsters.

"Best of three?" Rex handed her a wireless controller.

"You're going down." She pressed the Start button. "Ready?"

"Ready and waiting."

The screen faded up on a craggy gray field with a jagged ravine running down the middle. Three bridges connected the two sides, one of which was in extreme disrepair. On one side, three military units gathered on yellow grass while a massive horde of gray-skinned undead trudged aimlessly in the muddy swamp on the other side. Since they both preferred the precision of the military over the horde's brute strength in the earlier versions, they let the game randomly determine sides. Cari drew the military first. She arranged her units evenly across the battle lanes with a smug smile. Rex, on the other hand, clumped his team in the bottom lane. Maybe it was out of spite at having the less desirable team, or maybe it was because he thought the overwhelming numbers would work to his advantage. But all it did was give her a larger target to aim at. By the time the five-minute timer ran down, the score was an embarrassing 57 to 18.

"Dammit!" Rex exclaimed as a knockoff version of the Star-Spangled Banner trumpeted from the screen's tinny speakers. "I don't know how you do those combos. Are you four-jointed or something?"

"It's quadruple-jointed," Cari said. "And no. I'm just that good."

She reached over to ruffle his hair, but he ducked out of her reach.

"Round Two," he growled. "This time, *I* get the military."

She shrugged. "Loser's option."

He scowled, and they started again. The military side gained an early lead as Rex battered her front line before he regrouped in the middle lane for a late surge. Cari pretended to grimace while her heart pounded exuberantly. As his team advanced, she moved one of her lurching monsters to stand in front of a breaching Humvee. A jerk of her thumb, followed by three quick taps of her index finger, and the monster grabbed the oncoming vehicle by the passenger door.

"What the—?" Rex's jaw dropped as the screen cut to a closeup of the creature flinging the car back toward the military side of the field. It hit the ground, flipped end over end three times, and took out a third of his team.

"Strike!" Cari yelled over the whooping siren that accompanied her sky-rocketing point total.

"What the hell was that?" Rex demanded, his thumbs mashing furiously at the buttons.

"Battle Bowling," she said. "It was a hidden feature in SF2. I looked it up in the library computer lab last week."

"Does your mom know about that?"

"Does *your* mom know about *this*?" Cari repeated the move, obliterating all but one tank and a handful of his soldiers.

"Son of a bitch!"

Her triumphant laughter was cut short by the sound of the door opening behind her. She turned in her seat as the mall greeter entered the lobby. "Oh...hi."

"Uh, hello," he said, his eyes transfixed by the morbid display on the TV screen. "I'm so sorry to interrupt—"

"Goddammit!" Rex yelled over an explosion followed by a chorus of high-pitched screams. "The military can't throw its own tank? Screw that shit."

"Drexel." Cari elbowed him in the ribs until he turned around.

"Oh! Uh, one sec." Rex fumbled with his controller. The screen froze on a close-up of a zombie's face, its mouth peeled back in a victorious sneer. "Can I help you?"

The greeter cleared his throat. "Actually, I was looking for Ms. Hembert. I didn't mean to disturb you, but I know the store is closing for good soon and there are a few things I'd like to purchase, if I may."

Cari frowned. "Is Holly not there?"

"No. At least, I didn't see anyone."

Her frown deepened. Whatever else Holly may be (and she was a *lot* of things), she took her job seriously. She wouldn't just walk off it without a good reason.

Then again, the store was basically closed. If there was ever a time for *carpe diem*-ing, this was it.

"Okay, then," she sighed. "I guess I'll be right over."

"Great. Thank you." With a smile in Rex's direction, he ambled out.

She handed Rex her controller. "Looks like I'm gonna need a rain check on that tiebreaker."

"Any time, any place." Rex dumped the controllers on the counter. "You want company? It's even deader around here than usual, and I'm due for a break."

She smiled. "A break from napping and getting your ass kicked, you mean?"

"It's harder than it looks." He flipped the TV back to showtimes. "I'll clean up here and be over in a few."

"Sounds good." She slid off her stool. Maybe it wasn't the most responsible thing in the world to bring a friend to work, but Suttermill was in its final hours. What were they gonna do—fire her?

Chapter Five

The greeter waited at the register, a neat pile of ties and sweater vests stacked on the counter in front of him.

"Thank you for cutting your break short," he said as she ran the scan gun over the tags. "I do appreciate it."

Her hand trembled, making it difficult to refold the sweater vest in her hand. She wasn't really sure how to respond to someone saying they appreciated her. For better or worse, it almost never came up.

"Is this really free?"

"Hm?" She glanced up. He was pointing at the present-offering elf. "Oh…yes. It's free. Everything in that section is free. The trees, the reindeer…and I think there's even a Santa costume in the back."

"Just this will do," he said, hooking an arm around the elf's slim waist.

"Of course," she said, stifling a giggle. With the elf in his arm, he looked more like Santa than usual, even without the suit.

She swiped his card and handed it back to him. The machines had never been speedy, and today they were slower than ever. She drummed her fingers on the counter. Maybe the Internet had decided to pull a Holly and duck out early. At last, it uttered a surly beep and spit out a curl of paper, which he signed.

"You're all set," she said as she handed him his bag. "Thanks for shopping Suttermill—what's left of it, anyway."

"Of course." He looped his elf-free hand through the plastic handle. "And thank you for your help, Ms. Hembert."

She pointed at her name tag. "Cari."

"Right, Cari." Sans name tag, he simply pointed at his chest. "John."

"John," she repeated. Her polite smile faded moment he turned his back. She had wanted to say, "nice to meet you," but what was the point? She was probably never going to see him again.

A sudden vibration in her pocket demanded her attention. She flipped open her phone to check the caller ID.

Home.

"Shit," she whispered as her stomach started to churn. Her mother never called her at work. She barely called at all—and when she did, it was only because she wanted something.

Bzz.

She could just not answer. After all, she was on the clock. It would be perfectly reasonable if she didn't answer.

Bzz.

But that would only be a stopgap, wouldn't it? A brief delay before the call. And the next. And the next.

Bzz.

With a sigh, Cari pressed the green button.

"Yes, Mother?"

"Cari dear! Could you pick me up a carton of Menthol Blues before you come home? I'm down to my last pack. I'll pay you back for it, obviously."

Over-enunciated consonants, t's and s's hit so hard they sounded like an aluminum bat against a pipe. Almost enough to hide the slur in her voice.

Almost.

"Fine." Cari gritted her teeth. A dumb question, one she shouldn't ask, escaped her lips. "Anything else?"

"Well, if you're offering…"

There it was, that oh-so-casual tone Cari had heard so many times before. She screwed her eyes closed.

"Can you grab me a six pack too? Nelson came over to help me recover from that little incident we had when I dropped you off at work this morning. You know how good he is when I'm in spiritual distress."

"Oh, I know," Cari said bitterly. *And I bet he brought his friend, Mr. Cuervo. Patron Saint of Distressed Spirits.*

Because he's good *like that.*

"Yes. And I want to be a good hostess in return. But as you know, I have nothing *here to offer him."*

Cari's cheeks burned as a low, painful thumping filled her ears. "So, it's true. You *are* drinking again."

Her mother spat out a bitter chuckle. *"Yes, Cari. Now I am."*

Cari sucked air through her nose as full weight of the moment slammed into her gut. Had she been wrong? Had Libby been sober this morning after all? Had her accusation hurt her mother so much it had jostled her right of the wagon?

Was this, in fact, *all her fault?*

On the line came a soft shuffling sound, followed by a hoarse voice. *"Forget it, baby. Hang up and get back over here."*

Cari gripped the phone so tightly the slim edges dug into her hand. Her mother continued talking, but she couldn't hear her—the thumping in her ears had turned into an assault of cannon fire.

Was it her imagination, or had the lights in the store gotten way brighter all of a sudden?

And her clothes…they'd fit this morning, but suddenly they felt two sizes too small.

She flicked her gaze toward the clock on the register—and nearly gasped. How was it almost three already? Her shift was nearly over, and her job at Suttermill was about to disappear.

After that…*this*. And only this. Forever.

"Mayhem?"

She blinked. Across the counter, dark eyes stared at her with intense concern. How long had Rex been standing there?

"Thank you so much, dear." Her mother's cloying voice grated against her eardrum. *"Oh, and one more thing: I'm probably not going to be able to pick you up tonight. I mean, I probably could, but we both know how you feel about that. You can get yourself home, right?"*

"Yeah, sure. Gotta go." Cari managed to slap her phone shut before she sank to the floor.

"Whoa, hey!" Rex's voice tumbled down from above as he vaulted over the counter and knelt at her side. "What's going on?"

"My mom, she…she…"

She…what? She can't pick me up? She's drinking again? Probably because of me?

She hugged her legs and buried her face in her knees.

"It's okay," Rex soothed, and Cari felt a whisper-soft touch graze her arm. "Just breathe. In and out, okay? In…and out."

He demonstrated. She did her best to follow. Her heart pummeled her lungs like a prizefighter, making it difficult to breathe at all, let alone deep and slow. Concentrating, she forced her lungs to inflate. They ached in protest. She let them relax, then pulled in another full breath, and another, until at last she could feel her muscles start to untwist and her heart return to its normal, non-pugilistic pace. She slumped back against the shelves, her head rolling sideways until it came to rest on Rex's shoulder.

"I don't know why you take her calls," he whispered, his hand still on her arm. "It just messes you up."

Cari shrugged and turned her head her further into him. His t-shirt smelled like popcorn and vaguely ocean-smelling deodorant. "She's my mom."

"I guess." He knocked his forehead lightly against hers. "You want to lay down in the back?"

"I can't," Cari whimpered as she dragged her head up. The wet splotch on Rex's shoulder surprised her. She hadn't even realized she'd been crying. "The movers will be here at three and I think Holly went home sick without telling me and—"

"Don't worry about it," Rex said as he stood up. "I worked closing day at the GameStop, remember? I think I can handle a few ugly sweaters."

She took the hands he offered and pulled herself up. "What about the movie theater?"

Rex shrugged. "The last movie doesn't start until four, and it's some Disney knock-off that's been out since Thanksgiving. No one's into it. I can pull double duty for a few hours."

"But why—"

"No, no. No more questions." He pushed her gently toward the back of the store. "I'll come get you if I run into trouble. Which I won't. Because I'm the best."

She rolled her eyes. "Fine, I'll go. But you'll come get me in an hour, right? I...need to catch the bus before it gets dark."

"Aye aye, Cap'n." Rex saluted.

"Dork." She turned away before he had the chance to see the full extent of her gratitude.

The manager's office contained a cluttered desk, an equally cluttered bulletin board, and a row of lockers where the once-numerous staff members had stored their personal items. A single frosted glass window provided enough light for Cari to see without turning on the fluorescents. Grabbing a tattered Yellow Pages, she slid the chair aside and ducked down into the desk's leg cavity. Heat wafted from the floor-level vent, making the small space much warmer than the rest of the room. Curling into a ball, she wedged the soft, fat book under her head. As the smell of ink and paper filled her nose, she allowed her eyes to roam around the sepia-tinted semi-darkness in the hope that they would eventually tire themselves out. Filing cabinet. The bottom row of lockers. Knockoff Chanel purse. Garbage can.

She yawned. It was working. Chair leg. Another chair leg. Back to the lockers again, and the purse, and the garbage can...

The purse...?

She drifted off before she could finish marveling.

Holly must have been pretty sick to forget her purse at a store that, tomorrow, would no longer exist.

Chapter Six

She swiped an item over the counter-mounted scanner. *Blip*. The line stretched away from her register, further and further, until it practically disappeared into the shadows in the back of the store. A row of people with their arms full of God knows what, shuffling forward only if and when she allowed them to. *Blip*. Another item. *Blip*. Another; something light and innocuous that slipped through her hands without leaving any impression at all. *Blip*. *Blip*. *Blip*.

"Have a nice day." She placed the plastic bag on the end of the counter. "Next."

The line shuffled out from the ether. She looked up at her customer.

He didn't have a face. None of them did. They wore normal clothes, had normal hair, stood like normal people, except that where their faces should be was nothing except static, gray and bubbling like an offline television.

The thing in front of her dumped its stack of items on the table. They looked like giant gray Legos, each one with a huge barcode stamped on one side. Her hands worked by themselves, scanning them through. *Blip*. *Blip*. *Blip*. Her hands gave him his receipt.

"Have a nice day."

He took his bags, turned, and dropped into a deep, dark chasm in the floor.

"Next."

"*Morning!*"

Cari's eyes snapped open. She wasn't at her register. She wasn't even standing up. She was still curled under the desk in the back office.

A dream. Silly her. Of course, it was a dream. They didn't even have a counter-mounted scanner at the front register. Only the guns.

She pressed herself upright, squinting at Rex through the bright office lights. "What time is it?"

"Closing time. You don't have to go home, but…well, you're a minor, so you probably do have to go home."

Cari scooted out from under the desk. Her legs were stiff, and the right side of her face was numb from being pressed against the phone book for so long. Good thing it hadn't been open, or she'd probably have the number for Chin's China Garden stamped on her cheek. "You let me sleep all afternoon?"

"What 'let'? You were *out*. I tried to wake you and got *nothing*. I would have thought you were dead if it weren't for the snoring."

She scowled at him. "I do *not* snore."

Rex winked. "Sure, you don't."

"Whatever." Rubbing her eyes, Cari checked her watch. Suddenly she was wide awake. "Shit! It's five to midnight?"

"Yeah, exactly. So, we should probably—"

But Cari was already out the door, wincing at the pins and needles in her shins.

"Hey!" Rex cried. As she dove behind the register to grab her sweatshirt and bag, she could hear him trying to catch up. The clop of his boots and the rattle of his wallet chain were nothing compared to his breathless wheezing.

When he finally reached her, his cheeks were flushed and shiny with sweat.

"Thank God that's over."

"Sorry," she said, and took off running again.

"Wait! Don't you need to lock the gate?"

"Leave it! There's nothing left anyway." Of course, that wasn't technically true—a shelf of junk lingered in the back, presumably because it couldn't fit on the trucks, and an army of mannequins stood at attention in the front window. But given the alternative, she was willing to risk a few swiped dish towels.

"Christ, May, what's the rush?" Rex groaned as they blew passed the sanguine Atlas fountain. "The doors are *already* locked. They have been since ten."

"The *primary* locks have been engaged since ten." She wrestled the straps of her backpack over her shoulder. "Those are one-way locks. They still open from this side. But there's a secondary lock that engages at midnight after *everyone* is out. Once it goes on, no one gets through it until six am. In *or* out."

"That's weird," Rex panted. "Still, there's gotta be a back entrance, or an emergency release in case there's a fire or something, right?"

"I don't know," she panted. *And I don't feel like finding out.*

She banked around the corner and passed the empty greeter's window. About ten more feet and she would overtake the east entrance. Six feet. Two. One—

A carton of Menthol Blues.

She stopped dead. Sensing her presence, the automatic door slid open. A tantalizing wisp of icy air brushed against her forehead before the door sealed itself once again. She glanced up at the digital clock above the door that dictated the mall's one true time.

23:57.

She rolled her shoulders, hoping she would feel the stiff corner of a cigarette carton dig into her back. But the bag was too light, too floppy. Too empty.

The doors slid open again, enticing her to accept her failure—and the inevitable punishment that would follow.

Rex shambled to a stop next to her and doubled over, one hand braced against his knee while the other grasped the waistband of his chain-laden jeans to keep them from falling down. "Thank...you," he wheezed. "Almost...died. Now let's...go wait...for the bus...the sweet, sweet bus...with chairs and...sitting..."

Cari took a step backward. The doors closed again. This time, they didn't reopen.

"We can't leave yet."

His face crumbled, and he folded even further over his knees. "Mayhem, you know how much I hate exercise. Can't we—?"

Cari ignored him, sprinting back down the East Hall, past the greeter's window and the the arched bridge, on and on until she reached The Buck Stop Convenience Store. The manager, having made peace with the dimness of the store's prospects long ago, had stopped locking the security gate in the hopes of a major robbery and a big insurance payout (or so Rex had once speculated). Unfortunately for Mr. Manager, almost everything in the place was too crappy to steal, thanks to its random and ever-changing inventory. It was the kind of place where you'd be more likely to find a stuffed squirrel and bag of kazoos than milk, bread and toothpaste. Luckily, booze and cigarettes were two things it always seemed to have in stock.

"Grab a sixer of Red Crown!" Cari shouted behind her as she wheeled around the counter toward the cigarette display.

"Seriously?" Rex panted. "Why do you want to drink that swill?"

"It's not for me." Despite the time crunch, Cari found she had a spare moment to shoot him a "I don't want to talk about this" look.

He nodded, indicating message received, and trotted away.

Cari returned her attention to the shelves behind the counter. They'd reorganized since the last time she'd been on this kind of errand, and the cartons were now on the second-highest one.

"They only have 12 and 24!" Rex shouted from across the store. "Unless you want bottles!"

"Fine!" Cari said. She stretched herself to her full length but couldn't quite reach. Jumping only served to knock them further back. "A little help please!"

Rex materialized next to her so quickly it was almost like magic. "Stand aside, little lady. I'll handle this."

He plucked a carton from the shelf without so much as standing on his toes. Grinning, he tossed it at her. "What would you do without me?"

"I shudder to think," Cari said as she stuffed the box into her bag and tossed a crumpled pair of twenties on the counter, with a mental wave goodbye. Yes, her mother had promised repayment—which meant it was as good as gone.

A siren blasted through the air, smashing the closed quiet to pieces. She'd heard that alarm before, on the many, *many* nights she'd loitered around the mall until the latest possible moment. It was the all-out warning. In 30 seconds, every door in the building would be locked and sealed until morning.

But back then, she'd already been on the outside, at the bus stop, waiting for the final run of the night. Now...

She looked at Rex. He looked back at her with mounting dread. "Don't say it."

"*Run!*"

They raced up the East Hall, Rex falling further and further behind her thanks to his sagging pants and complete lack of athletic ability.

That's okay, Cari told herself. I just need to trip the sensor. Prop the door open, buy some more time. Only ten more feet.

Six.

Two.

One.

The siren cut out. In the lingering echo, she lifted her eyes to the clock above the door.

00:00.

Too late.

She raised her hands as she barreled full speed into the glass. The impact made her wrists spark with pain as they jammed back in her sockets. The doors, on the other hand, barely shuddered in their tracks.

"Dammit!" She slapped the door a few times, prompting another flash of pain down her arms. No response. Exhausted, she leaned back against the glass to catch her breath.

"Ugghhhhh." Rex lay sprawled on his back across the cobblestones, arms outstretched as he gulped greedily at the air. His eyes drooped closed and his cheeks glistened with sweat.

Cari narrowed her eyes. "You saw the clock, didn't you?"

He nodded. "What can I say? I wasn't running that fast."

"And you didn't think to tell *me* before I smashed into the door?"

"I'm sorry! My brain isn't getting enough oxygen. All I knew was that I could *finally* stop."

"Yeah, well, thank God you're such a lightweight. If you were in any better shape you would have slammed into the door. And me. With a six-pack of beer in your arms."

"Glad I could help." He peeled himself off the ground and joined her at the door, the six-pack dangling heavily in his grip. "Your mom's gonna kill you, isn't she?"

"Nah. She probably hasn't even noticed I'm gone," she said. And it was true. Given her mother's likely the state of mind at this late hour, she probably wouldn't notice her daughter had yet to come home. But she *would* take offense to the missing beer and cigarettes. For that heinous transgression, the punishment was sure to be severe. And from how Rex was staring at the ground, he knew that as well as Cari did.

"Anyway." Rex ran his free hand through his hair. "You're sure there's no way out?"

She scanned the walls around the door. No buttons, no switches. Nothing that even resembled an emergency release. "If there is, I don't know about it."

"Ah." Rex stood silent for a moment, possibly deep in thought. "Well then…if we're stuck here anyway, how about a movie night? I happen to know there are a couple of those old Universal monster movies in the projection room crawl space. *Dracula, Wolfman,* and I think *Frankenstein* might be up there too. I'll make popcorn, we can scare up some blankets from that tomb of a store you got over there, and we'll have a marathon." He hefted the beer. "We can even toast to your last day."

Cari smiled wistfully. In the chaos of their attempted escape, she'd nearly forgotten that this was her last day.

Suddenly, being stuck in the mall on this particular night didn't seem like such a bad thing. "Okay. I'm in."

"Alrighty then, you juvenile delinquent. Let's go!" He swung an arm around her neck in a loose headlock and half-dragged, half-shepherded her toward the rotunda.

"I am *not* a delinquent!" Cari squealed, delivering a light uppercut to his ribs.

"Stealing beer and cigarettes, Ms. Hembert? Oh, it'll be hard time for you, mark my words."

"Others will follow! My revolution will live on! Beer and cigarettes forever!"

"Tell it to the judge."

"I will." She wriggled out of his grip and sprinted toward the theater.

"Oh God, not more running."

She laughed but didn't slow down. Despite his protest, she could hear the heavy jangling of his wallet chain start up again. She sped up, but only a little. He was far too exhausted to chase her down, and she didn't want to be too mean. She reached the theater while Rex remained at the far end of the rotunda, loping along slowly as his pants gradually slipped further and further down his narrow hips. She giggled as a strip of bright yellow boxer shorts appeared above his waistband.

Her laughter morphed into a shriek as a thunderous noise shook the building to its steely bones and the room plunged into darkness.

Chapter Seven

"Mayhem, I'm coming! Stay there." Rex's voice echoed like there were ten of him as the jangle of his wallet chain increased in speed and volume. When he said her name again, it was from just a few feet away. "Are you alright?"

"Yeah, I'm fine," she said, tensing as his invisible fingers brushed her forearm. "What happened?"

"I can't say for sure, but I think the lights went out."

She scowled. "You can't see it, but I'm rolling my eyes."

"Yeah, I know."

They both yelped as a second metallic thud lit up the room with a dim, greenish glow.

"Ahhhh, okay," Rex said with a self-assured smile. "They probably turn off the main lights overnight. Nothing to freak out about."

Cari smiled. Under his nonchalance, there was a distinct tremble in his voice. "Either way, you're coming with me to get the blankets."

"For protection?"

"Yes. If there is a homicidal maniac running around, I wouldn't be able to live with myself if he killed you."

Rex swooned as he unlocked the movie theater. "My hero."

Cari waited in the lobby while he started the popcorn machine. "Let's make this quick," he said as they headed for Suttermill. "That thing is about a thousand years old and buggy as hell. It takes forever to warm up, and when it finally does, it goes from zero to Lake of Fire in three seconds flat."

"Why are they letting a minor operate something that dangerous?"

"They aren't. Not as far as they know."

She paused. "You lied on your application?"

Rex sighed and slid an arm over her shoulder. "I guess it's time you knew the truth. My name's not Drexel. It's Aladdin Matahari. And I'm not a high school freshman, I'm a post-graduate at Calbrion University Law School. So, whatever you do, don't fall in love with me. There's only one woman in my life, and that's sweet lady justice."

Cari pressed her lips together to keep from laughing. "It'll be hard, but I'll do my best."

With no lights and no inventory, traversing the empty shell that had once been Suttermill now felt like walking through a hollowed-out pumpkin three days after Halloween. At the back wall, they combed through refuse for something suitable, rifling through mismatched dish sets and kids' toys until they finally found a lime green king-sized quilt tucked in the corner. It was hideous, but it looked cozy and big enough for both of them.

"Did you really fill out your job application as Aladdin Matahari?" she asked as they retraced their steps back to the front of the store.

"Affirmative," he said, swinging the plastic case holding the quilt back and forth in a wide circle.

"And *nobody* questioned it?

"May, I've said it before, and I'll say it again: people in this town are idiots."

She chuckled. It was hard, if not impossible, to argue with that.

At they left Suttermill, she dug in her pocket for the store keys. Might as well lock up the nothing like she was supposed to, now that she had the time. She struggled the stiff metal gates in place and prepared to twist the key for the last time when a flicker of movement drew her attention to the army of unshod mannequins.

Smack in the middle of the blind, faceless horde, a magenta blouse shimmered beneath a mop of feathered blond hair.

Cari frowned, squinting in the dim green-hued light. "Holly?"

"What's that now?" Rex asked, briefly taking his eyes off the movie theater. Apparently, he was more concerned about the flammability of the popcorn machine than he let on.

"It's Holly," Cari returned as she slid back through the busted gates. They snagged shut the moment she cleared them. "She's…still here, I guess."

"Why?"

"How should I know?" Cari said exasperatedly. She rose to her tiptoes in an attempt to see around the dense thicket of plastic body parts. "Holly! It's me, Cari. What are you doing in there?"

Holly didn't answer. She didn't even move. A chill raced down Cari's spine. Carefully, she slid past the first row of mannequins toward her boss. "Holly? Holly, I swear to God, if this is a joke, it is not funny."

"Why do people always say that?"

Cari looked over her shoulder. Rex stood outside the security gate, arms still wrapped around the Day-Glo quilt. "Say what?"

"In slasher movies, right before the person gets murdered, they always tell the murderer lurking in the shadows to quit messing around and, quote, this isn't not funny. But who in their right might would joke-murder someone? That's how people get shot. Nope—nine times out of ten it's just a plain old murderer."

"Shut up, Rex," Cari grumbled, forcing her brain *not* to replay every horror movie where the dumb kid goes to investigate the creepy thing and ends up getting her head chopped off.

The further she went, the more packed-in the mannequins became, as if forming a protective circle around Holly. They're only plastic, she tried to tell herself. Hollow and light enough to knock over. So why was she bending and twisting to avoid even brushing against them?

As crazy as it sounded, she didn't want them to think she was rude.

Finally, she managed to sidle within arm's length of her target. Now she could hear something that had been too soft and far away for her to hear before—
breathing, stuttered and brittle, like someone shivering in the cold. But Holly's form remained static, her arms pinned to her sides, her shoulders a solid line of pink against the darkness beyond her.

"Holly?" Cari ventured. She reached out, much as she had when she'd roused Holly from her doodle-fugue. Her fingers brushed the back of her silky blouse...

Holly pitched forward, toppling the mannequins in front of her like bowling pins. Cari yelped as they bounced against the linoleum in a massacre of dismemberments and projectile beheadings.

"What?" Rex yelled. "What's going on?"

"N-nothing! I mean...I-I don't know," she called back. Holly had done nothing to break her fall. Her arms hugged her sides as she lay face-down in a pile of plastic torsos. Except for the shallow rise and fall of her back, there was no movement to her at all.

Cari stooped low, and with timid, shaking hands, she grabbed Holly's shoulder. Her body felt warm, but rigid. Rolling her over was trying to roll a log, but Cari didn't stop until Holly faced the ceiling. Her pink painted lips were slightly parted, her nostrils flaring ever so slightly, and—

Cari froze, her breath fleeing from her lungs. It couldn't be. She squeezed her eyes closed. Maybe it would disappear, the way it had before.

She opened her eyes.

Not this time. Both of Holly's eyes were still as black and slick as oil.

Holly's chest stopped moving. Her eyes and mouth opened wider and wider, stretching until it seemed the skin around them would snap. And the sound she made...like a pig being eviscerated between the grill of two semi-trucks. A gut-wrenching, inhuman screech.

"Christ on a cracker! What the hell *is* that?"

Somehow, Rex's voice cut through the noise. Grabbing onto his words like a life preserver, Cari fled. Plastic bodies flew in every direction as she scrambled toward the exit, manners now the furthest thing from her mind.

She yanked on the gate with every drop of her adrenaline-fueled strength. It creaked and snapped encouragingly, but ultimately did not budge. She kept throttling it, unconcerned with anything but getting as far away from whatever the hell was going on in this store.

"We need to call an ambulance," she panted at Rex. "Or the police. We need—"

The pig noise cut out, the sudden silence freezing her mid-throttle. Turning slowly, she expected to see the black-eyed Holly bearing down on her.

All she saw was the decimated mannequin village. No monsters. No magenta blouse.

"Where'd she go?" Cari squinted into the pile of bodies. "Rex, did you see—?"

The words died in her throat. Standing behind a confused Rex was the largest, most hideous creature she had ever seen. A vaguely humanoid mass of mottled brown clumps, it towered at least three feet over Rex's five-ten and was about as wide as a car. Its arms were so its knuckles dragging on the floor. From the top of its broad torso, a misshapen, featureless sphere drooped toward the unsuspecting boy below. If it weren't for the fact that it didn't have eyes, she would have thought it was watching him.

"Oh my God..."

At the sound of Cari's terrified whisper, the massive arms shot forward and wrapped themselves around Rex's waist.

"No!" She flung herself at the gate with renewed force. But after twenty-something years of abuse and neglect, the gate had apparently grown tired of being pushed around; no matter how hard she rattled or pried, it refused to move. "*Rex!*"

His only response was a strangled gurgle. The thing hefted him off the ground as if he weighed no more than the quilt pressed into his chest. It began to squeeze. Rex's eyes bulged and his jaw sagged, but all he could manage was a short, harsh gasp. His face had turned the color of raw liver. Shaking from head to toe, Cari looked frantically from left to right, searching for...what? What could hurt it?

What the hell *was* it?

With a drunken groan, the thing's head recoiled into shoulders like a turtle. A jagged line of what looked like raspberry jam appeared over the top of its skull as if it were grinning from ear to non-existent ear. With a wet pop, the line split like a Venus flytrap, revealing a crimson chasm spiked with row after row of broken yellow teeth.

Rex's eyes bulged even wider from their suffocating sockets, mouth open in a silent scream. And yet somehow, despite the certain destruction hovering right next to his ear, he managed to draw his gaze back to Cari. His hands and fingers twisted frantically in the air, unable to move any further under the weight of the gargantuan arms. Reaching for her. Begging her to do something. Save him.

Her fists slid helplessly down the metal gates.

"This can't be real." Her voice, but she hadn't said it. She couldn't have. She wasn't there. She was somewhere else, lost in grief and fear. Lost with him.

The thing's mouth sagged towards Rex. A snaggled tooth lacerated his forehead. Tears bathed her cheeks as the taste of iron flooded her throat.

She was about to watch her best friend die.

A loud splat shuddered her brain. Rex slipped to the ground, the left side of his head coated in a paste of raspberry jam and what looked a lot like mud. Cari's stomach lurched and her knees turned to water. Was that it? Was he dead? He must be. The thing had done whatever it had been trying to do.

And now it would come for her.

"Jesus…"

Rex inhaled the word with a dry, ragged breath. His eyes opened and found her almost immediately once again. The whites were webbed with red and his lips were almost purple, but he was alive. She exhaled for the first time what felt like years, unsure if the next breath would bring laughter or sobs.

It was neither. Instead, she screamed as the grotesque mass collapsed onto the floor next to Rex with a squishy thump. Where the pointy mouth had been was now nothing more than a slimy patch of what looked like bright red pumpkin guts streaked with chunky brown liquid. The only thing more disgusting than the look of it was the stench. It was as if that screaming pig from earlier had been left to rot on a sunbaked desert highway. And yet it barely registered. All she saw was Rex, alive, injured, and in need of help.

"Help!" she cried, rattling the stubborn gate. "If anyone is out there, please, somebody, help us!"

"Stand back."

A black hunk of metal came flying out of the shadows toward her. She jumped back as it struck the seam of the gate with an authoritative clang, then retreated into the darkness. Cari tested the gate. One side was still frozen up. The other, while still refusing to slide, had popped off its track far enough for her to bend it open and escape.

She fell to her knees, looping her arms under his and dragged him as far as away from the gruesome thing as she could manage. Coaxing the flattened quilt out from his arms, she slid it under his head like a pillow. "Are you okay?"

He smiled, his eyes opening and closing languidly. "Never better."

"Goddamn Creeps," came a voice from the shadows. "I just cleaned this floor too."

"So, clean it again. That's, like, eighty percent of your job, isn't it?"

Two voices. One woman, one man. And Cari recognized them both. From behind the impossible corpse emerged the pair she'd seen talking to Sam earlier that day. Grace and Cooper, she recalled, though their appearance had been slightly altered since that morning. Grace had tied the arms of her coveralls around her waist, revealing a tank top that might have been white once but was now streaked with a dull rainbow of stains. She wore a pair of brown suede workman's gloves and carried a sledgehammer at least three times larger than any Cari had seen before. Cooper had remained in his full security uniform, except now he'd added a black cargo vest, the pockets of which appeared to be quite full. In his right hand he held a long gun with a round magazine hanging below the stock. Both wore safety goggles, and neither seemed to be the least bit surprised by the giant monster oozing at their feet.

"You don't understand," Grace continued. "Whatever they make these bastards out of stains like a bitch. I literally have to go over the entire floor with bleach and a toothbrush to do a proper job."

"You could request better equipment."

She stared at him as if he had three heads. "And give Sam an excuse to lecture me on profit margin and solvency and whatever? Pass."

"Oh! I almost forgot." Cooper pulled a flat object wrapped in a wax paper bag out of his pocket. "For covering my shift last week. Allie's way of saying thank you."

Grace weighed the package suspiciously in her free hand.

"It's a cookie," Cooper supplied. "Peanut butter with chocolate drizzle. Her specialty."

"Not bad." She used her chin to nudge the package open. "Though you know that neither of you would have to thank me if you'd just hire a plumber."

"I'm married. I *am* a plumber. And an electrician, and a mechanic."

"Sounds like you need to unionize." She took a bite of the cookie. At their feet, the creature groaned. Without hesitating, Grace stomped a booted foot on the monster's back and dropped the business end of her hammer into the thing's misshapen skull. It made a sound like an underwater accordion as the last of its juices drained from its head. Cari watched the brown goop slither into the sunken grout between the cobblestones.

"Mm!" Grace exclaimed. "Not bad for peanut butter."

"What in the goddamn fucking *shit*?!"

Cari shrank back at Rex's roar. He rolled himself up and tried to stand. His shaken body had other ideas. Cari managed to wedge her shoulders under one of his arms before he collapsed completely.

Grace gave them a once-over, a bemused smile on her lips. "I think we're going to have to reverse direction on that, seeing as how, out of the four of us, Cooper and I are the only ones that are *supposed* to be here." She crossed her arms over the handle of her hammer. "We did last rounds at about ten to midnight and there was no sign of either of you. So! Who the hell are you, and what the hell are you doing here?"

Cari looked at Rex. He uttered a surly grunt before his head drooped forward dizzily.

Looked like she was on her own.

"Um, well…I'm Cari, and this is Drexel. Rex. I work…worked, at Suttermill, and I fell asleep in the back office, and I slept too long and then we were trying to leave but I had to get this…stuff for my mom, and—"

"Okay, okay. Honest mistake. Got it." Grace hefted the dripping hammer off of the monster's smashed head. "I'm Grace Henry, and this is Cooper. And this—" she nudged the beast with her foot "—is a Creep. That's what we call them, anyway. Don't know if they have a proper name. They're constructs, built out of dirt and rocks and shit and whatever else they can find. They make them big, strong, and stupid. Then they send them up here to…play."

Cari felt the hair on the back of her neck stand up. "Who's *they*?"

Grace glanced at Cooper, who tapped his watch.

"Later," she said. "We need to get you two somewhere safe. You obviously can't handle being out here on your own."

"Hey!" Rex said indignantly. "That thing got the jump on me. We could've wasted it if we'd known."

Cooper arched his eyebrow. "That's quite a statement coming from a kid who can barely stand."

"Dude, I'm not a kid. I'm sixteen. And as for the other thing…" Rex dropped his arm from Cari's shoulder and lurched forward. His knees looked ready to buckle again, but he kept himself up. "Eh? Pretty incredible, right?"

A loud, wet pop brought the conversation to an abrupt end It was quickly followed by a second, then a third.

"Uh," Cari groaned, her mouth as dry as lint. "Please tell me that's not what it sounds like?"

"'Fraid so." Gripping her hammer in both hands, Grace nodded at Rex. "Alright then, Mr. Incredible. We've seen you walk. Now let's see how good you run."

Chapter Eight

Cari's mind reeled. Was this really happening? Or was there a chance she was still asleep? She wanted to believe the latter so badly. But that noise assaulted her ears, wet and painful and undeniably real. She couldn't tell if the volume was because of increasing proximity or the number of creatures. Hopefully it wasn't both.

Something thumped against the back of her shoulder, not to injure but to spur movement. Turning, she saw Grace standing at her side.

"You can wrap your mind around it later," she said, grabbing the arm of her sweatshirt. "Right now, we've got to *move!*"

Grace yanked her forward, pulling her into a stumbling run. Next to her, Rex groaned as he forced his unsteady legs into yet another unwanted jog.

"No way we make it to the bunker!" Grace yelled to Cooper, who had assumed the lead.

"We gotta try!" he shouted over his shoulder. "We can't protect two civilians—two *kids*—against—"

His words petered out as a gargantuan creature emerged from under the arch. It was the same as the first one, inhumanly tall with a jellied mouth full of beige shards. Its deliberate steps shook the ground. Unlike the first, however, this guy hadn't come alone. Another behemoth plodded right behind him…and another, on and on until six behemoths crammed the mouth of the archway. Even at this distance, the smell was practically unbearable.

Cooper skidded to a halt. "Okay. No bunker." He turned to Grace. "Hi-Low. I'll take left, you take right."

"What about the kids?"

"They'll have to hide."

"Like hell we do!" Rex protested.

Grace ignored him. "Where?"

"How about the movie theater?" Cari supplied. She cocked her head toward the open doors.

"That'll work," Grace said. "Find a place with no windows and be as quiet as you can. If we don't…if they make it through, find something to throw at them. Sharp and heavy works best. Aim for their mouths if you can. Their bodies can be damaged, but they will regenerate. One good hit to the mouth will put 'em down ten times faster."

"Kind of like a video game," Cari said.

She raised her eyebrows in surprise. "Yeah, kind of like that." She lifted her hammer and looked at Cooper. "Ready?"

Cooper cocked his gun.

"Okay—*go!*"

Grace charged forward, screaming like a banshee at the advancing wall, while Cooper ran at full speed toward the fountain. He bounded over the lip of the basin and leaped upward, hooking his hands around the strongman's shoulders and scaling the statue like a monkey.

"I don't know about you, but this is *not* the chill going-away party I had in mind," Rex quipped as Cari helped him limp into the movie theater as fast as he could. Once inside, he dropped to his knees. Her heart spluttered briefly but settled when she saw he was only fastening the doors floor lock. Even so, his hand shook so bad he could barely turn the bolt. He was trying so hard to look not afraid she didn't have the heart to point out that a single glass door was not going to provide much protection against those things, locked or otherwise.

"Okay, done," he said, using the door to help himself back to his feet. "Now what?"

"We can barricade ourselves in the projection booth," she suggested. "At least then we should be able to see them coming."

"Sounds solid to me."

They hadn't gone more than halfway across the lobby when the first ratchets of gunfire drew them back. Stationed on top of the marble globe, Cooper blasted away at the left side of the enemy line, slowly turning the giants into something that resembled a chocolate-strawberry shake. On the other side of the hall, Grace twirled her hammer like a baton, taking out a creature at its knee-like equivalent before delivering the death blow to its vulnerable face cavity as it writhed pitifully on the ground.

"They look like they have it under control," Rex said. But Cari heard the unmistakable tremble of doubt in his voice—the same doubt that had been rising in her own mind. Cooper and Grace could fight, no question. But the enemy line was still advancing; in the time it had taken Rex to lock the door, it had closed half the distance between the archway and the fountain. There were so many of them, and so few of Grace and Cooper. It would only take one bite, one swipe to the leg, one hit to the head to turn the tables.

Rex cleared his throat. "So…you wanna hide?"

"Maybe." She arched an eyebrow at him. "You got a better idea?"

"Maybe." Grinning, he reached into his back pocket and extracted a slim paperback book. An image of an upside-down American flag dominated the tattered black cover.

"I knew it!" Cari exclaimed as Rex thumbed through the dog-eared pages. Another crackling blast from Cooper's gun made her wince.

"Hey, keep it down out there!" Rex yelled. "Can't you see I'm trying to read?"

Cari bounced on her knees impatiently, her gaze shifting from Rex to the ongoing battle. Working her way from right to left, Grace sprung from the mashed corpse of one Creep onto the shoulders of the next, wrapped her legs around the thing's fat neck, and plunged her weapon hilt-deep into the serrated mouth. It gagged as she twisted the handle and ripped it out, along with a huge chunk of the thing's throat. They'd almost gotten them all. Cari felt relief flood through her veins. Maybe they didn't need any help after all.

Then she saw a second line advancing out from the darkened archway. Only four this time, but still enough to drag her buoyed heart back to reality. *Of course,* it couldn't be that easy.

She turned back to Rex. His skimming had stopped on one of the last pages, which he was studying intensely. "I take it you found something?"

He clapped the book closed. "Nope. This book is total bullshit."

She frowned. "Then why do you look so happy?"

He cocked his chin at something over her shoulder. It didn't take long to see what he was referring to: the smoke was practically pouring out of the popcorn machine, the smell of burning oil so pungent she was a little embarrassed that she hadn't noticed it earlier.

"Okay," she said. "So…what are you thinking?"

His grin widened. "I'm thinking we should go bowling."

Chapter Nine

Cari pried the caps off the beer bottles with her keys and poured the contents down the sink, shaking each one vigorously to remove as much liquid as she could. Somewhere in the back of her mind, logic whispered sweet nothings in an attempt to rouse her sense of rationality. *This is crazy. This is impossible. This can't be happening. You're acting insane!*

She did her best to tell it to shut up. Insane or not, the danger certainly appeared to be real. If logic didn't want to help, it needed to stay the hell out of her way.

Meanwhile, Rex ransacked the entire kitchen to find what he needed—duct tape, a funnel, and a pair of thick rubber gloves. As soon as she set an empty bottle on the counter Rex swiped it up and placed it under the crackling popcorn hopper. With one gloved hand and a delicate touch, he tipped the hopper. A thin stream of bubbling brown liquid dribbled into the bottle.

"That gun of Cooper's," Rex said as he grabbed another empty. "Do you think that's an actual AA-12?"

"A what?"

"It's a kind of shotgun. Full auto. It's military-grade assault weaponry."

"Sounds illegal," she murmured, shaking the last bottle dry.

"Oh, it's *very* illegal. That's my point. AA-12s are not exactly standard issue for rent-a-cops, especially at a mall on life support. How the hell does *that* guy have one?"

Cari snapped on her own pair of gloves and took one of the bottles gingerly by the neck. Even through the rubber she could feel the heat of the bottle as she sealed the mouth with a square of duct tape. "If I had to guess, I'd say it's probably to deal with all the monsters."

"Fair point." He jiggled the hopper to drain it of its last drops of oil. "That's it. Three and a half bottles."

"Do you think it's enough?"

"*Grace!*"

Cooper's terrified shout tore through the air, prompting both Cari and Rex to race for the entrance. Cooper remained on top of the fountain, in the process of ejecting his clip and grabbing a fresh one from one of his vest pockets. Two Creeps remained on the left side of the hall, still on their feet and approaching in long, slow strides. On the right side, Grace swept the hammer over her head, preparing to drop it into the face of the Creep gnashing its teeth on the ground below her. Her hammer had already smashed its legs to pudding, but that hadn't stopped it from wrapping a massive hand around Grace's calf.

"Son of a bitch," Rex exhaled. "That thing's gonna bite right through her."

But Grace wasn't going down without a fight. Steadying herself on her free foot, she adjusted her grip until she held her weapon like a golf club. The hammer sliced through the air and landed with a spine-tingling crack in the middle of the giant fist. The thing screamed.

And so did Grace. She collapsed to the ground, clutching her now free but smashed shin, the pain blinding her to the monster lingering close by, alive and seething at her.

"Looks like we're up. Here." Rex handed a bottle to Cari. "Your aim has always been better than mine."

"Okay," she said, blushing slightly at the compliment. She unlocked the door while Rex retrieved the other three bottles. "Ready?"

He clinked the bottles together. "Ready and waiting."

She threw the doors open and ran forward at full tilt, sliding to a stop in front of the fountain. Twenty feet away, Grace lay on her back in a slick of monster goo, still too out of it to see the impending destruction looming over her. The thing had practically ripped its own skull in half at the prospect of sinking its teeth into her.

The bottle shook in Cari's hand. If she misjudged the distance, she would hit Grace. It would hurt. She would have scars.

But that was better than being ripped to shreds by a hell giant, right?

She inhaled and pulled her arm back. A burst of breath, and she let it fly.

"*Incoming!*" Rex bellowed.

Grace didn't move. Above Cari, Cooper looked up from struggling with his weapon and saw the bottle arching through the air. "Grace, cover!"

She snapped into a fetal position without hesitation. The bottle landed smack in the middle of the Creep's back and shattered. It roared like a gutted grizzly as the boiling oil gouged deep rivers into its swampy flesh, thrashing its arms as if trying to fend off the attack. Grace scrambled out of the way before a flailing boulder of a fist could further crush her injured leg. At last, the Creep collapsed into a smoking, deflated lump.

"Another!" Cari held out her hand. Rex slapped a second bottle into her palm. This time she aimed for the two remaining Creeps on the left, the ones still on their feet.

It landed between them. Droplets of oil sprayed their legs.

They barely flinched.

"Dammit," Cari grumbled. "Another!"

This time she targeted the rightmost Creep's torso. A direct hit. The thing let out a long wheeze, like someone who had been punched in the gut. As planned, the bottle broke.

Then it exploded.

"Shit!" she screeched as the Creep disappeared inside a pillar of flames. "How did *that* happen?"

"Who *cares*? That freak is on fire!" Rex thrust the last bottle into her hands and bolted back to the movie theater before she could ask where the heck he thought he was going. Above her, Cooper's magazine finally clicked into place. Taking deliberate aim, he nudged the trigger and fired a single round into the mouth of the burning Creep. It staggered and fell—straight into the Creep next to it.

Shouldering his gun, Cooper stepped off the globe, casually dropping the ten feet to the ground. He landed next to Cari as the second Creep joined its comrade in a fiery death.

"One side, people!" Rex streaked past them, wobbling under the weight of what appeared to be a bag of unmixed concrete. He tossed the grainy white contents over the blaze, subduing the flames.

"How did you do that?" Cari asked, surprised—and, if she had to admit it, impressed.

Rex held up the half-empty bag so she could read the label. *Commercial Popcorn Salt. 50 lbs.*

"You don't have hobbies like mine without learning a thing or two about fire safety," he said as he dropped the bag onto the floor. "You're welcome."

"Seeing how you started the fire, I'm not sure thanks should be necessary," Grace said as she joined their circle, leaning on the handle of her hammer like a cane. She was covered in dark sludge and smelled like she'd swam fifty laps in an Olympic-sized Porta-Potty. Compared to the stink of the room at large, however, her individual odor barely registered.

Cooper nodded at Grace's shin. "Bad?"

"It's certainly not good," she said.

Then Cari noticed the puckered red wounds streaked across Grace's forearms and chest.

"Oh my God. Did I hit you?"

Grace looked down at her arms. "Huh, will you look at that? I didn't even notice."

"You didn't notice a grease burn?" Rex frowned. "What's wrong with you?"

She glared at him. "Oh, I'm sorry. I was a little distracted by the giant monster trying to kill me, you, and everyone in the room. My bad."

A crackle of static made them all jump.

"Team Selene, report," demanded a distorted, static-ridden voice.

"It's about time," Cooper muttered as he unclipped a chunky hand radio from his belt. "Selene here. Where have you guys been?"

"Sorry, Coop. A Maw opened right outside the bunker and it interfered with the signal. Team Helios jumped on it ASAP but took heavy damage and had to return to base. Maybe if you'd circled back—"

"If we'd circled back?!" Grace yanked the radio to her mouth, prompting a grunt from Cooper. "Did you see what we've been dealing with out here? Where was *our* backup?"

"Um, well…like I said, the signals were interrupted, so the cameras have all been out too. I'm rebooting the system now."

Grace snorted. "You mean you unplugged it and plugged it back in."

"Uh, yeah, basically. It should be up in another half a minute or so. Okay? I promise. Stand by."

The stuttering voice cut out.

"You shouldn't yell at him like that," Cooper said. "You know he's got anxiety issues."

"What's the point of having a head of surveillance if he doesn't help you when you need him?" she shot back.

"Wait a minute," Cari said. "You mean there's more to this than you two?"

Grace and Cooper exchanged a questioning look, as if trying to determine who should say what. Before they could decide, the radio crackled again.

"Cameras coming back online. One more second and…oh good God."

"My thoughts exactly," Grace said.

"You're on the live feed?" Cooper asked.

"Affirmative."

"Then in addition to the mess, you can see that we've made some new friends." Cooper pointed to the top of one of the rotunda's columns and the intermittent red blink of a security camera. "Say hi, kids."

Cari waved sheepishly at the camera. Rex cocked two finger guns.

"Shit," the radio squeaked.

"Yes, Simon. I think we've pretty well covered that the situation is shit," Grace said.

"No, not—well, yes, that, but we've got a bigger problem. It looks like there's another Maw forming."

Something in the radio's tone made Cari's scalp squirm. Cooper must have felt it too; when he spoke again, his voice was grave. "Where?"

The entire room began to shake. For one fanciful moment, Cari allowed herself to think it was an earthquake. Nothing supernatural, just a nice, normal danger that could be defended by ducking in a doorway and waiting for it to pass. Then she saw the air on the opposite side of the fountain in front of Ripped! Fitness start to...the only word she could think of was *throb*. It was as if someone had stretched plastic wrap over the entrance and was intermittently pulling on the edges of it, expanding and contracting the facade in even, steady pulses. With every expansion, the center of it grew a little darker, until the entire doorway was nothing more than a big purple bruise suspended in space.

Cooper groaned. "Ripped again? That's the third time this month."

Grace shrugged. "That's Creeps for you. Big, strong, and stupid."

A metallic screech made them all cover their ears as a shaft of crimson light punched through the middle of the shadow like a red-hot machete.

"Take cover!" Grace shouted, hobbling into a crouch with her back against the fountain. Cari joined her, followed by Rex. The floor vibrated beneath her palms as the crack in the shadow widened. Now she could see things moving on the other side. Big things. Tentacled things.

Evil things.

"Selene, come in. We've got problems. Helios is out of commission, and the Doc is gearing up but... shit, guys, I think you're gonna have to figure this one out on your own."

"Great pep talk, Simon. You should coach little league." Grace snapped. She peered over the rim of the fountain. "It's not fully formed yet. Can we take it out before it stabilizes?"

Cooper studied the thickening blade of light. "Maybe. But I've only got the one magazine left. Bullets alone would take three full clips, even when it's at half strength. Maybe if we had something extra. Something with...a blast radius."

Cari felt their eyes zero in on the last bottle, still clenched in her fist.

Grace cocked her head at Cooper. "Hm?"

"Hm," he answered. "Yeah. Worth a shot, anyway."

"Roger that." Grace turned to Cari. "Can you hit it?"

Cari gaped at her. "Me? Uh, I, um...I don't know..."

"Let me put this another way," Grace cut her off. "My leg's busted, Cooper's basically tapped out, and this kid is...also here. If you don't hit that target, they are going to kill us, break out of here, and then...then things get really bad. So, I'm going to ask you again. Can. You. Hit. It?"

Cari looked from Grace to the bottle. It pulsed warm in her handle, bubbling with unleashed firepower. She *was* two for three. But the second one had been way off, and the first one, though a hit, had been off kilter enough to splash Grace. And those things had been *huge*. The...Maw, or whatever it was called, clocked in at half their size at best. Not to mention that, if Cooper really planned to shoot it in midair, the timing needed to be perfect.

A second shearing growl roared through the air, making the floor tremble violently. Grace yelped as she lost her balance and collapsed into her bad leg.

"It's getting stronger," Cooper said. "If we're gonna do this, it has to be now."

Cari's eyes darted from Cooper back to Grace, her face scrunched in pain, and finally to Rex. He knelt on all fours next to Grace, and while his face was composed, his eyes were glassy with fear.

"It's only half full," Cari said softly.

"I know." His eyes ticked up toward the glowing perforation. The red light danced across the marble floor like sunlight through stained glass. "But I think I've had enough fun for one night. Don't you?"

She giggled despite her nerves. "I think if I have any more, it'll kill me."

She shot Grace a look—more of a question, really—that she hoped the older woman would understand. Grace's bobbed her head once in response. After Cari turned away, she heard scuffling behind her as Grace dragged Rex back toward the entrance of the movie theater. She breathed a sigh of relief. Crouching by the edge of the fountain, she nodded to Cooper. "Let's do it."

"10-4." He tucked the stock of the gun to his shoulder so the scope was level with his eye. Cari followed its trajectory. The ragged hole hung suspended three feet in the air, about fifteen feet away.

Or was it eighteen?

"Ready?"

She bit her lip, unable to answer such a ridiculous question. Of course she wasn't ready. Who in world *would* be?

Another tremble buzzed through the floor. Unlike the previous tremors, this was softer, subtle, almost pleasant.

Why did that make it so much more terrifying?

"Cari?" Cooper prodded.

Ready or not, something was coming.

She gripped the bottle by the neck and nodded. "Ready."

"Aim."

She inhaled, letting her arm hang back as she crouched on the balls of her feet.

"Fire!"

She sprang up like a jackrabbit. The red light stung her skin like a swarm of angry hornets. Her arm shook, then locked. Now that she had a full, unobstructed view into the portal and the things on the other side, she could see that they were...not so bad. Not so bad at all. The light wasn't red, but the brilliant gold of a sunny sky. And the big things were not monsters, but trees. Beautiful, lush trees with velvety blue flowers that somehow, she knew would smell like jasmine. And the tentacled things were not tentacles. They were vines that led up to the giant trees where happy little squirrels and birds and butterflies frolicked to no end.

She stumbled as her front foot slid a few inches forward. There was a place for her there. She felt that keenly. She would be welcome. She could leave this town and this world and this life behind her. She could escape for good. She would never have to feel alone or scared or unhappy ever again.

Her back foot wobbled, aching to move as well. She vaguely heard someone calling her name, but it was secondary. Then tertiary. Then a total non-issue. All that mattered was the light, and the beautiful, horrible things inside it.

Mayhem...

The word tickled the back of her neck. She shook her head, trying to drive it away. Instead, it dug in deeper and brought the rest of the world crashing in with it.

"—now! Mayhem! Throw it *now!*"

She shook her head, and the spell dissipated. Squinting her eyes against the hypnotic light, she pulled her arm back and shot it forward, releasing the bottle at the top edge of the arc. All sound fell away as she watched the bottle sail end-over-end toward its target.

She undershot it.

Or wait…no, she overshot it.

Or maybe…

The bottle dropped into the direct center of the Maw.

"Yes!" She punched the air.

A mountainous arm shot out from the void, wrapping the bottle in its thick, rocky fingers.

She dropped her hand. "Oh, come *on*!"

"Cari, get down!"

She flopped onto her stomach and covered her head as Cooper let loose at the clenched fist. Small divots appeared in the surrounding floors and walls, but both the fist and the Maw seemed unaffected.

"It's a Gladiator!" Cooper growled in frustration. "The skin's too thick, I can't penetrate."

"Hold your fire!" Grace yelled from inside the movie theater, her arm still wrapped around Rex's neck. "It's gonna move. It has to. Wait."

They did. Sure enough, the hand with the bottle was followed by a shoulder, and then a head. But this one was different. Instead of a blind mouth, this one had eyes—if the two purple-veined, ventricle-strapped lumps pulsing in craggy sockets could be considered eyes. But eyes or hearts or something else, they didn't survive for long. With a frustrated roar, Cooper unloaded at them with the last of his arsenal. The creature reeled back, losing its grip on the bottle as it did. The gun clicked empty, but not before the bottle exploded in a torrent of glass, oil, rocks, and goop. The edges of the Maw spasmed, then snapped, vivisecting what was left of the now-faceless Gladiator. The building shivered from the impact before settling into a silence as cold and deep as a grave.

"Nice arm."

Cari turned around. Grace wasn't smiling, but the soft glow in her dark eyes made her look slightly less annoyed.

"Thanks," Cari said. She had barely regained her balance when Rex swooped in and wrapped her in a big hug.

"That was amazing!" he crowed, swinging her like a child swinging his teddy bear. "I said you had the best aim. Didn't I say it?"

"Yes, you did. Now put me down," Cari squealed until he released her. "I promise I'll never make fun of you being a total psycho anarchist ever again."

"Outstanding!" The radio whooped on Cooper's belt. *"We're gonna have to remember that trick. What on Earth do they keep in that theater? Dynamite?"*

"Not recently," Rex said under his breath. Cari elbowed him in the ribs. If she could barely tell when he was being serious, how could they?

"We're clear out here, Simon," Cooper radioed back. "You see any more activity?"

"Nope, we're all good. Come on in."

"Roger that. Over and out." Cooper clipped the radio back onto his belt. "Let's try this again, shall we?"

Chapter Ten

They picked their way through the swampy muck and body parts with Cooper in the lead and Grace bringing up the rear, struggling to slide the head of her hammer-slash-cane over the uneven ground.

As Cari surveyed the carnage, each step grew heavier and harder to take. This was nothing like a theme park or a video game. This was *real*. Monsters were real. Hell—if that's what that place had been—was real.

What was she supposed to *do* with all that?

"Everything okay up here?"

Cari tipped her head up as Grace fell in step with her. "Yeah…well, I mean, no. Not really." She shook her head. "How could I have missed this? I've been working here since June, and I never even…how could I not notice?"

"Because we you weren't supposed to," Grace said. "We spend a lot of time and energy making sure people don't notice. I wouldn't lose too much sleep over it."

"Yeah, May," Rex said. "I've worked all over this dump for two years and I didn't notice anything either."

Cari smirked. "Yeah, but you're kind of an idiot."

Rex chucked her on the chin. "You're so sweet to me."

Grace groaned. "Jeez, get a room why don't you?"

Cari burst out laughing. A few seconds later, Rex joined her. The thought was too ridiculous to take seriously.

They reached the arch. Cooper held up his hand indicating they should wait. He leaned around the corner, took a quick look in both directions, then waved them forward.

"Grace, take the lead. I'll cover you. Make sure nothing's on our tail."

"What's wrong?" Grace asked, sliding further forward. "You think we forgot something?"

Chk-chk-chk-chk-chk.

They all froze. Somewhere in the carnage behind them, a quiet skittering punctured the stillness.

"What the hell was that?" Rex hissed.

"I don't know," Cooper said, turning his empty gun in his hand until he held it like a baseball bat. Shifting as much weight as she could to her good leg, Grace dragged her hammer off the ground with a soft, pained grunt.

Chk-chk-chk-chk-chk.

The same noise. Louder. Closer. And undeniably up.

Did we forget something? Cari repeated the question as they slowly shifted into a back-to-back circle. *Did we forget something...*

The realization hit her like a bucket of ice.

"Rex?"

"Yeah?"

"We *did* forget something." She curled her fingers into the sleeve of his t-shirt, struggling to keep her voice steady. "We forgot about Holly."

A skin-shriveling screech shattered the silence. All eyes drew up as the black-eyed thing that used to be Holly flung itself off the balcony. Stunned and frozen in both movement and thought, Cari could only watch as her former boss plunged toward her, arms extended and fingers curled into claws. Her cracked lips split into a joker smile punctuated by slick, stained teeth.

"Everybody belly flop!"

She didn't have to be told twice. Her chest hit the stones as the air above her exploded. She looked up in time to see Holly fly smash into the far wall, her body crumbling to the floor like a bag of sticks. In the ringing silence that followed, Cari searched the room for the person to whom she owed her physical non-deformity, if not her life.

When she found him, standing in front of the east entrance, she recognized him immediately. It was impossible not to—she saw him every day. Now, with the smoking shotgun in his hands and a cold sneer on his face, he looked less like Santa Claus and more like Santa's mobbed-up twin. Saint Nicky Scarface.

"John?" Cari whispered.

His sneer disappeared as his eyes crinkled into a smile. He lowered the gun. "Indeed. A pleasure as always…Cari, right?"

"Yeah." She was as surprised by his recall as she was about the gun.

"Dammit, John!" Grace limped up to him, sounding more incensed than she had all night. "That was a covert you just shot. Now we have a whole other kind of mess to clean up."

"You would rather I let her rip into you like she did poor Mr. Jackson?"

"No," Grace sighed, her anger losing some of its edge. "How is Charlie anyway?"

"Doing well, all things considered. Out of surgery and doing quite well I'm told. A week or two in the hospital and he'll be good as new. Except for the eye, of course."

"Well…good. I'll be sure to send flowers. In the meantime, what are we supposed to tell people when *this* one doesn't show up for work?" She jerked her head in Holly's direction.

"She doesn't work here anymore." Cari piped in. "She was my boss at Suttermill. Today was her...our...last day."

"There, you see?" John said. "Nothing to worry about. Besides—"

Across the hall, Holly groaned and rolled onto her back. Cari shrank behind Rex at the sight of the two-dozen tiny, bleeding wounds scattered over Holly's cheeks and chest.

"She's fine." He patted his gun. "Loaded it with birdshot. Disarms and injures, but rarely kills."

Grace shook her head. "Risky move, Boss."

"This isn't my first rodeo." He extended his hand to Cooper. "Lieutenant O'Bannon, if you would be so kind?"

Cooper sighed. "Is that really necessary?"

"If we want to get her down to the bunker without incident, it is."

Cooper trudged over to the groaning woman, suspended the gun stock down above her temple, and dropped it with a cringeworthy crack. The groaning ceased. Slinging the gun onto his back, Cooper hefted the unconscious Holly in his arms.

"Thank you," John said. "You can put her in Cell One. I'll assess her there and see if there's anything we can do for her other than the obvious."

"The obvious?" Cari asked.

"You know." Grace pointed a finger at her temple and snapped her thumb down.

"Oh." Cari looked at her feet, embarrassed. That *was* pretty obvious.

John led the way past the east entrance, down a short hallway that ended at the mouth of a sporting goods store. Instead of proceeded all the way to the locked gates, he veered left through a narrow archway that led to the restrooms. Halfway down the hall two sets of plain gray double doors faced each other. John opened the doors on the left, with the words Security Staff Only written in peeling black paint. The set on the right was labeled simply Maintenance.

Inside, Cari recognized the arched window of the greeter's desk, only now she was looking at it from the inside out. On the opposite wall were three grainy closed-circuit televisions and a tall filing cabinet, on top of which stood the solicitous little elf John had acquired earlier in the day. It might have been cute except that he was backward, the tails of his green jacket facing out as he offered his gift to the wall.

"This is the bunker?" Cari asked.

"Sort of," John said. "Three exterior cameras might be enough to satisfy our friends at corporate, but our purposes require something a bit more robust. Luckily, Ray was good enough to allow my input regarding the renovation this place underwent seven years ago. I managed to slip in a few little upgrades underneath the new paint." He slid open the second drawer of the cabinet. Instead of files, it contained a keypad. He punched a series of numbers, then stepped back as the cabinet swung out to the left, revealing a descending staircase. Except for a faint blue glow, Cari couldn't see the bottom. Now the elf made sense—with the cabinet swung out, he could now greet all those brave enough to venture down the stairs.

"Does Sam know about this?"

"No," Grace said testily, "and he's never going to."

"Why not?"

"Because knowing him, he'd probably want to charge admission."

Cooper descended the steps first, angling his body to avoid knocking Holly's head into the cement wall. Grace approached next, but John stepped in to block her way.

"What happened there?" He pointed at her leg.

Grace looked sheepish. "I had to smash it."

His gray eyebrows rose. "You *had* to smash it? There wasn't any other option?"

She raised her chin defiantly. "Tell you what. Next time a Creep is about to turn me into a human juice box, I'll tell him to hold up until you have the chance to weigh in. Besides, it's not even broken."

He struggled to suppress a smile. It would only encourage her. "How can you be sure?"

"I know what a broken bone feels like."

"Yes, I know you do," he sighed. "Go the med station. I'll check it after I finish assessing the convert."

Grace rolled her eyes. Her attention fell back to Cari and Rex. "What do we do about them?"

He studied them, rubbing his chin thoughtfully as a plan began to form. Not a grand plan, but certainly an obvious one. "Our best fixer *is* in the hospital, and the rotunda *is* covered in liquefied Creep. Seems like we could use a few extra hands."

Grace frowned. "They're awfully young."

"Maybe. But they saved your bacon tonight, didn't they?"

She shook her head. As much as she tried to appear stern, he spotted a subtle hint of something other than irritation behind her eyes. If he didn't know better, he'd said it was pride.

"It's your call, Boss," she said at last.

"Thank you, Ms. Henry." He stepped aside. "Off you go."

Grace disappeared down the stairs, leaving Cari and Rex along with John. He continued to study them, his jovial face growing more serious until he was nearly scowling. Cari felt her shoulders tighten in anticipation of an outburst.

Instead, he sighed and lowered his eyes to the ground.

"I'm sorry," he said softly. "I'm sorry you got pulled into this, and that you can't unsee what you saw tonight. But more than that, I'm sorry that what you saw is the tip of an extremely dangerous iceberg."

He extended his hand to Cari. She was dazed enough to accept it. He shook her hand warmly, then offered the same to Rex. "Welcome to Virgil Security and Maintenance. I hope you two know your way around a mop."

He began to descend the stairs.

"Wait!" Cari called after him.

He paused but didn't turn more than his head. "Yes?"

"Why…why is this happening?"

John's entire posture shifted once again, this time becoming as cold and hard as granite. "Because even good people can make bad decisions."

Cari's lower lip quivered. She wanted to say something, to address the huge, horrible emotions lurking below the surface, but she couldn't find the words.

"Now what the hell does *that* mean?"

Good thing Rex always did. She smiled at the ground as he threw up his hands in disgust. "I swear to God, I've had it up to here with the cryptic language and significant glances. If someone doesn't give us a straight answer soon, I'm seriously gonna lose it."

John blinked, the cordial smile returning. "Young man, I'm afraid the straight answer isn't always the short answer. Stick around, and I promise, you'll hear it all."

He retreated down the stairs.

Rex snorted. "Can you believe the balls on that guy? Assuming we'd join their weird little club without even *asking* us first?"

"Yeah, totally lame," Cari agreed. It *was* pretty arrogant. And yet the longer they stood there, the more she found herself drawn to the secret door and its cool, comforting light.

"Although…"

"Yeah?" Cari turned to Rex. She was relieved to see he was still pondering the door too.

"Well, tonight *was* pretty fun," he continued. "And we did kick a lot of ass."

She snorted. "Oh yeah, it was lots of fun. Remember the part where you almost died? That was awesome."

Rex held up a finger. "*That* doesn't count. Like I told you before, I wasn't ready."

"Sure, keep telling yourself that," she said with a wink, trying to keep the tone light even though the memory of it made her want to throw up.

He rolled his eyes. "My point is, under the right circumstances, I could see us doing more of…whatever this is."

Cari nodded. "Yeah. Me too."

"Cool. In that case…" He extended his hand toward the door. "After you."

She was about to step forward when her body began to vibrate. She let out a shriek.

"What?!" Rex whipped one way and the other, his arms drawing back in a ninja attack stance. "What is it?"

"I don't…oh," She withdrew her buzzing cell phone from her pocket. Rex's shoulders relaxed, but only a little. She didn't have to check the caller ID to know who it would be.

"Don't answer it," he said.

Cari stared at the shaking metal square. "I have to."

She flipped the phone open.

"Yes, Mother?"

"Cury…"

No over-enunciation this time. The syllables were so soft and wet they barely resembled a word. Guilt gnawed at her heart.

This is my fault. I did this.

"Wur the hell ur my cig'rettes? I've been so usset all day, and you wur sposed ta get um an—"

I did this, didn't I?

Or did I?

"I need um anni need the recrown an—"

"Get it yourself?"

The words were out of Cari's mouth before she realized she was speaking. Rex's jaw dropped as her mother's drunken spluttering filled her ear.

"Whu the—"

"You heard me," Cari said, her heart racing like a steam engine as her mouth gained speed. "If you want to drink yourself stupid, fine. I don't *care* anymore. But I'm not going to help you do it. If you need beer, or cigarettes, or condoms for your nasty two-timing hypocrite boyfriend, you can drive your own *ass* down here to the Buck Stop and get them yourself? Here, I'll even help you out."

Cari hurled the phone out the guest relations window as hard as she could.

"Jesus!" Rex cried as it snapped in half against the far wall. "What the hell was *that?*"

"It had to be done," Cari said, slightly out of breath. "Otherwise, she'd have kept calling."

Rex nodded. For a moment neither of them spoke. They simply stood side by side, staring out the window at the pieces of Cari's destroyed phone scattered across the cobblestones of the East Hall.

"She's gonna kill you," Rex said at last.

"She can try," she said, sounding spiteful and meaning it for once. She knew he might be right. Maybe her mother would retaliate. And so what if she did? Cari had faced death tonight and won. She could do it again. And again. She'd do it a thousand times if she had to. But that was a problem for another time. Right now, in this moment, she better than she had in years.

Taking a deep, satisfied breath, she turned to Rex. Even though they hadn't left each other's side for more than a few minutes all night, Cari felt like she hadn't seen him in ages. His eyes were still bloodshot, his face and clothes caked in all manner of gunk. There were new lines etched around his mouth and forehead, either from shock or trauma or plain old exhaustion. She knew his face she knew better than anyone else's, and it looked as though it had aged ten years.

"Ready?" She held out her hand.

He grabbed it and threaded his fingers with hers. "Ready and waiting."

Together, they walked through the door.

Book II

VEILED THREATS

Chapter One

The bus trundled through the darkness toward the Four Winds Trailer Park. In the rearmost seat, Cari squinted through the dingy glass as the rusted, rickety arch drew near, its twin lamps glowing nebulously in the pre-dawn fog. She clutched her backpack, the canvas soaking up the sweat from her palms. She'd never stayed out all night before. Hopefully she would be able to sneak in without her mother noticing. Libby had sounded more than a little tipsy when she had called to demand her cigarettes, and that was hours ago. With any luck, she'd be fast asleep by now. Cari could sneak into her bedroom, pretend she'd been there all night, and her mother would never have to—

But the sight of a scrawny figure wrapped in a tattered pink bathrobe slumped against one of the arch's crooked pylons put an end to Cari's short-lived fantasy. She slid low in her seat in a weak attempt at hiding. But it was no good. As the bus's only occupant besides Elmer, the white-haired driver, it didn't take her mother more than a few seconds to spot her. Reeling up to stand, Libby whipped her hands from Cari toward the arch, her lips flapping furiously. The words weren't audible through the glass, but they rumbled through Cari's head all the same. *Carina May Hembert! Get your ass out here right now!*

Cari's shoulders shriveled up to her ears. The *one time* it would have been nice if her mother had been passed out drunk.

Elmer jiggled the door release, scowling impatiently at Cari in the rear-view mirror. With a heavy sigh, she got to her feet. Might as well get it over with. Yet as she trudged down the aisle toward the door, part of her—the part that refused to know better no matter how many times reality smacked her in the face—wondered if her mother had been waiting out there because she was worried about were Cari had been, who she'd been with, and if she was okay.

But once again, that stupid biological twitch was sorely mistaken. She didn't even make it off the bus before her mother grabbed her arm and ripped her off the steps so forcefully she nearly cracked their heads together.

"Where the hell were you?" Libby hissed, her breath sweet and rotten on Cari's face. "I have been waiting for my cigarettes since—" The fury drained from her eyes, replaced by pure revulsion. "Jesus! You smell like a *pig*."

"I can explain," Cari pleaded, her cheeks burning as she writhed against her mother's bony grip.

She arched an eyebrow at Cari expectantly. "Okay. Explain."

"I…uh…"

A heavy sense of dread consumed her as she realized that she, in fact, could not explain. What was she supposed to say? That she had spent the night fighting Creeps and mopping their pureed dirt-and-shit corpses off the rotunda floor? She had a strong suspicion that a story like that would only make things worse.

She bit her lip and said nothing.

Libby snorted smugly. "That's what I thought."

She dragged Cari into the weathered double-wide three units down from the main gate. For a woman who looked like a light breeze could snap her in half, she was painfully strong. Banging open the screen door with her elbow, she practically threw Cari inside.

Cari gaped at the trailer's interior with shock and disgust. The normally cluttered-but-clean combination living-room-dining-room-kitchen was a total disaster. A cascade of pizza boxes obscured the counter and stove, and a film of cigarette ash clung to everything. A minefield of empty bottles lingered under the table, and the smell of sweat and fermented sugar hung in the air like jungle heat.

"What the hell happened in here?" she whispered, though it was mostly rhetorical. If there had been any question about her mother and the so-called wagon, it was gone now.

A soft thud at the front of the trailer made Cari turn her head. The door to her mother's bedroom was closed. Her stomach clenched. That door was never closed.

She glared at her mother. "Is *he* still here?"

Libby swayed as if she'd been hit. Her rage dissolved, and Cari could see the regret and shame as clear as the wrinkles in her forehead and the blood-red veins in her eyes. Despite her better judgment, her heart prickled with sympathy.

"It's okay," she ventured, her tone soft and cautious as if speaking to a feral kitten. "It's not your fault. If he got you drunk, and did something to you—"

Cari cried out as Libby's hand twisted the skin of her arm until it burned.

"Shut your mouth," she growled. "Filthy little brat. I am your mother, and you will respect me."

She yanked her toward the bathroom.

"Mom, stop!" Cari flailed with her free hand, grabbing at the handles on the fridge, the oven, the microwave—anything that might slow her down. "I didn't mean—"

"Shut up!" Libby shouldered open the door to the tiny bathroom and shoved Cari at the shower. She yelped as her toe snapped back against the lip of the shower pan, making her stumble forward. Her shoulder and cheek smashed into the tiled wall and she crumbled, whimpering, into a pile.

Libby twisted the nearest knob all the way around, sending a frigid torrent slamming into Cari's chest and face. She opened her mouth to scream, but the water was sharp enough to bleed the air from her lungs. Her hands and knees slipped on the plastic basin as she tried to scurry away, but Libby stooped down to block her path.

"Mom, please…" Cari wheezed as her mother's fingers dug into her shoulders.

Libby did not seem to hear her.

"There is foulness in you," she murmured, her eyelids sagging as if she were about to fall asleep. "You must be cleansed."

In the moment before her mother shoved her back into the brutal cascade, Cari wondered who she was really talking to.

Chapter Two

Even with her zeal fortifying her resolve, Libby could not withstand the combination of vomit-inducing stink and lack of ventilation forever. She was barely out of the room when Cari slapped the doorknob's button lock down with a wet, shaking palm. She leaned back against the door, one hand wrapped around the knob, breathing in shallow gulps through her mouth until she calmed down. When she was certain her mother wasn't planning to return for round two, she adjusted the water temperature to a more humane level, peeled off her soaked clothes, and resumed the shower on her own terms. Her mother might be a lunatic, but she was right about one thing—something *had* to be done about that smell.

She tried everything from lavender soap to diluted bleach, scrubbing her skin with a sponge, a loofa, and then a pumice stone before the smell finally abated. After she was finished, she dug a threadbare quilt out of the linen closet and curled up on the floor. Her mind grew fuzzy and distant as she listened to the soft murmur of muffled voices and television jabber coming from the heart of the trailer. Sometimes the words would morph into silence, followed by a few minutes of harsh grunting. She covered her head with the blanket then, pressing the thick fabric against her ears until it stopped. Occasionally, a light knock on the door would punctuate her relative solitude. Cari didn't answer. She kept still, safe behind the one lock in the house, until she heard the metallic snap of the screen door closing. She listened for the follow-up squeak of a return entrance, but it didn't come. Only then did she get to her feet.

Time to get ready for work.

Tucking the quilt under her armpits, she studied herself in the scratched, splotchy mirror. Her skin throbbed bright pink from her mother's scrubbing. That would probably go away soon. So would the four thin bruises wrapped around her right bicep, which were already shifting from purple to brown. They barely even hurt anymore.

She retrieved her backpack from where it had fallen beside the toilet, then padded back to the door. Holding her thumb over the button, she twisted the knob until the lock released.

The soft drone of a news anchor from the portable TV mingled with a gentle snoring. Careful not to make a sound, she poked her head around the doorjamb. Her mother sat upright at the dining room table, eyes closed and chin resting on her chest. On the table in front of her sat a half-empty pizza box and a pink plastic cup with a matching curly straw. Beyond her, the door to her bedroom stood ajar.

It was as clear a coast as Cari could hope for.

She slipped down the hall into her bedroom. It had originally been a storage closet, but her late father had converted it to a bedroom shortly after they'd moved in. It wasn't much, all chipboard walls and a bare overhead bulb, but it was warm and functional, and even a little cozy. A twin bed and nightstand took up most of the space. At the foot of her bed was a wooden box where she kept her everyday clothes—ripped jeans, ratty tees, and old sweatshirts, all acquired from thrift stores or dug out of various lost and founds. A rod affixed above the trunk gave her a place to hang the crisp button-up shirts and linen pants she had worn to work at the Suttermill Department Store. Nicer stuff. More professional.

But that job ended yesterday. And this new job…

She dropped her eyes to the chest. If last night was any indication, she would be better off in something less formal and easier to clean. Or, more likely, replace.

A snarling snore shook the thin walls. Cari stiffened. Had her mother somehow sensed her intentions? She checked her alarm clock. 8:14 pm. The bus would be arriving in ten minutes, and it wouldn't be back again until after nine. There was no telling what her mother might be up to by then—or more importantly, who would be up to it with her. With any luck, she would stay asleep. But Cari had already rolled the dice on that once today and lost. Double or nothing did not feel like a safe bet.

Opening the chest slowly so the hinges wouldn't creak, she dug out a pair of jeans, a baggy black sweatshirt, and faded black tank top featuring Ms. Pacman chasing a trio of ghosts. She dressed quickly, tying up her dark blond hair in a messy bun and covering it with her hood. She'd be cold, but it was the best she could do. Her hat was in the kitchen, as were her gloves and scarf.

She finished by swiping on some eyeliner and mascara, which she kept hidden in an old cookie tin under her bed. Her mother had never expressly forbidden the use of makeup, but given her bouts of religious hyper-devotion, it didn't seem wise to test her on it.

She grabbed some extra clothes from the chest and stuffed them under the blankets, shaping them until they roughly resembled her. It wouldn't fool most people. It wouldn't even fool most idiots. But depending on the circumstances, maybe it would fool her mother.

She strapped on her backpack and switched off the light. In the dark, she crawled across the bed to the wall where a panel allowed access to the outdoors. It had been nailed shut by her father as part of the conversion. Since then, she had pulled the nails out and installed a combination lock, kept the hinges well-oiled, and practiced opening it every week, both with the light on and by the glow of her keychain flashlight. Her father had sealed it to keep her safe. She had unsealed it for the same reason. It was her escape hatch, to be used when she needed a little air. After being trapped in a windowless bathroom all day, air was exactly what she needed.

She slipped out of her room without so much as a whisper. Her feet crunched the dead leaves as she sprinted toward the entrance gate, keeping to the shadows until the bus's headlights bounced to a stop on the other side of the dilapidated arch.

Elmer eyed her narrowly when she signaled for a stop at the mall's east entrance. It was almost nine, which meant the mall was only open to the public for another hour. She felt him track her progress down the aisle, his frizzy white eyebrows drawing closer together with every step she took. But he didn't try to stop or question her, and the moment she dropped from the final step to the sidewalk he yanked the doors shut, proclaiming the end of his involvement. She smiled sadly. That was the thing about life in Halcyon— ever since the mine died eight years ago, almost everyone was so fixated on their own lives that any concern they had for anyone else was brief and academic. As long as you kept your head down and minded your own business, you could do whatever you wanted. Everyone else would be too busy keeping their own heads down to care, or even see it happen at all. Most of the time, Cari found the situation depressing. But as she watched the bus trundle back onto the highway, she had to admit that the blindness of self-interest had its useful moments too.

John sat at his usual post behind the greeter's desk when she entered the building, engrossed by a paperback novel with a tentacled six-headed monster ensnaring a submarine on the cover.

"Cari!" He stood as she approached, tugging at the bottom of his maroon sweater vest. "I wasn't expecting you for another forty-five minutes at least."

His smile warmed her from head to toe. Compared to the cold night, not to mention the events of the day thus far, the sudden shift overwhelmed her, and she had to lean against the counter to keep her balance.

"Oh, yeah," she said, trying to sound unaffected. "I was just sitting around the house so I figured I might as well come over and see if there was…anything I could do."

His smile retracted, giving way to stoic pride. "Proactive," he said, adjusting his wire-rimmed spectacles. "Good. That's very good. You're most welcome, of course. You can head downstairs if you like, or you can join Mr. Ranganathan and the others."

Cari's lips perked up at the corners. "Rex is here already?"

"Yes, he arrived before dinner so he could formally resign his position at the movie theater as well attend to some things downstairs. He is with the Lieutenant and Ms. Henry in that…karate studio, I suppose, next to the fitness and supplement shop. You know the place?"

Cari nodded. She had walked by the Black Lotus Defensive Arts Academy every day on her way to

Suttermill. "I didn't realize we were allowed to be in there after hours."

"That was Ms. Henry's doing. I think she has a special arrangement with the owner." Smiling conspiratorially, he bent forward until he was almost to her level. "But between you and me, sometimes I find it's better not to ask."

The studio, if it could be called that, was a wide square room with a woven beige carpet, floor-to-ceiling mirrors, and just enough equipment to give it a blush of legitimacy. In front of a rack of free weights stood a row of benches where Grace sat, doing bicep curls with kettlebells the size of cantaloupes. Her kinky black hair was tied back in a short ponytail, and she had belted the sleeves of her green overalls around her waist. Her right leg stuck straight out in front of her, displaying the shin wrapped in thick black bands. A remedy for the bone-smashing injury she'd suffered—or rather, had inflicted on herself—the night before.

Along the right wall, Cooper and Rex were engaged with one of a half dozen over-used, saggy canvas punching bags. Cooper wore his security uniform and black utility vest, his forest green baseball cap turned backward over his close-cropped blond hair. He was the picture of control, holding the bag steady at arm's length while Rex attacked it in a style that could only be considered "free form." Like Cooper, Rex was also in uniform, albeit a less conventional one—the baggy black jeans and black t-shirt with the words *Never Say Die* slashed across the chest were exactly the sort of thing he'd worn every day when he worked concessions at the movie theater. He'd tossed his black combat boots under the bench, and Cari giggled at his orange-and-blue-striped stocking feet. His wavy dark hair flopped messily, and his hairline glistened with sweat. Apparently, they had been at this a while.

Of the trio, Rex spotted her first. His wave of greeting morphed into a flurry of chops followed by roundhouse kick that was thrown way off-kilter by his heavy gauge wallet chain. "Yo, May, check it out! Cooper's teaching me kung fu. Pretty good right?"

"Teaching is a bit generous," Cooper said, his green eyes glinting with amusement.

"So is good," Grace added.

"True," Cooper agreed. "Mostly I'm here to make sure he doesn't hurt himself."

Rex yelped as one of his hands bounced off the bag and smacked into his own forehead.

"Too much," Cooper qualified.

"Reminds me of the time you tried to teach me karate."

Cari jumped as Simon's voice leaped from the radio tucked in a duffel bag under the bench.

Cooper grinned at the security camera mounted over the front entrance. "What are you talking about? This is totally different. For one thing, you were way worse."

"That's not true!"

"The first time you hit the bag you sprained your wrist."

"Okay, fine," Simon huffed. *"Maybe I did suck. But that's only because you're a crap teacher."*

Grace cackled with delight as Cooper's cheeks flushed red.

"No! Wait, I—sorry, I didn't mean that. It's not your *fault that you're crap. You just...have too much natural talent to be able to teach it."*

Grace shook her head at the camera reproachfully. "Kiss ass."

Cooper arched his eyebrow at her. "You and I have very different ideas of what constitutes a compliment."

"Please." She dropped her weights to the ground. "The only thing you ever 'taught' me was how to curl up and protect my organs when, and I quote, I'm 'being punched and kicked into submission.' I swear, I don't know how your soldiers didn't string you up by your underwear."

"Because when I told them to drop and give me fifty, they actually did it," Cooper said. "I assume if I tried that here you'll laugh at me."

"Absolutely we would." Pressing a hand towel to her neck, Grace turned to Cari and cocked her head at the bag. "Wanna try?"

"Me?" Cari's stomach sprouted butterflies. "I don't know…"

"Why not? Even if you're terrible, you'll still be miles better than The Whirling Dervish and The Invisible Manchild."

"Hey!" Rex shouted, executing one last jump kick that nearly hit Cooper in the face. "That would be an *awesome* wrestling duo. You in, Simon?"

"*Pass.*"

"Your loss." Rex gamboled over to Cari. "Looks like you're up."

He clasped her by the wrists. She shot a pained look at Grace. She shrugged with an amused grin. No help there.

With a sigh, Cari allowed herself to be led toward the bag.

"Don't worry," Cooper said. "It is actually a lot easier than he makes it look."

"Jealous." Rex scoffed.

Cooper ignored him, hugging the bag closer now that the threat of impact had passed. He nodded at Cari. "Let's see what you got."

"Um, okay." Curling her fingers into loose fists, she raised her hands to her chin as if she were trying to hide behind them. The droopy bag swayed gently in Cooper's arms. It looked calm, peaceful, maybe even a touch pathetic. It had never done anything to her. Why would she strike it?

No sooner had the question crossed her mind than an image flashed in the bag's yellowed canvas.

Her mother's face had been calm too.

She shivered as ghostly, frigid water rushed down her neck and back. Libby had held her daughter down, listened to her screams for mercy, on and on for hours…for *years*… and through it all her face remained placid and deaf, like a statue.

Like porcelain.

Cari's knuckles cracked into a fist and she lashed out at the phantom face. It exploded into a million confetti-sized pieces that flew away and faded into oblivion.

"Oof!" The bag swung into Cooper with enough force to back him up a half-step. He and Rex exchanged surprised glances. "Uh, not bad. Let's see if you can do it again."

"Okay," Cari said, a flush of excitement warming her cheeks. That felt amazing. Much better than she'd expected. She felt strong. She felt *free*.

Cooper recovered his stance, dropping a bit more weight into his heel this time. She pulled her fist back, eager to unleash another blow or two. But a sudden trembling in the soles of her feet made her stop. She looked up as the overhead fluorescent lights began to flicker and strobe erratically.

"What's going on?" Rex asked. The bags swayed on their mounts as the free weights rattled in the rack.

"Don't move." Wobbling onto her good foot, Grace snagged a ten-pound dumbbell from the rack and held it in two hands, the same way she held her hammer. "Something's coming."

Cari jumped as Rex's hand brushed against her wrist. She grabbed it and held tight as the shudders swelled around them. It was almost here. Almost—

Pfffft!

The punching bag in front of them split down the middle with a flatulent groan. Cari grimaced as dark goop oozed from the gash, plopping onto the floor in heavy black globs. The shaking and flickering stopped.

"Oh, great." Grace dropped the weight so she could clap sarcastically. "Nice job, idiots."

"What *is* that?" Cari asked.

"Epic failure." Cooper gave the dripping bag a wide berth as he came around to the middle of the studio. "They were trying to open a Maw and it fizzled."

"I guess they got scared off by Iron Fist over here." Rex nudged her with his elbow.

She dropped her gaze, her cheeks prickling with pride—and a little shame. Yes, she had done well, and yes, it had felt good. She just wished it hadn't involved punching her own mother, even if it was only pretend.

"Does that happen a lot?" she asked, hoping to change the subject.

"Not really," Grace said. "Their best chance at opening Maws is between midnight and one in the morning, and while they may be evil, they're not stupid. They know that any attempts to punch through outside Power Hour usually ends up in excremental embarrassment."

"I think you mean exponential embarrassment," Cooper said.

"I know what I said," Grace shot back. "I mean, if they needed to use the facilities, they should know by now that it's one floor up and across the hallway."

"You keep saying that," Cari said. Next to her, Rex tried to poke at the gelatinous hemorrhage. She shoved his hand away. "*They* need. *They* want. *They're* not stupid. But you still haven't told us who *they* are."

"Patience, Grasshopper." Grace pressed her hands together and bowed. "Soon all will be revealed." She extracted a bottle of baby powder from her duffel and tossed it to Cooper, who sprinkled it over the mess. The blob seized like a slug. A wisp of smoke rose from the center, along with a squeal like a boiling lobster.

"What are you doing?" Rex asked.

"Old trick," Cooper said, powdering the bag as well before he handed the bottle back to Grace. "It neutralizes any low-level nastiness that might be hanging around. We'll scoop it up and toss it in the incinerator later."

Grace smirked. "I love it when you say 'we,' Coop. It almost sounds like you really believe you're gonna help."

"I do believe it. But something more important always seems to come up. It's weird."

"A true mystery." Grace hobbled toward the exit. "How about you make it up to me by doing last rounds while I kick things off downstairs?"

Cooper nodded. "Sounds fair, what with your gimpy leg and all."

Grace scowled at him from the door. "Why don't you come over here and say that?"

"I'd pretty much have to, wouldn't I?"

"Shut up." She turned to Rex and Cari. "Let's go, or we'll be late."

"Late for what?" Cari asked.

"Orientation."

Grace flipped off the lights. In the sudden darkness, the puddle glowed green for a second before fading like an afterimage on the back of her eyelids.

Grace clapped Cooper on the shoulder as he exited the dojo and headed right toward the West Hall. Rex left next, and Cari was about to follow him when Grace held up her hand. Cari complied, her heart pounding as Grace looked her up and down.

"You seem…pinker than normal tonight."

Cari blushed. "It was that Creep smell. I spent most of the day in the shower trying to wash it off."

"Uh-huh. And knocking the wind out of a juggernaut like Cooper? What was that?"

From his place a few feet out the door, Rex inhaled sharply, undoubtedly preparing to say something stupid. Cari fixed him with a warning look until his shoulders slackened out of his defensive posture. She returned her attention to Grace. "I don't know what that was. But I'm fine. Just…really happy to be at work."

Grace studied her carefully, her brown eyes gradually narrowing into slits. Cari's limbs itched with the desire to fidget, but she forced herself to keep still. Grace could stare all night if she wanted to. She would *never* find out what had made Cari punch so hard.

At last, Grace broke the stare. "If you say so." Pivoting on her good leg, she limped out of the studio. "Come on. Simon gets even more squirrelly than usual when we're behind schedule."

Chapter Three

John still sat at his desk when Grace, Rex, and Cari entered the office.

"Good workout?" he asked without looking up from his book.

"Fabulous," Grace said. She opened the second drawer of the filing cabinet, revealing the concealed keypad. "Thought it appears we owe Sensei Liebowitz a new punching bag."

John frowned. "Why?"

"Epic failure."

"Ah." He nodded and turned the page. "Make sure I get the receipt."

"Will do." She tapped out the combination, then stepped back as the cabinet swung away from the wall. Before descending the steps, she stopped to pat the head of the gift-bearing elf on top of the cabinet. Rex jumped up and slapped the gift like a high five. Cari lowered her eyes reverently as she passed beneath it into the darkness beyond.

Unlike the secret staircases of her childhood daydreams, this one was neither winding nor inordinately long. In fact, it looked like any other basement staircase except that it ended in a tiny landing bathed in blue light with a knobless steel door and another keypad on the opposite wall. The three of them squeezed together in the small space as Grace entered the second combination, squinting to make out the numbers in the dim light.

The steel door zipped into the wall with a whoosh, revealing a short hallway lined with eight cage-like lockers. As the newest recruits, Cari and Rex's lockers were at the end of the hall furthest from the door. Even though it had been less than a day, Rex's locker was already as crammed with junk as his locker at school, with a few extras that were (she hoped) unique to this location. Alongside the crumpled papers, empty soda bottles and inside-out potato chip bags, a bundle of fireworks sat wedged in between several jugs of bleach. In the lockers closer to the entrance, the diamond-patterned metal doors revealed the handle of Grace's sledgehammer as well as the retrofitted rack that held Cooper's shotgun. Her own locker, on the other hand, remained empty. As the launchpad for Rex's chemistry experiments, the only thing she needed in her locker was the hazmat suit, and even that was useless until John ordered one in her size.

She slipped off her backpack and hung it on one of the hooks. Still not great, but better than nothing.

Her eyes wandered from the hall of lockers out to the rest of the bunker.

At one point during their initial tour the previous night, John had mentioned that the mall's surveillance and security systems had been upgraded eight years ago, in conjunction with a round of cosmetic renovations. Once glance at this room had her calling B.S. The kitchenette to her right, with its avocado-colored appliances and gold-fleck Formica counters, might have been considered cutting edge in the late days of disco. The rest of the room contained a few plastic chairs and a worn corduroy couch that served as a lounge. A shaggy orange throw rug covered a large swath of the parquet floor, and waist-high bookshelves filled with dog-eared paperbacks and old magazines lined the walls. The only things that looked newer than the eighties were the huge wall-mounted flat screen (to which Rex had already connected his gaming console), and another sliding steel door, similar to the entrance located in the middle of the far wall between two bookshelves.

But then she'd turned her attention to the left side of the room, and what had once been the detention area. The cells most likely had been simple cages when the mall was first built, more than capable of subduing a teen-aged hooligan or petty criminal. Now, only the doors were made of bars. The walls between the cells had been bricked up with concrete.

Except, that is, for the wall bordering the main room, which was inset with a pane of floor-to-ceiling shatterproof glass. The cell inside was dingy white and bare except for a single cot bolted to the floor in the middle of the room. Lying on that cot was Holly, ex-Suttermill manager and ex-human being. She didn't move as Cari approached the window. Her lifeless black eyes stared up at the ceiling, and her limbs were completely rigid. If it weren't for the subtle rise and fall of the straps fastened over her chest and stomach, Cari might have thought she was dead.

Which might not have been such a bad thing.

Guilt gnawed at her stomach. Maybe she wasn't as immune to the Halcyon syndrome of minding one's own business as she thought. Holly had been off all day yesterday, and yet until the moment she dove at Cari with the intention of wearing her face as a hat, it had barely registered.

Then again, how could she have known, especially when the early stages of demonic possession were apparently the same as the flu? And even if she had recognized it for what it was, who would she have told? Would it have been the custodial staff? She doubted it.

Holly's head twitched, then rose, as if her forehead were being pulled by a puppeteer's string. She stared at Cari, her black eyes twin pools as her lips cracked open in a drooling, idiotic smile.

Cari shrank back in disgust. Barely a day had passed, and yet Holly's teeth were as stained and rotted as those of a decade-long meth addict.

"Everything okay?"

Cari spun around. John stood in the mouth of the entryway next to her locker, a pinched look on his face.

"Yeah, fine," Cari turned back to the cell. Holly's head lay on the pillow once again, her eyes bugged and staring at the ceiling in slack-jawed fascination. "How is she?"

"It's hard to say." John joined her at the window. "I've kept her sedated, but given the way her physiology is changing, that won't be a viable treatment forever. This last round of barbiturates was enough to knock out a linebacker, and yet they barely managed to subdue her mania. I've got a few panels I can try, a combination of anti-psychotics and ARVs and a few other things that might be able to slow things down…but to be honest, I'm not hopeful."

Cari bowed her head. "How long does she have?"

"I don't know. A week? Maybe a month? I can't say for sure." He smiled mirthlessly. "They didn't exactly cover demonic transmutation in med school."

She swallowed hard. "And if we have to…you know…what then?"

He pulled his shoulders back. "Then we make sure we have our story straight. This was the last place she was seen so this will be the first place they'll come looking when they realize she's gone."

"That might be a while. Her social network was...limited."

She and Holly had worked together for six months, long enough for Cari to know that Holly's parents had both worked at the Halcyon mine before it went under—her father as a foreman and her mother as a secretary. They never recovered from the shock of the mine going bust, and both died of organ failure before Holly turned twenty. She had no siblings, and the only "friends" Cari ever heard her talk about were men. A new one every weekend, whose visits Holly would describe in an uncomfortable level of detail. If those were the only people that kept track of Holly's existence, then it might be months before anyone realized she was gone.

In typical Halcyon fashion, Cari didn't know whether to feel incredibly fortunate or horribly depressed.

She jumped as a hand fell on her shoulder.

"You don't need to worry," John reassured her. "I promise I am looking after her as best I can." He steered her away from the window toward the lounge. "Go on now. They're waiting for you."

Chapter Four

Grace perched on top of a low bookshelf next to the flat screen, munching on an apple. Next to her, a rolling whiteboard displayed a mess of scribbles punctuated with the occasional sepia-toned photo. Rex had settled himself in the middle of the red sofa with his arms draped across the back. As Cari sat down next to him, she noticed that the three of them were not the only ones in attendance. Tucked in the far corner sat a dark figure dressed in a black duster, jeans, and cowboy boots. Except for a black and silver goatee, his face was obscured by the brim of a black cowboy hat. He slumped low in his chair with his legs spread wide and arms folded across his chest. He seemed completely out of place, except for the winged lock patch on the left chest panel of his coat that indicated he was indeed an employee of Virgil Security & Maintenance.

"Who's that?" Cari whispered.

"No talking!" Grace bellowed, spraying bits of apple across the floor. "Class is now in session. Silence your cell phones, spit out your gum, and please engage the safety on all your firearms."

She slapped the button on the bottom of the television. A man appeared, thin and pale with matted brown hair and a scruffy beard. A blue-white glow lit him from below the chin and spilled onto the surrounding clutter of disassembled home appliances and desktop computers. Like the man in black, he also wore the VSM winged lock logo, sewn to the breast pocket of his navy-blue cotton t-shirt. As soon as he saw them, he dipped his face toward the white-blue light, his eyes trailing back and forth as if reading something.

"Oh, hello. I didn't see you there," he recited, pushing his horn-rimmed glasses up his nose. "My name is Simon Mackie, head of surveillance for Virgil Security & Maintenance, and I will be taking you through your new employee orientation."

Cari smiled with recognition. Apparently, the disembodied voice on the radio had a face after all.

Rex groaned and flopped his arms against the couch cushion. "Orientation? Seriously? Don't we have better things to do? Monsters to vanquish? Damsels to rescue? Napalm to—"

"Complaining will only make it longer," Grace said. She jabbed a finger at the screen. "Watch. Listen. We'll make this as quick as we can. Go ahead, Simon."

"Right." Simon's shoulder had shriveled during the interchange. Bowing his head again, he tapped frantically at his keyboard. His face disappeared behind a full-screen graphic of heavy black letters.

Welcome.
Everything You Know Is Wrong.
Cari sucked in her breath. This ought to be good.

The words faded, and a photo appeared. It was a ripped, yellowed document with *The Founding of Halcyon* written in looping script at the top.

"The year is 1851."

"Oh my *God*." Rex slapped his hands over his face, prompting another stern look from Grace.

"Anyway...the year is 1851," Simon continued. "A group of settlers led by the Reverend Lawrence Fludd was traveling from New Orleans, heading for a new life on the California frontier. On a day in the middle of November, under threat of an impending snowstorm, they stopped early to make camp. One of the settlers went to get water from the nearby creek when a shaft of light broke free from the clouds and struck the water, illuminating a bevy of gold nuggets in the riverbed. Lo and behold, the settlers had stumbled onto one of the biggest veins of gold in the region, and the city of Halcyon was born. The town and the mine flourished for over a century before the vein was depleted, at which point the mine folded, and the town shriveled until it was nothing but a withered husk of its former glory."

Simon's face reappeared on the screen. "I assume this all sounds familiar?"

"Add a mullet, a pencil mustache, and a smoker's cough, and you'd be the spitting image of my third-grade teacher, Mrs. Rauschback," Rex said, propping his feet up on the chipped coffee table.

Grace snorted laughter. "Mrs. Rauschback might be the pinnacle of knowledge at Bishop Elementary, but did she know which three parts of that story are lies? Because we do, starting with the reason they stopped at this spot in the first place. It wasn't because of the weather. It was because they ate a few people."

Cari's breath caught in her throat. Grace had said it so casually she truly wasn't sure she'd heard her right. "They *ate* people?"

"No way," Rex scoffed.

"'Fraid so. You can read it for yourself in the founders' journals." Grace pointed at the shelf below her. Nestled between pulp novels and some National Geographics that looked older than Grace herself were five or six unlabeled leather books of different colors and sizes. "The Reverend's is here. So is his wife's, and his brother's, and a few other people."

Cari frowned. "I thought those belonged to the Halcyon Historical Society."

"They *belong* with people who are going to *read* them. All the Historical Society did was shut their eyes and tout that stupid Founder's Day fable while keeping the truth locked up in a pretty little glass display case. It was staring them right in the face for decades and—"

"Hey!" Simon cut in. "This is *my* presentation. You told me you were going to *assist*."

"I *am* assisting," Grace said. "Your presentation has all those visual aids and stuff. I'm doing the short version."

"*This* is the short version?" Rex moaned.

"Anyway, if you want me to stop so badly, you could always come out here and *make* me." She fixed Simon with a mocking smile.

He scowled back. "For your information, I *was* planning to come out there, but I...changed my mind."

His eyes shifted toward the couch.

Grace rolled her eyes. "Really, Simon? It's not like they're gonna bite you."

"Won't we?" Rex chomped his teeth at the screen.

"Kids, play nice," Cooper said as he slid into the empty space to Rex's left. In place of his gun, he held a blue foam lunch bag. "Grace, this is Simon's presentation. Let him conduct it how he wants."

"Fine." Grace huffed. She collapsed back against the wall and crossed her arms. "Go ahead, Simon. Lie number one."

"You've ruined it now," Simon pouted. "I was going to do a dramatic reading, with period voices and musical accompaniment and everything. But you've all got things to do, so whatever. Let's skip it." His face disappeared, and the screen rolled furiously through a dozen slides of weathered pages and faded handwriting. "The Reverend's party had been traveling for months when they encountered a small tribe of indigenous people. Seeing that the party's stores were growing thin, the tribe offered to share what food and supplies they could spare. In return, the Reverend tried to convert them to Christianity. As you might imagine, they declined. Here the details get a little fuzzy—it's unclear if he killed them alone or if he had help. Either way, the tribe disappeared. After that, he divested several bodies of their flesh, and provided that as sustenance to his congregation to see them through the rest of their journey."

The slides kept coming.

"Wow," Rex muttered. Pressing his palms together, he bowed his head toward Grace and mouthed an exaggerated *thank you*. Cari didn't blame him—she could feel her own eyes starting to glaze over.

At last, the scrolling stopped, and Simon reappeared. "Between the unsanitary conditions, and the fact that it is generally a terrible idea to eat human flesh, the entire group fell ill with a parasitic fever so severe that they were physically unable to continue. Essentially, they stopped here to die."

"If only they *had* died," Grace said. "Would have saved us all a lot of trouble."

Cari gasped as the floor jerked beneath her feet. Above them, the lights flashed, then faded to almost nothing. Everyone stopped talking as they searched the room and each other to verify that this was actually happening.

She let out a soft sigh of surprise as an icy finger drew itself across her throat.

Then it was over. The lights returned to normal, the room stilled, and the cold contact disappeared.

"W-what was that?" Cari stammered. It hadn't lasted more than a second or two, and yet she couldn't seem to stop shaking.

"Simon?" Grace asked.

"Yeah, I'm on it. Stand by." His head twitched in several directions, his pale skin absorbing the glow from what appeared to be dozens of monitors. "Uh, nope. No indication of a breach. We're all good. Now—where were we?"

"They came here to die, but they didn't," Cari supplied. She rubbed her arms to chase away the last of the chill.

"Right. Thank you," Simon said. "Which brings us to Lie Number Two: How They Really Found That Gold."

He clicked the mouse. Another weathered document appeared.

"Sweet baby Jane!" Rex exclaimed as he helped himself to a fistful of Cooper's potato chips. "When are we going to talk about the lie you told *us* when you said this would be interesting and it's actually terrible?"

Simon ducked as if Rex's words might come through the screen and clobber him.

Grace smiled sympathetically at the screen. "You want me to take this one?"

Simon slumped in his chair. "Fine, go ahead."

"Okay." She leaned toward the couch, her eyes glittering with menace as if she were about to tell her favorite campfire story. "So, it's the middle of the night. The Reverend is on his deathbed when suddenly a man appears at the door of his tent. Only it's not a man. He stands on two feet like a man, but his skin is the color of soot and he has burning embers for eyes, and on his head are a pair of iron ram's horns. He tells the Reverend that he's a Courier, who comes when others do not, to deliver the wretched from their anguish. He swears to the Reverend that he will not only to spare all their lives, but he can make sure their mission is a grand success for eight score years and one day. The Reverend asks what the Courier wants in return for all this bounty. And the Courier says, oh, nothing really. A mere trifle. Your signature, that's all. Out comes the big leather book, and the sharp little knife. The Reverend pricks his finger, signs his name, and the rest, as they say, is history. The next morning, he wakes up to find a camp full of miraculously healthy people and a river full of gold." She shook her head. "For someone who claimed to be a man of God, he didn't know shit about what a deal with the Devil looks like."

Cari shuddered as another tremor rolled through the room.

"Not again," Rex groaned. "We're never gonna get this over with."

She braced herself for the cold touch. Instead, the vibration shimmied through her like a tuning fork, making her teeth hum and her skin itch. A dry patch formed on the back of her tongue. She coughed to clear it, but that only seemed to make it worse, spreading the dryness until it felt like she was wearing a wool turtleneck on the inside of her throat. Once again, the rumbling passed in a matter of moments, but her dry mouth remained. She tried to breathe and ended up doubled over her thighs in a hacking cough.

What the hell was *happening*?

"Here," Cooper said as he passed her his half-empty juice box. She aimed the straw at her tongue and squeezed, coating her throat with soothing cherry-lime goodness. "Specs? Anything?"

Simon's eyes flicked left and right, up and down. "Nope. Still nothing."

"You okay?" Rex asked as she swished the juice in her mouth.

She nodded, swallowed, and drank some more. Despite her assurances, Cooper gave her an additional half-minute of observation before he turned to Simon. "Go ahead."

"We're almost done." Simon tapped the keys. "Now— Cari and Rex. This is for all the marbles. Do you have any idea what Lie Number Three might be?"

Cari chewed thoughtfully on her straw. She glanced at Rex, but he was too busy digging the M&Ms out of Cooper's trail mix to bother with the question. She doubted he would have been able to answer any more than she could anyway.

"The mine wasn't depleted."

She turned toward the man in the corner. His posture hadn't changed, but he had pushed his hat back, revealing gray eyes and long sideburns in addition to the goatee. His voice was coarse and smoggy, a perfect match for his appearance, with a hint of a Spanish accent.

Grace extended her hand to him. "Something you want to share with the class, A.J.?"

The cowboy ducked his head and touched the brim of his hat graciously before continuing. "The mine wasn't depleted. Not naturally, anyway. There would have been signs. Studies and reports. Things would have been scaled back, an exit strategy plotted out. But there was none of that. One day, everything was fine. The next—poof!" He snapped his fingers. "*Perdido*. All gone." His contribution concluded, he pulled the brim of his hat back over his eyes.

"Correct," Grace said. On the screen, two dates sat stacked on top of each other. November 12th, 2011, and November 11th, 1851. She pointed to the upper date with a marker. "We all remember this day, don't we?"

Cari nodded, as did Rex. "That was the day the mine closed."

"Correct," Simon said. The graphic morphed so it looked like a subtraction equation. The solution faded in below the line. 160. An ominous shiver rolled up Cari's spine.

"A score is twenty years," Grace said. "Eight score is one-hundred and sixty years. Plus a day." She tapped the 12. "The term of the deal had expired, and the Courier came back to collect what was his."

"Let me guess," Cari and Rex exchanged a knowing look. They'd both seen enough horror movies to know what signing in blood typically meant. "He came to reap the Reverend's soul."

"And circle gets the square," Grace said. "But the Courier was a Faustian, wheely-dealy kind of guy. He couldn't resist trying to double down first."

"So, what did he do?" Simon jumped in. "He paid the mayor a visit. He adopted a more era-appropriate look, of course, but the deal was the same—another sixteen decades of prosperity in exchange for the mayor's name in the book. The problem was that, instead of offering his deal to a sick man dying in the desert, the Courier was now dealing with a savvy politician in the pink of health who presided over one of the wealthiest towns in the state. Where the Reverend had seen a bargain, the mayor saw lunacy, and he told the Courier to get lost. Which he did—but not before collecting his original fee. And just like that, the years of prosperity came to an end."

Rex's hand shot up.

Grace sighed. "Yes, Rex?"

"As *fascinating* as all this is, what does it have to do with giant mud monsters and the pooping punching bag?"

He reached for a peanut butter chocolate chip cookie, but Cooper shielded it with his arm. "Not the dessert."

"The reason this is important is here." A sepia-tinted photo appeared on the screen. In it, a group of people in frontier attire stood in front of a covered wagon, staring at the camera with intense conviction. "Twelve settlers joined Reverend Fludd's mission. Five men, three women, and four kids under the age of thirteen. They weren't damned outright when he signed his name, but his deal—to say nothing of what they'd done to the tribe—cast a shadow. Made them more susceptible to the Courier's enticements. And one by one, each of their names ended up in his book."

"So what?" This time, Rex didn't bother raising his hand.

"So, this." Reaching past the TV, Grace slapped the button on the wall next to the steel door. It whooshed open, revealing a second set of doors made of iron and held closed with thick chains and no less than six padlocks. The room beyond was cylindrical, dimly lit by a pair of simple iron sconces, and empty except for a single rough-hewn table in the middle. On the table sat a lectern—and on that lectern, a leather-covered tome opened to a page about two-thirds of the way from the end. Cari was too far away to read the words, but the reddish-brown scrawls were unmistakable.

An ear-splitting shriek made them all swing their heads toward the back of the room. In the first detention cell,

Holly bucked and thrashed against her restraints, screaming not words but long, throaty roars that made Cari's lungs throb sympathetically. A moment later John appeared at the door to the cell, a jangle of keys in one hand and a syringe filled with an opaque whitish liquid in the other that he had most likely acquired from the med station across the hall. The sight of him only made Holly thrash harder.

"Ms. Henry, if you would be so kind," he called, his voice even as he turned the key in the lock.

Grace pressed the button again, sealing the room shut. Holly's screams faded into subdued, angry whimpers. Only then did John descend and calmly slipped the syringe into her neck. Her noises cut out, and the room relapsed into silence, save for the gentle buzz of the overhead lights.

"Like Simon said," Grace said, easing herself off the bookshelf. "Twelve souls bound to that book and damned to the depths. Now, they're trying to claw their way back out." She swiped her hand across the whiteboard, reducing several doodles to smudges, and began to write out a numbered list. "Their goal is simple: To get out and wreak havoc in our world. That makes our goals pretty simple too."

She stepped back and recited what she wrote. "One: Don't Die. Two: Don't Let Them Out. And Three: Don't Say Anything. To Anyone. Ever." She underlined the last word twice before tossing the marker back in the tray. "The only people who pay attention to this kind of thing are fake psychics and real psychiatrists, and neither one is any good to us. If you find yourself in a situation where you must speak, do your best to come up with a plausible explanation. Otherwise, keep your lip zipped and let the senior staff members do the talking."

She wiped her hands. In the distance, the all-out alarm announced midnight. "Now that you know what we're really up against, consider this your last chance to opt out. If you can't or don't want to follow these rules by any means…*any* and all…you know where the exit is."

She hopped back on the bookshelf, crossed her arms and watched them carefully. Cooper focused intently on the last crumbs of his meal, his body as still as death.

Cari looked past him to Rex. He regarded her with pressed lips and a furrowed brow. He was battling his own nature, that chaotic streak that prodded him to dive in and damn the consequences. She'd played the part of his reason and rationality many times, but never had the role been more critical than it was in this moment.

She closed her eyes pictured her home. Her rustic non-bedroom. The sticky counters and cluttered floor. The woman passed out at the table. The thump on the other side of the bedroom door.

The noises she'd tried so hard to block out with a quilt.

She opened her eyes and considered the bunker. The steel door guarding the unholy book. The demon in her cell. The phantom scratching at her throat. Grace and her busted leg.

Grace. And Cooper. And John. And whoever the guy in black was. And Rex, of course.

Danger lurked in both places. But here, she didn't have to face it alone.

She smiled at Rex as the alarm cut out. "At least we don't have to kill each other in a battle royale-style tournament to save our families."

Rex grinned back. "We'd be the exact wrong people for that job anyway."

"Touché," she agreed. With his constant string of discordant and often bigoted foster families, Rex was the only person she knew who could reasonably claim to have a worse home life than she did.

They both turned back to Grace. She raised her chin, and while she didn't quite smile, her eyes glimmered with pride. Dismounting the bookcase once again, she reached down to the bottom shelf and withdrew a thick three-ring binder. Even from across the room, Cari could see that the winged lock logo took up most of the grubby white cover.

"You're gonna have to share, I'm afraid," Grace tossed the book on the coffee table next to the remains of Cooper's food. Cari craned her head to read the upside-down words: *Virgil Security & Maintenance - New Employee Handbook.* "John's always making changes, so he only maintains the one copy. Read it early, read it often. There will be a quiz later."

Another quake throttled them. This time, the shudders were so violent Cari had to brace herself in the corner of the couch to keep from bouncing off. From the television speakers came the squeal of a siren, similar to the all-out alarm but faster, higher-pitched, and way more unsettling.

"And by quiz, I mean…"

Cooper eyed the screen. "What say you, Specs? Still nothing?"

"No such luck, Lieutenant," Simon said, his face drawn. "Major incoming. East Hall near the Buck Stop."

Metal screeched against faux wood as A.J. burst out of his chair. "On it!"

"Can we go too?" Rex clasped his hands and pouted at Grace. "Please, boss? Pretty please?"

She and Cooper exchanged a look. "If you go, we all go. I don't want you irritating the crap out of Team Helios."

"Probably a good call," Simon said. "This is gonna be a big one."

"Copy that," Grace said, mimicking A.J.'s sprint toward the lockers as best she could on her partially-functioning leg.

Cari hung back as the others grabbed their weapons. Grace swung her hammer back and forth while Rex snapped on a pair of plastic gloves and began stuffing disposable sports bottles into his canvas messenger bag. They looked like they were filled with water, but the stinging, bleachy smell hinted that they were anything but benign.

"Do you need me to take one?" Cari asked, glancing self-consciously at her weaponless locker.

"Sure," Rex said. He handed her the last bottle. "They're easy to operate. Just pop the top, aim and squeeze. But don't get it on your skin. It burns like hell." He flipped the top flap over the mouth of his bag, revealing the word *RAGE* written in jagged red letters.

Cari screwed the lid a little tighter before slipping it into the front pocket. Down the hall, A.J. hefted a massive rucksack onto his back. Half a dozen flat black gun stocks protruded from the top and sides, making him look like a giant goth peacock.

"So," Cari said to Grace as she slung her hammer over her shoulder, "A.J. is on Team Helios?"

Grace her locker shut. "Are you kidding? Look at him. A.J. *is* Team Helios."

Chapter Five

They jogged past the greeter's desk, the arched bridge, and the abandoned shell of a Mrs. Field's Cookies until they reached the ragged perforation hovering at the far end of the East Hall. Simon hadn't been exaggerating—even partially formed, the Maw was already as big as an elephant, its semi-transparency staining the midnight mosaic behind it a rotten-plum brown. Cari kept her eyes pinned to the back of Grace's head. The last time she'd looked directly into a Maw, she'd frozen up. That wouldn't happen again. Whatever abomination awaited them this time, she was not going to give it the benefit of her hesitation.

As if sensing their approach, the droopy Maw snapped into a taut circle of swirling red light. Grace gripped her hammer like a baseball bat while at the front, A.J. reached into the folds of his coat and unsheathed two short flat-bladed swords. Despite her nerves, Cari smiled appreciatively. Storing both pistols *and* a pair of mini katanas on his belt was a feat of fashion engineering the likes of which she had never seen.

A keening moan sliced through the hall. The red light constricted like a pupil in the sun before flooding the Maw with deep, black nothing. Setting her feet in a pitcher's stance, Cari gripped the bottle and braced herself for the phalanx of monsters that was about to come marching out.

Instead, a small bundle of black fur tumbled out of the depths and landed with a plop and a whine on the gray cobblestones.

"What the hell?" Rex muttered, voicing her confusion as well as his own. They leaned forward to get a better to look. A fuzzy lump huddled near the base of the Maw, blinking its green eyes and whimpering in distress.

Cari frowned. Was that a *kitten?*

Before she could fully comprehend the first fuzzball, several more emerged, tabbies and calicoes and even a teeny tiny Scottish fold. The edges of the Maw blurred with each arrival, slowly receding until only the motley litter remained, stumbling and mewling in precious disorientation.

"Awww," Rex cooed, edging past Cari toward the pile. "Look at 'em. They're so—"

A blast of compressed air cut him off as a fine mesh net descended on the kittens, quickly entangling itself in their uncoordinated limbs. Cari whipped her head toward A.J., who shoved the net gun back into the arsenal on his back, then dove forward and scooped the net off the ground, trapping the squirming brood in the makeshift sack.

"Why'd you do that?" Cari startled herself—it wasn't like her to yell at a man with the backpack full of guns. "They're just kittens."

His eyebrows drew together beneath the shadow of his hat. "Kittens? You think so?"

Without waiting for her answer, he wound up and smashed the sack against the floor in a symphony of thunks, crunches and heart-wrenching yowls.

"No!" she shrieked.

But A.J. continued to smash. The bottle slipped from her fingers and smacked against the cobblestones as she clamped her hands over her face. Two hits became three, and then more, until it sounded like a wet towel being flapped against the ground. She choked back a sob, chasing away visions of what the poor things must look like now.

"Christ, man, isn't that enough?" Rex said. He was doing his best to sound gruff, but she could hear the brittle waver in his voice. At last, the horrible noise stopped.

"Look now," A.J. said, slightly out of breath.

Cari shook her head, pressing her palms to her tearing eyes. Her imaginings had been bad enough. She didn't need to see it for real.

She jumped as something brushed her elbow.

"It's okay." Cooper's voice this time, as soft and comforting as a down quilt. "It's not what you think. Trust me."

His tugged gently at her arm. Shaking, she relented. Dark liquid smeared the cobblestones. She was about to cover her eyes again, or possibly vomit, when she noticed the color. She squinted and leaned forward ever so slightly to make sure she was seeing it right. Sure enough, the liquid wasn't red, but purplish black.

"What the...?" Taking a deep breath, she coaxed her eyes toward the mangled mass suspended from A.J.'s fist— and recoiled instantly. Instead of kittens, the smashed-up carcasses of a dozen basketball-sized spiders hung ensnared in the nylon netting. Between their size and the leathery blue-green plates covering their bodies, they looked more like dinosaurs than bugs. All of them were shattered, and most of them were dead. The few that remained glared venomously at A.J with faceted yellow eyes, their broken limbs twitching as they gnashed at the air with long, slick teeth.

"Oh my God." Cari covered her mouth. Bile burned the back of her throat again as a new series of visions floated through her mind. She saw herself reach down to scratch behind a fuzzy kitten ear. Saw its mouth open. Wider, and wider. And then the teeth…

She shook her head. If it hadn't been for A.J., she would have lost a hand.

Rex looked just as rattled. He stared at the bag, eyes perfectly round, one hand buried nervously in his hair. "Why would they *do* that?"

"To send a message," Cooper said. "A little hello to the new kids on the block."

"How thoughtful," Rex said bitterly. "Maybe we should get something for them. Like a fruit basket full of scorpions."

"I wouldn't recommend it," Grace said. "But I like the enthusiasm."

She lifted her hammer as A.J. set the bag on the ground. One of the few survivors flopped onto its back, squealing and spitting purple as Grace approached. Its barb-tipped feet scraped against the stone as it tried to right itself, but it was no use—too many of its legs were broken.

"Word of advice, kids," Grace said, "Never underestimate anything that comes out of a Maw. No matter how cute or appealing it looks, it's all the same nightmare underneath."

She raised her weapon. Once again, Cari averted her eyes. She was by no means sad to hear the hammer come down, and yet she couldn't help wincing a little at the thick, wet crunch.

"All Teams, report."

Cooper unhooked the radio from his belt. "We're clear, Specs. They popped a Trojan horse, but we neutralized it."

A.J. arched an eyebrow. "We?"

"Correction. *Helios* neutralized it. And the Maw appears to have disintegrated on its own."

"*Um...are you sure?*" Simon asked, his voice barely audible over the still-shrieking siren. *"The heat sensors are still picking up activity in the area. Looks like there's another one out there."*

Cari swiveled her head up and down the hall, along with everyone else. Except for the giant smear of spidersaurus guts on the floor, nothing appeared out of the ordinary.

"We've got no visual," Cooper said. "Can you re-confirm the location?"

"Um, that's the thing, Coop. It's sort of...moving."

"What are you talking about?" Cooper demanded. "Maws don't move."

"I don't know what to tell you, friend. This one does."

"What's its position?"

"About fifty feet west from your current position, near the rotunda arch. And I think—yeah, it's definitely heading your way."

They all looked again. But there was still nothing there.

"We don't *see* anything!" Grace shouted.

"It's there, dammit! It's coming right at you!"

Cari's heart raced. Her eyes flicked back and forth, searching the storefronts, the faux second-floor windows, anywhere that a Maw might hide. She saw nothing. More importantly, she *felt* nothing. No shaking floor, no cold fingers, no dry throat. Everything was completely normal.

And then everything was gone.

Chapter Six

She woke up on her back somewhere dark. Dark, hot and damp, with gray-green fog that stunk like gym socks and rotten bananas. It clung to everything—her skin, her eyelids, her lips. She wished she could hold her breath forever. Sipping the sweaty-tasting air through her mouth, she took in the thicket of lumpy gray tubes that surrounded her. They looked like giant misshapen sausages with smaller sausages sticking out of them, stretching high and out of sight into the impenetrable shadows above.

"Ugh…"

"Jesus!" Cari screamed as Cooper emerged from the murk next to her. The jolt of adrenaline made her vision go fuzzy. "You scared the crap out of me."

"Sorry." His brow furrowed she massaged her pounding temples. "Are you okay?"

"I'm fine," she said. "What happened? Are we…in hell?"

"No." Cooper took a knee, feeling around the ash-colored moss at their feet until he found the radio. He pressed the button, but nothing happened. "First of all, we don't even know if the Maws technically open into hell. We're about ninety-nine percent sure, but there's no way to confirm. Second, the only way a human successfully passes all the way through a Maw is if they choose to. Unwilling captives are ejected almost immediately."

Cari gestured to the bizarre forest. "*This* is ejected?"

"Yes and no. A couple of years ago, some of the settlers started using Maws for short-wave teleportation. They suck us up from one place and dump us out in another. It's the underworld equivalent of making a quarter disappear. They do it mainly to divide our ranks and create confusion, but it also has an added bonus of inducing a veil, or a shared dream state." He knocked one of the formless lumps with his knuckle. Despite being at least twenty feet tall, the entire thing quivered as if it were made of paper. "All this might look and smell and taste real, but it isn't. Physically, we are still in the mall somewhere. We just have to wait for the others to find us. With Simon's array, it shouldn't take long. An hour, at most."

"Great." Cari shivered as a slimy breeze licked at her neck. "What are we supposed to do until then?"

A leonine growl ripped Cooper's answer apart. From between two tree lumps emerged a lanky, shadowy figure. Long black hair rippled from its skull, joining with the hair on its face, shoulders, and torso like a scruffy hooded sweatshirt. It wore a loincloth made of silver scale mail and its legs were covered in short black fuzz that ended in padded feline feet. Its eyes were perfectly round white orbs, punctured through the center with a bullet of black. It looked like an upright lion. Or a demonic Chewbacca. Cari's heart thrummed with fear and, weirdly, regret. She wished Rex was here. He'd know exactly what glib pop culture reference to make.

The creature lifted its arms. In each hand, a thin crescent of steel glinted in the foggy light. It tipped its face up to the inky sky and roared again, revealing every one of its fang-like teeth.

Cooper unholstered his gun. "And you thought we'd be bored."

"Simon, I'm coming in!" Grace yelled at nothing in particular, bouncing impatiently on her good foot as she waited for the painfully slow filing cabinet to swing away from the wall. He didn't answer, but that didn't mean anything. Simon had the place wired halfway to oblivion. There was no way he hadn't heard her.

At last, the cabinet opened enough for her to squeeze through. She gripped the banister and propelled herself down the stairs. Her injured leg throbbed in protest, but she barely noticed. She was too busy trying to convince herself what had happened hadn't really happened. Her hands shook so badly it took her three tries to plug in the first number of the keycode. Luckily, John opened the door from inside before she had to deal with the rest.

"What's going on?" he asked as she pushed past him. "I thought I heard Mr. Mackie yell something about a shuttle. Is it true?"

"Maybe," Grace tossed over her shoulder as she peg-legged her way past the kitchenette and down the dim hall that led to the Surveillance suite. She twisted the knob, but it was locked. Of course. "Simon, open up!"

From the other side came the scrape of metal, followed by a flurry of frantic rustling. "I, uh...do you have to? I mean, it's not like this has never happened before."

Her fingers curled into fists. "Now is not the time, Simon. Open this door or I swear to God I will rip it off its hinges."

A loud clatter and more rustling served to rile her further. Was he actually *barricading* the door?

"Can't you watch on the main viewer? I'll loop you in on everything, I swear."

"You see?" she demanded from John, who now stood next to her, slightly winded from chasing her down. "*This* is why you don't accommodate madness. Because it ends up *biting you in the ass.*" She unleashed a flurry of fists on the wood-paneled door until John slipped his hands over her arms and stopped her.

"This is not productive." His voice itched like antiseptic on a paper cut. "Mr. Mackie can perform his duties however he sees fit in order to achieve the best results. There's nothing you can do in there that you can't do from the lounge."

"Fine," she grumbled. Shaking his hands away, she stumbled back down the hall. If Cooper was here, he'd probably say the same thing. Compared to some of the other crap they dealt with, shuttle recovery was about as routine as it got.

They just had to figure out where the bastards had dropped them off first.

She lumbered toward the lounge's flatscreen, where Simon had already thrown up a black and white high-angle view of the East Hall. Between the high-def cameras and the 4K resolution, she could clearly see the remains of the first Maw, a distorted shadow lingering in the air like unnaturally bounded mist. Other than that, and the dark smear on the floor, the hallway was empty.

"Call Team Helios," Grace barked at the screen. "Patch him through the TV mic."

A series of beeps ensued before a voice came through, distorted but easily recognizable. "*Team Helios reporting. What's up, home slice.*"

She rolled her eyes. "Rex, give A.J. back the radio."

"*No can do, Boss. I'm under orders to, and I quote, answer your questions and stay the hell of out the way.*"

"You let him go on a recovery mission?"

She winced at the skeptical tone in John's voice. "He wouldn't take no for an answer. I figured it was better to have him being useful out there than bouncing off the walls and distracting us down here. Besides, Cari is his girlfriend, so—"

"*Friend!*" Rex's voice piped in. "*Not girlfriend. She and I, we're just friends.*"

"Fine. Whatever. Either way, you're highly motivated. What's your position?"

"*On the far end of the mall, near the south entrance. We're working our way back towards you.*"

"And?"

The uncharacteristically long pause that followed irritated her more than anything Rex could have said.

"*Nothing yet.*"

"Son of a bitch." She slapped the chair in front of her so hard it nearly fell over.

"*Don't worry,*" Simon interjected. "*We'll find 'em. Give me a second.*" The view screen flashed blue, followed by a rapid parade of images from different parts of the mall. The east entrance. Spartan Sport and Range. The Atlas fountain. The bathroom sinks. Her eyes probed each one, searching for Maws, for movement, for anything that looked out of the ordinary. The gamut finished with a series of exterior angles, useless for the current purpose, and the cycle started from the beginning. Her heart galloped, spurred on by adrenaline and dread. Aside from the occasional glimpse of A.J. and Rex prowling the halls it was the calmest Power Hour she had ever seen.

Chapter Seven

The dire Wookie hunkered down, shifting back on its heels as it launched into a run. It didn't get more than a few feet before Cooper fired a blast that made Cari's brain shimmy in her skull. The creature doubled over with a howling scream as the scattershot ripped through its abdomen.

"Behind me," Cooper hissed. He accentuated the point by grabbing her wrist and shepherding her to his side as two more creatures, each an exact copy of the first, emerged from the lump-line. She slapped her hands over her ears as the knee of one exploded in a wet burst, followed by half of the other one's head.

"Reversing!"

She jumped back, avoiding Cooper's feet by mere inches. He swung his gun toward another emerging threat and fired. Another backstep was followed by another shot. She kept pace, her fingers curled lightly into the back of his utility vest as her eyes darted left and right, wary of more enemies. The burn of gunpowder joined the humid stink of mold and meat, making the place smell like the world's worst barbecue. Another step. Another shot. The ground sloped upward as their progress led to the top of a mossy gray hillock. It was high enough for her to see over the top of the tree-lumps to the edge of the forest—if the forest had an edge, that is. But it was just a bunch of lumpy gray nodules, packed together like a rotten head of broccoli, on and on until finally surrendering to the murk and disappearing from sight.

She shot a glance over her shoulder. Pair after pair of white orbs with black dots blinked into existence between the trees behind them.

Her fingers dug further into Cooper's vest. They were surrounded.

They were trapped.

Undaunted, Cooper retrained his weapon. The thick air grew thicker with gun smoke and black bloody mist as he perforated the hairy army, and yet the carnage did nothing to stem the tide. No sooner had he dispensed with one enemy than the eyes of two more snapped open behind their comrade's mangled corpse. Unleashing a lion-like growl of his own, he spun in a full circle, firing his weapon into the field below as she tried to duck and crawl into invisibility. How long had the wave been coming? How long would it be before it broke?

"Cartridge!" he yelled over the roar of gunfire and enemy screams.

She stared blankly up at the back of his head. What did that mean? Like for a printer? Or a video game? And what did that have to do with the peril at hand?

"Left side pocket." He stopped firing long enough to jiggle his gun. "Running low!"

Oh. Right.

She reached into the indicated vest pocket and withdrew a drum of bullets. He ejected his cartridge, taking another step backward so he could reload. She stepped with him—and felt something thin and sharp zip tight around her ankle.

Crap.

The world did a somersault. Her stomach flipped as her lungs slammed into her ribcage. She landed hard, her back slamming into the cold, wet dirt.

"Cari!"

Cooper's voice rang out from somewhere high above her. High and far away. She tried to reach toward the sound, but her bones ached from the impact and logic flitted in and out of her grasp. She managed to drag her head up enough to see a rough black cord wrapped around her ankle. It snaked down the hill and disappeared into the garlands of fog. A snare of some kind, and she had walked right into it.

The rough rope bit into her skin. She screamed as it wrenched her bones and tendons, dragging her several feet closer to the fog where another pair of eyes danced out at her. But these eyes were not like these others. These were not black, but a bright, bloody red.

"Take cover!"

The order bypassed her rattled mind and surged straight to her arms. They wrapped themselves around her head as a spray of bullets assaulted the rope and surrounding ground. When the barrage ceased, she unraveled her arms and looked up. Cooper stood over her, staring at the ground with a mix of fury and disbelief. It didn't take a genius to figure out why—except for a small pockmark or two, the rope looked absolutely no different.

"Dammit!" she cried, her disorientation smothered by a blanket of rage. She yanked herself forward and clawed into the rope with her nails. But it was no use. Even the slick of blood seeping from the gashes in her ankle did nothing to soften the steely black fibers.

Another sharp tug threw her backward once again. The fog at her feet thinned just enough for her to see the thing that had her in its clutches.

There were two of them, one standing up, one crouched with the rope in its hands. That one looked like all the rest—same hair, same eyes, same fury. The upright beast was some kind of albino, with a silvery white coat and rabbit red eyes. Instead of the dual scythes, it held a long ivory staff topped with a curved silver blade.

It grinned at her. Her lungs withered at the sight of his zippered teeth. It shifted the sickle to both hands. The grip was nauseatingly similar to how Grace had held her hammer before crushing the bag of hellish spiders. It hadn't been pretty, but at least it had been quick.

Cari had a feeling she wasn't going to be so lucky.

The albino grunted at its cohort. She would have screamed, but shock had cauterized any faculties she had left. When the underling yanked on the rope for the third and final time, her body closed the distance between them as limp and helpless as a rag doll.

The albino's grin widened. The blade rose. Half-dead with fear already, it took all the strength she had left to close her eyes.

She'd been cut before. A razor nick on the back of her knee. An errant chop of a carrot. Even one or two blood-brother-type promises she'd made before she was old enough to know how stupid that was. She assumed being stabbed would feel similar. A thousand times worse, of course, but on the same spectrum. So, when she felt a massive crushing weight fall on her instead, it startled her just enough to make her eyes pop open.

She found herself staring directly at Cooper.

The sickle came down. He bellowed as the tip of the blade impaled his shoulder.

Her jaw fell open, but she was too stunned to make a sound.

"Run," he muttered through gritted teeth. A drop of blood clung to the corner of his mouth. "Now."

"How? I'm—" She was going to say trapped, but a roll of her ankle proved her wrong. When they had released her, or why, she didn't know. She wriggled away as the albino wrenched the blade from Cooper's flesh. He grunted in pain. A rope flew out from the darkness and snagged him around the neck. She could see streaks of blood—her blood—coating the black fibers.

Apparently, one human sacrifice was as good as another.

She slid back as more demonic eyes flickered to life among the trees. A few glanced her way, but not many. They were much more interested in Cooper.

No. Not interested. Envious. Eager. They wanted to play with the new toy too.

"Run," he spluttered again. His fingers clawed at the wet earth. "*Run!*"

Her heart told her to stay, but her feet were less convinced. She was at the bottom of the hill before she knew it, dragging her bleeding ankle as she headed for a not-yet-lion-infested section of the monstrous forest. She barely made it ten feet past the lump line before the fog became so thick that she couldn't see far enough ahead of her to take the next step. She slowed but kept moving, taking step after blind, mangled step. It felt like progress, and yet every noise that came from behind her—every impact, every scream, every satisfied feline chuckle—seemed as loud and gut-wrenching as if she were standing right next to him. Just when she thought she would lose her mind if she heard one more sound, the torturous noises cut out like someone had hit the Escape button.

She stopped dead. The fog pressed in, sealing up the remaining visibility and packing her into dark, silent nothingness. Her usurped brain regained its authority, and with it came a hefty helping of guilt. Cooper had saved her life by offering up his own. No one had ever done that for her before. And she had returned the sacrifice by leaving him to be ripped apart by devil lions.

Her cheeks burned as she stared reproachfully at the void in front of her. Whenever she and Rex played co-op games, she never hesitated to throw herself into the fray, to take a few hits for the good of the team. And yet now, when she'd had the chance to do that for real, she'd run scared. She'd never thought of herself as the kind of person who would turn her back on someone in need...

...and she wasn't. She never had been, and she wasn't going to start now.

Raising her chin, she glanced over her shoulder at the foggy nothing behind her. Without the screams, she couldn't be sure she was looking in the right direction. Or that she wasn't already too late. But then again, there had been no death rattle, no clear moment of expiration. The screams hadn't faded. They had simply stopped. As far as she knew, he was still alive.

It was reason enough to try.

She turned until she had made what she guessed was a full about-face.

"I'm coming, Cooper."

Taking a deep breath, she stepped back into the fog—and emerged somewhere completely different.

The video reached the end of its cycle for what felt like the eightieth time. Grace rubbed her eyes. She'd shimmied closer and closer to the screen with every repetition. Now she was practically kissing it. It gave her one bitch of a headache, but without any obvious clues as to where the Maw had deposited Cooper and Cari, she had to look for the non-obvious ones. A stray sneaker. A scuffed tile. A drop of blood. If it was there, she was not going to miss it.

"Helios, report," she said without taking her eyes off the screen.

"Yeah, we're here," Rex answered after several long seconds. *"We're finishing up in the West Hall. I never realized how big this place is before tonight."*

She frowned. His earlier rambunctiousness had evaporated, and his voice was tight and fraught with concern.

Clearly, there was no point in asking if they'd found anything.

The video continued to scroll through the empty corridors. She chewed her thumbnail, dreading the question she knew she had to ask.

"Simon, is there any chance that they...aren't here anymore?"

"What?" Rex cut in before Simon could respond. *"What do you mean, not here anymore? Where would they go?"*

The screen flipped to Simon's indignant face. "No way. They'd have to agree to it, and Cooper would never let that happen."

"Let what happen? Will someone please tell me what's going on?"

John leaned forward on the couch, his fingers steepled below his chin. "Lieutenant O'Bannon served in Iraq," he said, his voice low, limiting his thoughts to her ears only. "He's had resistance training. They could beat him into dust, and he would never give himself up."

"I know, and normally I would agree with you," Grace muttered back. "But it's not just him out there this time.

Like you said, he *is* a soldier. You think there's anything he wouldn't do to protect an innocent kid?"

John's deep sigh was answer enough.

"*Boss?*" Rex ventured, his voice brittle. "*Hello? Can anyone hear me?*"

She glanced up at Simon, then back at John. Their pained expressions told her they were going to be no help.

She rubbed her forehead and closed her eyes. Why couldn't the Maw have taken her instead? She was a blunt instrument. She should be the one out there bashing up the bad guys. It should be her life that got traded to save another—not that it would have come to that if Cooper were in charge right now. He was the tactician. The man with the plan. If the situation were reversed, the way it *should* be, he would have no trouble bringing her home.

But she wasn't about to say any of that to Rex. The last thing she wanted to do right now was make a sixteen-year-old kid cry.

A harsh rasp terminated the tense silence. Grace jumped and nearly whacked her head against the screen. She whirled to face the noise.

While they had been searching for the missing pair, Holly had managed to wriggle out of her restraints and now squatted like a frog on top of her rumpled cot. She fixed them with a black-eyed stare as a dry wheeze grated out of her rancid, grinning mouth.

A few stunned moments passed before Grace realized that she was laughing.

Chapter Eight

Cari gulp in short, shallow breaths through her nose as she tried to get her bearings. The pine-scented air and warm, buttery light were a far cry from the sickly fog of her previous surroundings. In fact, the only thing that remotely matched her previous surroundings was the large oil painting hanging on the wall behind the expansive mahogany desk. The hairy beast resembled the sickle-wielding albino very closely, except for the bulbous nose and fleshy chin that made him look more human, and therefore even more horrifying. He seemed both revolted and enraptured to be devouring the arm of a headless human corpse. She didn't know the name of the painting, but it looked familiar, as if she'd skimmed over it in a textbook. She wouldn't have lingered on it, that's for sure.

In front of the desk were two mottled pink leather chairs, and at their backs was a red velvet settee where Cooper lay sprawled out, disheveled and barely conscious. Short, deep gashes covered his face and arms, and a thick purple bruise wrapped around his neck. His shoulder bore such a striking similarity to hamburger meat that looking at it made her feel sick. But most concerning was the dark splotch the size of a softball spreading across the left side of his utility vest.

"Cooper?" She laid her hand delicately on an unscathed section of forearm. He shivered at the contact.

"I told you...to run..." he wheezed around bright pink teeth. "Now...it's...too late."

"Why? Where are we?"

Groaning, Cooper managed to heave an eye open. "His office." He jerked his face toward the desk. Between two fountain pens sat a slim black nameplate inscribed with gold letters. *Reverend Lawrence Fludd.*

She frowned. "I thought he was from the 1800s."

"He can be...whatever he wants...in here." He flopped his arm until his fingers found the sleeve of her sweatshirt. "Listen...he's gonna try to convince you...to join him. He'll use logic, and bribery, and when that fails, violence. And it's gonna hurt. He won't kill you, but you'll wish he would. That's what he's counting on. Because for you to really be his, he needs your permission. Say yes and the pain will stop. But it will only be the beginning."

Grunting, he shifted his other arm so he could take her by both shoulders. His green eyes pierced hers with their cold, dim light. "You have to say no. As loud as you can and as many times as you can until they come for us. And they will come...I promise..."

His hands slipped from her shoulders, and he fell back.

"Cooper?" She tapped his arm. No answer. She fumbled with his wrist and felt around for a pulse. Was that his blood she felt or her own?

She had decided that the slow, irregular thump was definitely his when the dark wood-paneled door creaked open behind her. Her body stiffened as the horrors of the evening marched through her mind in a dark parade, culminating with an image of the painting above the desk. If their little romp in the woods had been the opening act,

Veiled Threats

then what rotten, madness-inducing hell spawn waited behind her?

"Well, hello there."

Low and slow, with a smooth southern drawl. She frowned. It didn't *sound* like the voice of a cannibalistic monster. But then again, how would she know? It wasn't like she had a huge frame of reference. Bracing herself, she turned to face him.

The man standing in the doorway looked...the only word she could think of was *rich*. He wore a deep black suit and a crisp white shirt with gold cufflinks. He had chestnut brown hair combed back from his widow's peak and a clean-shaven, pasty white face. There were a few wrinkles on his forehead and at the corners of his dark eyes, but he didn't look old. Forty-five, or maybe a bit older. If it weren't for the circumstances—and that painting looming at the edge of her vision—she would have been tempted to call him handsome.

He nodded hospitably at Cooper's unconscious-or-worse body. "Lieutenant O'Bannon. By all means, make yourself comfortable. And you." He turned to Cari. "You must be the little one I've heard so much about. Reverend Lawrence Fludd. A pleasure to make your acquaintance."

He extended his hand. At first, she thought he was offering it for her to shake. She was about to slap it away when he swung his arm wide. He was gesturing at the sideboard lined with crystal decanters, arranged according to the hue of their contents, from golden honey to licorice brown. "Can I offer you a drink?"

"I, uh...no," Cari stuttered. "I don't drink."

"As you wish." He poured a healthy amount from one of the darkest distillations into a beautifully engraved tumbler. "I hope you'll forgive me if I don't offer one to the Lieutenant. He doesn't seem in any state to

148

accommodate a stiff libation at the moment, wouldn't you agree?"

Cari looked back at Cooper. Except for the deep red of his wounds, he was desperately pale. "Is he dead?"

"He's walking the path, sure enough." Leather creaked as the Reverend settled into the chair behind his desk. "Whether or not he reaches the end, however, depends on you."

"What do you mean?"

The words came from Holly, but her lips didn't move. She stayed frozen in her froggy pose with her mouth open in a perfect circle. The only thing that moved was her throat, spasming and clucking like she was trying to cough up a furball. The words retched out of her as if she were a loudspeaker.

"*I mean that, with the Lieutenant indisposed for this tet a tet, you are the only one who can supply the second tet.*"

"What's happening?" Grace cautiously approached the bars of Holly's cell door.

"I don't know," John said as he joined her. "This is the first time she's said anything coherent since we subdued her."

"*I...I can't do that. I'm not...I don't have—*" Holly coughed, cutting herself off. Her eyelids ratcheted into a narrow glare. "*He will die if you don't. I won't have to do a thing. We'll sit here, quietly, and watch him slip away. Is that what you want?*"

"What the hell is she talking about?" Grace shook the bars in frustration. "What the hell are you *talking* about?"

Holly cocked her head at Grace, who stiffened. Those black eyes were vicious enough to cut right through her.

"*No!*" Holly's high-pitched shriek made Grace's bones itch. She gripped the bars tighter and scowled, refusing to show the unhinged bitch even one iota of the unease bubbling up inside her. *"Don't hurt him. Yes, okay, fine. If that's what you want, I will speak for him. For us."*

"Dear God," John exhaled. "That's Cari."

Grace glared at him. "How can you tell?"

"How can you *not?* It sounds exactly like her. She must be talking to someone, and the conversation is being…broadcast somehow, to us, through Holly. It's…incredible."

"Yeah, I'm positively giddy with excitement," she sniped. "Can you tell which one of them she's talking to?"

"No." He leaned forward. "But whoever it is, they obviously want us to hear what they have to say."

"Have a seat."

Cari considered the chair in front of his desk. The pink leather was too pale to be dyed, yet it didn't look like any natural leather she'd seen before. Its mottling reminded her of her mother's face after she'd had a few, how the ruddiness in her cheeks faded into rosy blotches at her temples and jaw, while the skin of her neck remained as white as milk. She sidled closer to Cooper. "I'd rather stand."

The Reverend arched an eyebrow over the rim of the crystal tumbler. Despite having taken several sips, the level of liquid had not receded a drop. "A bit squeamish, are we? It's not as though the chairs bite." His lips split into a toothy grin. "Not anymore, anyway."

Her stomach lurched. She clenched her jaw and tried to look tough. "Tell me what you want."

"Very well." He set his glass down. "I want the good doctor."

"John?" She frowned. Besides a pony, that was the last thing she expected him to ask for. "What do you want with him?"

"Well, it's like this." He clasped his hands on his desk. "I assume they told you how I arrived at this sorry state of affairs."

Considering the lush office, she couldn't see what he had to be sorry about. But she kept that observation to herself. Why drag this out any more than necessary? "Yeah. So what?"

He chuckled to himself. "If you need to ask, it means they must have left out some critical details. Specifically, the name of the man who refused to extend the Courier's bargain."

His knowing smile sent a shiver down her back. She shook her head.

"Now, now," the Reverend said gently. "There's no need to get upset. After all, who would expect a child to recall the name of a single town magistrate from ten years ago? No, the fault isn't yours. It's theirs. They kept it from you to hide his shame. Doctor John Virgil, former mayor and man of medicine, sent my soul to the devil to preserve his own."

He looked so smug that she had to turn away so she didn't throw up on the thick burgundy carpet.

"He didn't know," she explained to her feet. "He thought it was a con. Or a joke. He didn't know."

"Didn't know or didn't care?" the Reverend pressed as he stood up. "Lest we forget, his dismissal did more than prompt the Courier to finish his business with me. It ruined your town. Stole your future. When you think about it, you're as much a victim here as I am."

Slipping his hands casually into his pockets, he ambled around to the front of his desk and perched lightly on the edge, appearing to be every bit the congenial southern statesman. "See, you and I, we're the same. We can help each other out. What do you say?"

He smiled pleasantly, his dark eyes soft and inviting like rich milk chocolate, or crushed velvet.

Or the fur of a kitten.

She smiled back.

"No."

The confidence drained from his face. "What?"

"We're *not* the same," she said, her smile flipping into a scowl. "You're a hypocrite and a murderer. You deserve everything you got, and everything you're ever going to get. We are gonna make sure of that. Me, and John, and all the others. Forever."

She glared at him defiantly, her head swimming with euphoria. That felt good. Better than good. Righteous. Liberating.

But her triumph fizzled at the Reverend's throaty chuckle.

"Wonderful speech, darling. And while I admire your loyalty to a master you've had for all of two days, I'm afraid you've missed my point. My soul was the lifeblood of this town. I sacrificed myself upon its altar so it would thrive."

"Oh, please." She was glad he was standing in front of her so she could spit the words in his face. "You were trying to save your own ass. The fact that you failed is nobody's fault but your own. Not to mention that you dragged twelve other people down with you."

He glowered down at her. "Regardless of my original intent or the *alleged* aftereffects, the soul I proffered *is* what made Halcyon great. That is an undeniable fact. Your dear doctor couldn't be bothered to make the same sacrifice. He failed to live up to his oath of office, to say nothing of his oath to good old Hippocrates. He took the town we loved and crushed it beneath his own cowardice."

His hands shot out too quickly for her to dodge. She shrieked and tried to wriggle out of his grip. But his hands, and in fact his entire body, seemed to be emanating a sharp, debilitating cold.

"Can you honestly tell me that a man like that deserves such fierce loyalty?" he whispered, latching his gaze onto hers. "Especially from someone like you. Someone he has already devoured?"

She tried to answer, but his eyes silenced her. They swam like whirlpools, dark and rich and blissfully endless. The cold feeling disappeared, replaced by a warmth as thick and rich as melted caramel. She could almost smell the toasted sugar.

"What do you want?" The words dripped from her mouth before she realized she was going to say them.

He put a finger briefly to her lips. Shadows blurred the edges of her vision, chipping away at her awareness until all she could see was him.

"There was never any hope, you know." He didn't say it to her, but into her. Through her. She was a secondary player, floating around the edges of her own consciousness, shunted to the side to make room for someone else. "All this time, you've been throwing rocks at an avalanche. It gets closer, and you rage harder, but it was always meant to engulf you. Whether you believe it or not doesn't make it anything less than gospel."

He ran his hands up her arms. Even through her sweatshirt, she could feel his clammy palms leeching into her skin.

"It's time, John. Accept it. Sign the book."

Grace's hands shook as her blood surged furiously through her veins. That slimy son of a bitch had not only kidnapped two people, he now had the balls to make *ransom demands?*

"That's insane," she growled. "It's insane, right John?"

She glared at him expectantly. He was staring at Holly with one arm crossed over his chest and the other fist pressed to his mouth as if he were going to be sick.

"John?"

He jumped as if he'd forgotten she was there. "Uh, yes. That is what—yes."

Shaking himself out of his ineloquence, he addressed Holly. "Even if I wanted to sign, the bargain is closed."

Holly sat with her face turned up to the ceiling, mouth wide and black eyes open. She hadn't fully blinked once since her fugue began, and the edges of her eyelids were raw and cracked. It didn't even look like she was breathing. Just when Grace thought the conversation had ended—or maybe Holly had given up and simply died—there came another wet rumble from Holly's throat.

"Then make a new bargain."

John inhaled deeply. "I can't. I'd need the Courier."

"Find him. It shouldn't be too hard. He has a nose for desperation."

"I—he...he's been missing for years. It's possible he might be...gone. Permanently."

The tip of Holly's chin dropped to her sternum, exposing the brown and green stains coating her throat. She emitted a wet burp as her puppeteer attempted to compose himself. *"Even if the Courier is missing or gone, as you say, whatever* employed *the Courier is not."*

John closed his eyes. "Perhaps."

"Good. A new deal, then. Your soul in exchange for my freedom, as well as the safe return of Lieutenant O'Bannon and the girl."

John rubbed his eyes. To Grace's horror, he appeared to be considering it. Slowly, he shook his head. "I can't."

Holly's black eyes narrowed into slits. *"You're the same coward you always were, Virgil."*

"You don't understand—"

"I understand perfectly. And as is usually the case, the price for your cowardice will be visited upon the young." Holly's mouth stretched into a freak show grin. *"The only difference is that this time, you're going to have to watch."*

Cari moaned as the warm, sweet feeling vanished beneath a plume of ice. What had the Reverend said? She'd heard him speak, but the words were formless, squishy sounds severed from any meaning. She wanted to run, but her legs were so weak that she had to lean into his grip to keep herself from collapsing.

"You can't kill me," she moaned in dogged defiance even as her head flopped back. Her peripheral vision was still non-existent, and her brain felt like it had been pureed. "Cooper said this isn't real."

"It isn't," the Reverend said. "This is merely a playground for the mind. But your body—your real body—is still somewhere." His eyes sagged momentarily closed. "And now, mine is there too."

"Huh—?"

Her words ended in a strangled gurgle as ten thick invisible fingers wrapped themselves around her throat. She clawed at her collar but found only her own skin. Chuckling, the Reverend let go of her shoulders. She dropped to her knees in front of him.

"Stop." Cooper stirred behind her. "Leave her alone."

The Reverend frowned and his eyes slid sideways. There was a loud wheezing grunt, and his gaze fell back on her. She waited for Cooper to protest further but heard only silence. Turning her eyes up, she twisted her jaw in a silent plea for him to stop, to let her go. To let her live.

He smiled wider.

"Who's the embarrassment now?"

Chapter Nine

Holly collapsed backward, squealing and clawing at her throat.

"Jesus," John gasped. "He's really going to kill her."

But Grace wasn't listening. She was thinking about the last words Holly had said before she'd started gagging. Soft words, almost too soft to hear.

Who's the embarrassment now?

Why did that feel so...familiar?

"We've got incoming!" Simon's voice blurted from the television in the other room.

"Where?" she shouted over her shoulder.

"Unclear."

She rolled her eyes. "One of those days, I guess."

"I can't take this," John said. She was about to ask him what that meant, but he was already running full speed toward the lounge.

And the book.

"John, wait!" Grace cursed her bad leg as she hobbled after him. "That isn't the answer. We'll figure this out. Give me one second to—"

"To what? You have no idea where they are. This is the only way." He stumbled through the scattered mass of chairs and closed in on the steel door.

"Stop!" Grace shouted. Her leg screamed at her to slow down. She ignored it and launched herself forward. Her hands landed on John's arm as his fingertips grazed the release button and yanked him away before he could press it, buying just enough time to scramble past him and wedge herself between the wall and his terrible ideas.

"What are you doing?" he demanded, the lenses of his bifocals magnifying the desperation in his eyes.

She arched her back and spread her arms over the wall, shielding the release button while maintaining enough distance to not accidentally bump it herself. John hesitated, his hands hovering in the air near her waist as he struggled with this new quandary. He still wanted to get to the book, but he was unwilling to violate the social mores of personal space. It was this exact dilemma she had been counting on to buy herself some time.

"He could have called her a loser," she said, breathless after her recent sprint. "Or a wimp. No offense, but either one would have made more sense. But he said embarrassment, even though she hasn't done anything that even comes close to embarrassing. So why would he…say that…oh my God, *that's* what this is all about?" Her skin prickled with understanding, and then fury.

"What are you saying?" John demanded.

"I know where they are." Grace craned her neck toward the television. "Simon, pull up the video feed for all the bathrooms."

"*Which ones?*"

"Any that look at the stalls."

"*Uh, well, we don't have any that look* into *the stalls, you know, for obvious reasons—*"

"I know that, genius," Grace snapped. "Just give me the best we've got."

"*Roger that. Standby.*" The screen cut to blue.

"We're wasting time," John brooded, moving away from her in favor of pacing the floor.

"Give me a minute." She turned to face the screen. "If this doesn't work, you can finger paint every single page with my blessing."

John snorted. The screen cut to a black and white image of a tiled room with three stainless steel stalls.

"Come on," Grace whispered as the images cycled in even more rapid succession than before. "Show me where you are."

The cycle started over.

And she saw it.

"Stop!" She stabbed a finger at the screen a wrinkled white thing flitted out from under a handicap stall. It withdrew just as quickly, leaving a faintly glistening trail behind it.

"What?" John's head nudged over her shoulder. He squinted desperately at the screen. "What do you see?"

"Wait for it," she said, her finger hovering over the spot where she had seen the movement. Sure enough, the white thing returned. This time it stayed there, stark and obvious against the dark granite tile. How could they have missed it?

If she had to guess, it was probably because it hadn't been there until a moment ago.

"Helios, report!" Grace shouted as John dashed across the bunker to his locker.

"*Helios-adjacent here. You got something?*" Rex said eagerly.

"Second-floor women's bathroom. Handicap stall. Be advised, there is at least one hostile." With that, she limped away after John.

"*How can you tell?*" Rex's voice chased her, but Grace didn't stop to answer.

He'd find out soon enough.

Cari gasped as the Reverend's invisible grip eased, letting in a trickle of air. He tilted his head, the corners of his lips twitching up with amused curiosity. Whatever the state of his real body, this one was perfectly composed. He stood with his hands clasped behind his back and a slight bend at his waist, looking down on her as if she were a child reciting a poem. He was enjoying this, watching her body try to heal itself, watching her hope rise, knowing all the while that he could crush them both at any moment.

"Please..." she begged, tears streaming from the corners of her eyes. "Please...stop..."

Dropping to one knee, he took her face in his hands, closing the distance between them until the tip of his nose nearly brushed hers.

"Don't worry." His breath was cloying and noxious, like sour milk. "Whatever world you go to next, you won't be alone for long. Your friends will be there soon. I promise you that."

"No..."

The invisible vice clamped down once again. Blood throbbed in her ears as she grasped futilely at her bare neck. Unless something stopped him, his hands would not leave her throat again.

The Reverend must have sensed her realization. He ran his tongue over his lips as his pupils fattened with pleasure. She rolled her eyes once before squeezing them shut. She might not be able to get out of dying, but she certainly didn't have to watch him get off on it either.

A soft electronic beep cut through the fog of static crowding her ears.

What the hell is that?

She peeled her eyelids up and glanced at her left wrist. The face of her digital watch peered back at her. 1:00 AM. End of Power Hour. Her racing heart skipped a beat. She had successfully stalled him long enough. Now he would simply turn to dust and she would wake up somewhere in the mall, she and Cooper both, safe and—

He doubled his grip, squeezing so hard she thought her neck would break. Her eyes bulged in their sockets, forcing themselves open, forcing her to look whether she wanted to or not. The Reverend's plump, rosy face had turned a sickly grayish white. It sagged from his jaw and cheekbones like the skin of an uncooked chicken. The color had drained from his eyes, turning from brown to bilious yellow, and his once upright frame was as bent and crooked as a crone.

The veil hadn't disappeared, but it *was* receding. Slowly, but perhaps enough for her to get away. She shifted back on her knees, but something flat and cold pressed against her back. A wall. Or a floor.

Her arms fell like lead to her sides. Veil or no veil, she was still trapped.

The Reverend's gray tongue lolled from his mouth as if tasting her defeat. He threw his head back to laugh.

Instead, he let out a long, multi-tonal shriek that made her throbbing eyes recede into her skull. The bands of iron disappeared from her throat. Coughing and spluttering, she peeled her sore eyes open.

After the soft glow of the Reverend's office, the overhead fluorescent lights were almost blinding.

She was on her back, her legs splayed out with her right temple pressed to the base of a toilet. To her left, Cooper lay sprawled on the floor, unconscious but no longer bleeding. His well-being would have been her biggest concern if not for the necrotic skeleton straddling her hips. She groaned as a torrent of greenish-white goo slid from the baseball-sized hole its chest down its stomach and onto her sweatshirt.

"Mayhem!"

The sound of Rex's voice made her want to cry. Behind the foul creature, the over-sized door of the handicap stall rattled on its hinges as something heavy smashed against it. It was then she noticed the smoking perforation in the door approximately level with the demon's gaping wound.

"We're here, May! We're coming for you."

The thing's mouth twisted into a sneer. She would have thought that losing most of his torso would kill him, or at least distract him long enough to give the others a fighting chance. Apparently, she had underestimated his commitment. He twisted around, sending another gooey flesh river cascading over her stomach. She choked back vomit as it slathered her belly what felt like liquefied fish guts.

Another slam against the door practically mangled the puny lock. Sneering, the creature shifted into a crouch, his ragged-nailed fingers curled into claws.

"May."

A thump near her feet made her crane her head downward. Rex was on his knees, a sports bottle in each hand, pressing his cheek against the floor so he could see under the metal partition. His drawn face lit up like Christmas when his eyes found hers. Her lips parted, but she couldn't quite manage to smile back.

Then Rex tilted his gaze upward. When he saw the thing on top of her, his eyes filled with a wrath that chilled her bones and warmed her heart.

"Son of a bitch," he growled.

One final slam and A.J. burst into the stall shoulder-first, brandishing a cocked pistol in each hand. Rex scrambled to his feet, popping the tops of the sports bottles as he went.

And the Reverend pounced.

Grace watched John slam through the bathroom door, his shotgun at the ready. Gripping the rubber handrail, she managed to drag herself over the last few steps of the stilled escalator when a series of blasts and pops froze her in place. Panting, she leaned back against the balcony railing to take the weight off her throbbing leg, waiting for any indication of the volley's outcome. But there was only silence. That left her with two options: wait and see who (or what) came crawling out and respond appropriately; or go in blind with guns blazing. One of those options was smart. The other was the only option for a blunt instrument such as herself.

She rammed the door with her shoulder and barreled around the privacy wall. Her heart plummeted into her boots as she watched A.J. and John drag an unconscious Cooper out of the handicap stall by his arms and ankles. Three bloody gashes ran down A.J.'s cheeks, from his eyelashes to his jaw. They looked fresh, yet his expression remained as stony as ever.

She held the door open as they carried him out. It was the perfect opportunity to assess his injuries, only there didn't seem to be any. Her anxiety turned to relief, then quickly soured into dread. If he wasn't injured, then why was he unconscious?

"What's wrong with him?"

"I don't know yet," John said, grunting under the top half of Cooper's weight. "I have to get him to the med station ASAP."

"Do you need help?" she asked, willing her leg to stop hurting.

"No," A.J. said. He cocked his forehead in the general direction of the sinks. "They do."

Grace nodded. As the two men negotiated their way down the non-functional escalator, she tiptoed further into the bathroom.

Cari sat on the far end of the counter with her back to the mirror. She had taken off her sweatshirt—a good call since it was covered in what looked like elephant snot—and had crammed it into the furthest sink possible. Rex had wedged himself between her and the wall. He had Cari's chin cupped delicately in his hand as he wiped grime from her cheek with a wet paper towel, his brow a cross-stitch of concern and anger.

Grace coughed and made sure to scrape her feet against the ground as much as she could as she came around the privacy wall. By the time she reached the counter, Rex had backed up almost all the way to the stalls, his hands jammed in his pockets and his eyes pinned sheepishly to Cari's feet. In the handicap stall across from them, Grace spotted the remains of a corpse sprawled across the linoleum. It looked about how she'd expected it would, based on the foot she'd seen sticking out from underneath the door: sagging skin, tattered brown suit, wizened eyes. The only surprise was its torso, which appeared to have been chomped in half by a shark—or more likely, an equivalent number of bullets. She observed it for a few seconds, but it didn't move. The corpse did, in fact, appear to be dead.

She turned her attention back to the kids. "So," she said, bending an elbow on the counter. "How's it going in here?"

"He choked her." Rex's eyes flitted to the mass of purple bruises and small, slivered cuts on Cari's neck. "He nearly killed her. While we were out there standing around doing *nothing!*"

"Okay, okay. Calm down," Grace said, doing her best to suppress her amusement. "I know this was upsetting. But this sort of thing *does* happen. These assholes don't play fair. They lie, they kidnap…they choke. They do whatever they think they need to do to get what they want. That means that sometimes, the people we… care about are going to be in danger, no matter what we do to prevent it. But the answer is not to snipe and point fingers. Separately, we stand no chance against them, and they know that."

She paused, waiting for the silence to grow heavy and awkward enough that they both had to look at her. "Whatever else happens, never, *ever* forget who the real enemy is here. Understand?"

Cari nodded obediently. Rex scowled at the floor.

"Good." She suppressed a groan of pain as she dragged herself up to stand. "Ready to go back downstairs?"

Rex shrugged. Grace turned to Cari. Her eyes had narrowed into dangerous little half-moons. Grace followed her gaze to the corpse where it lay, still immobile, its rank fluid puddling around it.

"Cari?" Grace prompted. "You want to go downstairs?"

After a moment, Cari shook her head.

"Then what *do* you want to do?"

The question seemed to freeze her to the core. Even her breathing stopped. Grace waited for what felt like an eternity, but no answer came.

"Maybe we should—" Rex began.

Cari didn't let him finish. Letting out a primal scream, she snatched Rex's bottle of God-knows-what off the counter and hurled herself at the corpse. The plastic crackled as she jammed it into the seeping mouth and squeezed as hard as she could. Rotted flesh and brain matter sizzled as the corrosive contents filled the body's orifices, then started making new ones. The small room filled with the stench of dead farm animal. But Cari didn't stop until the bottle was crushed and empty, and what had once been a body was nothing but a putrid gray puddle slowly spreading across the linoleum.

"Better?" Grace asked, wiping at her watering eyes.

Cari nodded, her arms sagging. "Better." Her voice was hoarse but steady.

Grace looked back to Rex. The only part of his face that his hands weren't shielding against the smell was his eyes, two shocked round circles centered directly on Cari. Grace smiled sympathetically. She knew that look. It had been aimed at her several times, and she'd even worn it a time or two herself. It was the look of someone who had just realized there was still an ocean of things he didn't know about his friend.

Chapter Ten

No sooner had she delivered Cari into John's capable hands than the full weight of the night's events fell on Grace like a three-story house. And she wasn't the only one; the moment they walked into the lounge, Rex collapsed face-first onto the floor.

"Are we there yet?" he moaned, his words muffled by the shag carpet. From back in the corner, A.J. chuckled around the sweet-smelling cigarillo between his teeth, the square peach-colored bandages sealed onto his cheeks distinct despite the shadow of his hat.

"Almost," Grace said, stepping over Rex on her way to the whiteboard. "You know we have a bunk room where you can do that, right?"

"I'm good, thanks." He gave her a thumbs up without lifting his head.

"Grace?"

She looked up as Simon appeared on the television screen. He seemed even more bedraggled and anxious than usual. His blue eyes were puffy and bloodshot behind his glasses, and his short brown hair stuck out at all angles as if he'd been tugging at it.

"What's going on? Everyone stopped talking to me. Are you okay?"

"Yeah, we're good," Grace said as she uncapped a marker. "Though there is a bit of a mess in the food court bathroom."

Simon grinned impishly. "I take it our guest was either very young or very old, huh?"

She shook her head. "I appreciate the setup, but after tonight I'm officially done with bathroom humor."

"Roger that." He clacked the computer keys. "Cameras are back on standard rotation now. I'll let you know if anything jumps."

"Cool. Thanks, Simon." She paused. "Sorry about all the yelling earlier."

He shrugged. "It's cool. I'm kinda used to it."

Grace chuckled. Whether it was relief or a by-product of the adrenaline draining from her veins, she felt charitable enough to favor him with a smile. In response, his cheeks flamed scarlet, and he dropped his flustered gaze to his hands. Another keystroke and the screen cut back to the security feed.

"He's weird," Rex told the floor.

Grace shrugged. "Who isn't?" She twiddled the marker in her fingers as she considered the list she'd written earlier that evening. Don't let them get out. Don't let them get you. Don't let anyone else find out. Defend, resist, lie. A classic list of three. But it was incomplete.

The marker squeaked as she wrote.

Rex dragged his head off the floor. "Whatcha doin'?"

"You'll see." She finished with a flourish and moved out of the way so he could see. "Rule Number #4. Don't Let John Do Anything Stupid."

Rex nodded thoughtfully. "Not bad. Might I make a suggestion though?" He clambered to his feet with a groan. Grabbing a red marker, he crossed out over John's name and wrote *ANYONE!!!* above it in big, sloppy letters.

Despite her exhaustion, Grace found herself smiling. "That works too."

After finally convincing Rex to abandon the carpet in favor of a bunk, Grace returned to the med station to check on the patients, only to nearly collide with Cari in the doorway.

"Uh, hey," Grace said. She eyed the thin layer of gauze wrapped around Cari's neck. "You good?"

Cari answered her with a shaky smile. "Yeah. I'm good."

Grace nodded, giving her a single pat on the shoulder. A gesture of comfort and congratulations on a job well done. But it was also a test. She needed to make sure that Cari was really there, that she had made it through. That she was, in fact, good.

Cooper, on the other hand, was a different story. He lay on an exam bed with his eyes closed as John ran a portable ultrasound over his bare abdomen. Under the flood of exam lighting, the long, sharp bruises on his torso stood out like ink stains against his wan skin. Worse than that was the pumpkin-sized purple and red splotch over his left shoulder, currently affixed with a large ice pack. Looking at it made her arm ache. No way he was going to be fit for heavy lifting—or anything else—anytime soon.

"How is he?" she murmured, leaning against the door jamb in an attempt to look casual.

"Stable," John whispered back. He put the ultrasound back in its place in an upper cabinet and joined her in the doorway. "No perforations or cuts. All his injuries appear to be subcutaneous, as is typical of violence performed in a veil. No signs of sepsis or gangrene. No internal injuries either, which is a minor miracle based on what he's recounted in his conscious moments. All in all, I'd say he's incredibly lucky."

"So, he'll recover?"

"Oh yes. A week or so off his feet, and it will be like it never happened."

"Thank God," Grace sighed. "With Charlie in the hospital and the kids training up, it would be hard to cover a long-term loss."

"Right. Staffing issues. Of course." John's grin was mischievous. And obnoxious. She glared at him until it went away. "I've given him codeine to get him through the worst of it. He'll sleep through the rest of the night and will be fine to go home in the morning."

"Can I talk to him?" she asked, in what was most definitely *not* a pleading tone.

"Sure. But be quick about it. He really does need his rest."

Cari turned away from the detention cell as John emerged from the med station, pulling the door softly shut behind him.

"How is he?" she asked.

"He'll survive," he said. "How are you feeling?"

"I'm fine." She tugged at the gauze around her neck. "This itches a little."

"That's the disinfectant. It will stop soon. But I was speaking in more of a psychological sense."

"I *said* I'm fine."

She winced at the sharp note in her voice. To compound her embarrassment, John held up his hands in a defenseless posture. "Okay," he said gently. "Good. I'm glad to hear it."

She sighed, her cheeks tingling. "I'm sorry. I didn't mean to yell at you."

"I understand." He joined her in front of the cell door. "You've had a rough night."

"Yeah…"

She trailed off as both their gazes turned to where Holly lay curled on the floor next to her cot. Her eyes were closed, and every so often she would emit a jarring, snotty snore.

"Did she really dictate our entire conversation?" Cari asked.

John nodded. "Both sides, verbatim. Or what sounded like verbatim anyway. She also demonstrated some of the significant moments of…um, physicality."

"Ah." Cari squeezed her eyes closed, fending off the shards of memory trying to force their way into her thoughts. She did not need to relive that. Ever.

"That's how Ms. Henry was able to figure out where you were," John continued, easing the conversation in a different direction. "Something about embarrassment and a scatological joke. I didn't follow it, but luckily she did." He shook his head at Holly. "I must admit, I've never seen anything like it before. I mean, we do what we can to prevent people from being taken this way. On the occasions when we have failed in the past, the subject has either wasted away or killed themselves within the first few hours. No one has ever held on this long before, and they've *never* presented with abilities like this. It's like…an evolution, or something."

Cari nodded absently. Despite John's academic fervor, she couldn't quite get around the sight of the woman lying on the floor of a prison cell, the tattered remains of her magenta blouse barely covering her greening skin and her blond hair hanging in greasy ropes over her face.

"I thought you were going to kill her if you couldn't bring her out of it."

John's ebullience faded. "I did say that."

"And now?"

"I don't know."

He wanted her to drop it, she could tell. But she had known Holly. They hadn't been friends—there had even been times when Cari thought Holly hated her. But that didn't make what happened to her any less awful. "Do you think she is suffering?"

He pursed his lips in a deep frown. "I've asked myself that same question many times. If there is any of the real Holly left—and that is by no means a guarantee—then she may be experiencing discomfort. But she's also a connection. One we've never had before. If they can broadcast to us, maybe we can figure out a way to do the same. Maybe someday we will even be able to communicate with them, in an open dialogue."

The bitterness of her laugh startled her. "I know I'm new here, but diplomacy doesn't seem to be their strong point."

"What is the alternative?" He glared at her, his voice rising. "They can't be killed. You can't kill what's already dead. All we can do, all we *are* doing, is stalling. We'll keep them shackled here as long as there are those of us willing and able to take up the fight. But after that…" He dropped his gaze to the ground.

Cari gaped at him in disbelief. Her hands curled into fists, shaking not with fear this time, but anger. "So, the Reverend was right? All that crap he said about how there was never hope—that was true?"

John's head sagged further. In the cell, Holly whimpered in her sleep. She seemed so peaceful. So *normal*. Cari could barely believe that this was the same woman who had tried to rip her face off not twenty-four hours earlier. But that wasn't Holly's fault. None of it was, not even the fact that she had been working in this mall. She was only here because she'd been seduced by something that never should have been allowed to set one diseased-ridden toenail on this plane of existence in the first place. And the responsibility for that—maybe not all of it, but some—could be laid at the feet of the man standing next to her.

"Why didn't you sign it?"

She could feel John bristle at the question, but she pressed on. "If you really thought the Courier was just a crazy weirdo, then what would have been the harm of giving him what he wanted just to make him go away?"

"Maybe I should have," John said, pressing his head against the bars. "I swear, I thought I was doing the right thing. And by the time I realized…what the consequences would be, it was too late. The deal the Reverend made with the Courier was closed for good."

"But *they* didn't know that?"

"I guess not. That's why this is so important." John's sapphire eyes flashed desperately at her from behind his glasses. "If I can find a way to reach them and stop all this madness, isn't that worth the sacrifice?"

"Maybe," Cari said. "But *we* aren't the ones making the sacrifice, are we?"

The color in his face deepened to a furious burgundy that made her recoil. She expected him to start yelling. Instead, he released a sigh like a pressure cooker letting off steam.

"I think you should go home," he said stiffly. His hands dropped away from the bars but stayed clenched. "You've been through a traumatic experience. Get some rest and come back tomorrow."

He turned and abruptly rounded the corner into the lounge. She stared after him in shock. Apparently, she had hit a nerve.

Moving from the med station door to Cooper's bed was the most difficult trek Grace had made all night. John has covered the worst of his injuries with a blanket, but that didn't make the flurry of bruises on his neck and face any less disturbing. He looked emaciated too, like the escapade had drained something from him. It was probably a combination of the stark lights and her own exhaustion, but the closer she got, the less sure of that she became. After being partners for nearly five years, she knew his face almost as well as she knew her own. There was a hollowness to his cheeks that hadn't been there before, and his eyes had retreated deeper into the darkened caverns that encased them. It was the first time that, if she looked at him from the wrong angle, she barely recognized him.

She tried to move silently, yet the moment she reached his side he turned his head in her direction. "Grace?"

She winced at the hoarseness of his voice. "Hey Coop," she said, placing her hand on the sheet near a lump that she assumed was his hand. His eyes barely opened, but it was enough for her to spot that familiar green sparkle that was somehow aloof and warm and tough and friendly at the same time. She swallowed a sigh of relief. Finally, something that looked right. "How're you feeling?"

"Like I was hit by a single-serving tornado," he said. "Give it to me straight—how bad is it?"

She ran her eyes up and down his body as if she hadn't been cataloging every inch of visible skin since they'd found him. "I don't know about bad, but..."

He groaned. "Great. How am I gonna explain this to Allie?"

Grace shrugged. "It's not the first time you've been injured on the job. What do you normally tell her?"

"That I was rousting punks behind the dumpsters, and they got salty." He nodded at his ice-bound shoulder. "Think that'll work this time?"

"Maybe if this were a '70s cop show."

His chuckle ended in a cough of pain. He reached for the cup of water on the table next to him. She nudged it over to meet his hand.

"Anyway, there is one good thing to come out of this," she said as he drank. "We finally found something you suck at enough to teach it to someone else."

"Ha ha."

"I'm not joking. Not totally. Cari never would have made it without your help."

"Only because she wasn't armed." He handed her the cup and wiped his smiling lips with the back of his hand. "She kinda reminds me of this girl I met about five years ago. She was young, puny, undisciplined—"

Grace arched her eyebrow. "*Was* young?"

He sighed. "And now, she's a real pain in the ass."

"Yeah, yeah." Grace put the cup back on the table and tugged the blanket up to his chin. "Let's hope that's where the similarities end, okay?"

He nodded, blinking slowly as his face slackened into a drowsy frown. "I think John's gonna put me on leave."

She bowed her head. "It's the right call."

"Maybe." He groped in the direction of her hand. "You'll look after them while I'm gone, right?"

"Of course. Just like I do when you're here."

"Very funny," he slurred. His eyelids drooped closed again. This time, they stayed that way.

"Coop," she whispered. "I'm gonna take off so you can sleep." She placed her hand on his forearm for exactly one second before sliding it away. "Speedy recovery."

"Thanks." His head sunk back into the pillow. "You too."

Chapter Eleven

Cari grabbed her backpack out of her locker when the sound of clumsy footsteps made her jump. She whipped around to see Grace hobble into the mouth of the locker-lined hallway.

"Oh," she said, swallowing a couple times to keep the dry rattle out of her voice. "Uh…hi. Sorry, I thought you were, um—"

"It's okay," Grace said. "Happens to all the newbies."

"Oh. Good. I guess." Cari kneaded the canvas bag with both hands. "Does it ever stop?"

"No. But it does get easier to tell the difference between friend and foe." She leaned back against the door of Cari's locker. "How are you feeling?"

Cari shrugged. "Like I've got strep throat. But the cuts have stopped hurting, and John said the bruises will clear up in a few days."

"Did he say anything about *those* bruises?" Grace nodded at the four long brown marks on her bare bicep.

"Oh, that." Cari rubbed the spot as if she were cold. "I guess the Reverend grabbed me pretty hard."

"It must have been *really* hard, since it made those marks all the way under your sweatshirt," Grace said. Her tone was easy and light, about as far away from prying as it could be. But the piercing gleam in her eye made Cari feel as if her head and chest had split open, spilling her darkest secrets all over the floor.

"Must have been." Cari muttered as she threaded her arms through the backpack's straps.

"Heading home early?"

"John said I should!" Cari blurted before she remembered that she wasn't talking to Holly, who as her supervisor had never asked a question that didn't contain some amount of accusation. "I mean, he said it would be better if I rested."

"Of course." Grace appeared unfazed by the outburst. "But seeing as how it's winter and the good Reverend is splattered all over what appears to be your coat—which we are going to have to incinerate, by the way—I thought you could maybe use a ride home."

Cari considered it. With all this talk about bruises, she wasn't in love with the idea. But Grace did have a point—the first bus wouldn't be by for at least another hour, and the January desert was no place for bare arms. "Okay."

"Fabulous. There's an emergency exit down the hall past Surveillance. I just have to get the keycard from John and we can go." She hobbled past Cari to her locker where she dug out her bag and car keys along with a fur-lined pink parka and a blue pullover with an image of a cavorting imp and *Halcyon Hellions* emblazoned in sunshine yellow over the chest.

"Here." She held out the parka for Cari to take.

"Oh, no!" Cari backed away as if Grace had offered her a basket of cobras. "I can't take that. You'll freeze."

"*I'll* freeze?" Grace looked her up and down before thrusting the deliciously puffy jacket into Cari's arms. "Please. I run warm anyway. Now put it on. I'll meet you at the door in five minutes."

Cari expected Grace's car to be something big and sturdy, like a weathered old truck. But when Grace pressed the button on her key fob, the round lights of a powder blue Volkswagen convertible flashed pertly instead.

"*This* is your car?" Cari asked, approaching the passenger's side with hesitation.

"Sort of." Grace shoved her bag in the back. "It belonged to a friend of a friend who didn't need it anymore."

Cari settled in the front seat. She surveyed the dust-free black leather dashboard, the uncluttered center console, and the yellow pine tree labeled Summer Sun hanging from the rear-view mirror. Maybe it was her imagination, but the fresh citrus scent felt cool and soothing against her scratchy throat. "Doesn't seem like your style."

"It's got four wheels and a working engine," Grace said as she tapped Start button. "That's enough style for me."

Grace guided the car down the highway and into Halcyon. Cari kept trying to think of conversation topics as they rolled through the empty main street, its cubed gray buildings as dark and silent as a graveyard, but she was too tired to come up with anything besides "go straight" and "turn here."

At last, the Volkswagen turned into the Four Winds Trailer Park. As the small car crunched over the frozen gravel toward Trailer #3, Cari spotted a pair of figures huddled together on the front stoop. She recognized the smaller lump as her mother. The second figure she also recognized but wished she didn't. He twisted away from the headlights as they washed over him, his hand dropping to the side of the small porch as if he had spotted a weed that needed pulling. His plaid shirt was tucked into his khakis, every strand of his sandy blond hair perfectly in place, his mustache neatly trimmed and combed. Her mother, on the other hand, looked completely disheveled, wrapped in a baggy pink robe with her mousy hair ratted around her head and her glasses nowhere to be seen. She withdrew against the light, her bony hands clutching a chipped coffee cup as if it were a life preserver.

"Crap," Cari grumbled.

"Who are these people?" Grace frowned as she shifted into park.

"My mother and her—friend."

"I see."

Leaving the lights on, Grace got out of the car and beckoned for Cari to join her. They approached the stoop side by side. One of Nelson's arms snaked around Libby's shoulders, while his other hand gripped her elbow. He squinted against the glare, his head twitching blindly back and forth. "Who's there?"

Cari scowled at the wet slur in his voice. She looked at Grace, who nodded encouragingly.

"It's me. Cari."

"Huh?" Libby stumbled as Nelson dragged her to her feet. "Where the fu—"

Cari nearly laughed at the facial gymnastics her mother endured when she realized Cari had an ally with her. Her angry sneer contorted into a narrow-eyed scowl of betrayal before she finally donned her go-to mask of maudlin relief.

"Oh my God, Cari!" she crowed, leaning against Nelson as if overcome by emotion. "Thank the Lord you're okay."

"Where on Earth have you been, young lady?" Nelson demanded gruffly. "Your mother has been worried sick."

Cari seethed at him, defiantly mute.

"Edensgate Shopping Center," Grace chimed in. "Working."

Libby's unsteady gaze wobbled over to Grace. "I thought she was fired yesterday," she said with barely concealed disgust.

Grace smiled indulgently. "Not quite, ma'am. She was let go when Suttermill closed. But as the store's top employee, we offered her a new position as a junior custodian with Virgil Security and Maintenance."

"Oh, so…she's a trash girl now." Nelson didn't bother hiding his amusement. Cari burrowed further into the parka's fur lining and wished she could die there.

Grace, on the other hand, grinned that much brighter. "It's a good job. Thirty hours a week, with full benefits for her and any…ah, dependents."

Libby's ears perked up. She looked imploringly at Nelson. "Benefits…that's good, right?"

He gripped her tighter, smiling the way a cat might smile at a canary that had slammed into the window one too many times. "Honey, you're not thinking this through. Custodial work is bottom rung, with very few prospects." He flung a condescending smirk at Grace. "No offense."

"None taken," Grace said. "In fact, you're right. There isn't much of a future in it."

"See?" Nelson said.

"Yes. And unfortunately, with the state of the town being what it is, we've had to reduce our starting salaries to $40,000 a year."

Libby nearly choked. "*What?*"

Cari had to admit she was just as surprised. As Nelson tried to reason with Libby, Cari cocked a questioning eyebrow at Grace.

"What?" Grace asked under her breath. "Did you think we'd ask you to do this job pro bono?"

"Well…yeah. Kinda."

"Why?"

Cari thought for a moment. "I guess I assumed...it was my moral obligation. Or something."

Grace smiled. "And that's exactly why you deserve every penny."

"Libby, please think about this." Nelson's already rosy cheeks had darkened considerably, and his voice squeaked with reined-in panic. "It's not proper for a young woman to be out cleaning toilets in the middle of the night, surrounded by who knows what sort of people. She belongs at home where she can learn quietly with all submissiveness like the Book says. And, you know, there's her safety to consider, of course..."

Cari bit back a bitter laugh. He put on a good show, pretending to be oh-so-concerned with her welfare. After all, he was Nelson Baines, community leader and shepherd to all the lost sheep. Who wouldn't take his compassion at face value? But he was no shepherd. He was a wolf, and Cari knew it.

Luckily, she wasn't the only one.

"There's no need to worry, sir," Grace said. Her smile revealed every single one of her teeth. "She will be well looked after. I *promise* you that."

Nelson shrank back a half step before his pride caught him. "Well, then...I suppose it's up to you, Libby. You're her mother."

Libby winced as he gave her arm another hard squeeze. "It's fine with me," she said softly. "As long as the checks clear."

"Excellent." Grace turned her attention to Cari. "Nice work today. Now get some rest. Tomorrow is another night."

She got in her car and drove off without given Nelson or Libby so much as a parting glance.

Cari watched Grace's cherry-colored taillights disappear behind a thin copse of trees before turning around, her smile slipping into a scowl.

Nelson also stared after the vehicle, his eyes flaming. Her mother, on the other hand, was looking at her. The anger that Cari had grown so accustomed to finding there had faded. In its place was the blank, worn-out stare of an alcoholic that had grown unintentionally sober.

"Well." Nelson cleared his throat. "It's late, and the girls will be up soon." He ran his hand up Libby's arm. She shuddered, her shoulders hunching even more dramatically than normal, as if she were trying to curl up inside herself. His hand lingered at her neck, and he leaned in slightly as if he were about to kiss her. Instead, his eyes roamed over to Cari. The challenge they held was clear. So, she was making real money. Money that might get her out of this hell hole—someday. But until then, he was still in charge—and if she wanted to test him on that, well, he'd like to see her try.

Her scowl deepened as she clenched her empty fists. If only they were at Edensgate. Then she would meet his challenge no question. But out here, in this icy, uncaring reality, all she could do was stand there. Stand tall and refuse to look away.

His eyebrow curved up with intrigue. Relinquishing Libby's neck, he sidled toward Cari. Despite her pounding heart, she held her ground. He wasn't much taller than she was, yet he loomed large as he closed the space between them. His eyes slipped down her body from collarbone to ankle and back again, making every inch of her scream with the desire to flee.

"You've sure grown up, haven't you?" His breath wafted across her cheek. Her tender throat spasmed at the smell of coffee and tequila.

He lifted his hands.

She jumped back, arms tensing in a defensive cover.

Smirking, he zipped his tan windbreaker up to his neck. "Good night, Cari. Godspeed on your new endeavor."

She relaxed her stance, cheeks burning with fury. Fury at herself for pulling away, and fury at him for being alive. He stood there for another moment, savoring his victory, then turned and disappeared into the dark.

"You should be nicer to him."

Cari heaved her attention toward her mother. Libby stared longingly after Nelson with the obedience of a kicked dog. "He's been good to us. He helps us out with rent, with groceries—"

"He gives you booze," Cari said, her voice trembling with righteous indignation. "That's why you like him. He helps out so you'll feel like you need him. Like you owe him something. Then he gets you drunk and…he's using you, and we both know it."

Libby's mouth dropped open. "How dare you? I am your *mother* and—"

"I don't care!" she cried, her words piercing the early morning stillness. "If I am paying the rent—and I will be paying *all* the rent now, Mom—then I get a say in what goes on in this house. If *ever* see him here again—"

"What? You'll do what?" Libby slurred. Her eyes flickered with their old anger.

And for the first time in her life, Cari ignored it.

"I'll leave," she said, her voice low and heavy with conviction. "And I'll take the money with me. Then you'll see how good Nelson really is when you're completely dependent on him for everything. Him and his *wife*."

Libby spluttered incoherently. She still looked furious, but now she looked scared too. Scared of losing the money, and her squalid but settled lifestyle along with it.

And maybe…maybe there was a part of her, some tiny part that wasn't swimming in alcohol and self-loathing, that was scared of losing her daughter too.

Cari sighed as the rush of anger faded into immense exhaustion. "I love you, Mom. I do. But enough is enough."

Libby's mouth snapped closed, her wide eyes growing wet with emotion and frustration. She stomped back to the trailer without another word and slammed the door. A moment later, the porch light blinked out.

"That went well," Cari whispered to herself. Shuffling cautiously in the moonlit semi-darkness, she made her way toward the undergrowth of burdock and clover next to the front stoop. Her fingers brushed pebbly earth, searching until she felt the kiss of cold glass against her palm.

She lifted the bottle from the weeds. It was too dark to make out the label, but she recognized it from the size, the rounded rectangular shape, and the long slope of its neck. Cuervo Especial. Judging from the weight, it was at least half gone.

She rolled her shoulders up to her ears, retreating like a turtle into the fuzzy-necked shell of Grace's parka. It smelled the same as her car, fresh and tangy, like lemon and saltwater and sunshine. It smelled like a completely different place. It *was* a completely different place, or at least a microcosm of one. It was new. It was a change. And it meant that other things could change too.

With a gasp she wished was a scream, Cari hurled the bottle toward the closest tree. It exploded against a trunk with a crystalline crash. She'd never heard a more satisfying sound.

Turning away from the shadows, she hopped the step up to the door, wide awake even though she had been up all night, and all day…and all night…and all day.

She paused, frowning at the screen door. That couldn't be right.

But it was.

She had been up for almost two days straight, and she didn't feel tired at all.

Book III

THE LONG MOON

*C*ooper ran. Every muscle in his body burned and his heart felt like it was going to bust out of his hazmat suit, but still he ran.

He ran and left them behind. Unconscious, helpless, maybe even dying. He hadn't wanted to, but his gun was empty. If he didn't get help, or bullets, or both, all of them were dead for sure.

He ran, stumbling over the uneven ground toward the exit. There were at least seven magazines in his locker. If he could make it back to the bunker, maybe—

He ran past the last tall shelf and ground to a halt near the checkout lanes. He should have been able to see the exit from here. But it was choked and invisible under the dense lattice of slick red and blue vines. No weak spots. Not even a keyhole's worth of space in the whole hideous tapestry.

Schluck.

His shoulders slid up to his ears at the sharp, wet sound, like a knife stabbing into meat. Above him, the normally yellow glow of the large pendant lights had turned purple as it fought to be seen the red vines and gray flowers twined through the surrounding the metal cages. The lights swung back and forth, making the beams wiggle like water. Between the light, his suit, and the thick air pressing down on him, he felt as if he were standing on the ocean floor.

Schluck. Schluck. Schluck.

His breath snagged in his throat.
She was coming...

Chapter One
Earlier that Night...

The old wooden stairs creaked beneath Cooper's feet as he descended. He hadn't wanted to leave the dark, warm quiet of the bedroom, but the smell of frying bacon and sugar had grown too tempting to resist. Yawning, he padded through the brief foyer into the large farmhouse kitchen. Allie stood at the white mid-century stove with her back to him. A spatula teetered absently in her hand as she supervised a squadron of steaming pans.

"Breakfast for dinner?" Cooper asked, stretching his arms over his head before placing them lightly on her shoulders.

"Mm-hmm. And blueberry pie for dessert."

"Wow." He felt her smile as he pressed his lips to her freckled cheek. "What did I do to deserve this?"

"You married me." She turned to give him a proper kiss. She looked adorable in her red sweats and one of his faded gray Army t-shirts, her raven hair tied in a high knot. He glanced at the shifty-eyed cat clock over the front window. Not even seven and already dressed for bed.

"Long day?" he asked, taking a seat at the table. It was a semi-rhetorical question—as a registration clerk at the VA hospital, every day was a long day.

"Long enough," she said as she piled scrambled eggs onto a plate. "Uncle Ray came in today."

Cooper stiffened. "How is he?"

She shook her head. "The pain is getting worse, and now he's having fainting spells. Doctor Conway said that stents might help, but at this point...it's a matter of time."

"How long?"

"Weeks. Maybe months." She lowered her eyes to the floor. "He's only sixty-three. It seems so...unfair. Doesn't it?"

He nodded at the rose-embroidered tablecloth. Not only was Ray a longtime friend of Allie's parents, and a retired army captain, but as the mall's previous manager, he had been the one to recommend Cooper for the night guard position at Virgil Security and Maintenance. For a man as good as Ray to die so young, and in such a way...

Cooper had never been very comfortable with the idea of a slow death. Granted, death of any sort wasn't exactly a pleasure cruise. But during his time overseas he could at least count on it being quick—most of the time, anyway. The thought of watching someone deteriorate over weeks or months, or even years...maybe it was harsh to think it, but what was the point?

"I'm sorry," was all he could think to say.

"We all are," Allie said. She piled his plate with home fries, two ham steaks, and a piece of buttered white toast, and handed it to him. "I had lunch with Jeanette at Mercy today," she said as she turned back to the counter.

"Oh yeah?" Cooper said, eagerly latching on to the change of subject.

"Mm-hmm. Sounds like Charlie Jackson is doing well. He should be released later this week."

"That's great," he said with genuine enthusiasm. "We're all looking forward to having him back."

He dug in while she prepared their coffee—black for him, decaf with cream for her—and sat down on the other side of the table.

"It's been nice having you home these past few nights," she said, tracing a cheerful green vine on the tablecloth with her finger.

He nodded, his mouth full of toast.

"Any chance we could make that permanent?"

He stopped in mid-chew, barely resisting the urge to slap himself in the forehead. He should have known this feast held an ulterior motive.

"We've been over this," he said. "John doesn't need a patrolman on during the day. He has that covered."

"Yeah, but…maybe he would give you his day post and he could take the night shift?"

Cooper chuckled into his coffee mug. "You expect a man pushing seventy to take night patrol so an ex-military youngster can sit at a desk all day? Somehow I don't think he'll go for that."

"No, he probably won't," she said sharply. Her point was as clear as a classified ad.

Cooper put down his fork.

"Another job won't pay as well as this one does. You know that. If you're serious about being a stay-at-home mom, we need this money."

"We need to conceive a child first," Allie shot back, "and unless I completely misunderstood eighth-grade biology, we *need* to be in the same place at the same time for more than five minutes to do that."

Her tone made Cooper's teeth ache. That high-pitched whine made his normally intelligent and sensitive wife sound like a spoiled brat. It bothered him so much he didn't even attempt to joke about that five-minute comment. It might have made her laugh under normal circumstances, but he had a feeling it wouldn't be appreciated at the moment.

"I know it hasn't been easy," he said as gently as he could, "but we knew there would be sacrifices when I took this job. As I recall we decided—*together*—that the benefits outweighed the drawbacks. The way I see it, this job is the only reason we're able to even think about having kids now as opposed to five or six years from now. Right?"

Allie glared at him. He was right and she knew it. But that didn't mean that she was going to admit it. Instead, she crossed her arms, pooched out her lower lip, and sulked.

"I wish I'd never told Uncle Ray that you were in the army. Then he never would have recommended you for this stupid job."

Cooper set his jaw, refusing to let her see how her words had cut him. "This stupid job matters to me. It makes me feel like I'm making a difference."

She rolled her eyes. "How? I'm sorry to be the one to tell you this, Cooper, but you're not a soldier anymore. You walk around an empty mall in the middle of the night. It's not exactly saving the world."

He bit the edge of his tongue to hold it in check. Allie said things like that when she sensed she was about to lose and wanted to get in one last shot. It took every ounce of willpower he had not to tell her how wrong she was. Not that it would help his case if he did. She would think he was crazy and would keep on thinking it until he proved it to her. As infuriating as she could be during their arguments, he would never expose her to that kind of danger.

Besides, it was against company policy.

He wiped his lips and tossed his napkin on the table. "I think I'll take my dessert to go," he said as he stood up. "It might not matter to you, but I don't want to be late for work."

Chapter Two

Cari zipped the parka up to her chin. She could still faintly detect the smell of sea salt and lemon in the fur lining. She'd been wearing the coat for over a week and Grace had yet to ask for it back, so she figured she'd keep on wearing it as long as she was allowed. It was a little big, but it was warmer than anything else she owned. Underneath it, she wore the standard combination of jeans, vintage logo t-shirt (Teenage Mutant Ninja Turtles this time) and a roomy hoodie—basically, her new work uniform. She checked her makeup one last time in her compact mirror. Eyeliner and mascara, with a touch of smoky silver eye shadow. It looked better than she'd expected. She smiled, and reflexively dropped her gaze. It still felt weird to be pleased with her own reflection.

Tucking the mirror into a side pocket of her backpack, she went into the trailer's main room. The tiny television on the kitchen counter spewed noise as a gaggle of red-faced pundits struggled to be heard over one another. Libby slouched at the dining table, a cigarette trailed smoke from her hand as she stared listlessly at the remains of a microwave turkey dinner.

"I'm going to work," Cari tossed at her. "Should be home by six."

Her mother dragged her head up. She sneered at Cari. "What's all that stuff on your face? You look—"

"What?" Cari glowered. "I look what?"

Her mother shrank back, eyes at once fearful and furious at being cowed by her own daughter. She grunted at her plate in disapproval. But Cari didn't really need her permission, did she? Not after her first week's paycheck had been enough to cover rent and groceries for the rest of the month. Pulling her shoulders back, she stalked past her mother and headed for the door.

"Don't forget my cigarettes," her mother mumbled after her. "Please."

She sighed, her proud posture slumping a little. She hated that she still felt sorry for the woman, and yet she was helpless to feel anything else. After all, she was her mother.

"I'll see what I can do," she said, and slipped out.

She didn't look back at the trailer until she was in her seat on the deserted night bus. Even from three trailers away, Cari could see her mother's shadow moving on the other side of the smoke-stained curtains. Ducking. Rising.

Pouring.

She wrinkled her nose. In the week since Libby had heard her daughter now made enough money to pay their way in full, Libby had cleaned up her act considerably. Cari hadn't seen a single bottle, empty or otherwise, anywhere in the house. The wine glasses hung in the cupboard above the fridge, and the shot glasses were gathering dust on the windowsill. Libby hadn't even asked about what had happened to the bottle of Cuervo tucked under the front porch. She must have realized that Cari had destroyed it, and yet she hadn't given her so much as a crooked glance in retaliation.

None of it meant Libby had stopped drinking, of course—even in a trailer the size of a cereal box, there were plenty of places to hide a bottle. But she was always in her room with the door closed by the time Cari got home in the morning and stayed sober, if hungover, until Cari left for work. It was ugly progress, but it was progress, nonetheless.

At least Libby had respected the most critical condition. Cari had neither seen nor smelled the presence of Nelson Baines all week. She hoped Libby had broken it off with him, but that seemed unlikely. After all, Libby didn't have an income, and Cari sure as hell wasn't giving her any spending cash. Where else would she be getting all that secret booze?

The mall rose into view, its illuminated marble facade glowing brilliant white against the midnight blue sky. Cari pulled on her backpack, rolling her shoulders as she let whatever was or wasn't happening in the trailer slip to the back of her mind. If Libby wanted to continue doing terrible things with a terrible man, that wasn't Cari's problem. Not until she saw him in her home again. Then she'd do what she'd promised—take the money and run.

Cooper watched the bus pull away on the tiny, static-choked screen as Cari entered the front doors, walking off the screen as her footsteps shuffled into reality. He swiveled in his chair and waved a finger at her. She waved back from the other side of the Guest Relations counter. He was the only one to offer a greeting. The others didn't seem to notice that she had arrived at all—not even Sam, who was apparently too focused on his clipboard to register the slim teenager standing at his elbow.

"Have the floors been polished?" he asked, frowning at the pages. With his chubby cheeks, beady black eyes and angular nose, he looked like an overfed ferret trying to do algebra.

"Yes, sir," John said.

Sam scalloped his pen across the paper with a flourish. "Burnt bulbs?"

"Replaced."

"Shelves?"

"Cleared and dusted."

"The security gates?"

"All fixed. We had to replace the tracks and the lock after those burglars mangled it last week, but it's done. Even ended up a little under budget."

"Excellent." Sam's jowls wiggled as he bobbed his head in satisfaction. Cooper had to admit, he was mildly impressed. When Sam had been promoted, Cooper had assumed he would follow in "Uncle Ray's" footsteps, and his entrepreneurial ambitions would quickly give way to disenchantment and absenteeism. But here it was, nine-thirty at night, and Sam was still running over his checklist like a pudgy, suburbanized Napoleon. That was the only reason Cooper was on monitor duty. Compared to the real surveillance suite Specs had rigged up downstairs, these early-90s tube TVs were fifty shades of redundant. But John had asked that they behave themselves in front of Sam, and Sam expected them to behave like janitors and mall cops.

So...

Cooper leaned back in his chair, laced his fingers behind his head, and tipped the bill of his baseball cap down over his eyes as if he were about to take a nap. He had never been one to disappoint expectations, no matter how ridiculous. He didn't intend to start now.

Sam turned his attention to Grace, who stood a few feet to John's right. On the surface, it appeared she had done her best to heed John's request for good behavior. With coveralls freshly washed and zipped all the way up to her neck and her black curls combed into a skull-tight ponytail, she was the picture of professionalism. But she stood with one shoulder slumped against the wall, chewing her thumb and staring vacantly into the middle distance, doing her best to pretend she was somewhere else.

"And the fountain?"

"Huh?" Grace startled as if she'd just been woken up. "Oh, yeah. Fountain is 100% blood free. No need to worry about *that*."

Sam raised an eyebrow. "Is there something else we should be worrying about?"

John opened his mouth, but Grace was too quick. "Well, since you asked, I don't think we're ready for site visits yet. There's some water damage near the base of the fountain, and those new flowers in the rotunda boxes are sprouting weeds."

Sam waved his hand dismissively. "The water damage is minor, and the flowers look fine."

"Okay, but…it's a full moon out tonight."

Cooper's outstretched legs stiffened. Where was she going with this?

"So?" Sam asked.

"So, is it a good idea to have a bunch of corporate execs over? I mean, what with them being vampires and all."

Cooper chuckled as the tension in his limbs eased. John's head dropped, though whether it was out of exasperation or relief, Cooper couldn't tell. "Werewolves," he muttered down at Grace.

Grace frowned back at him. "What?"

"Werewolves are the ones that come out at a full moon. Vampires can be out whenever as long as it's at night."

"*Whatever.* I still think this is a bad idea."

"Be that as it may," Sam said, "tomorrow morning at eight is the only time the Jillian's reps have available for the next six months. Things might not be perfect, but we have to try. We need a new anchor store, and we need it *yesterday*. Otherwise, corporate is going to sell this place and we'll all be out on our asses. So, when they reps get here, all I ask is that you be professional. Polite. *Don't* call them werewolves."

"Gotcha," Grace said. "And where did we land on vampires?"

Sam pinched the bridge of his nose. "Just don't say anything, okay?"

"Hey-o!" Rex's voice carried over the whirr of the automatic doors. He sauntered over to Cari, who had been lingering on the sidelines while the grown-ups talked and slung an arm over her shoulders. "What's the good word, y'all?"

Grace coughed and pressed her hand to her mouth. Unable to see over the counter in his reclined state, Cooper pretended to yawn and stretch so he had an excuse to straighten up. Printed on Rex's t-shirt were the words Corporate Revolt in blocky white letters.

So much for behaving.

Sam turned his irritated scowl back to John. "And can we please keep the Mickey Mouse Club out of sight? I know you're threading the needle on child labor laws, but let's not highlight that on the first visit."

"Who are you calling a child?" Rex demanded. He extended his hand to Sam. "Aladdin Matahari, Calbrion Law School. Nice to meet you."

Sam shot John a pleading look.

John cleared his throat. "I'll take care of it," he reassured. But there was no mistaking the subtle tremor of laughter in his voice.

"Great." Sam snapped up his clipboard. "I'm going to do one more sweep, and then I'm out of here."

"Wow," Rex whispered as Sam marched toward the rotunda. "Who tied *his* thong in a knot?"

"He's just worried," John said. "Jillian's is the biggest luxury department store chain left in the country. Signing them to the old Suttermill space would keep us all in business."

Grace snorted. "Yeah, it's a dream come true. Except for the long moon."

His brow knotted. "Yes, that is unfortunate."

"What's that?" Cari asked.

"The first full moon after the winter solstice." He lowered his voice, eyes flitting toward the arched mouth of the rotunda. "Moon phases affect the virility of our...lowland counterparts. The fuller the moon, the more power they have. Combine that with our side of Earth being tilted so far away from the sun, and the effect can be...unpredictable."

"In English, please?" Rex asked.

"Long night plus full moon equals bad shit," Grace said. "Clear enough?"

A high-pitched scream answered her, followed by a hearty crack. Not gunfire, but close enough to send Cooper's blood racing. He rocketed out of his reclined seat and dashed out the door, meeting up with Grace as she vaulted the counter and raced into the rotunda. Sam knelt the far edge of the Atlas fountain, holding his clipboard face down against the flat marble ledge. His arms shook and his eyes were glassy with fear.

"I-I-I was j-j-just bending down to check on that water damage," he stammered, "and when I looked up, there was a...a..."

"It's all right," John said as he jogged up behind them. "Let's have a look."

With a steeling breath, Sam lifted the clipboard. A ribbon of red and blue slime stretched long from the paper to a wet lump smeared across the stone. Crushed gray legs twitched like broken metronomes. Had they been intact, each one would have been about the size of a cotton swab, except for the two on the very end, which looked closer to pencil-length.

"Oh, God..."

Cooper turned to see Rex press the back of his hand to his mouth, his golden-brown skin turning the color of pea soup.

"You okay?" Cooper asked.

Rex bobbled his head circuitously, then let it hang down. Not a clear answer, but Cooper didn't push it. He didn't want to embarrass the kid.

Grace squatted next to the fountain to examine the remains more closely. She poked the blob with a finger. It shuddered, maybe more than it should have, and the spot where her finger touched turned black.

She grinned. "Well, hello Sylvia."

"What?" Sam demanded, scratching the back of his neck.

"*Sylviana scolopendra,*" John interjected quickly. "The wilderness centipede. They live in parts of the deep Mojave. We see them in here occasionally, especially on cold nights like this."

"Fantastic," Sam said, doing his best to flick the slime off his clipboard. Rex groaned softly into his hand.

"It's nothing to worry about, sir," John continued. "We never get more than one or two, and as you can see, they are too lethargic from the weather to do much of anything. They are quite harmless, I promise you. Now why don't I walk you out? Big day tomorrow, after all."

Sam nodded, apparently dazed by the soothing tone of John's voice, and allowed himself to be shepherded out. "Well, if you're sure…"

"I am. We will take care of everything, don't you worry."

"Okay. Thank you, John."

"It's no trouble, sir. No trouble at all."

"Yeah, right," Grace whispered as they walked out of hearing range. "You ask me, trouble is all we got."

"Long moon?" Cari asked.

Grace nodded. "Shit gets stronger and lasts longer. Everyone needs to be on their guard tonight. That includes you, Barfy McGee."

Rex flushed. He snatched his hand away from his mouth. "Don't worry about me, Boss. I'm dandy. I just…don't like worms is all."

"A centipede isn't a worm," Grace said. "They're arthropods with segmented bodies and elongated mandibles, not to mention dozens of teeny tiny legs, while worms—"

Rex held up his hand, his face losing some of its recently reclaimed color. "Fine! I don't like worms, or worm-like creatures, or anything that reads as *worm*. Can we please move on?"

Grace nodded around an impish smile. Cooper, on the other hand, felt sorry for him. He looked like he was moments away from keeling over—until Cari's hand fell onto his forearm. Then he forced himself to stay upright.

"Anyway," Cari said, her tone daring someone to stop her from changing the subject, "what is Sylvia *really?*"

"Sylvia Bishop," Cooper said as Grace pulled a pair of plastic gloves from her pocket. "Younger sister of Mary Fludd, nee Bishop."

"The Reverend's wife?"

"Bingo," said Grace. Taking a rag from her back pocket, she began wiping the slimy mass into a pile. "According to the journals, Sylvia was a teacher who accompanied Mary and her husband on their journey west. She set up the first schoolhouse here."

"*She's* the reason Halcyon High was built in the middle of a freaking swamp?" Rex directed his question at Grace's shoes.

"That was the good Reverend's doing. He never liked Sylvia and wanted to keep her activities as far away from the rest of the group as possible. He suspected that she lived an un-Christian life back in Louisiana as a politician's mistress, or worse. He didn't have any proof, but when has that ever stopped a man of God from persecuting people? He even accused her of luring children into devil worship. The man either had no sense of irony, or a *very* good sense of it. In any case, as Halcyon's mayor his authority was unimpeachable, so he banished her to the mountains."

"Uh-huh," Cari said as if she knew where this was going. "I assume that was a big mistake."

Grace tapped her nose with her slime-free index finger. "A young woman alone in the wilderness with no food, shelter or protection from the elements…it doesn't get much more desperate than that. So, it didn't take long for the Courier to find her. She made a deal for ancient knowledge of the woods and wilds, presumably so she could take revenge against the man that had wronged her. Unfortunately for Sylvia, having made his own bargain, the Reverend himself was untouchable. Her sister, however, was another story. Mary stood by while her husband acted as her sister's judge, jury and executioner. In Sylvia's eyes, she had just as much to answer for as the Reverend. She decided Mary would do the suffering for the both of them."

Cari shivered. "Do we even want to know how she did it?"

"You're looking at it." Grace held up the sticky ball of rag and guts, drawing a grimace from Cari and a nauseated groan from Rex. "Six of these things crawled into her bed while she slept. Her screams woke up almost everyone in town. The doctor managed to rip them out before they ate too much of her. Nothing he could do about the venom though. Full body paralysis took hold almost immediately, but death—that didn't come for three days. Conscious the entire time. I swear, if it were me, I would have let them keep eating. It would have been quicker."

Rex shook his head. "It just goes to show you: never banish a weirdo to the woods. They never come back *less* crazy. And they *always* come back."

"Amen," Grace said.

Cari grinned at her. "So, let me get this straight: You know all about this stuff, but you don't know the difference between werewolves and vampires?"

"So?" Grace scoffed. "That's like saying I know all about car repair, but I don't know where unicorns come from. I'd rather focus on stuff that's relevant, not ridiculous." She eyed the sticky ball thoughtfully.

"Something on your mind?" Cooper asked.

She shrugged. "I mean, I know she's a witch of the wild, but still—centipedes? With a med station chock full of anti-venom? Doesn't that seem like small potatoes for the long moon?"

"You complaining?"

She winked and shot the lump of fabric into the nearest garbage can. "Better dead than bored, that's what I say."

"And I'm sure Sylvia will be happy to oblige." Cooper started back toward the mouth of the rotunda. "Small potatoes or not, everyone's on the floor tonight. Grace and

Cari will take the West Hall, Rex and I will take the East, and—"

He cut himself short as John stepped into the archway, blocking their path.

"Lieutenant, may I have a word?" His voice oozed warmth, with a steel plate underneath. "You too, Ms. Henry."

Leaving Rex and Cari in front of the Guest Relations window, John led them to the corner near a bubbler that looked like a miniaturized version of the Trevi Fountain. His bespectacled eyes landed on Cooper first. "While I appreciate your enthusiasm for due diligence, Lieutenant, I feel I must remind you of the absence protocol."

Cooper's heart sank, burning with frustration the whole way down. "You've got to be kidding me. It's a long moon, for Christ's sake."

"You've been out for a week. That means your first shift back is off the floor until we're sure your performance is unhindered. You can take my spot in the med station, and I will partner with Rex."

Cooper ground his teeth together. Aside from empty whining, he had no real argument. And it *was* protocol. "Yes, sir."

"Thank you." John turned to Grace. "And speaking of performance issues, we need to talk about Cari. Assisting with munitions was fine at first, but she's not…progressing as quickly as she needs to."

Grace scowled. "She can take care of herself."

"Really?" John's eyebrows rose halfway up his forehead. "Need I remind you that the Lieutenant almost died trying to protect her?"

"Well…"

She looked at Cooper. Her eyes begged him not to confirm this. He sighed mournfully. Yes, it was his job, and yes, he had been happy (or as happy as any dying man could be) to do it. But the fact remained: If Cari had been carrying her own weapon, he might not have gotten hurt, and he wouldn't be benched now. Reluctantly, he ticked his head to one side and then the other.

Grace slumped in disappointment.

"Fine," she snapped. "So, she's a little behind. But she's getting better. I've been running her through some boxing moves and her right hook is *bonkers*."

"And that *is* something," John said. "But the fact remains that she needs her own weapon proficiency."

Cooper gaped at Grace. "You mean she doesn't have one yet? What have you been doing all week?"

She glared back at him. "Busting up walls of Creeps with two teenagers. What have *you* been doing?"

"That's enough," John said. From the pocket of his cardigan, he withdrew a single iron key and extended it to Grace. "I'll radio Mr. Guillermo and have him meet you over there. Maybe he can help move things along."

Grace frowned at the key. She looked nervous, and Cooper didn't blame her. He'd been lucky enough to come to the job with a pre-existing proficiency, not to mention his own weapon. So had Rex. So had A.J.—or at least Cooper assumed he had. Those that didn't have one coming in needed to adopt one. Quick. As someone who'd gone down that path, Grace knew that better than anyone. It didn't make the process any easier, or the consequences of failure any less severe, but it did make her uniquely qualified to guide someone else through it.

At last, she took the key from John's hand. "10-4, Boss. Consider it done." She stalked back toward the loitering teens. "Cari, can you come over here please? We have an...errand to run."

Chapter Three

When they came within sight of Spart Sport and Range, Cari recognized the black-clad figure loitering by the front entrance almost instantly.

"How did you get here so fast?" she asked A.J when they got close.

He fixed her with a deeply solemn stare. "I know where I'm needed."

"Oh." She nodded. "Right. Of course."

His eyes lit up as the stony expression crumbled. "Nah, I'm only kidding. I was already here restocking when I heard John on the radio."

"Oh!" Cari said, startled by the shift in demeanor. "Okay, sure. Um…sorry."

"Don't apologize," Grace said as she sauntered past him. "He does that to all his new friends. It's the hat, I think. It goes to his head."

"It's a good hat. Not my fault if people make assumptions about what's underneath. Still, I'm sorry if I made you feel foolish." He touched the brim of the item in question and spread his other arm wide. "Ladies first."

Smiling shyly, Cari obliged his request.

So much for the mysterious man in black.

Having never considered herself the "sporty" type, Cari had never been inside Spartan Sport and Range until now. It was the size of a basketball court and divided into three sections by aisles that led to the back of the store. The middle section was narrow and full of circular clothing racks, while on the left and right, tall black shelves stretched almost all the way up to the pendant cage lights hanging from the bare metal rafters. As Grace led them past the checkout lanes, Cari noted the sparse clothing selection, bare shelves, and deflated, outdated equipment.

Apparently, the store's name worked on multiple levels.

They stopped outside an unassuming door in the back next to the dressing rooms. Cari expected Grace to use the iron key she kept fiddling with, but A.J. pulled out a ring of his own instead.

"Where'd you get those?" she asked.

"My day job." He opened the left side of his duster. Pinned to his black shirt was a simple white name tag with his name and the word "Spartan" in cornflower blue letters.

"Wow." Cari shook her head. "Do you ever sleep?"

A.J. looked at Grace before answering. "Do you?"

"Actually, no," Cari said, shifting her weight timidly. "I haven't slept since I started working here."

Another wary look floated between the two adults.

"When you say you haven't slept," Grace said, "do you mean you haven't needed to, or that you haven't been able to?"

Her caution made Cari feel self-conscious, as if she'd done something wrong. She took an extra moment to think before she answered. "I guess…I didn't feel tired, so I didn't even try."

"Oh." Grace's concerned expression dissipated. "Yeah, that's normal. Didn't you read the employee handbook?"

Cari shook her head. "We've been so busy this week, I haven't had time yet."

"It's all explained in there. John has a fancy word for it. *Somnia* something or other. You go into REM sleep for three days straight twice a year, and other than that it's purely recreational. The actual dates you will sleep are based on a number of factors. Your age, the date you started working here…astrological sign, probably. Cooper's got a whole chart on it."

"Why?"

"Because he's a control freak."

Cari rolled her eyes. "No, I mean why does it happen?"

"We think it's caused by proximity to the book," A.J. said as he unlocked the door. "And a condensed sleep pattern is only the beginning. You might also see improvements to healing, strength, dexterity—basically any skill or feat you'd find in the Player's Handbook."

Cari tilted her head curiously. "You're into D&D?"

"I have many interests." He grinned at her. His joy was so infectious she was almost helpless to do anything besides smile back.

The door opened into a cramped manager's office. Across from the desk was a single locker big enough for a grown man to stand in. A.J. spun the combination lock, unhooked it, and stepped inside. A week and a half ago, Cari would have been shocked to see him push the back panel open. Now, the revelation of another secret passage barely made her heart flutter.

Unlike the bunker, this one led to a narrow ramp scarcely illuminated by dim overhead bulbs. It declined so steeply that she had to walk on her toes to keep from leaning backward. They descended at least twenty feet to the end of the hallway and a bank vault, with a central wheel, combination lock, and lever handle.

And a keypad.

And a keyhole.

"Wow," she whispered. This was even more security than the bunker had. Whatever they kept on the other side of that door, they wanted to make absolutely sure no one got in by accident.

Grace slipped her key into the keyhole, turned it once, then entered a series of numbers on the keypad. "02. 19. 93" Grace recited to Cari as she entered them. She nodded to A.J., who spun the combination lock wheel right, left, and right again.

"10. 31. 15," he said, then threw his weight against the wheel, grunting as he turned it to the right and cranked the lever down. Even pulling as hard as he could, the door opened slower than a boulder covered in molasses. Eventually, a crack appeared between the concrete wall and the thick steel door. Cari tried to peek inside but saw only darkness.

Grace went first, beckoning for Cari to follow. She stepped inside, the darkness swallowing the ambient light from the hallway. Luckily, she only had to walk a few feet before banks of overhead fluorescent lights started to slam on, revealing the room yard by curious yard.

The three of them stood in the middle of an aisle. On either side, rows of shelves and racks contained every kind of weapon Cari had ever seen, heard of, or could possibly imagine. Rifles and shotguns, great axes and broadswords, maces and morning stars, all stacked or hung in a neatly labeled slot. They kept walking until the aisle opened into a wide, empty space, allowing her to see how far the rows stretched to either side. The room was as wide as a football field, with a shallow ceiling and gray concrete walls. On the left, in a corner still draped with shadows, Cari could make out the lumpy outline of a cannon, and—

"Holy crap, is that a trebuchet?"

Grace looked up from a rack of longbows. "Yeah, but it's pretty much ornamental, for obvious reasons." She arched an eyebrow at A.J. "Not sure why we have that to be honest."

"Belinda found it." A.J. wandered in the direction of the war machine. "She was overseeing an estate auction at a Scottish castle and sent me a picture. I thought it would be funny to bid on it, so I did. Anonymously, of course. Never expected to win." He patted the worn wood affectionately. "Not enough people share my appreciation for medieval weaponry."

Cari ran her hand over the bamboo handle of a katana sitting on a shelf with seven or eight similar swords, stored neatly but unceremoniously, with less concern for visual impact than access. Next to them sat a pair of sai, a couple bo staffs, and several varieties of nunchaku. The only other time she had seen similar weapons (other than the in the Ninja Turtle cartoons) was during a third-grade field trip to the Carson City Museum of Natural History. But these weapons didn't look like they'd been unearthed from a shrine or a grave. She slid the sword off the shelf. It felt surprisingly light in her hand as she freed a few inches of the blade from its sheath. Clean and sharp but notched along the edge where it had connected with something hard and angry.

This wasn't a museum. It was an arsenal, and a well-used one at that.

She turned to Grace. "Who pays for all this?"

Grace peered at Cari through the scope of an unloaded crossbow. "John, mostly. He had family money and a thriving medical practice before the mine went down. He fronts the cash, and we keep our eyes on the flea markets and estate sales. And A.J.'s wife helps out quite a bit."

"Unbeknownst to her," A.J. said with a heavy sigh.

"Right." Grace either didn't detect the regret in his voice or chose to ignore it. She turned to Cari. "Do you know why we're here?"

Cari shook her head.

"John doesn't think you can defend yourself, and that's grounds for termination." Grace handed her the crossbow. "We are here to find you a new favorite toy."

Cari's mouth went as dry as summer. The varnished wood of the crossbow slid in her palms as her hands started to sweat. Aside from Rex's half-baked concoctions, she'd never held a weapon before.

It was a milestone she surpassed in excess.

Aisle by aisle, Grace selected weapon after weapon and thrust them into Cari's arms. A pair of pistols. A short bow. Another, chunkier handgun. Just as Cari thought she would buckle under the weight, Grace steered them back toward the empty space where she grabbed a box of bullets from a shelf and a fistful of arrows from a basket on the floor.

"You know, I thought my job was more of a…support role," Cari said, fumbling with her load. "I didn't think I would have to kill people."

Grace chuckled. "You're forgetting a critical point. These things *aren't* people. They're weeds, with roots a hundred feet deep. We whack 'em down, but they always pop back up."

"I know." Cari bit her lip. "But…John said he might be able to find a way to communicate with them. Maybe even negotiate peace."

"Yeah," Grace said with a small sigh. "I can see why he would want to believe that. It's a mistake though. These assholes are allergic to peace. But if it makes you feel better, this isn't only about saving your own ass. It's about protecting others. We hold our own to keep each other safe. Anyone who can't do that puts everyone else at risk."

An image of Cooper's bloodied face and body rose in Cari's mind. She blinked it away. "I know."

Grace bobbed her head in satisfaction. "Good. Now let's begin with some target practice, shall we?"

A row of waist-high benches stood at ten-foot increments in front of three targets stationed along the back of the warehouse. Monster heads, Cari saw when they got closer, or crude approximations of them. They varied in size, with the smallest about a foot across and the largest spanning about three or four feet. Each of them had beady black eyes and toothy, gaping mouths with thick gray tongues. Boil-covered slimy-looking skin extended to their mid torsos, barely covering the gelatinous yellow jelly over which it was draped.

"There." Grace pointed at the bench closest to the middle dummy.

Cari dropped her artillery on the table. Now she could see the damage that had been inflicted upon the monster substitutes. Bullet holes, gashes, even a couple scorch marks, all of them causing the faux flesh to peel away, revealing a congealed blood-like substance and more ballistics gel.

"Like 'em?" Grace asked, arranging the weapons in a line. "Simon makes them for us to practice on. Building these things is one of his *many* longstanding hobbies. At least this one is borderline useful."

"I haven't had any complaints."

Simon's voice boomed godlike around the giant room. Cari looked around for a screen. Instead, she found a clover of speakers hanging in the corner near the ceiling.

Grace rolled her eyes. "Anyway…once John brought him on, he came down and worked on these during his days off. Still does, I believe."

"They're really horrible," Cari said, aiming her smile at the speakers. "And I mean that as a compliment."

"Thank you. Always glad to hear someone appreciates my work."

Grace finished lining up the weapons and ammo as A.J. wandered over with a few more weapons to add to the proceedings. He surveyed the line-up and selected a small handgun. "We'll start out with something simple. This is Eddie's favorite."

He popped the clip, loaded it with bullets, and slammed it back with his palm. Then he handed the gun to Cari. Her hand began to shake. It felt a lot heavier now that it was full of death.

"Who is Eddie?" she asked, distracted by the unfamiliar feeling of the textured metal grip biting into her delicate skin.

"My boyfriend."

She frowned at him. "I thought you were married?"

"I told you—I have many interests." He winked at Cari. "Luckily, I found others who share them."

She blinked, trying to absorb this new information. *Wrong again.* A.J. was deeply mysterious. Just not in the way she'd thought.

She looked up as Grace cleared her throat. "As much as I hate to break up this gabfest, let's not forget: Long moon. Big night. Can we focus please?"

"Disculpame, jefe." From a cubby beneath the table's surface, A.J. withdrew three pairs of safety goggles and headphones. With their gear situated, he guided Cari into a proper shooting stance. She did her best to follow his

instructions. It felt like she was posing for a Cubist painting.

"Good," A.J. said. He leaned down so his cheek was next to hers and pointed at the target. "Focus on the front sight when you aim. Try to fire at the bottom of a breath. That's when you're steadiest. The kickback is always stronger than you expect this first time, so be prepared for that. Don't hit yourself in the face, and do *not* let go of the gun. Got it?"

Cari nodded, trying to listen, process and apply the knowledge at the same time. Stand. Hold. Sight. Breathe.

Breathe…

"Okay." A.J. slid her headphones over her ears. All sound cut out except for her racing pulse. He tapped her shoulder once.

"Ready!" He was shouting, but his voice was muffled.

Inhale.

Another tap.

"Aim!"

Exhale.

Tap.

"Fire!"

The shot blasted through the cavernous room, its echo both endless and horribly final.

Chapter Four

Cooper rapped on the wood-paneled door under the peeled lettering that read Surveillance. Three taps. Pause. Two taps. Pause, then three more. From the other side of the door came a shuffle of papers, followed by a series of snaps as multiple locks disengaged. Finally, the door swung inward.

"Hey, Specs." Cooper high-stepped over a pile of partially decimated electronics scattered in the entryway.

Simon raised a hand, his attention never wavering from the floor-to-ceiling screens. Pads of paper, pens in various states of gnawed ruin, and dozens of empty Chinese takeout trapezoids littered the desk in front of him. The place smelled like corn syrup and sweat socks that Cooper had not had the pleasure of experiencing since his days in basic training. Simon didn't let a lot of people into the inner sanctum. Not willingly, anyway. But for some reason, Cooper was an exception to the rule. Not only did Simon welcome his entry—and had even gone so far as to assign him his own knock code—but Cooper was the only one who could use Simon's nickname with any hope of getting him to answer.

"What's up, Coop?" Simon asked when Cooper finally managed to fight his way through the clutter and reach the desk. His greasy brown hair framed a face covered in at least four days of stubble, but at least his t-shirt looked clean. His eyes flitted hummingbird-fast between the screens, but never went so far as to look at Cooper directly.

"Not much, pal," Cooper said emphatically. He'd spent the last few hours keeping an eye on Holly, laboring under the assumption that an incarcerated hell spawn would require at least some amount of supervision. But except for a couple of growling ripsaw snores, she hadn't stirred from her cot. He'd had to come up with another way to occupy his time.

"I did an inventory of the kitchen, and the cupboards are bare. All we have is Red Vines and gummy worms, so I figure I'd start an order." He held up a pen and a pad of paper. "Any special requests?"

Simon shrugged. "I'll take those Red Vines and gummy worms if you're offering."

"Great." Cooper flung the pen and paper onto the desk. Couldn't say he didn't try. He retrieved a second rolling chair from the corner and, shifting a stack of motherboards from the seat to the floor, pulled himself up next to Simon.

Simon's hand twitched on the joystick, and the screen in front of them swapped views with the screen to their left. Two figures advanced down the West Hall near the snarl of ropes and plastic tubes that had once been the Mount Olympus Playland. The taller, bulkier one wore a brown sweater and carried a shotgun. The other had a black messenger bag slung over his shoulder and a holster around his narrow waist. Instead of a gun, it a sports bottle full of toxic-looking green liquid.

"How they doing?" Cooper asked.

"Okay." Simon pressed the joystick forward and the focus tightened in on the pair. At this level of detail,

Cooper could see Rex's sports bottle was a little more than half full. "There was a small Maw in the southern corridor leaking bugs. The kid nearly blew chunks, but he kept it together long enough to shut it down."

Cooper nodded. Under the desk, his fingernails bit his palms in frustration. He should be out there, not in here taking lunch orders. Maybe he didn't have full extension in his shoulder, and maybe he still tasted metal when he coughed. But so *what*? He was fine, dammit. Fine enough to fire a gun anyway.

A sharp vibration on his wrist snapped him out of his pout. Simon looked down as his own watch beeped a melody that sounded a lot like the theme song from the old Batman TV show.

"Oh-one-hundred and all's well." Simon pressed a button on the side of his watch face. The beeping stopped. "Maybe they decided to take this moon off."

"Yeah, maybe," Cooper said. "How are things in the Armory?"

"Let's find out." A couple of joystick jigs, and nine different angles of the Armory's firing range appeared on the center-most screens. In the middle was an eagle-eyed view of A.J. and Cari standing at a bench near the targets. In her hands was a brick of a handgun. Colt .45, Cooper thought. Possibly something bigger. She pointed it down the lane, but her attention was on A.J. as he pointed sharply at the gun, then the target. A little further down the bench was a cache of weapons arranged in a haphazard clump. Grace stood a few feet behind the pair, one arm crossed over her chest while she rubbed her temple with the other hand.

A.J. stepped behind Cari, his eyes on the target. Cari's shoulders rose, then fell. Her hands jerked back as she fired.

Cooper's eyes darted to a closeup view of the targets. None of them so much as shivered. On the middle screen, Grace jolted forward, arms flailing.

"That doesn't look good," Simon said.

"No kidding," Cooper agreed. "Can we get the audio going in here?"

Simon tapped the keyboard again. The room filled with the voice of Cooper's partner.

"—been over this a dozen times. You can't hold your breath while you shoot. You will pass out before you get the chance to kill anyone. Now try again."

"Yeesh," Simon groaned under his breath. "Definitely not good."

"You said it," Cooper agreed.

Cari resumed her firing stance. Simon cranked the volume knob all the way down as she blasted away, emptying her clip at the wall surrounding her target. Grace pounced on her as soon as the shooting ceased.

"Okay. Clearly, this one is a no go." She snatched the gun out of Cari's hands.

"Does this work?" Cooper pointed to the desk-mounted microphone in front of him.

Simon eyed him skeptically. "Of course, it does. I don't keep broken things around for no reason."

Rather than point to everything in the room around them, Cooper repositioned the mic and pressed the Talk button.

"Maybe you should try a different target," he said. "Like a barn. Broad side first, then go from there."

Simon covered his mouth, his eyes wrinkling behind his horn-rimmed glasses.

The on-screen trio looked up. A.J. smirked. Cari seemed embarrassed. And Grace was downright livid.

"Don't you have something better to do, O'Bannon?" she demanded of the ceiling.

"No, actually. I do not. Feel free to let John know."

"Oh, I will." Despite her irritation, he appreciated the underlying sympathy. "Now stop distracting us. We've been at this for hours and we're nowhere."

Cooper frowned. "What have you tried so far?"

"Everything!" Grace threw up her hands. She glanced back to Cari, who was toying pitifully with the handle of a short sword and took a few steps away. Her voice dropped into a whisper. "Seriously, I don't know what's happening here. The second we put a weapon in her hand, she turns to Jell-O. It's...concerning."

Cooper's heart sank. That was the last thing he wanted to hear and was about to say as much when Cari's wounded look stopped him. No such thing as whispering on a loudspeaker. Whatever he said, Cari would hear it too.

He released the Talk button and slumped back in his chair. On screen, A.J. handed Cari a small mace and led her to the target. He mimed a swing that should have sunk the spikes deep into the dummy's jiggly flesh. But when Cari imitated it, the iron ball bounced harmlessly off the skin a foot to the left of its mark.

"Son of a bitch," Cooper muttered. He rubbed his chin. This was more than simply not good. This was a disaster.

A series of impatient raps on the door made him swing around in his chair. "Who is it?"

"The Easter Bunny and his imaginary friend. Who do you think?"

"Sorry," Cooper called back to Rex. "Long moon. Better safe than sorry."

"Do we have to let them in?" Simon had his hackles up.

Cooper sighed sympathetically. He never pushed Simon for information about his agoraphobia. At five-foot-five with delicate features and a slim build, he had probably endured more than enough bullying to do the trick. But sometimes, like now, it needed to be mitigated. "The team has grown, Specs. I know you don't like change, but you're gonna have to see them eventually."

Simon's head drooped, obviously unhappy. Even so, Cooper pressed the button and let the door release.

"Thanks a lot," Rex said as he entered. He looked to be on the verge of making another sarcastic comment when his attention snagged on the piles of electronic paraphernalia. His eyes went as wide as saucers. "So, *this* is where you keep the good stuff."

Cooper glanced over at Simon. He didn't say anything, but the muscles in his shoulders ease. For as oblivious as the kid could be, he'd managed to pay Simon the best compliment possible.

Rex dropped into a cross-legged seat on the floor to get a better look at a remote-controlled car from circa 1986 while John joined the other two men at the desk.

"How's the action out there?" Cooper asked. Even he could hear the note of desperation in his voice.

John patted him on the shoulder. "You're not missing much, Lieutenant. Anything going on in here?"

Cooper's jaw tightened. He gestured to the monitors. "See for yourself."

They watched Cari's second attempt at striking the monster. The miss was so drastic that she nearly impaled her own leg.

"Oh, dear," John said as Grace wrenched a weapon out of Cari's hand for the second time. "That's concerning."

"That's what Grace thought. What we all thought, really."

"Any chance she's faking it?"

"I don't think so. What would be the point? I'm sure Grace explained what was at stake here."

"M-maybe she wants to get fired," Simon interjected timidly, his face never turning away from the screens. "I mean, this job isn't exactly a cakewalk. Maybe she...decided it's not for her."

"No way."

They all turned toward Rex, who still sat on the floor. "She needs this job. Not wants it. *Needs* it. There's no way she'd screw it up on purpose. Trust me."

"I do," John said. "Which leaves one explanation: She is simply incapable of performing the duties this job requires. Which means that, unfortunately, we'll have let her go."

Rex jumped to his feet. "You can't do that. It will kill her."

"I know it will be difficult, but I'm afraid there's nothing else we can do."

Rex narrowed his eyes. "Does this have anything to do with what she said to you last week. The thing about Holly?"

John's jaw hung loose for a moment before he snapped it back up. "Of course not."

But Cooper didn't like how pale his face had become. "John, what's he talking about?"

"It's nothing, Lieutenant," John said brusquely. "An ethical dilemma on which she and I happen to hold opposing views. But I would *never* retaliate against an employee simply because they disagreed with me. This is a safety issue. Nothing more."

Turning from the fuming teenager, John leaned over Cooper's shoulder toward the microphone and pressed the Talk button. "Ms. Henry?"

Cooper saw Grace's entire body go stiff. "Yeah, Boss?"

"Will you and Ms. Hembert please report to the med station at once?"

Grace nodded solemnly. Behind her, Cari's shoulders crumbled.

"This isn't right," Rex muttered. He shot Cooper a pained look. "You know this isn't right."

Cooper shifted uncomfortably. His thoughts pooled around the dull throb in his shoulder. "I know you care about her. But continuing to employ her is risky. For her as well as the rest of us."

Rex snorted furiously as if Cooper's words were the height of betrayal. He whipped his head back to John. "If she goes, then I go."

John sighed. "I'm sorry you feel that way, Mr. Ranganathan. You're a good employee and a fascinating young man. We will be sorry to lose you. And…for what it's worth though, I do sympathize with your loyalty."

Rex laughed bitterly. "Yeah, right."

Before he could say more, the lights in the room flickered and a squawking alarm put an end to all conversation.

"Crap," Simon said, tapping the joystick. "We've got incoming."

"Where?" Cooper asked.

The tapping slowed, then stopped. Simon sat completely still, staring at the screens in disbelief.

Cooper's stomach filled with dread. "Specs, where *is* it?"

Simon swallowed hard.

"Everywhere."

"What's happening?" Cari shouted over the shrieking alarm.

"Do I look like I have a periscope for a head?" Grace shouted as she sprinted toward the exit. A.J. had stationed himself next to the door, pistols drawn, scanning the hallway for enemies. Without breaking her stride, Grace snatched a stocky hammer from a nearby shelf. With a scratched handle and a pitted charcoal-colored head, it looked as if it could be Mjolnir's brother from another, less-royal, mother.

"What should I do?" Cari asked, trotting a few paces behind Grace.

"Stay here."

"Are you sure? It sounds like you need all the help you can get."

"Yeah…I know."

The words hit her like a roundhouse kick in the gut. She stopped running. "And the only way I can help is to stay out of the way."

Grace slowed but didn't turn. "It's only for now, until we have a chance to figure out a good…trajectory for you. Put you on a path to—"

"He's gonna fire me, isn't he?" Cari blurted out. She hadn't wanted to say it out loud, but the words would not be stopped. It was too important.

Grace skidded to a halt.

A.J. whipped his attention away from the hall. "*Qué pasa? Escuchaste lo que dijo Simon. Hay una monstruo enorme. Necesitamos—*"

"*Un segundo!*" Grace snapped. She turned back to Cari, her face stony but confident. "We'll figure something out. I promise."

Cari nodded at the floor. She wasn't sure she believed that any more than she would have believed an outright denial.

Grace pointed at a red button next to A.J.'s elbow. "Press this once we're out. Then door can only be opened from this side. When I—or whoever—come back to get you, listen for two long knocks, then four short, then two long. That's how you'll know it's safe. If anything tries to get in without knocking, shoot it…or, you know, do the best you can."

Even in the dim light, Cari could see Grace's cheeks flush. Normally, Grace's embarrassment would have been a rare treat. In this case, she couldn't even smile. Not when she thought about what would most likely happen to her if something got through that door.

Grace nodded at A.J. "*Vaminos, vaquero.*" She slapped the beat-up hammerhead into her palm.

A.J. grinned, his white teeth glinting in the shadow of his hat. "*El gusto es mio.*"

His duster billowed out behind him as he raced up the ramp, guns pointed forward, a cold greeting for anything that made the mistake of getting in his way. Cari's palm lingered on the springy red button as they disappeared down the hall, her body buzzing with fear as well as frustration. They were off to save the world—or at least the town—and here she was, weak and unreliable and probably a few hours away from being fired. If that happened, it was all over. The tenuous influence she held over her mother, the modified drinking hours, Nelson's banishment—all of it would disappear. She would be right back where she started, except that now they would be really, *really* mad. Especially Nelson. She didn't know what that would mean for her exactly, but she knew she would be helpless to stop it. And she was *so fucking sick* of being helpless.

She smacked the button. The door slammed closed.

Maybe she was on the road to getting fired, but she wasn't fired yet. There was still time to fix this.

She marched back to the range.

Chapter Five

Cooper bolted up the stairs as stealthily as his bulky frame would allow. Distracted by the current predicament, John hadn't noticed Cooper retrieve his AA-12 from his locker, and Cooper wanted to keep it that way. His hopes were nearly dashed when he reached the top of the steps. John and Rex had stopped dead not three feet away from the top of the stairs, barely leaving enough clearance for the cabinet to swing closed behind them. Cooper was about to ask what the hold-up was when he saw it for himself. Above the greeter's desk, a lattice of writhing red vines choked what had been the window to the hall. Smooth, slick, and streaked with veins of maroon and midnight blue, the vines looked less vegetable and more vascular, like a knot of boneless, skinless veins.

"Well. That's new," Rex whispered, wringing the strap of his messenger bag.

John tucked the butt of his rifle to his shoulder. Rex fell in step beside him, rummaging through his bag for an aerosol can affixed with a Bic lighter. Cooper followed with his back to them, gun at the ready.

The corridor between the office and the East Hall was dark and empty. As soon as they rounded the corner, however, it was clear where the vines had come from.

Maws ran up and down both sides of the hall every ten feet or so, with thick purple trunks sprouting from each one. Though the Maws couldn't have been open for more than a few minutes, most of the trunks already stretched halfway to the ceiling. Vines flowed from them, snaking along the walls, threading through the gates of abandoned storefronts, encountering vines from other trunks and weaving themselves together until the building's features could no longer be seen beneath an ever-expanding meat-vine sweater.

"Keep to the middle," John whispered as the trio ducked under a spray of vines wriggling down from the arched bridge. "Don't get close to these things."

Cooper nodded, prompting a bead of sweat to roll down his neck. He wiped his forehead, and his hand came away slick. Not out of fear, but because the hall had ground as hot and humid as a jungle. When they entered the rotunda, he could see why. Above the fountain, where the straining Atlas now held a vine-strapped globe, a ring of flowers bloomed from the tallest plants. The petals were thunderhead gray with a knot of tiny pink and red stamen in the center of each one. They swayed gently as if kissed by a breeze even though the air was suffocating in its stillness. Every few seconds, one of the flowers spasmed and coughed out a fine purple mist. Some of it fell to the ground, but the majority slid up the sides of the rotunda to the apex, forming a pendulous cloud.

"Cooper."

He jumped. Grace hadn't been yelling, but between the stillness and the vine-skinned walls, even normal speech seemed louder and closer than usual. He turned around as she trotted toward them. Instead of her usual sledgehammer, she held a squat, beat-to-hell hammer in two hands like a tennis racket. A.J. followed her, weapon-heavy rucksack strapped to his back and his pistols up. Cooper waited for the third member of their party to appear, but it didn't happen.

"Where's Cari?" he asked when they got within whispering distance.

"In the Armory with the door locked," Grace said. "I didn't know what we were dealing with, so I figured it was best to keep her out of it. Clearly, I was right." She glanced at the foliage, flowers, and fog. "Sylvia's learned a few tricks since last time, I see."

"Long moon," John said. They all nodded in agreement. Even Rex—though judging by the stunned look on his face Cooper doubted the words had truly registered.

"You see her yet?" A.J. asked.

"No," John said. "But this amount of manifestation could never be accomplished remotely. Not even on the long moon."

"How do you know?" Rex asked.

"I just do," John said, his tone clearly indicating that now was not the time for a seminar. "She's here. Believe me."

Still suspicious, Rex looked at Cooper, who nodded his support.

A brittle crack shattered the stillness. Cooper looked up. Webbed cracks had formed in one of the pink glass panels of the dome where a particularly ambitious vine had dug in with its suckered feet.

"That settles it," John said. "We gotta get rid of these things before they bust through the ceiling."

"How?" Grace asked. "We can't exactly shoot them, and I'm fresh out of Round-up."

"We cut them off at the source." He nodded at the nearest trunk. The Maw it sprung out of was barely bigger than the trunk itself. "Collapse the Maws. The vines won't disappear, but it should stop them from getting any bigger. Mr. Ranganathan, if you please?"

"Are you—!" Rex started to yell, then dropped his voice to a whisper when the unnaturally loud volume made him wince. "Are you kidding me? There's got to be a hundred of them. Does it look like I have a hundred of *anything* in here?" He rattled the canvas bag.

Another crack bounced off the walls. John glared upward as a second vine sunk into the glass. "Then start with the tallest ones and go from there. Now, *if you please.*"

Grumbling, Rex dug through his bag for almost a full minute before extracting a dozen aerosol cans that he had painted with bright green bull's-eyes. "How about these? Toss one in and boom!" He cocked his finger at one of the green dots and snapped his thumb. "Planty go bye-bye."

"It'll do." John extended his hand to Cooper. "You're the tactician here, Lieutenant. We'll follow your lead."

"Yes sir."

As he scooped up the cans, Cooper couldn't help feeling a little bit smug. To think John had wanted him to stay on the bench for this.

While A.J. supplied Grace and Rex with handguns from his Helios arsenal, Cooper walked the perimeter of the rotunda, located the five highest reaching vines, and traced them back to their origin points. When he was sure he had the correct five, he placed an aerosol at the edge of each Maw, moving cautiously so as not to provoke them. The trunks seemed to stiffen as he approached and resumed their undulations the moment he stepped away. Compared to the others, these five seemed lumpy and swollen, as if they'd eaten a big meal. He lingered a moment, watching the colors and fibers flow out from the Maw. The trunks were super saturated, almost velvety in the middle, with the vines growing lighter the further they stretched, fading from maroon and eggplant to lavender and rose. He might have called them pretty if he didn't know about the vile swamp that their roots called home.

"Set?"

John's voice brought him back to task.

"Set." He slipped his gun from his shoulder, wincing a little at the lingering stiffness in his injured muscles. He took aim at a can. Out the corner of his eye, he saw his four compatriots do the same.

"On my signal," John called out. "Ready."

Cooper readied.

"Steady."

He trained his sight on the bright green bullseye.

"Fire!"

The shots rang out as a single unified blast, rolling into every nook and cranny of the building.

Cooper had thought it was a good plan. And technically, it did work. Every one of the five Maws snapped closed, slicing the trunks clean through the process.

He never expected the stumps would start bleeding.

And he never, *ever* expected the blood would be made of centipedes.

A gurgling screech grated against Cooper's ears as Rex finally lost his long-suffering lunch.

"Retreat!" Grace screamed. She was quickly drowned out by the dry *click-click-click* of a billion stick legs skittering across the tile.

He should be running. But his brain wouldn't let him. Not until it was all caught up.

Trunks. Sliced at the base. Closed the Maws. Killed the trunks. Good plan. And now—bugs? Giant bugs. Giant bugs...with giant bug teeth...

There's a giant bug on my foot.

Panic squeezed his lungs. His leg bucked, and the thing went flying. Not that it mattered much—there were roughly a hundred more, streaming from the base of the severed trunk.

Okay. Now *you can run.*

His gun banged against his sore shoulder as he tore off down the hall. He gritted his teeth and kept going, passing first A.J., and then Rex, who looked pale and dazed, as if he had crash-landed in his worst nightmare. Cooper caught him by the arm and together they fell in line next to Grace—just in time to see a centipede as big as a banana and as fast as a rocket launch itself from a nearby vine and land on the back of John's upper arm.

"Boss, watch out!" Cooper cried as the creature ripped into his sweater with its pincers. John whipped his arm, trying to shake the thing off. But it was too late. He let out a roar of anguish as it buried its head in his flesh.

"No!" Grace wailed.

John stumbled, but he didn't stop running. Reaching around with his opposite arm, he clamped the squirmy thing in his fist and yanked. There was a sucking sound as its head came free, then a crunch. Rex groaned at the sight of the blue and red goop oozing from between John's clenched fingers. Cooper felt the muscles in the boy's arm go limp.

"Stay sharp, kid!" Cooper yelled, shaking him as hard as he could. Rex whimpered, but he kept his balance, and his eyes stayed open.

"I'm okay," John called over his shoulder. But Cooper could see through the rip in his sweater that the crescent-shaped wound was already starting to swell. He shot an alarmed look at Grace, who nodded. She saw it too.

They reached the corridor outside the office before John's knees buckled. Letting go of Rex, Cooper managed to hook his good arm through John's uninjured elbow before the older man collapsed. Sweat soaked his shirt and his cheeks had turned the color of moldy Swiss cheese. Grace looped herself under John's other arm, and together they dragged him into the office. The wall of vines covering the window was even denser than it had been when they had first seen it. With the window inaccessible, the only way the little bastards could get to them was through the door. They had created their own bottleneck.

How ironic.

"A.J.! Cover us!" Cooper shouted into the hallway.

"Sí, Teniente!" came the enthusiastic response, followed by the pop of pistol shots. Meanwhile, Rex slumped against the office wall, his face ashy and his eyes affixed to John. He looked completely terrified.

"He'll be okay," Cooper said as Grace yanked open the cabinet drawer. "The med station has everything we need. Once we get him downstairs—"

The firing stopped.

"Mierda," A.J. hissed over the ratchet of a shell being chambered. A chorus of high-pitched little screams accompanied the next blast.

"Oye, chico de rabia! Rex! *Ven aquí! Necesito el fuego líquido!"*

Grace didn't look away from the keypad. "Sounds like you're up, kid."

"Oh...uh, right," Rex fumbled in his bag, his expression shifting from one of fear to one of determination. Retrieving his makeshift flamethrower, he took a steeling breath. His eyes fell on John, and to Cooper's utter amazement, he grinned. "This one's for you, old man."

He whirled out the door.

John chuckled. "I guess he's forgiven me for my...uh...my..." He trailed off as his head snapped back on his neck.

"John?" Grace shook him, but he didn't respond. From the hall came a whooshing sound, along with a blast of residual heat. Apparently, Rex had provided the inferno monsoon A.J. had requested. But would it be enough?

"Can you manage him on your own?" Cooper asked Grace as the cabinet door opened. "No offense, but I think a shotgun might be more useful than a hammer in this case."

Grace scowled. "Only because they're advancing in a group. If they were coming at us in a straight line, I would crush it. Literally. The whole thing."

"That's the real problem with centipedes. No discipline." Cooper extracted himself from John's elbow. "Anti-venom's in the lower middle cabinet. Second shelf."

"I remember," Grace tightened her grip around John and trundled into the stairwell. His body remained limp, but his eyes were bright and rolling furiously to all sides. Cooper wondered how long it would be until he couldn't even do that.

Until he was nothing more than a living corpse.

He shoved the thought from his mind as Grace disappeared down the stairs. Centipede venom was quick, but so was the anti-venom. Besides, John had only been bitten once, and in an extremity. It could have been so much worse.

A thud echoed from the hallway, followed by a grunt of pain.

"*A.J.?*" Rex cried.

Cooper flew out the door. Rex had laid waste to the advancing horde, the three-foot flame reducing the tiny legion to charred and shriveled briquettes. At his feet A.J.

writhed on the ground, straining for the shotgun just out of reach while simultaneously trying to rip a munching centipede from his collarbone, apparently unaware of the other three currently wriggling their way up his belly. Before Cooper could yell at him to move, they ducked their heads and tore into him. His scream could have woken the dead.

"Rex, I'm coming!" Darting into the hallway, Cooper grabbed A.J.'s outstretched arm and dragged him into the office. Rex followed, continuing to lash the horde with flames until he had crossed the threshold of the office and slammed the door behind them.

Whipping out a switchblade, Cooper attended the bug in A.J.'s shoulder first. It squealed as he sliced it in half. Gritting his teeth against the pain, A.J. dug the severed top half of the creature out of his neck and flung it as far as he could. It was the last thing he did before his arm locked up. Cooper repeated the process with the three in his stomach, tossing the the bisected remains across the room where Rex stomped on them with great relish.

"Over your phobia, I see." Cooper hefted A.J. off the ground, draping one of his arms over his shoulders.

"They're trying to eat us alive." Rex said scraped his boot across the floor, leaving a lumpy red trail behind. "How is being afraid going to stop *that*?"

John was already sitting up on his own by the time Rex and Cooper stumbled into the med station with the paralyzed A.J. suspended between them. Grace looked up from John's arm as they dumped him into the next bed over. Her expression turned from concentrated to terrified.

"Jesus," she whispered, leaving John to finish wrapping his own arm. "How many got him?"

"Four," Cooper said.

Her fingers brushed her lips in shock. "John, I think we should—"

"Go ahead" John rose from the cot and grabbed a glass vial from the tray next to him. He slipped a syringe from its protective plastic sleeve and poked it through the vial's stopper. Meanwhile, Grace pushed A.J.'s hat back on his head so she could hold his immobile face between her hands.

"A.J.," she whispered.

His eyes rolled up to her. A tear slipped down his cheek. Wiping it away with her thumb, she lowered her mouth until it was next to his ear.

"Barre Burrata."

His eyes shuttered. She lowered him to rest on the pillow, repositioning his hand tenderly over his eyes.

"What does that mean?" Rex asked.

"Christ, doesn't *anybody* read the handbook?" Grace grumbled. "It's a kill switch. A nonsense phrase we introduce during periods of condensed sleep. It induces a coma-like state, for when someone is incapacitated or possessed...or in unnecessary pain."

"Wow." Rex shook his head. "I mean, I know you guys are hardcore, but incepting people? That's insane."

"Call it whatever you want," Grace said as John swabbed the skin over A.J.'s carotid. "You're getting one of your own the next time you fall asleep."

Rex's jaw dropped. "You wouldn't."

"We have to," John said. "It's as much for our protection as it is yours."

"Figures *you* would say that."

"*Rex,*" Grace hissed. "Not the time."

Rex scowled but shut his mouth. The three of them watched in silence as John inserted the syringe into A.J.'s neck and pressed the plunger. They all held their breath in anticipation. But except for a minor quickening in the rise and fall of his chest, nothing happened.

"What's wrong?" Grace asked.

"I don't know. He had more bites. A lot more," John said. Retrieving a pair of scissors, he cut open A.J.'s shirt and proceeded to sterilize the shallow divots scattered over his abdomen. "But I think we caught it in time. It will just take the anti-venom a little longer to work. And of course, there's the kill switch to consider."

"It takes about an hour to wear off," Grace said in response to Rex's confused look. "Assuming the anti-venom works, he should wake up feeling like he was on a trip to Jamaica."

"Lucky him."

Cooper barely realized the words had come from him. His mind had been elsewhere, in a different med station, in a different desert, in what felt like a completely different world. But standing over a brother in arms lying in a hospital bed, unconscious and full of holes...that was the same.

"Uh, guys? We may have a problem."

Grace groaned up at the ceiling. "Don't you know any other songs?"

"What is it, Specs?" Cooper asked around her outburst.

"Uh, well I hate to say this in light of everything, but...it's Cari."

Everyone froze. John's hand hung suspended over A.J., the iodine swab dribbling turmeric-tinted liquid onto his chest. Next to him, Rex squeaked like a gutted mouse. Cooper lowered his gaze to the floor, momentarily unable to look the kid in the eye. "What happened?"

"Nothing yet. But the centipedes...they're moving toward Spartan."

"All of them?"

"Pretty much. A lot of my cameras have been obscured by those vines, but all the bugs I can see are heading that way."

"We've got to do something," Rex insisted, his voice shaky and fragile. "I know we're all down on helping people who can't help themselves right now, but...shit, man. We've gotta go get her." He sighed. "One last time."

Cooper nodded. The kid was right.

"I'll go."

He said it at the same time as Grace.

"It's my responsibility," she insisted before he had the chance to make his case. "I made the call to leave her there. I should be the one to bring her back."

"And you're my partner," he countered. "I go where you go."

"You're still recovering," Grace pointed out. "If your immunity is compromised and you get bit by one of those things, or more than one—"

"This isn't up for debate. It's protocol. Right?"

He glared at John, daring him to contradict his own favorite refrain. John's gaze swiveled from Cooper to Grace with an evolving frown that began with irritation and ended with deep concern. He wouldn't be able to talk either them out of going. Cooper figured that much was obvious. But more importantly, Cooper suspected he didn't want to. Sure, Cari's combat skills might fall short of perfect. Cooper knew that better than anyone. But when it came to the Maw-dwellers, no one—*no one*—was an acceptable loss.

"I want you both in hazmat gear," John said, his tone uncompromising. "Suits and boots, and gloves too. Seal the seams with duct tape. That might buy you enough time if those things get on top of you." He paused. "And if you see Sylvia..."

"We'll give her a big kiss for you," Grace said.

As they made their way to the lockers, Cooper heard the squeaky stomp of boots coming up behind them.

"And where do you think you're going?" he asked as Rex brushed past him.

Rex turned on Cooper with a look of such fearless sincerity it made Cooper feel awed, and even slightly afraid.

"You go where your partner goes, right?"

Cooper nodded.

Rex opened his locker and grabbed his suit. "That makes two of us."

Chapter Six

*C*ari? Can--hear--?"

Cari lowered her latest trial weapon, a Glock 19, and raised her eyes from the depressingly intact target to the speaker bank. "Simon?"

"*Yeah.*" His voice was garbled and clipped with static. "*There—a—interference because—the activity—don't know—stay open, but I wanted—reach you—still can. We—problem.*"

She groaned inwardly. "Is that how you start every conversation?"

"*Huh?*"

"Nothing. Sorry," Cari said. She'd been hanging out with Grace too much. "What's the problem?"

"*—coming—*"

"What?"

The only response was an unintelligible burst of noise. She rolled her eyes. If he wasn't going to be helpful, the least he could do was not distract her.

She lifted the gun, squinting through the sight to line up the shot. It looked perfect. But the thought of squeezing the trigger sent a series of spasms down her arm that made her hand ache and her bones turn to liquid. There was not a doubt in her mind that the bullet would go winging off on whatever trajectory it felt like taking. She slammed the gun on the bench. What the hell was *wrong* with her?

"*—centipedes.*"

"Simon…if you need to tell me something, you gotta fix that signal. It sounded like you said centipedes."

"*That's—said. Hundreds—giant—coming——now.*"

The static overtook his voice, then cut out, leaving her alone once again in the big empty silence.

At least, it would have been silent, if not for the faint scratching noise behind her. A spindly shiver wriggled across her neck as she recalled the creature smeared over the back of Sam's clipboard. Seeing it dead had been harrowing enough. The thought of a live one crawling in her direction…

And Simon had said hundreds? Hundreds. Giant. Coming.

Now.

The scratching continued, her fear amplifying the volume to jackhammer level. She looked down at the gun in her hand. How giant was giant for a centipede? Probably not big enough for her to hit it. Not unless it was the size of a horse— and if that was the case, she would have bigger problems.

But she cocked the gun nonetheless. Taking a deep breath, she turned as slowly as she dared and faced the door. It was still locked up tight. She exhaled a sigh of relief, but it lodged in her throat halfway out. In the shaft of light at the bottom of the door, a shadow squirmed. The scratching kept on. It was definitely getting louder now. Louder, and faster.

What was it doing?

She took a step forward, gun theoretically pointed at the shadow. The closer she got, the more details she could make out. It looked like a hairy snake. Except she knew those weren't hairs. They were legs. A hundred of them, or close to it. And antennae. And pincers as sharp as razor blades.

The barrel of the gun shook. She clamped her free hand around her wrist. Freaking out wasn't going to help her accuracy. Besides, there was nothing to be afraid of. It was just a bug.

Then the noise changed. The light, brushing curiosity condensed into a sheering sound like metal through bone. She stared in horror as a pair of blood red pincers sliced through a crack at the bottom of the thick metal door, followed by a pair of long, prickly legs.

"That's impossible," she spluttered. A scream bubbled in her throat, but she clamped her lips closed. It wouldn't do any good. No one would hear her. For better or worse, she was on her own.

She leveled the gun and fired.

In the time it took to suit up and return to the main floor, the East Hall had shifted in appearance from an alien jungle to the inside of an alien's heart. The heavy purple cloud that had been gathering at the top of the rotunda had grown fallen, scattering striated patches of purple fog throughout the hallway. The vines weren't moving as fast anymore now that they had suckered to every visible surface, including the floor. Cooper stepped on a thick red rope and felt it squish under his boot. For a moment he thought he felt it—or something inside it—squirm under his weight. Picking up his feet, he led Grace and Rex down the hall toward Spartan.

Inside the sporting goods store was no better. The walls were eclipsed by dozens of massive trunks, each one as round and bulbous as a whiskey still. Their distended skins were snare-drum taut and semi-translucent, revealing the pulsing, squirming broods inside. Even through the plastic hood of his hazmat suit, the sound of wriggling legs and clacking pincers was cacophonous.

"Holy shit," Grace whispered, easing her sledgehammer off her shoulder and slowing her pace to a cautious sneak. "There's gotta be a million of them."

Cooper was inclined to agree. And those in incubation were only part of the number. Reclining on the distended trunks was the rotunda horde—the part of it that hadn't been splattered, sliced up or cremated, anyway. They clung to the bark like nursing piglets, immobile except for the occasional, lethargic twitch of antennae.

"What are they doing?" Cooper asked.

"As long as they're not doing it to one of us, I couldn't care less," Grace said. Rex nodded in agreement, his suit rustling vigorously as he practically strangled the strap of his duffel bag.

They stopped outside the manager's office so Cooper could unlock the door. Thanks to the cumbersome gloves and the fact that he had to keep wiping drops of purple mist off his face window, negotiating the correct key out of A.J.'s key ring was not as easy as he had expected. He cursed his fat fingers as Grace and Rex stood guard.

"It's weird," Grace mused. Cooper glanced back at her—she was looking up at the gray-petaled flowers that hung from the ceiling, their foggy belches raining purple mist onto the lumpy crimson hillocks that had once been clothing racks.

"You don't say?" Rex shot back.

Grace sighed. "No, I mean…I've read every letter and journal the founders wrote, and I don't remember any of them talking about flowers that spit fog."

"But they talk about centipede-spawning flesh vines?"

"Mary died from centipede venom. That's close enough." She paused as another flower sprinkled them with mist. "What do you suppose it does?"

"Would you like to find out?" came the raspy, gurgling response.

Cooper's hands froze in mid-fumble. *Who the hell was that?*

He whipped around. Two barbs of dark purple mist hovered above Grace and Rex, their pointy heads twitching as they swayed subtly in the air. Though they didn't have faces, it still seemed as though they were watching, biding their time, waiting for the right moment.

Apparently, that moment had come. Before Cooper could utter so much as a gasp of warning, the barbs reared up and plunged into the backs of his compatriots' necks.

Rex screeched, the confusion in his voice quickly turning to panic. "It's in my suit! Jesus Christ, it's in my fucking suit!" He clawed at the plastic with rubber-tipped fingers as the scream faded into a wet, gasping cough. Grace, on the other hand, didn't make a sound. She simply fell to her knees, her hands swiping at the clear plastic panel over her face. A pearly lavender fog filled her helmet, obscuring her completely.

"Grace!" Cooper rushed forward, driving his knees into the vines next to Grace and dragged her head onto his lap. The weight of her was somewhat comforting. He had half-expected to discover that she had turned to smoke.

"Hold on." He fumbled with the helmet release, his fingers even less effective now that they were coursing with adrenaline. "Hold on, Grace. Stay with me."

Finally, he managed to free the helmet from her suit. Her skin and lips were ashy, and her normally warm brown eyes had frosted over with a white haze. But she was still here. Still breathing. Still alive. He trailed a plastic finger along her cheek. "Thank God."

"No."

That voice again, raspy and heartless. Cooper turned in its direction. The invading mist lingered near Grace's discarded helmet, coiled up like an angry rattlesnake.

"What did you say?" he demanded.

"No. No God. Only power."

It shot across the room like a switchblade, drawing every bit of ambient moisture into itself, clearing the air but for this one lavender comet.

Cooper slid his gun from his shoulder to his hands, trying to get the nose of the streaking cloud in his sights. He didn't know if bullets could kill this thing, but he had to try. Except that it was moving too fast, racing across the walls...and piercing the distended trunk-sacs as it went. Cooper's stomach plummeted as each one deflated like a punctured balloon and the brood inside tumbled out.

He reoriented the shotgun toward the closest trunk outside the office door. They would be the ones to reach him first, and while he knew he couldn't hold them off forever, he sure as hell wasn't going down without a fight.

But the centipedes didn't seem to notice him. Instead, they juked left, flowing along with the others until some secret instruction made them all juke again, toward the middle of the room. Cooper traced their progress with his gun as they grouped in the center aisle. They started to climb, not onto any structure but on top of each other like an inhuman pyramid. The ethereal blade that had freed them reverted to mist, swirling thick around the pile like frosting on a cake.

Cooper blinked. For a second, a divot in the mist looked like the sleeve of a cloak. And that...that was a mouth. But not a human mouth. It was round, and rigid, flanked by a pair of sharp pincers.

A bug's mouth.

The gun seemed to fire on its own. Bullets tore into the base of the squirming tower. It bobbled to one side, then the other, trying to keep its balance in the slick of red goo oozing from the base.

The gun clicked empty. He reloaded and kept firing. The tower kept tilting, the puddle beneath it kept expanding. But the waves of centipedes kept on coming. And no matter how many times he reloaded, no matter how many rounds he pumped into it, the tower kept growing. Six feet. Seven. Eight. The gun clicked again. He reached for another magazine—and came up with nothing but air.

The floor started to vibrate. His soles itched as all around him, every waiting centipede burst into a tiny cloud of purple ash. The mist stopped swirling and fell, draping the tower like a heavy purple cloak. A pair of black antennae emerged from the top, stabbing curiously at the air. They were followed by a flat, eyeless black shield, and a pair of hornlike jaws that looked big enough to swallow his head without provoking so much as a hiccup. Instead of hair, segmented black plates rolled down its back and disappeared into the neck of the cloak, which began jerking and pulling in all directions. The first razor sharp leg punched through the cloak and bury itself in the thick, juicy floor.

Schluck.

That's when Cooper ran.

Cari's breath grew labored and shallow as more and more bullets flew from the gun. They threw up sparks as they hit the door, the floor, the walls—everything, it seemed, except the mini-demon struggling to get inside. She adjusted her aim—lucky her, the target was getting bigger with every passing second—and fired again.

The centipede didn't even flinch at the ruckus. It kept on flailing as it inched further and further toward freedom.

"Son of a bitch," she growled. She needed to do this. She needed to kill this thing. She needed this job. More than any of the others did. It wasn't fair.

The bug trilled excitedly. With one final yank, it rocketed free from the door. Cari's heart raced as it squiggled and zigged down the hall, its body rippling like water as it closed the distance between them. She kept squeezing the trigger until the bullets stopped coming.

The thing hadn't even slowed down.

"It's not fair!" Letting out a furious, frustrated scream, she hurled the empty gun at the skittering monster. Not exactly the height of maturity, but besides scrambling up one of the tall shelves like a cartoon elephant running from a mouse, she was officially out of ideas.

The gun landed. Not with a bang or a clatter, but a crunch. She watched in stunned silence as the creature flailed its front legs, trying to drag itself out from under the heavy lump of metal that had crushed its back.

"Huh. That's…lucky."

She frowned. Was it lucky? Or was it exactly how it should be?

Leaving the Glock in the puddle of guts, Cari jogged back to the shooting range. She found the Colt A.J. had given her to try first near the bottom of the discard pile. It felt dense and substantial. That would work.

She ejected the magazine and popped the bullet from the chamber like A.J. had taught her. Setting herself in front of the middle target, she flung the Colt end over end down the range.

The Colt hit the dummy right between the eyes, and kept going, slicing through the gel and smashing into the wall with a loud crack. She giggled as the head peeled apart and collapsed to either side like a deranged Jell-O mold melting in the sun. There was no spasm of doubt this time, no sudden muscle weakness. In fact, she'd never felt stronger in her life.

"Just like the bottles," she murmured. How could she have not figured it out sooner?

"*Hey! What—doing?*" cracked Simon, his indignity strong enough to momentarily overwhelm the interference. "*Man, now I—new one.*"

But Cari was too busy staring at her right hand in wonder to respond. Throwing the guns had felt exactly like throwing oil-filled bottles at Creeps on her very first day. And she had nailed her target almost every time.

But guns were not made to be thrown. She needed something built for the purpose.

"Simon, I need you to find something for me," she said as she sprinted for the shelves. "I don't know if there's a database you can search, or if what I need is here—"

"*Oh, I'm—here,*" Simon cut in, along with a cackle of keystrokes. "*A.J.—one of everything. What—need?*"

She told him. Just saying the words made her grin uncontrollably. "And obviously, I'm gonna need more than one."

Chapter Seven

*S*he was coming…
…and now she was here.

With his back to the solid tapestry of vines that had once been the store's entrance, Cooper watched the witch approach. Her back legs crept over the uneven ground, while the other half curled in front of her, partially concealed by her robe. The only two he could see were the extra-elongated top set protruding from what would have been a person's shoulders like sharp chopsticks that had been snapped in half but not completely separated. They pierced the ground as she walked, leaving wounds in the vines that quickly filled with fluid. Her antennae twitched in anticipation as her head bobbled vindictively. She was proud of herself. Why wouldn't she be? She'd already taken down two of them and was undoubtedly going to take the third.

Even so, he wasn't going to let her off easy. He tore off his hood to regain his peripheral vision and raised his fists. She hissed, mandibles clicking hungrily. She would kill him, but not before he ripped off a leg or two. Maybe even crushed her jaw. If he did enough damage, it might give the others a fighting chance.

"Go on then," he growled. "Take your best shot."

She surged forward, sharp feet kicking up spurts of blood. Her jaws parted, revealing a circle of pointy little teeth lining the entrance to a ridged purple gullet. The thought of seeing it up close was almost enough to make him lose his nerve.

She reared back and screeched. A battle cry. He pulled back his fist and prepared for her to enter his range.

But it didn't happen. Instead, she froze in mid-back bend, her antennae flailing wildly and her front legs swiveling in their sockets, stabbing desperately at the air behind her.

Cooper lowered his arms. That hadn't been a battle cry. It had been a scream of pain. But from what? Keeping one eye trained on her front legs, he slid a step to the left to see what made a monster stop dead in her tracks. Between the third and fourth segments of her back protruded a silver handle, almost invisible under the glut of thick black blood.

And there, standing outside the door to the office, was Cari, her arm extended from the throw. On a thick leather belt around her hips, five silver tomahawks glittered in the dim light, each one delicate and deadly sharp.

Despite the gigantic creature gnashing away in front of him, Cooper felt a wide smile spread over his face. Maybe he wasn't totally screwed after all.

Cari didn't know what the hell she was aiming at when she let the ax fly. Even now she couldn't really tell what it was other than huge and bendy and draped in dark clothing, with stick-like arms that were trying unsuccessfully to dig the smarting little thing out of its back.

"Cari!"

Cooper's voice broke her daze. She scanned the room and found him on the other side of the giant lump. His face held a combination of surprise, relief—and awe.

That's right, she thought, hands on her hips in her best hero pose. I saved your ass.

The thing twisted, and she saw it for what it was—a huge freaking centipede.

Unfortunately, it saw her too. Its pincer-like jaws clicked rapidly, strands of drool dripping from the mouth.

Her smugness vanished. Maybe she hadn't done quite as much ass-saving as she'd thought.

She ripped another ax from her belt and chucked it straight in the centipede's sharp, wet face. Its head slammed back around from the force of the impact.

Direct hit! Her heart took flight. Now all she had to do was stand back and wait for it to fall down dead.

Instead, it swiveled back around, the silver ax in its mouth glinting like a metal filling. If anyone had told her that centipedes could smile, she would have rolled her eyes and called them an idiot. But as it crushed her weapon like tin foil between its jaws, Cari swore she saw the rigid face jerk into such an expression. And the sound it made after it spat the mangled ax across the room sounded a lot like a dusty cackle.

She grabbed another ax. In response, the beast threw itself onto all fours—or rather, all one hundred. It zagged toward her, winding around the clothing racks that now looked more like giant red mushrooms than furniture. She stood poised to throw, her head twitching all over as she tried to keep up with the creature's rapid movement.

"Her legs!" Cooper's voice thundered from behind the bug. "Take out her legs!"

She scanned the ground below the beast, but all she could see was a billow of dark fabric. Crouching down, she flung the ax like a Frisbee, keeping it as parallel to the ground as she could. The butt of the ax struck the creature's left front leg at what was proportionally the ankle. The creature grunted and slowed, shaking the affected leg as if its foot had fallen asleep, and resumed unhindered and even more pissed off.

"Shit," she cursed under her breath. Even if she had time to line up another shot, she had no idea what to aim for.

Rising to her feet, she withdrew two axes from her belt, feeling a little silly as she did so. Except for a few boxing moves, she had no training in hand-to-hand combat. She had no business attempting it now. But trained or not, the moment for projectile attacks had ended. Time to fight or die.

And she had zero interest in dying.

The centipede reared back into a looming mass of angles and teeth. It tapped its pincers together and uttered a wet snarl. A streak of terror tore through her, but she refused to acknowledge it. Baring her own teeth, she snarled back. Its pick-legs shot toward her. Her back tensed in anticipation. She raised the axes over her head, blades up. If she was going to get impaled, at least she wouldn't be the only one.

The centipede snapped forward the same time she did. One of her axes got tangled in the billowy fabric of the cloak. The other made it through with enough force to crack one of the segmented plates of the thing's torso. She waited long enough to see the trickle of violet blood slide down the thing's armored skin, then squeezed her eyes shut as she braced for her own impact.

But it never came.

"Cari!"

She opened her eyes and looked up. Cooper clung to the centipede's back, his arms looped around its long front legs, holding them back as he struggled to lock his ankles around its torso. "Cooper? How did you get up there?"

He grunted as the centipede jerked to one side and he nearly lost his grip. "Good question. Let's discuss it at length—right after you kill this bitch, okay?"

"Right. Sorry." She focused on the bleeding abdomen in front of her. The fabric squirmed as the thing's legs twitched in furious panic. Now she was grateful for the cloak's bagginess. It was easier to wrap her mind around the whole business when she couldn't see the full effect. She raised her weapons once more.

Something slammed into her side and sent her flying. The axes slipped from her hands as she crashed to the ground. She landed hard on the protruding roots, sending bolts of pain through her hip and shoulder as her temple scraped against the floor. Her vision darkened, first with disorientation and then with blood. She shook her head and willed herself not to pass out.

"Behind you!"

She tried to turn. Not fast enough. Another blow barreled into her. Unlike the first hit, this one persisted, grinding her sore body further into the roots. She squeezed her eyes closed and bit her tongue to keep from screaming.

The thing on top of her laughed. The sound turned her blood to ice. Not because it was so horrible, but because she recognized it. Slowly, she lifted her head.

Straddling her hip was Grace. Her eyes were as pale and slippery as boiled eggs, and her rosy brown skin had drained of color. Her helmet and gloves were gone, and something had slashed the top of her hazmat suit to ribbons. When their eyes met, her flaked lips split her face in a wide, drooling smile.

"No," Cari whispered, as if a single word could wipe this horrible vision out of existence. This couldn't be happening. She must be seeing things. The Grace she knew would never—

Grace slapped Cari across the face. Cari grunted as ragged nails bit into her cheek. She tasted blood.

And she saw red.

As Grace showered her with more cruel laughter, Cari felt something inside her break open. White hot rage flowed from her chest down her legs, through her arms, into her fists.

Grace lifted her hand to take another shot. Her pale skin caught the light, and she didn't look like herself anymore.

She looked exactly like Cari's mother.

Cari felt her arms rocket upward. She saw her hands wrap around Grace's neck and squeeze. Grace's hand fell, her eyes bugging in surprise. The world spun. When it stopped, Cari found herself sitting upright. Now Grace's shoulders were pinned to the uncomfortable floor. Her nails raked at Cari's arms, drawing red, numb rivers from her skin. Her vision had shrunk to a pinpoint centered on Grace's maniacal face. All sound, including what might have been a man screaming her name, faded below the monotone mantra pounding in her ears in time with her furious heart.

No. More. No. More. No. More.

One of her hands grabbed Grace by the tattered plastic collar and jerked her upward. Grace's head snapped back in a nasty whiplash, but the insane grin never wavered. Cari's other hand dropped to her side, Dragging the last ax from her belt, she brought the blade to Grace's throat.

"*Don't...*"

Cooper's voice meandered through her perception, then faded out again. Both of her hands were visibly shaking—with fear, with exhaustion, but most of all with fury.

"No more."

The hand holding the blade begin to press down, hard enough to draw blood and then harder still. She suspected she meant to cut Grace's throat, and would have, if a giant centipede had not crashed onto the floor next to her. She jumped backward, flinging Grace as far away from her as she could. Both women landed on their elbows a few feet apart. Grace's rheumy eyes centered back on Cari almost immediately. Flipping onto all fours, she began to crawl in Cari's direction. Cari tried to stand, but the ground was too slick with vine goo. The best she could do was slide backward on her forearms as Grace approached, elbows out and belly low.

Just like a centipede.

"Grace," Cooper grunted from beneath the writhing behemoth. Despite having a fifteen-foot centipede fall on him, he had not relinquished his grip. Grace's head ticked in Cooper's direction like a stuttering record, but she kept coming. Her Grace's mouth split into a snide grin, a coating of purple saliva staining her teeth.

"Mr. Edelman's Piano Lesson."

The horrible smile cracked. Grace's jaw dropped open, her eyes rolled closed, and she collapsed face first onto the sticky floor.

"Holy shit," Cari whispered, trembling with relief.

The moment was short-lived, shattered by the centipede's furious roar and Cooper's cry of alarm. She turned in time to see the beast roll itself halfway up, then slam down. The back of its head connected with Cooper's chin as his skull smacked into the floor. He groaned, his limbs finally slackened, releasing his foe. Cari winced at the sight of the inch-long red circles lining the inside of his calves and thighs. It appeared the monster's smaller feet had been digging into his flesh the whole time he'd been holding on.

The centipede wriggled, testing its rediscovered freedom. Saber legs pierced the ground as it regained its balance. It swiveled its plated head in her direction.

She clutched her last ax in an iron grip. Throwing it wouldn't do any good—that thing would chew it up and spit out again like a wad of silver gum. That left one option: Direct attack. Now. While it was still on its back and she still had the upper hand.

Then again, could a single ax against a giant centipede *really* be considered the upper hand?

The thing must have sensed her reluctance. It let out a high-pitched warble that made the nape of her neck shriveled into her scalp. That didn't sound like anger or frustration. It sounded like elation. Like victory. Winning was a mere formality now. All the *real* threats are gone, and soon you will be too.

She narrowed her eyes. Everything in her peripheral vision blurred, then disappeared, until there was nothing but her, and the monster, and the ax. Dozens of tiny legs rippled, beckoning her to come a little closer. She ground her teeth.

You got it, bitch.

She raced up the subtle incline of its torso. Its exposed belly was both hard and springy under her feet. On all sides its legs jabbed at her, poking her sneakers, trying to make her fall. One snagged on the cuff of her jeans and sent her pin-wheeling off course. A vision of her body skewered by a dozen of those sharp little feet flashed before her eyes. With a cry she threw the whole of her weight in the opposite direction of the stumble. By some minor miracle, she managed to stay upright. Her heart slammed in her chest as she passed the last set of tiny legs. All she could see now was its head, and its rigid, pin-filled mouth.

Its torso rippled upward, stealing her momentum. She stumbled backward as the creature pounced on her with its long front legs. But they were stuck fast, buried too deep in the undergrowth.

Cari grinned. "That's what you get for making a mess."

Planting her feet on its stomach, she rode the movements like a surfboard as it tried again to wrench itself free from the irony. Now it was her turn to laugh victoriously. She did the best she could—it was hard to laugh and swing the blade at the same time.

The blow split its brittle skull in two. The ax disappeared into the newly created rift with a thick, wet slurp, taking her hand along with it. She cringed as something cold and snotty coated her fingers. Her peripheral vision returned, along with flickers of red light as, all around the room, the Maws snapped closed. Their severed vines withered almost immediately.

She yelped as the beast she stood on started to sag. With a final burst of strength, she yanked the ax from the skull. She expected it to be coated in bug guts. Instead, feathery gray mold frosted both her hand and the weapon. The hard, bouncy surface beneath her cracked, and she jumped off the carcass mere seconds before it collapsed into a pile of ashy white dust.

"Ach!" came a noise from inside the pile.

Cari yanked her hand back, ready to strike. But it was only Cooper, coughing as he clawed his way out from under the pile of pulverized exoskeleton. She lowered her weapon and ran to him.

"Are you okay?"

"Oh yeah, I'm great," he wheezed. "I always wanted to know what deep-fried cockroach tasted like."

Spitting and brushing floury bug bits off his suit, he wobbled over to the unconscious Grace. As he knelt next

S.G. Tasz

to her, Cari felt something sharp poke her in the ribs. She'd barely cut her. A scratch, at most. But that was only because Cooper had intervened. Otherwise…

Cooper ripped off his gloves and ran his fingers over Grace's neck, feeling for a pulse. A layer of sweat had coagulated on her face, neck and chest, so thick it looked like she'd been dipped in glass. Cari frowned. It wasn't that hot in here, and Grace had been passed out for a while. Why was she sweating so much?

And was she crazy, or did the sweat look a little purple?

"What's wrong with her?"

"Infection," Cooper said. He stripped off the remains of her hazmat suit until she wore only her tank top and leggings. "She should be able to fight it off now that Sylvia is gone."

Cari sighed. "Good. I was worried that…for a minute while we were fighting, it seemed like she was going to turn out like…well, Holly."

"She might have if the infection had been allowed to escalate. It would have scrambled her brain and tricked her into giving herself over. That's why we build in the kill switch."

"You mean that thing you said?"

"Yeah. It shuts the brain down and gives it a fighting chance. Or at least stops the infection from advancing. If it didn't—"

A bright round projectile sailed through the air and collided with Cooper's neck. He doubled over with a grunt, rubbing the back of his skull. The projectile fell to the floor, struck the edge of a vine with a fat, rubbery bounce, then boomeranged backward with such force it nearly hit Cooper again. It ping-ponged over the unpredictable knots scattered across the floor and dribbled to a stop a few feet away from Cari's toes. She arched her eyebrow. With all the

259

firepower at their disposal, who would be rash enough to lob a basketball instead?

Her heart sank. As if she even had to ask.

She looked up to see Rex raise his fist above Cooper's prone head, eyes bleached and face stretched into a Joker-esque sneer.

"Cooper, watch out!"

Cari found her voice at the last viable moment. Cooper managed to roll away before Rex's arm drove downward. The energy of the punch and the lack of impact caused Rex to pitch forward, giving Cooper plenty of time to counter the move by wrapping his elbow around Rex's neck. Flecks of white foam flew from Rex's lips as he clawed the air behind him, trying to get at Cooper's face.

"Easy!" Cooper bellowed in his ear. "Struggling is only gonna make it worse." He clamped his free hand around Rex's wrist and twisted it up behind his back. Throaty snarls morphed into a whine of agony.

"Stop!" Cari wailed. "You don't have to hurt him. Why don't you switch him off, like you did with Grace?"

"Christ, why do we even *have* a handbook?" Cooper sighed in exasperation. "He hasn't had a hypersomnia episode yet. We haven't had the chance to implant a kill switch."

"Then...what are you saying?" Cari's voice shook. "There's nothing we can do?"

Cooper's jaw clenched. "There is one thing."

"What?"

He tilted his head toward her apologetically. "Extreme physical shock."

She frowned, uncomprehending. He jerked his head down again.

He was looking at her ax.

"No…" she moaned as his request became clear. "I can't do that. Not to him."

"It's either that or you hold him down while I punch him in the face ten or fifteen times." Cooper's green eyes had turned steely. He wasn't bluffing or joking. He was tired and angry, ready to do what needed to be done so they could all get the hell out of there. Part of her could relate.

The other part of her *really* didn't want to slice up her friend.

Cooper swung Rex around so his free arm faced her. "Take it."

She did as instructed, cradling his wrist as gently as she could while still holding it still. Carefully, she sliced through the duct tape attaching the yellow plastic sleeve to his glove. His normally golden skin had turned a sickly beige, and it was as hard and smooth as a ladybug's shell. She rotated his arm so the inner wrist faced out. With a shaky breath, she brought the blade down.

A rumble of warning rolled out of his throat. As the silver touched his skin the noise changed, shifting and shrinking into a very small, very human whimper.

"Please."

Her breath caught in her throat. That was Rex's voice, only smaller and more terrified. "Please, Cari. Please don't hurt me."

She looked up at him, hoping to see a sign of recognition, or maybe even affection. Instead, his milky eyes snapped onto hers so fast it made her dizzy. In the center of each white orb hung a circular brown stain, like a drop of tea on a peeled egg. He let out a rapid, high-pitched giggle.

Her eyes narrowed to slits. "You of all people should know: My name is Mayhem."

The ax scratched like a butter knife over marble as she carved a long, shallow line in his flesh.

He screamed and wrenched his arm away from her, blood streaming from the wound.

Dark, purple blood.

"Quick!" Cooper untwisted Rex's other arm from behind his back. She dove for it, gripping him by the forearm while narrowly escaping the clawed fingers that attempted to grab her by her ponytail. The ax snagged on the plastic sleeve. She yanked until it ripped. The skin was already much softer on this side, and she had to take extra care not to cut him too deep. He grunted half-heartedly in discomfort. Then his head sagged forward, and he went quiet. She dropped his arm. "Tell me that's enough."

"It is." Cooper nodded at the first wound. The purple blood was already streaked with arterial red.

Rex's head rolled on his neck. "Damn…"

Her entire body shook with exhausted relief. Not a hell growl. Not fake human. That was his voice. Her friend's voice, for real.

She wrapped her arms around his waist. Cooper loosened his hold, and Rex slumped into her. His cheek bounced against her shoulder as the rest of him threatened to slide to the floor.

"Rex," she said, hooking her arms under his to keep them both upright. "Rex, can you hear me?"

"Ahh…" he sighed, his breath tickling her neck. "Wha…what happened?"

"You got hit." Cooper stooped down to lift the still-unconscious Grace. "You both did. I was able to, as you would say, inception Grace. For you, we had to take a less humane approach."

Rex's feet finally accepted responsibility for his weight. He stood up and took a good look at his arms. "Jesus. Is that why I look like I belong on a 72-hour psych hold?"

Cari bit her lip. It wasn't funny, but her chest rumbled with adrenaline-fueled giggles anyway. Or maybe they were sobs. She clung to him for another moment, then pulled away. "Give me your arms."

He held them out obediently. Aiming her gaze resolutely at the floor, she shrugged off her sweatshirt and draped it over his wounds, looping the sleeves twice and securing them with a tight knot. "This should slow the bleeding until we get back to the med station."

He tried to shift his arms. They barely moved under the tourniquet. "Jeez, Mayhem. First you cut me and now you cuff me? What did I ever do to you?"

"For your information," Cooper interjected, "the only reason that pretty face of yours is still in one piece is because she intervened when she did. You should be thanking her."

"Maybe I will," Rex retorted, and Cari assumed that was the end of it.

Instead, Rex turned to her. He tried to take her by the shoulders, but his arms were bound so tightly he only got as far as placing one hand on either side of her collarbone. It was a struggle for her to meet his eyes. When she finally managed it, she was surprised to see a scatter of flinty silver speckles near the irises. A remnant from his possession? Or had they always been there? And if they had, why hadn't she noticed them before?

"Thank you, Mayhem."

She shivered. It wasn't the voice of a monster, but it wasn't her goofy friend either. It was the future. A hint of the man he would someday become.

Then he waggled his eyebrows, yanked her close, and proceeded to cover her face in sloppy kisses. "Thankyouthankyouthankyou!"

"Ugh, get off!" Cari slapped at his shoulders until he let her go. She should have known. "And you're welcome. I guess."

"Grace?"

They both turned to Cooper, who still held Grace in his arms. Her body had contracted into a fetal position, with the side of her head pressed tight against Cooper's chest. The semi-purple sweat had thickened into an opaque gray pudding that clung to every visible inch of her skin. She shivered like a wet rabbit.

"Holy crap," Rex said. "What's happening to her?"

"The infection's turning," Cooper said. "It's trying to retake control. I've gotta get this stuff off her ASAP. Are you guys—"

"Go," Cari looped her arm through Rex's. "We'll be fine."

Chapter Eight

Cooper raced through the office and down the stairs. Instead of heading to the med station, he veered into the right hallway and kicked open the door to the barracks. Grace whined in his arms like a child being woken prematurely from a nap. It quickly devolved into a series of grunts when her body began snapping back and forth. He winced as her nails dug into the tender muscles of his shoulder.

"Don't do this," he pleaded, holding her tight to suppress the spasms. The gray goop made his hands itch, but luckily the hazmat suit did a fine job of protecting the rest of him. He sidled between two rows of bunk beds toward the showers. Falling to his knees in the first narrow stall, he let her slide onto the tiles as he grabbed the taps and opened them all the way up. A spray of water spewed from the calcium-crusted shower head, dousing them both. It was lukewarm at best, yet Grace screamed as if it were molten. She scrambled halfway out of the blast zone before Cooper wrapped his arms around her waist and hauled her back under.

"Oh no you don't," he said, sitting her down between his legs. "You're not going anywhere until every teaspoon of that crap is off you." He propped the soles of his boots against the beige tile across the shower and pressed his back to the wall, effectively boxing her in. One of her flailing hands smacked him in the head. Undaunted, he closed his arms around her and pinned her back against his chest. She slumped, defeated, and allowed the water to do its work. After a few more minutes, she stopped shaking.

"Okay," she said, her voice hoarse but human. "I'm good. You can let me go."

Satisfied that she was no longer a flight risk, he released her.

"Thanks." She ran her hands over her face and shoulders, scrubbing the last of the stuff off her skin. When she raised her arms over her head, he assumed it was to make sure she was thoroughly rinsed. Instead, she peeled off her shirt and tossed across the room.

"What are you doing?"

"What does it look like I'm doing?" she asked as she wriggled out of her leggings. "I don't know if you know this, but most people shower without clothes. Besides, this shit is *everywhere*." Her pants joined her shirt on the floor. She tilted her head so the water could run over her face.

"Uh…right. Okay," Cooper said, trying to keep his voice steady. He should leave. But that required standing, and with the shower being as small as it was, there was no way he could do it without knocking her over, or at least brushing against her. Given how he was sitting, that was the last thing he wanted to do.

She ran her hands over her face and down through her hair, her fingers twisting through the wavy black curls. Water streamed down her neck and over her narrow shoulders. The paste had faded, revealing the light brown hue of her natural skin.

"Damn," she said, her fingers kneading the back of her neck. "I feel like I've been trampled by an elephant. What happened out there?"

He cleared his throat, focusing on a tiny gray smudge still lingering near her right shoulder blade. "You got hit. You and Rex. Fog first, then fever."

Her fingers stopped moving. "Did I hurt anyone?"

"No. I switched you off before you could do anything."

"Good. Thanks."

He nodded at the smudge. His hands twitched, itching to reach out and wipe it away.

"Is Rex okay?"

"He will be. Cari too." He smiled. "Actually, she turned out to be quite the asset."

"Really?" She twisted around to face him. Water sluiced down her back, and the smudge disappeared. "What did she end up with?"

Robbed of his focal point, Cooper directed his gaze to his own kneecap. "Tomahawks."

She slapped herself in the forehead. "Of course. I should have thought of that. And she was good?"

"She was fantastic. You would have been proud."

"I am." He could hear the sincerity in her voice. She turned away from him, and he felt like he could breathe again.

"Jesus! Cooper, you're hurt."

He looked down. The inner seam of his yellow pant leg was streaked red and ripped in half a dozen places where Queen Bitch's legs had pierced him. He had to admit, it looked bad and it hurt like hell.

"Oh, that. It's nothing."

"Yeah, right." She brushed her fingers over the wounds. Her touch sparked a warm shiver that started in his thigh and surged upward. He squeezed his shut. Why couldn't the water have been twenty degrees colder?

She turned again, leaning into him a little more than last time, or so he thought. Her arched eye caught his and would not let go. "What did you do?"

He shrugged. "Nothing you wouldn't have done."

The mocking look faded beneath a reluctant smile. She dropped her eyes but didn't turn away. Nor did she remove her hand. His brain throbbed with so many ideas, the most powerful of which was the desire to laugh. It was funny, after all. It was funny that they'd worked together for five years and she had never touched him for more than a second or two at a time. Funny that he'd never thought anything of it until this moment. And really, *really* funny that now it was all he could think about. That, and how badly he wanted to change it.

"Cooper? Is everything okay?"

Simon's voice bounced off the ceramic walls. To Cooper's simultaneous disappointment and relief, Grace retracted her hand. He averted his eyes as she got to her feet.

"Yes, Simon," she called. "Everything is fine. We're just getting washed up."

"We?"

"Yeah. Me and Cooper."

"Oh, I see—no! I mean, I understand. We don't have cameras in there, so I don't see *anything. Obviously."* Simon cleared his throat. *"Anyway, John wants everyone to report to the med station ASAP, so head on over there as soon as you're, ah…done."*

"It's not like that!" Cooper shouted over Grace's giggles as Simon clicked off. He pulled himself up, careful of where he placed his hands and his eyes. "Why would you say it…like that? Now people will talk."

"Relax." Grace grabbed a bar of soap, her tone as casual as if they were discussing their favorite restaurants. "Everyone knows you'd never cheat on Allie. You're too much of a boy scout. That's what makes it funny."

He snorted, hoping it would mask the shame gnawing away at his heart. Funny, he thought as he dragged himself out of the stall. Yeah, right.

"I see my sister put you through the wringer again."

Cooper glared in Holly's direction. Soaking wet and painfully distracted, he didn't realize he had meandered within speaking distance of her. He had seen her a few times around Edensgate before she had become a victim of their hospitality. One of those typical Halcyonites who thought that, because she was born rich and moderately good-looking, she had the right to behave as nasty as she wanted to, especially when she didn't get what she wanted. Now, with her jaundiced yellow eyes and her once-pretty face covered with weeping sores…maybe it was mean, but it seemed like a better fit.

However, it didn't look like Holly herself was currently at home. Instead of the popped-hip, bow-to-me stance he remembered, she looked as if she were trying to hide in plain view. She knelt with her head bowed low so that ratted clumps of greasy blond hair obscured her face, clinging piteously to the bars with scabby, pistachio-tinted fingers.

He stopped walking.

"Hello, Mary."

Her head ticked up. Behind the blond strands, cracked lips twitched in amusement.

"She's been workin' on this ever since you put her down the last time," she said in a hoarse Louisiana drawl. "Waiting so patiently for the solstice to make sure she had enough oomph to do it. Poor thing. All that time and effort, just to be dogged again."

Cooper grunted, trying not to stare at her with blatant fascination. John had told him about her role during their encounter with the Reverend, how the words had spooled out of her gaping mouth like a speaker. Now, though her lips were still stiff, her jaw moved up and down in time with the words like an animatronic puppet.

They were learning.

"Working on what?" he asked.

"Transubstantiation," she mimed. "As I understand it, she wanted to bring herself into the living realm—as we all do—only not as herself. She wanted to be powerful. Godlike. But she couldn't come barreling through fully formed. I know you think we're brutes who just want to tear holes in your drapes, but it's not as simple as that. Believe me, I wish it was."

Cooper nodded. "She couldn't come through as one big thing, so she came through as a lot of little ones."

A finger bounced against her nose. "She used the small crawlies as transports, each one carrying a little spark of her inside it. The vines were a sort of conversion factory, and—"

"And the flowers were the smokestacks that let her spirit out," he sighed. "Great. Something new to worry about."

"But that's not the only thing, is it?" Her head lifted. He followed her gaze toward the open door of the med station. Rex lay on one of the cots, chattering incessantly. His animated gestures seemed particularly agitating to John as he tried to work a needle and thread through the long crimson gash on Rex's left arm. His right arm was already bandaged from wrist to elbow. That's where Cari stood, next to his shoulder, holding her ax out for him to inspect.

He smiled at it enthusiastically, apparently oblivious to John's work.

The same could not be said about Cari. Every few seconds her eyes jigged over to Rex's exposed injury. Even from across the hall, Cooper could see the ax shimmer as her hand trembled.

"She needed to toughen up," he said.

Holly's shoulders jerked up in an approximation of a shrug. "A little leather in the spirit is a fine thing. It's the only protection we have against the horns of the world. But thick skin doesn't grow up and out, does it? It grows in. It replaces soft with hard little by little until one day you realize that what you've done is toughened your very soul. Your compassion, your empathy, your heart, they're gone, and now there's nothing left but anger and fear and hatred. And then you're no better than my husband. Or me." She sniffled pathetically.

Cooper almost laughed in her face. Like he was going to fall for that. Still, he couldn't blame her for trying. He was the big, strong soldier. Who better to try the damsel-in-distress act on? Too bad he'd been around long enough to know better.

"But this isn't about me."

Now *that* was a new one. He shot her a dubious glance. She peeped out from behind her filthy blond locks. The white film over her eyes had receded, replaced by two sparkling emeralds.

He knew better. But he couldn't help himself.

"If it's not about you, then what *is* it about?"

She tipped her chin toward Cari. "Your girl. She sliced someone open tonight. The one she calls her best friend, no less. And she nearly decapitated another. An angelic face is the perfect disguise for steel and fire. The only thing holding that in check is her heart. If anyone ever rips that out of her, then God help you all."

She collapsed into a coughing fit, likely prompted by the taste of the sacred name on her infernal tongue. Pus-colored spittle sprayed the concrete floor. He took a step back as a spasm lifted her upright. The white film had slipped over her eyes once again. She staggered back to her cot and curled into a ball.

He had expected her to attack, or coerce, or at least appeal to his sense of decency. That's what these things did. They exploited every weakness to serve their own ends. But she hadn't done any of that. She'd simply given him advice and asked for nothing in return. If he didn't know better—and he did—he would think she had genuinely wanted to help.

"*Teniente.*"

He turned from the cell as A.J. emerged from the med station. His duster had been replaced with a blue button-down shirt with the Virgil Security & Maintenance logo on the breast pocket.

"Helios," Cooper responded, noting the discontent in his voice.

A.J. paused. A look of concern darkened his shadowy features. "Something the matter?"

"Nothing specific. Shouldn't you be resting?"

"It looked worse than it was. Besides, John said everyone not dead, undead, or suffering from crippling social anxiety is needed on the main floor. It's a disaster area up there."

"Roger that," Cooper said. "How's the kid?"

"Hyper." A.J.'s smile broadened. "He's *very* excited about the weapon our little *lanzadora* has chosen for herself."

"I think we all are. Though I have to say, I'm a little surprised no one thought to try something like that sooner."

"Understandable. But let me ask you this. Why do you think John doesn't want us bringing our families here, or telling them anything about what we do?"

Cooper uttered a harsh laugh. "Isn't it obvious?"

"Fair enough. But it's not just that. Think about it. We all found this place in different ways, and none of them involved a Help Wanted sign. These are strange forces at work, my friend. Some of them are destructive. We know that to be true. But there are others too, and if you're paying attention, maybe they put something in your path that only you can pick up. Who knows—if Grace or I had suggested axes, they might have turned out as badly as all the rest. Then where would we be?"

Cooper smiled ruefully. "Short-staffed."

"Right." A.J. clapped him on the back. "*Bien está lo que bien acaba*, eh? But I will say this—under no circumstances can we let her carry a gun."

"Yeah," Cooper said, resisting the urge to glance back at Holly's cell. "That's probably a good call."

Chapter Nine

The full force of Virgil Security & Maintenance—minus its head of surveillance, of course—emerged from the basement ready for a very different kind of battle. Everyone had divested themselves of their weapons—everyone, that is, except Cari. Since she had to retrieve her discarded axes anyway, she'd told John that it was only reasonable for her to keep her belt and its sole tenant with her, and John had agreed. Pretty quickly, in fact. As she paused to admire the way the single ax on her hip shone in the dim light, she wondered whether guilt had played a role in his decision. After all, she had kinda-sorta saved the day right as he was about to fire her. A minor concession was the least he could do. She just had to promise it wouldn't be in the way.

As they proceeded into the East Hall, and Cari realized her weapon would be the furthest thing from "in the way." Sylvia's monstrous figure may have turned to ash, but her vines lacked the same courtesy. Thick clumps of vegetation sagged from the balconies clung to the walls in twisted hedgerows. The whole place stunk of dirt and rotting fruit.

"Damn," Grace murmured. She backtracked to the door across from the office marked Custodial and began passing out mops, push brooms and, amazingly, rakes. "A.J, could you run to the Armory and grab a couple machetes? I think we're gonna need them."

"Sure." A.J. hoisted a back-mounted vacuum cleaner onto his shoulders, wincing as one of the straps scraped the bandage on his neck. "Might as well handle *la bruja* while I'm there too."

"I can go with him," Cari said. "I need to get my axes anyway."

"Hang on a second." Grace paused, her eyes roaming from Cooper to A.J. to John. They all nodded at her. From one of the metal shelves, she retrieved a puffy paper bag. "We were going to wait until you were through your first ninety days, but…well, after tonight, you've earned it."

She held the bag out to Cooper, who reached in and extracted two bunches of forest green fabric. One was puffy and thick, the other slim and soft. He handed the first to Cari, and the second to Rex. "Welcome, Team Eos."

"Oh, hell yes!" Rex shouted as he unfurled his gift and held it up for all to see: A t-shirt with a winged lock plastered over the entire front and the name of the company written in paint-splattered letters. "That's what I'm *talking* about. Do yours, May. Do yours!"

He elbowed her in the arm until she complied. It was the same logo, but with more classic lettering, printed on the back of a cotton fleece sweatshirt. She did a quick inventory. Metal hardware. Stitched-in thumb holes. A phone pocket with a grommet where she could run headphones, if she ever got a phone that played music. It was by far the nicest article of clothing she owned.

She raised her eyes to Grace, who smiled. "Try not to destroy this one for a least a week, okay?"

Cari nodded, resisting the urge to hug her. She didn't want to risk ruining the moment.

"Holy shit…what the hell *happened* in here?!"

The exclamation rumbled toward them like a freight train. John's face puckered in misery while Grace's eyes flamed. They all peered around the corner as if any sudden moves might provoke an attack. In front of the entrance doors, Sam gaped in horrified wonder at the gnarled vines clinging to the walls and piled around his feet.

"Son of a bitch." Cooper voiced the thoughts of the group. He had whispered, but still it caught Sam's attention. The puffy circles under his eyes glowed blue against his saggy pale skin, and his stocky legs wobbled precariously.

"What is…how…who is responsible for this mess?"

"Uh…what mess?" Grace asked. Cari stifled a laugh, while Rex and A.J. couldn't quite manage. Scowling at the lot of them, John eased himself out of the group. He approached Sam with his hands out in a defenseless posture.

"Sir, what are you doing here? It's four in the morning."

Sam's mouth opened and closed several times before any words came out. "I couldn't sleep, so I figured I'd come down and do another walk-through, to make sure there was…nothing left to do." His glassy eyes roamed the destroyed hallway, and Cari thought she saw his lower lip tremble.

"I thought the doors were locked until six," Rex muttered. "How did he even get in?"

"Sam insisted on having a key made for emergencies," Cooper said. "John didn't want to give him one, but Sam didn't give him a choice. He threatened to terminate our contract."

"Oh, that's just great." Grace hissed. "What's the point of locking doors if anyone can walk in whenever they want?"

"He does run the place."

"Ugh, fine." Grace crossed her arms over her chest. 'But if he thinks he's gonna make this a regular thing, he's in for a rude awakening."

"Understatement of the century, am I right?" Rex nudged Cari in the arm. She smiled in acknowledgment but kept facing forward. She hadn't been able to look at him since the med station. The cuts hadn't been deep, but they were jagged, ugly, and almost certain to leave scars. Sure, she'd done it to save his life, and he was grateful to her now. But what about a year from now, when he had to wake up every day and had to choose whether to wear long sleeves or deal with all the weird looks and questions? How was he going to feel about it then?

"—seeds of a pernicious desert ivy in the rotunda flower beds."

In the hall, John was doing his best tap dance. "It seems they'd been dormant until tonight. But we had an air filter malfunction, and something must have gotten through and activated the seeds and, well, here we are."

Sam narrowed his eyes. "You're telling me a group of kids scattered an invasive desert plant into our flower beds as—what? A prank? Some kind of…eco-graffiti?"

John shrugged. "Is there any other explanation?"

Sam's mouth clamped shut. The atmosphere tightened as everyone else's breathing grew shallow. Cari wanted to grab Rex's hand. She settled for digging her fingernails into her own palms. There was no way he could believe such a ridiculous excuse. And yet, like John said, what else could it be?

After an eternity, Sam sighed and rubbed his eyes. "I can't reschedule this tour, John. They won't be able to come back for months. So…could we at least get the Suttermill space presentable and maybe…I don't know, hide the rest?"

"Of course," John said eagerly. "That's no problem at all. We'll clean up the store first, then drape a canvas over the entrance. Tell them we are painting or something."

Sam nodded in slow motion. "Yes. Yes, that could work."

"Excellent." John beckoned to the rest of the crew. He regarded them with wide eyes and lifted brows, an expression that Cari read as both "He bought it!" and "Let's not give him too much time to think about this."

"Ms. Henry and Lieu—uh, Mr. O'Bannon will start cutting up the bigger pieces, and Mr. Guillermo and I will load them into bins for incineration. Cari and Mr. Ranganathan will do the finishing work. Sweeping and mopping, dusting and arranging. How does that sound to everyone?"

"Sounds good, Boss," Cooper said while everyone else nodded along.

"Then let's get to it. As for you, sir—" John turned back to Sam, who was still studying the room as if it were a surrealist jigsaw puzzle. He jumped when John touched his shoulder. "If you'd like to accompany me to the office, there are a few chairs where you can sit down and put your feet up, maybe catch a few winks…"

Sam allowed himself to be steered toward the relatively vine-free office. Cari felt the tension drain from the room with every step he took.

"Now that *that's* done." Grace clapped her hands. "Rex, Cooper and I are in Suttermill. A.J. and Cari are still on machete duty."

"And axes." Cari supplemented.

"Right, axes. Bring those too. Ready, and break!" She pumped her fist and bounded off.

"How does she still have that much energy?" Rex groaned.

"Subverting authority is her Red Bull," Cooper said. He followed her route at a much less enthusiastic pace.

"Guess I'll see you guys in a few," Rex said. He turned to A.J. "Keep your eye on this one, man. She's crazy."

"Takes one to know one, psycho," Cari shot back, doing her best to ignore the pang of guilt and shame his words caused. She hoped with all her heart he didn't believe that.

She turned to A.J. as Rex disappeared through the arch. "Think Sam believed John's story?"

A.J. shrugged. "People believe what they want to believe."

"It didn't look like he wanted to believe that."

"Then they believe what they have to, so they don't go insane." He bent his arm and offered it to her. "Shall we?"

She smiled and accepted. "Lead the way."

Chapter Ten

When Cooper saw Allie's gray Civic in the garage, his heart dropped. She worked six-to-six, which meant she was usually gone by the time he got home. The only time that didn't happen was when he got off early, or when she'd gotten bad news.

And he wasn't home early.

He pulled his truck into the spot next to her, but left the engine running. Once he went in, the mask would have to go on. He wouldn't be Lieutenant O'Bannon, Scourge of the Underworld. He'd be an almost-middle-aged mall cop, and nothing more.

But what if he didn't turn off the engine? What if he jammed this old bucket into reverse and drove away? Headed for the border. Jumped a train. Joined the circus.

Or did something even dumber than either of those things.

His hand shot out, grabbed the key and killed the engine.

He really was a boy scout at heart.

Allie looked up from her coffee mug as he entered.

"Uncle Ray is dead," she said flatly, dabbing at her red-rimmed eyes with a crumpled tissue.

Cooper's bag slipped from his shoulder and landed on the floor with a seismic thump. "I thought they gave him month?"

Her face crumpled and she shook her head. "He had a massive cardiac event in the middle of the night. Doctor Conway called a little while ago and told me. Didn't want me getting blindsided when I got to work."

Cooper eased himself into the chair next to her. Emotions washed through him so fast he couldn't keep up. But that was okay. In this moment, there was only one thing that mattered, one thought he felt was worth expressing.

"I'm sorry," he whispered, reaching for her hand. "About Ray, and…about this morning."

She uncurled her fingers and let him take her hand.

"I'm sorry too," she said, smiling through her tears. "I mean, I stand by what I said, about making time to be together and all that. But I'm sorry I was so nasty about it. You have every right to do something that you care about. I just…I wish we could have everything we wanted and nothing we don't."

She rolled her eyes at her own ridiculous statement. "Anyway, if you want to keep working at Edensgate, you should. But maybe we could try to make a little room for…you know, us. Okay?" She peered up at him, her doe eyes shining.

He sighed and squeezed her hand. She knew he wouldn't say no.

Sniffling, she leaned her forehead on his shoulder and laced her fingers through his. He studied them, his thick and calloused from work, hers smooth and thin, like a surgeon or a pianist. They didn't match, and yet the more he looked at them, the less he wanted to let go.

"So, listen," she said. "Doctor Conway said I could come in a little late if I needed to. I know you're probably exhausted, but...would you mind if I joined you upstairs for a bit?"

He tilted his chin down to her. She confirmed the invitation with a wink.

"You're sure you're not too upset?" he asked.

She rose from her chair. Even in a bulky sweater and flannel pajama pants, the way she moved made him much less tired. Running her fingers through his hair, she leaned down and kissed him. He closed his eyes, breathing her in. She tasted like peppermint, sweet and invigorating. He wrapped his arms around her waist, pulling her closer. She smiled against his lips the way she had every time he'd kissed her goodnight when they were dating. That was barely six years ago, but it seemed longer. Almost like it had happened to someone else.

Breaking away, she stood up and tugged him gently toward the doorway. "Come on. Who knows when we'll get another chance?"

It was hard to argue with that. Wrapping his hand around hers, he followed her upstairs.

Sunrise stained the world cotton candy pink. A rare treat for Cari, considering her ride home usually took place in the early morning dark. After the night she'd had, a treat was exactly what she needed.

Suttermill had been in a worse state than Spartan. She hadn't thought such a thing was possible. But with barely anything inside to divert their growth, Sylvia's vines had all but packed the empty department store. It had taken all five of the VSM staff to drag the foliage into the rotunda. The amount of work had prompted John to request that everyone stay a few extra hours—at overtime rates, of course. In the end, the Jillian's tour had proceeded as planned, with the only hiccup being that the reps would not be able to see the rest of the mall thanks to a miscommunication with the painting crew and toxic fumes. When the reps left, promising to "carefully consider the opportunity," Sam had been too relieved and exhausted to do anything besides stagger to his Lexus and drive away.

Cari pressed her head against the window, letting the condensation cool her work-weary forehead. Swallowing the weed prank story was the path of least resistance, and that was a path that most Halcyonites could walk blindfolded. But Sam wasn't from Halcyon, a fact that he would be the first to point out. How long he continued to buy the story without question remained to be seen.

The bus pulled up to the rickety metal arch at the mouth of the trailer park. Elmer's head drooped almost to the steering wheel as she hopped off, as if he were still half-asleep. Unnerving behavior for a driver, but fortunate in the given moment. She didn't have to worry about concealing the weapons dangling from her hips. She had meant to put them in her locker before she left, but in the chaos of the cleaning blitz she'd forgotten all about it. Her brain had been so fried by quitting time she had barely remembered to grab her mother's requested cigarettes. It wasn't until she was on the bus and felt the five hilts jab her in the thigh that she realized she was still wearing her belt. She was surprised at how quickly it had become a natural extension of herself, like her hand or her sense of smell. And like a limb or a sense, she imagined she would feel equally strange to be without it.

The wheeze of the bus faded in the distance, leaving only the crunch of her footsteps. There were no birds, no voices, not even the hint of a breeze. She frowned. It was solidly morning now. People should be getting up, watching the news, making coffee. Starting their cars. But she heard nothing but dead silence, as if she were the only person left in the world.

She shivered, quickening her pace as she mounted the steps to her trailer. Despite the cheerful sunshine, the air had turned bitterly cold. With a trembling hand she inserted her key into the lock and opened the door.

She nearly collapsed under a wave of overripe Old Spice. Coughing, she stumbled backward and nearly fell off the porch.

I made a mistake. The shivers returned, stronger and more overwhelming than before. *I stayed away too long and left an opening for the wolves that lurked in the shadows.*

In the half-second before the door fell all the way open, she found herself wishing she'd stayed at the mall. Raided the break room fridge. Played video games. Watched TV. She could have crashed in the bunker like Rex had chosen to do. She could have rested somewhere dark and quiet. Somewhere safe.

But the door opened, and the sunshine cut through the brown darkness inside, illuminating the full ashtray and the empty bottle, and it was too late to turn back.

Despite the searchlight brilliance of the open door, the inhabitants of the trailer remained undisturbed—though in Libby's case, that was understandable as she appeared to be out cold, her head resting face up on the back of the kitchen banquette. And maybe it was understandable for the other occupant as well, distracted as he was by what he had deemed a willing partner. The rest of the scene flashed as discreet images, all high contrast and fuzzy, like badly composed photographs.

A pudgy hand tangled in a mass of mousy blond hair.

Another hand roaming the peaks and valleys of a blue knit sweater.

A mustache pressed against a pale, exposed neck.

Nelson's face tilting in her direction, hair disheveled and mouth hanging open.

Teeth. Long and slick, and streaked with crimson. Eyes too bloodshot to be merely drunk.

Fury. Excitement.

Hunger.

"No," Cari moaned as she pressed a hand to her chest. Her heart was pounding so hard and fast it felt numb. Hollow. Like it wasn't even there. She stumbled back against the door jamb, her knees weak and her eyes burning with furious tears. She wanted to scream, or cry, or throw something.

Her free hand fell to her hip.

No more.

She wanted to throw something, and that's exactly what she did.

Book IV

THE
MOURNING SUN

Chapter One

Grace vaulted down the stairs toward the bunker so fast her boots barely touched the steps. John's words chased her the whole way down.

"Ray's dead."

She'd been home for maybe ten minutes when he'd called. Barely enough time to shove a handful of crackers in her mouth and toss her work clothes in the laundry.

Well, not all her clothes. Her tank top, bra, leggings and underwear had been donated to the incinerator thanks to the infected purple goo-sweat they'd been stewing in for the last four hours. Even if they'd looked at all salvageable, there was no way in hell she'd risk introducing that crap to the city water supply.

Then the phone rang. Not her cell, but the ancient rotary phone stuck to the wall over the narrow peninsula that separated her kitchenette from the living room/bedroom/rest of her tiny bungalow. The jangle of the old-timey bell filled her with dread. Three people in the world had that number, and they only used it when something was really, really wrong.

Which, of course, something was.

Ray's dead.

She landed at the bottom of the stairs with a thud. Her fingers flicked over the keypad without hesitation. She raced past the lockers toward the detention cells, where a drooling Holly pressed her puke-green cheek against the first window. Grace wrinkled her nose at the undead thing stroking the double-thick plastic with her tattered fingertips, her yellowed eyes fluttering in a droopy-lidded half-coma.

At last, she blasted through the door of the med station. John's head shot up from the cot where he was smoothing out a new sheet. The sight of his bloodshot eyes, pasty skin and sloping shoulders hit her like a bucket of ice. Based on his reaction, her own appearance wasn't much better. She'd left in such a hurry she'd barely had time to wrap her uncombed black curls into a handkerchief, and she wore the faded backup coveralls she kept balled up in her closet for emergencies. She hadn't even had time to shower, and her light brown skin looked ashy, even a little purple still, from the previous night's exploits. But it didn't matter. Nothing mattered except being here.

She shambled across the room and collapsed into his arms. "What happened? I thought he had time." Her voice, buried in the shoulder of his cinnamon-scented sweater vest, sounded soft and small, even to her own ears.

"We all did," John murmured. "Massive coronary. There was nothing they could do."

"Did you call Mimi?"

"A few minutes ago. I offered condolences to her and to Lola, who I'm told is on her way back from Honolulu now to help with the arrangements. She said the funeral will likely be next weekend. A small service, just family and a few close friends."

"Good," Grace whispered, unwilling to ask if that included her. Beyond the walls of Edensgate, the three of them appeared to be nothing more than colleagues: she, a mid-level employee; John, her boss; and Ray, the manager that had contracted them to fulfill the mall's security and maintenance needs—until last week, that is, when he'd retired due to his failing health. It was a business relationship, and a past-tense one at that. If anyone knew the real history of their bond, not only would she and John be invited to the funeral, they would be seated in the front row.

Or run out of town on a rail.

She gave John one more light squeeze around the waist, then extracted herself from his arms. "And there's no way to know if this will affect…you know, this place?"

"No." He sighed and rubbed the back of his neck. "We'll have to keep an eye out for anything—"

The insistent buzz at her hip made her cringe. John stared at her pocket like it was full of snakes.

"…strange."

Grace's hand shook as she checked the caller ID. A local number, but no contact name associated with it. *Please,* she prayed as she pressed the green button. *Please be a solicitor. A wrong number. Even—*

"Hello, my name is Polly with the Green Sun Initiative."

"Oh, thank God," Grace exhaled, her arms and legs going liquid with relief.

"Oh my! Well…thank you very much. I'm glad to be speaking with you too. Would you agree to take a quick 10-minute survey about a proposed bill regarding—"

"Grace!"

She nearly sent her phone flying as she whirled around to face the door, and the trembling ball of black and blond streaking toward her.

"Cari?" Grace braced herself for impact, but the younger girl skidded to a halt mere inches from the collision point. "What's wrong?"

"I second that," came a voice from the doorway. Grace looked from Cari as Rex wandered into the room, clad in sweats, a tattered black t-shirt and extremely dingy socks. The white gauze bandages wrapped around both forearms practically glowed against his russet skin, evidence of his own trials from the previous night. "I was about to slay RenoKing78 at MegaBall, so this better be good."

Grace rolled her eyes, made sure the call was disconnected, and turned her attention back to Cari. The girl's delicate body heaved, presumably from exertion, as she struggled to catch her breath. Then her blue eyes turned upward, and Grace saw the real reason for her breathlessness.

Panic.

"I think...I think I may have killed someone," Cari heaved.

Grace's knees buckled. Luckily, John had the presence of mind to grab her by the elbow before she could fully collapse.

"Sorry, I think I misheard you." Rex ambled in to join them, smiling to disguise the tremble in his voice. "From where I was standing it sounded like you said you killed someone."

"Who?" John prompted as Grace composed herself. "Who was it?"

"Nelson Baines. My mom's...um, boyfriend, I guess. He was there when I got home, and he was doing...something, to her. So, I threw an ax at him." She bit her lip as her eyes filled with tears. "I didn't mean to do it. Or…I don't know, maybe I did. It's hard to remember. Everything sort of went black and brown and fuzzy. One second my hand was empty, and then I had the ax and then…it hit him." She swallowed like she was trying not to be sick. "It hit him in the face."

"Damn," Rex muttered, his smile long gone. "Are you sure he's dead?"

"Well…I'm sure he *was* dead. He just didn't…stay that way."

The words lingered in the air like the smell of rotten meat. Rex gaped at Cari as if she'd slapped him across the mouth. Grace could feel her mind trying to untether itself from her reason, and she was tempted to let it happen. She wanted to disappear, to let the panic overtake her.

What made her yank her wits back into her head was the terrified puppy look on Cari's face, her huge eyes darting between John and herself, pleading silently for their help.

She's one of us now. Whatever happens, we can't let her go through this alone.

Grace took a breath, shook John's hand off her, and forced herself onto her own feet.

"Okay," she said with as much surety as she could muster. "Where is Nelson now?"

"My house," Cari said. "I locked him in when I left."

"And your mom?"

"In the car. She was unconscious so I dragged her into the back seat."

"And the car is…?"

"In the parking lot."

Grace frowned. "I thought you couldn't drive."

The left corner of Cari's mouth tugged down, and she stared at her feet. "Um, well…"

"It's okay," John cut in, placing his fingers lightly on Grace's shoulders. "I think we can leave moving violations on the back burner for the time being. Take us to your mom."

Nodding, Cari booked it out of the room with Rex close on her heels.

"After you, Boss." Grace swept her hand in front of John like a footman in front of a king. "Wouldn't want you to cut me off twice in a row."

He rolled his eyes as he jogged passed. "Am I wrong?"

She grunted her acquiescence. Of course, he wasn't wrong. A half-beheaded demon-murderer trapped in a rickety trailer was the definition of bigger fish to fry. But she wasn't in love with the thought of Cari whipping down the pitted desert highway in her mother's junky little coupe either.

They emerged one by one into the pale pink dawn. The smell of frost hung in the air, edged with the foul stench of scorched rubber and gasoline. As they cleared the wide columns of the entrance, they confronted the source of the smell: a rusted red car, its front wheels popped over the curb and its face hugging a lamppost.

"Damn, Mayhem," Rex said, waving the acrid fumes away from his face.

"Told you," Grace mumbled in John's direction. He glared a few half-hearted daggers at her, then approached the crumpled vehicle. Both doors were closed, and the windows were coated with gray condensation so thick it was impossible to see inside.

Grace turned to Cari. "You said Nelson was doing something to her when you walked in?"

"Yeah." Cari nodded, her freckled forehead a patchwork of worry lines. In front of them, John leaned down to try and get a better look through the rear passenger window. "At first, I thought they were just...you know, making out or whatever."

"Ew!" Rex grimaced.

"I know. But then he stopped, and he looked up at me, and--"

A muffled growl rankled the quiet morning, followed by a dull thud as the face of Cari's mother burst into view inches from John's nose. He yelped and sprang backward like a spooked cat.

Grace dashed forward, fists up and ready for blows. Luckily, the window was stronger than the rest of the car, because it hadn't even cracked. Screaming in frustration, Libby Hembert slammed her forehead against the glass again. Still, it held strong as a puddle of thick, black liquid seeped from the torn patch of skin on her forehead. Gnashing teeth squeaked over the glass as gangrenous palms slapped and smeared the fog. Her eyes weren't black, as Grace had expected, but swirling gray and opaque. They reminded her of the thick ominous murk that lingered in the air over a deep canyon, disguising the reality that there was, in fact, no bottom.

From behind her came a soft, fragile whimper. Without turning, Grace slid a foot or so to her right, putting herself between Cari and the growing black blotch on the glass.

"What now?" she whispered at John.

"Same as always." He slid a hardback leather case from his pants pocket. Unzipping it revealed a set of hypodermic needles and a small vial of red liquid. "Sedation, then isolation protocol."

The stoniness of his words chilled her to the core. "That only ends one way."

"We don't have another option." John sucked the red liquid into the needle. "I don't know how, but the Edensgate perimeter has been breached. We have to limit the number of casualties." He slipped the case back in his pocket, held the syringe needle-up, and flicked the chamber. "You go left. I'll be the distraction."

"Fine. But make it quick. The kid's been through enough already." She pivoted in place toward Cari and Rex. "Keys."

Cari fished the ring out of her pocket and tossed them at Grace. Though Cari's eyes never left her toes, Grace had no problem snatching the projectile out of the air. The girl had truly remarkable aim.

Grace dropped into a squat and duck-walked toward the parking lot. When she was sure those hazy eyes had lost track of her, she doubled back, circling the car, and hunched next to the front wheel. Meanwhile John inched closer, hands up, muttering placations in a soothing tone. When he was about three feet away, he stopped. Grace ventured a look upward. Libby's ghoulish face was still suctioned to the window, completely absorbed by John's unwavering stare. She grinned at him and flicked the tip of its blue-gray tongue against the glass like a snake.

Shivering, Grace returned her attention to John. He held up an index finger. Stretching long, she hooked a hand under the cold metal car handle. He held up a second finger, the muscles in his legs and arms tensing ever so slightly. With her other hand, she located the unlock button on the car's key fob.

He held up his third finger.

She pressed the button and yanked the door open. Libby tumbled forward; her huff of surprise was quickly subverted by a spiraling screech as she smashed face-first into the cement.

John descended and plunged the syringe into her neck. She spasmed, emitted one last pitiful croak, then crumbled into a lumpy, sweater-and-jean-skirted heap on the sidewalk.

"Mom!" Grace heard Cari scream. She looked up in time to see Rex grab her by the arm, halting her rush in their direction.

Grace caught his eye and jerked her head toward the door. He winked in solemn understanding, then gently ushered Cari inside.

Satisfied, she turned back to the twisted mass of semi-humanity in front of her. Libby's head lay on her right ear, face turned in Grace's direction. Most of her front teeth were cracked or broken. Black blood flowed from both mouth and nose as well as forehead. But at least those eyes were closed now. She listened for a moment to the wet, ragged breath wheezing from that destroyed mouth.

"Breathing," she muttered. "Like *people* do. That's a good sign, right?"

"I don't know." John rolled the unconscious woman onto her back before gathering her up in his arms. "We don't know what we're dealing with yet, so...maybe. But don't get your hopes up."

"Copy that," Grace said. His voice was as hard as granite, but she knew where to spot the glimmer of hope in his eye.

He rose to his feet with little difficulty, as if Libby weighed no more than a sack of sponges. "I'll take her downstairs and run the usual tests. You go out to the trailer and figure out what's going on with Nelson."

She held up her hands. "Nothing would make me happier than taking that bastard for a ride on the Pain Train. But if it's information you're after, you know I'm not much of a diplomat."

"Good point. Have Mr. Guillermo meet you there. He'll have everything you need for a proper...ah, summit."

"Not Cooper?" she asked. "I mean, I'm sure A.J. *could* do it, but Cooper has actually handled hostile interrogations before. Wouldn't he be a better fit to take the lead?"

"Normally, yes. But as you may recall, the Lieutenant is still on restricted duty after his encounter last week, and I doubt last night's antics helped his condition."

He had a point. Between the stab wound from a scythe-wielding man-lion and facing down a twenty-foot centipede-witch, Cooper had earned a break, and A.J. was perfectly capable. No logical reason to feel disappointed at all.

She tipped her chin at the battered car. "I assume you have a plan for this?"

John shrugged. "No one's going to give a tiny smash-up like this much attention, assuming anyone even comes this way today at all. We'll leave it for now. Perhaps Mr. O'Bannon can get it running long enough to drive it into the delivery bay when he gets in tonight."

"Copy that." She unwound Cari's house key from the ring and pocketed it. Her eyes wandered from the broken car to the bloodied woman, then back to John.

"By the way," she said as she tucked the keyring into his hand, "that strange stuff we were supposed to keep an eye out for? I think we may have found it."

Chapter Two

Cari's knees felt like pudding and numbness dulled her thoughts. At least the myopic fury that had consumed her in the trailer was gone. She'd felt it flare up when she saw her mother hit the ground, but Rex's hand on her arm had snuffed it out. His touch penetrated the fog, light but steady on her right shoulder, as he guided her past the lockers and into the bunker.

"How 'bout a cup of Joe?" he practically yelled, steering her into the kitchen so quickly his toes caught the back of her sneakers and she nearly fell over. Behind them, John's body-laden steps thunked in the opposite direction.

She spun out from Rex's grip and tore after him.

"Mayhem, wait!" Rex called after her.

She didn't listen as she rushed past the entryway toward the holding cells. Out the corner of her eye she glimpsed Holly crushing herself against the bars of her own cell, her beady black eyes practically popping out of her head as they tried to follow John down the hall. Cari blinked, and Holly disappeared. All she saw now were the slim, swaying arms and legs that hung limply from either side of John's wide frame.

"I want to see her!" she wailed.

John paused in front of the second cell on the left but didn't turn around. "I can't let you do that, Cari."

White-hot rage filled her. She bobbed to the right, attempting to sweep around him, but John pivoted left and blocked her.

"Mr. Mackie, Cell Two!" The bars in front of him slid back and he plunged into the room. Before she could rush in after, a slim hand wrapped around her wrist and held her back.

"Let me go!" She wrenched against Rex's grip.

"No can do," he said, grunting as he struggled to hold on to her flailing limb. "You don't need to see that."

"Yes, I do!" she screamed in frustration as the bars slammed shut. "I want to see my mom!"

"She's not your mother!"

John's words froze her to the core. He finished securing his burden to the cot in the middle of the room and turned to face her, his body strategically positioned to block her view.

"She's not your mother," he repeated. "Not right now. I'm going to do everything I can to get her back for you, but until I do, it's best if you stay away. The first sedative is going to wear off soon, and when she wakes up, I'd like to keep her as calm and unstimulated as possible. You're the last person she should see."

The words stung like a hoard of bees, painful and burning. She had a right to be there, to stay by her side and see her through this. But John had put on his vacant, self-assured doctor face, the one that reminded her of the marble statues of Socrates and Plato staring up from the pages of her long-abandoned textbooks. She sulked in defeat. All the screaming in the world wouldn't do any good—there was no arguing with a stone. "Can you at least tell me how she is, *Doctor*?"

"When there's something to report, you'll be the first to know. I promise."

"Great," she snarled and stalked back to the kitchen, Rex at her heels.

"Sorry about that, May," he mumbled sheepishly as she slumped into a chair. "That dude is kind of dick, but in this case, he probably knows what he's talking about."

"Whatever," she snapped before inserting the tip of her thumbnail between her teeth and biting down angrily. Maybe Rex had been trying to help, but that didn't mean she was going to forgive him for being John's co-conspirator.

"Uh, well, why don't you just sit there and try to chill out and…watch me make the coffee?" He turned and busied himself at the counter.

As reluctant as she was to heed any instruction he gave her, her eyes followed along as he filled the pot with water and dumped it in the back chamber, then grabbed the filters from the upper shelf. Gradually the tense muscles in her neck started to loosen, and she let her hand fall back onto the table.

The nascent serenity was shattered by a furious scream, followed by a cascade of Holly's sadistic laughter.

Rex yelped. The coffee filters went flying as he twisted the knob on the coffee grinder. "Fresh beans!" he yelled over the roar of the gears. "Nothing better than fresh beans, that's what I say!"

As usual, Rex had all the subtlety of a Mack truck. A wave of appreciation swept over her, and she had to take several deep breaths to keep the hysterical giggles from tumbling out. Looking down, she saw her hands clenching the edge of the table so tight her knuckles were white. Her eyes welled, not with tears of sadness or worry, but guilt. She could've made a break for her mom's cell if she wanted to. Rex was slower than she was. He wouldn't be able to stop her. But she'd held herself in place with all her strength instead.

Because she didn't really want to see her mother. She just wanted to know that everything was going to be okay.

They'd been right to stop her.

The grinder ran until the hopper emptied, and beyond. Almost a full minute. By the time Rex shut it off, the disturbance down the hall had faded. She shoved her hands in the front pouch of her sweatshirt and focused on Rex's hands, dipping and waving like a magician as they performed their tasks. She closed her eyes. The next thing she knew, the smell of roasted chicory wafted across her nose.

"Here we go." Rex placed a mug in front of her. "What do you need? Cream, sugar...Xanex, maybe?"

"Black is fine."

He arched an eyebrow in surprise but said nothing, scooping three mountains of sugar into his own coffee before settling into the chair across from her.

"So...um, how are you doing?"

She bit her lip. They both knew it was the dumbest question ever in the circumstances. Still, he cared enough to ask it. For that, she owed him an honest answer.

"I'm scared."

He nodded solemnly. "Me too."

There was something on his mind, she could tell. Letting the silence sink in, she brought the mug to her lips. The coffee smelled like a house fire and tasted like burnt chalk, but she would endure it for as long as it took him to get the words out.

"You killed a guy with an ax today." He addressed the words to the tabletop.

She sighed, running her finger around the smooth ceramic lip. "I didn't kill him. I threw an ax at his face and the blade got lodged in his skull."

"That's usually the same thing."

"Not this time." She downed the contents of her cup in a single gulp. It wasn't so bad if you drank it fast enough.

"Still." He squirmed in his seat. "Are you…are you sorry you did it?"

"No."

She surprised herself at how quickly she answered. That's not what a normal person would do, would they? A normal person would at least feel somewhat conflicted about striking to kill, even if it was in self-defense—or in the defense of another, as it happened in this case. But as soon as the word flew from her lips, she knew she'd never said anything more honest in her life. "I'm not sorry I did it, and I don't feel bad at all."

She pushed her empty cup toward him.

"More coffee, please."

Chapter Three

Grace jogged to her car, her phone bobbling in her hand as she swiped through her contacts for A.J.'s number. He answered on the fourth ring.

"Hola?"

"I need you to meet me at Four Winds as soon as possible."

"Why, what's—?"

"A summit. I assume you know what that means."

"Dios mío." He sounded as if he'd been punched. *"Okay, I'm on my way."*

"Trailer Three. See you soon."

She hung up and selected another contact from the list. It barely rang once.

"Edensgate Security Office. Simon Mackie speaking."

"It's me. Has John briefed you on the situation?"

He snorted. *"If you're talking about the second rotting corpse now stinking up our holding cells—"*

"Her name is Libby." She cut him off with a snarl. "She's Cari's mom. Libby is her name. Understood?"

"Oh, r-r-right." Simon stammered. *"C-c-copy that. Sorry."*

"I'll let you make it up to me." Grace dug in her pocket for her keys. "I need you to get me some background on a local man. First name Nelson, last name Baines. Bravo, Alpha, India, November, Echo, Sierra. Got it?"

"Baines with a Bravo, 10-4," came the answer, followed by the chatter of computer keys. *"Anything specific you're looking for?"*

"Anything specific would be great," she said as she fastened her seatbelt.

"Roger. I'll call you when it's done. And...Grace?"

"Yeah?"

"Try not to do anything...you know, too stupid."

She smiled. "Thanks pal. Talk to you soon."

Grace burned rubber through town, slowing down only when the wobbling metal archway to Four Winds came into view. She entered the trailer park with the engine running at a low purr and cut the wheel to the right. The VW Bug lurched over the uneven mounds of dirt that served as a combination yard-driveway in front of the first trailer. Luckily, it appeared to be abandoned, as did many of the units near the entrance. When the mine kicked, the trailer park had expanded away from the road to accommodate all the citizens who could no longer afford the upkeep of their cushy in-town McMansions. Only the true hard cases still occupied the small, dumpy front units.

She spurred the vehicle toward the narrow thicket at the edge of the park and wedged it between a pair of spindly bushes, hoping the minty green paint job would help it blend into the scenery. She continued on foot, keeping to the tree line until she reached Cari's trailer. A perimeter check confirmed all windows were intact, and the door remained latched. Leaning against the rear wall, she released a tense, shaky sigh. She might not have the What or Why on Nelson, but at least she had a reasonable expectation of Where.

Before the morning air had time to chill her to the point of shivers, the crunch of heavy tires broke the silence. Peeking around the edge of the trailer, she spotted A.J.'s mud-splattered Jeep Cherokee rolling down the center drive. His head swiveled to either side like a surveillance camera until he caught sight of her. She rounded the trailer to meet him as he pulled in behind it, killed the engine, and hopped out. He wore his typical ensemble: black shirt, black jeans, boots, and duster. Everything except his cowboy hat. His salt-and-pepper hair fell across his forehead in wet, freshly showered strands, and his stubble was no less prominent than it had been a few hours ago.

"Feel like telling me what this is all about?" he asked, dark eyes brimming with concern.

Keeping her voice low, Grace filled him in on the events of the morning, from Ray's passing to Cari's return to the state of Libby Hembert—or what was left of her, anyway. A.J. nodded along, hands perched on his hips, his face as still as sandstone. It was only when she told him about Nelson's reported behavior that his forehead started to pinch, and his lips looked as if he'd sucked on a lemon.

"You're sure this all happened outside of Edensgate?" he asked, a subtle but distinct tremor in his voice.

"Simon's checking on Baines's history now, but as far as we know he's had no significant contact with the mall or anything in it."

He stared at her, eyes sloped and pleading, as if begging her to say it ain't so. She looked away, back toward the trailer—and saw the corner of one of the drawn shades flutter.

She smiled. "What say we go ask him ourselves?"

They circled around to the front door, pressing their backs to the trailer wall so they couldn't be seen from the windows. A.J. went up the stoop first, examining the door as Grace waited on the ground.

"Should be easy enough." He reached inside his duster and produced a rubber-handled stiletto knife, which he passed down to her, then turned his body perpendicular to the door and put his fists up. "You might want to stand back. There could be shrapnel."

"Easy, Chuck Norris." Grace held up the house key Cari had given her. "No need to wake the neighbors."

A.J. pouted but dropped his hands. "Fine. It's a shame though—my high kick is a thing of beauty."

"I'm sure it is," she murmured as she slipped past him. To her surprise, the key turned fluidly in the rusted-out lock. She glanced over her shoulder. "I'm left. You're right."

He nodded and assumed a runner's stance. From beneath his coat, he produced a second stiletto and held it point forward, ready to impale.

She opened the door a crack, her body tense and ready for an onslaught.

"And...go!"

She charged inside. Her eyes sprinted over the bottle-littered table, then darted left, searching the fouled kitchen and narrow hallway for movement. Nothing. She whipped right. Also nothing, except A.J.'s back as he performed a similar sweep of the small living area.

"Clear?" he hissed back at her.

"Clear." Squinting in the unlit space, she examined her side of the trailer more carefully. "There's a couple closed doors down this way though."

"Yeah, I've got one on this side too."

Which window had been the one with the fluttering shade? She tried to picture it, but the vinegary stink of old wine made it difficult.

"Yours first," she said at last.

They shuffled down the narrow walkway between two tattered banquette couches, A.J. on tiptoe while Grace slid flat-footed in reverse, her eyes pinned to the opposite side of the trailer, until she bumped up against him.

"On a three count," he said. "Uno. Dos. *Très!*"

She turned around as his foot connected with the flimsy door in a powerful thrust that was, in fact, quite beautiful.

What they found on the other side of the door, however, was the exact opposite.

A cheap dresser and vanity took up space to the left and right of the door, both made of the same fake-wood veneer and piled high with what could only be called "sex junk:" a plastic feline face mask, five or six pairs of lace panties in a variety of Day-Glo stripper colors, half-melted candles, and a dozen or so empty flask-shaped bottles. But the truly unsettling part of the room was the bed. Except for two pairs of fuzzy pink handcuffs hanging on either side of the wrought-iron headboard, it was bare. No pillows or blankets, not even a fitted sheet, the satiny blue finish of the mattress dulled by a mottle of dingy brown stains. Most of them looked like water damage except for the patchwork of smeary, mud-colored slashes across the upper middle of the mattress.

"Jesus." A.J. passed a hand over his forehead, chest, and shoulders. "What the hell went on in here?"

"I *do not* wanna know," Grace said, sweeping the room for their quarry. The furniture took up almost all the floor space, the bed frame appeared to have a solid base, and there were no other doors to indicate a bathroom or closet. To see anything more would mean traversing that mattress, and she would rather set her hair on fire than get any closer to that abomination. She turned back toward the main room. "Come on, let's go check the other—"

Her words died. Outside the open bathroom door lurked Nelson, drooling and snorting like a bull.

At least, she assumed it was Nelson. It was hard to tell with the ax buried in the left side of his face. His once perfectly coiffed blond hair clung to his saggy cheeks, heavy with sweat, and his trim mustache was caked with gooey black blood.

"Graaaaaaace," he rasped, sinking into a low forward crouch.

Her vision tunneled as she cataloged the area between them. There was no alternate path, no room to maneuver, and no possible way to outflank him. At Edensgate, she could almost always count on at least one of those things. But here...

Her lungs evacuated as all further brain function came crashing to a halt. The hand holding the knife squeezed the handle in a death grip. If there was only one road to take, then why wait?

She sprang forward. He reeled back and pounced. A bound and a half later and she was close enough to smell the stink of alcohol oozing from his skin. His hands landed on her first. She heard the zip of fabric ripping as he clawed at her chest and shoulder. A picketed line of teeth hovered over her, white and black and red all over. That was it. A face and hands. The rest of him was hollowed out as he arched backward. Out of striking distance.

Her lips pulled back in a snarl. That son of a bitch meant to grab her, hold her, and rip her throat out, all without ever giving her an opportunity to counterattack.

Except...

The plan coalesced in her brain a half second before her body obliged. Turning her fist from a stab to a punch, she lashed out with a jab as beautiful as A.J.'s high kick, if not more so. When it landed, they both screamed: Grace from the impact that crushed her fingers and sizzled up her arm; Nelson from the additional inch and a half of ax blade she had drilled further into his skull. Grabbing his face, he collapsed to the floor.

Grace fumbled a dishtowel out from the refrigerator handle with fingers numb from the blow, then dropped down to straddle the drooling, whimpering man-demon. "What did you do to her?" she growled, twisting the towel between her hands.

Nelson giggled, gray spittle bubbling from between his clenched teeth. The edge of her vision turned red.

"Wrong answer, dick." She shoved the towel into his mouth and pressed the butt of her hand against the back of the ax. Another half-inch of blade disappeared into his face. He roared against the gag as more blood spurted from the wound in small, oily arcs. "Tell me what the hell you did to her!"

"Grace, stop!"

Strong, non-negotiable arms looped below hers and dragged her to her feet.

"He needs to tell us! I'll make him talk. Let me go!"

Her flailing arm smacked A.J. on the side of the head. He grunted, but his grip didn't weaken. "No, *querida*. Not like this. Now, be quiet. There's been enough screaming as it is."

She groaned, flopped her arms a few more times in protest, then gave in. A couple deep inhales of A.J.'s leather-polish-wildflower soap went a long way in cooling her fury.

"Better?" he asked as he withdrew his arms.

"I guess." She glared down at the bleeding, semi-conscious Nelson. "My way would have worked, you know."

A.J. indulged her with a smile. "Perhaps. But why don't we try the easy way first?"

Nelson wheezed something at them.

The fact that he thought he had the right to say anything without permission filled her with fresh rage. "*What* was that, asshole?"

His eyes fluttered and he whimpered again. A tenuous chain of words stumbled out of his semi-unconsciousness.

"Thank you…sir. Thank you."

A.J. swooped down and grabbed Nelson by the ankles, his eyes smoldering. "Give me twenty minutes. See how thankful you are then." He looked up at Grace. "Come. Help me drag this *pedazo de mierda* to the bedroom."

A.J. returned from the truck as Grace finished locking the second fuzz-covered metal cuff around an unconscious Nelson's left wrist. From the duffel bag in his hand, he extracted a length of rope and handed it to her. "Bind his ankles too. We need to restrict his movement as much as we can."

"It's your show, friend," she said, and looped the rope around Nelson's legs.

A.J. sidled around the right side of the bed and began unpacking the rest of the bag. She watched out of the corner of her eye as he laid a leather-covered blackjack on the dresser next to their two stiletto blades, followed by a crucifix, a syringe, a pair of pliers, what appeared to be a surgical-grade scalpel, and a whole host of other sharp and shiny implements.

"Are you really going to use all that?" she asked as she tied off the last knot.

"For the most part, no. It's psychological. If he's still any part human, it'll send a pretty loud message." He held up a handful of glass vials full of clear liquids with small, inscrutable writing, all identical except for the label color. "These, on the other hand, are our silver bullets, for when the conversation needs a jump-start."

"Uh-huh." Her task complete, she backed into the doorway. "You know what else makes a good silver bullet? An *actual* bullet."

"Perhaps. But threats of brute force could backfire depending on his state of being. Sometimes you need a more nuanced approach." He lined up the bottles on the dresser and pointed at the one with the green label. "Ketamine, to sedate and to relieve pain." Then the red label: "Platypus venom to bring that pain back times ten." Finally, the purple label: "Sodium pentothal, or what some call truth serum. Doesn't always work, but it rarely hurts...too much."

"Wow," she said, genuinely impressed. "And here I thought you were just the weapons guy."

"Knives and guns aren't the only weapons, Grace."

"No, but they are the best ones."

He smiled serenely. "We'll see."

The buzz of her phone sent her heart racing. "It's about time!" she said as she pressed the call button. "Simon. What have you got for me?"

"Quite a bit, actually. You ready for it?"

"One sec." She curled a finger at A.J., then stepped into the hallway. She was about to put the phone on speaker when A.J. stopped her hand.

"It's better if he doesn't know what we know," he whispered, tilting his head back toward the man shackled to the soiled mattress like a demented Jesus.

"Fair enough." She angled the phone upward so they could both hear. "Go ahead, Simon."

"Alright. Nelson A. Baines, born February 10th, 1971 at St. Agnes right here in Halcyon to Elizabeth and Abner Baines. He is the oldest of three. Sister Felicia was born 1973, and brother—"

"We don't need the family tree." A.J. cut him off before Grace could, and with a far less abrasive word choice. "Skip ahead to the last nine or ten years or so. What was he doing before the mine fell, and what has he been doing since?"

"One sec...okay, yes. He was head of security at First National Bank of Halcyon. When it shuttered in 2011, he got a job at the Stop-n-Go on the south side of town. His wife, Leeann, was and still is a Civics teacher at Halcyon High. He's got two kids, both girls. Kate, 17. Chloe, 15. Kate's on the basketball team at HHS, and might have a decent shot at a scholarship next year. Otherwise, college isn't looking good for either of them, according to their report cards."

"How did you get access to their report cards?" Grace asked.

"Uh...do you really want me to answer that?"

She smirked. "Withdrawn. Keep going."

"Nelson worked at the S-n-G for about three years, then quit to devote all his time to his community outreach. Property records indicate that the family sold their house and moved to Four Winds around that time as well. Number #17, a triple-wide on the back hill overlooking the river. I guess he's the type that needs to have the nicest house on the block, even in a trailer park."

Grace nodded along. "And when you say, 'community outreach,' you mean his substance group-slash-circle jerk?"

"I think you mean prayer circle," A.J. corrected.

"I know what I mean," Grace shot back. "Simon?"

"Uh, he does run a prayer circle and substance support group...in theory. But the only record I could find connecting him to any church is from before 2011, when he was a deacon at Our Lady of the Mountains. Since then, he's had no affiliation with any church in town, and his group isn't listed on any event calendars. They have a single-page website that says they meet at seven every night, and it gives

Nelson's house as the address, but other than that I haven't found any employment records or volunteer sign-ups, and there's nothing in his bank accounts that would indicate a donation to—"

"We get it," Grace said. "Considering Libby's alcohol addiction, I think we can safely assume that's where they met. Do you have a sense of when they started seeing each other *outside* the group?"

"Negative."

"Dammit!" She caught A.J.'s reproachful glare and corrected herself. "Sorry, Simon. That's not your fault. Any adulterer with half a brain would be careful not to leave a paper trail—which in this case is appropriate, given that half his brain is—"

"*Anyway*," A.J. interjected. "Now we know that the mine fall impacted Nelson in an extreme way."

"Well, no shit." Grace rolled her eyes at him. "It's not like everyone else won a car and a trip to Bermuda. But he's the only one that's gone full-on Cocoa Puffs."

"Exactly my point. Simon, you said he worked at the bank?"

"Affirmative. And he was good at it too. Even got a commendation from the governor when he helped foil some crazy hacking attempt back in '08. I tell ya, under different circumstances I could picture us hiring this guy."

"Right," Grace said around clenched teeth. The idea of working with Nelson made her want to throw up.

"Simon," A.J. chimed in as she recovered, "can you tell if he was in the bank when the news of the mine hit town?"

"One second…hold on…yes! His work schedule has him opening the bank that morning."

"That's what I thought." A.J.'s brows joined over his angular nose.

"What?" Grace asked, covering the phone with her hand. "What does that mean?"

"The bank was the first place most people went after they heard the mine was dead. A big group showed up several hours before it opened. The employees didn't want to let them in, so they broke the windows and stormed the place. That's where the first fatalities occurred."

"First of many," Grace said bitterly, thanking her lucky stars that she'd already been at Edensgate when the week of violence had kicked off. "You think one of the settlers got a hold of him there?"

"I suspect he experienced a uniquely horrific trauma on that first day, and it has led to something worse. I can use that." He brushed her hand away from the microphone. "This has been helpful, Simon. *Gracias.*"

"Oh well...de nada."

She shook her head as A.J. returned to the bedroom and closed the door. *What a bunch of nerds.*

"Simon, one last thing. That Bible study thing he runs—do you have a member list for it?"

Simon whistled through his teeth. *"That's a little trickier. Substance support groups, religious or otherwise, don't take attendance or keep member lists. That's how they can use the 'anonymous' tag."*

She smiled. "I'm sensing a 'but' coming."

"Buuuut, this is Halcyon we're talking about. Playing Six Degrees of Separation never makes it past round two. Give me a few days. I'll find who was in that group."

"10-4," Grace acknowledged. "Thanks. Would you mind patching me through to John's phone? I want to give him the update."

"Sure thing. Stand by."

She sat down on the cracked leather couch as a series of beeps and buzzes disrupted the line.

"I'm afraid we have a situation, Mr. Baines."

She looked up as A.J.'s voice filtered in from the other side of the door. "One that involves you, and the woman who lives here, and now, unfortunately, me. We have a problem we need to solve, and to do so, I'm going to need your help." The rubbery snap of a medical glove punctuated his words.

"Ms. Henry?"

She dragged her attention back to the phone. "Hey, Boss. Wanted to let you know we've got Nelson restrained. And good news: I don't see any indication that he left the trailer or had contact with anyone else since Cari left him."

"What's his condition?"

She cringed. "Yeah, that's the bad news. He's conscious, but his condition is…pretty much what Cari said it would be."

"And by that you mean…?"

"Demonically possessed with an ax in his head."

"I see." His voice tightened. *"And his chances of recovery?"*

"In the toilet."

"Understood."

The word sounded so heavy it hurt her back to hear it. "Anyway…how's Cari holding up?" She wanted to ask about Libby too, but she had a feeling she wasn't going to like the answer.

"As well as can be expected. She's in the break room with Mr. Ranganathan, playing some sort of pugilistic video game."

"Well, next time you see her, let her know that Nelson has been handled, and that she doesn't have anything to worry about."

"That…might be a bit premature."

She stiffened. "What do you mean?"

"If his chances are truly, quote-unquote, in the toilet, is it safe to assume there would be no benefit of further detainment, or awaiting a possible antidote?"

"Correct," she said, resisting the urge to comment further. Eight years of nothing but goose eggs and he still would not let go of that stupid antidote idea.

"In that case, he will need to be dispatched."

"Tell me something I don't know," she said with an irritated sigh. "We can handle it, Boss. We've both done the vanishing dance more than once."

"Your skills are not my concern."

He paused. A fresh surge of anxiety kicked her heartbeat into overdrive. He was choosing his words. He only did that when he was about to deliver the worst news.

"It's like this," he continued at last. *"Nine times out of ten, when someone from Halcyon disappears, it's because they simply up and moved. They decided to try their luck somewhere else, and who could blame them? It's unfortunate they didn't say goodbye, but everyone understands. That's good for us, because when that tenth time happens, it's dismissed out of hand like all the rest. Nelson Baines, however...he was part of whatever fabric still makes up this community. He had status. He had a family. When someone like that goes missing, people notice. They ask questions—and they will aim their suspicions at whoever saw him last."*

Grace did her best to suppress a shiver. "Simon didn't find any records that tie Nelson to Cari, and his affair with Libby was a secret, and a very well-hidden one it looks like. There's no reason anyone would think he was here last night."

"That's something at least," John said. *"But prying eyes don't always make the front page. Sometimes you don't know who saw what until it's too late."*

She rubbed her temple. "If we can't dispatch him, and we can't keep him alive, then what the hell *are* we supposed to do with him?"

"As I said, your skills are not my concern. I'm sure you will find the perfect solution."

"Thanks for the vote of confidence," she sniped. "I gotta go. I'll call when we have more."

"Thank you. And be careful."

The call cut out. She sat there for a moment, staring at the raggedy banquette across from her and wondering what she had been thinking when she had answered her landline that morning. After a moment she groaned, slapped her knees, and hauled herself up to stand. Might as well give A.J. the good news.

"Don't feel like talking?" His slow, deep baritone stopped her outside the door. "Given the headache you must have I can't say I blame you. What do you say I help you out with that, and then we can try again?"

Nelson's gagged screams shook the trailer to its metal bones. She opened the door as A.J. wrenched the ax from Nelson's face.

"Hey! You busy?"

"Marginally." He joined her at the foot of the bed. "What's the news?"

"Not much. John has every faith in us, he's looking forward to hearing what we discover—oh, and we can't dispatch him."

He stared at her as if she had told him it was currently raining ketchup. "But we can't keep him alive."

"I am aware of that."

"Mierda." He tossed the blood-greased blade at Nelson's feet and rubbed his forehead in frustration. "You know who we could really use for this?"

Grace held up a warning finger. "Uh-uh. Don't even think about it. We are not to get him involved. Boss's orders."

They turned to the shivering creature strapped to the mattress. His tar-black eyes roamed over A.J.'s tools, the blades and bottles a stark omen of vicious things to come.

The injured side of his face tilted skyward, revealing the cleaved flesh of his cheek. But it wouldn't stay that way for long. The wound had already started to suture itself, forming a jagged line of black jelly from the middle of his cheek to his eyebrow. A small bulge in the ocular cavity indicated a growing eyeball.

"Huh." A.J. tilted his head and frowned. "That's strange."

"Is it?" Grace asked over the buzzing of her phone. Unknown Number. She pressed the button to silence it. "Cari split his melon and a few hours later he's up and at 'em and trying to eat me for breakfast. Regeneration isn't that surprising."

"That's not what I mean." He turned his head slowly to either side, as if looking at Nelson from a slightly different angle would reveal the answer. "I have the strangest feeling that I've met him somewhere before. And not that long ago, either. Somewhere..." He trailed off, his expression befuddled and annoyed.

"It's a small town," she supplied. "We've probably both seen him dozens of times and not even—"

Her phone buzzed again. Unknown Number again.

"Do you need to take that?" A.J. asked.

She smirked. "As critical as my opinion is, I'm sure the Green Wind Initiative will survive without it." She hit decline, then silenced her phone. "Sorry about that."

"*De nada.* We should probably get started though. There's a lot of ground to cover, and I don't want to find out what happens to this *monstruo* once it gets dark."

Chapter Four

Rex mashed the buttons of his controller. A series of audio embellishments whooshed from the television, punctuated by some ninja-esque exclamations. On the screen across from the couch, a frog and a gorilla dressed in *gi* and headbands tossed each other around in a Technicolor blur.

"Watch this, Mayhem! I got him now."

Cari lifted her head from the arm of the couch, attempting to feign interest. She'd been watching Rex play for hours, and her eyes throbbed.

"Dammit!" Rex yelled as the gorilla grabbed the frog by its ankles and tossed it into a rock wall at the back of the playing field.

"And *boom* goes the dynamite!" Simon's scruffy, triumphant grin replaced the combat on the screen. "Give it up, young Padawan. You cannot defeat the master."

"Lucky shot." Rex pouted, rolling his thumbs over the joysticks impatiently. "Best of twenty-one."

"If you insist. Get ready to be owned once again."

"You wish." Rex thrust his chin at the spare controller on the table. "You sure you don't want to play, May?"

"No, thanks." Her legs ached as she slid off the couch. "I think I'm gonna go for a walk."

He tore his eyes off the selection screen to look at her. She shrank away from the worry creasing his face. "You, uh, want me to come with?"

"No, that's okay," she said quickly as she hurried away. "I just…want to be alone for a minute."

She dashed out of earshot before he could say anything else. It wasn't that she didn't appreciate the offer. But his desperation to paint this as a "a normal day" had begun to grate on her nerves. Nothing about this was normal, and she feared she might start clawing her skin off if she had to pretend it was for one more second.

When she reached the lockers, she slowed to a shuffle, letting her attention wander down the hallway toward the detention cells. Her ears strained to catch any noise. More specifically, she listened for words, or even intelligible grunting—anything that resembled human communication. Instead, she could only make out the occasional click of metal on metal and a shivering but steady breath.

"He won't save her."

The words swooped in from out of nowhere, piercing her skin and filling her veins with fire.

"And how would you know?" she snapped at the barred door of Cell One.

Holly giggled. She sat on the floor, her back pressed tight against the wall and her legs splayed long across the stained concrete. Milky gray eyes rolled in their sockets, and everything else had taken on a slightly seaweed tone, from her ragged skin to her matted blond hair, even her tattered jeans and blouse. She looked dried out, like a husk ready to crumble at any moment. Everything except for her mouth, where her perpetually splitting lips oozed brown fluid like self-renewing lip gloss.

"I know," she croaked, prompting another micro-split in her bottom lip, "because of *who* did it to her."

"I was there." Cari lowered her voice to a whisper and tiptoed closer to the cell, shooting a glance down the hall as she did so. She had a feeling John wouldn't like her talking to Holly. "I saw Nelson do it."

Holly rolled her head side to side and hacked out another chuckle. "You think because you and your friends beat back the waves night after night that makes you safe? We made this place. We are the eyes in the trees, the shadows and the light, the water and the sand. We are the soul of Halcyon, and that can never be undone. Not by you, or them, or anyone."

"Then why are you all still here?" Cari sneered. "If you're so big and tough, you should be able to flick us aside and walk out the front door. Instead, you lose. Night, after night, after night."

Holly growled and slammed her skull back against the blocks. The resulting crack made Cari reel back.

"Maybe we're a little...waylaid, at the moment." Her eyes narrowed with vicious delight. "But who's to say that some impotent little morsel didn't break free, and find a cozy nook somewhere to squirrel away in, all coiled up like a rattlesnake, waiting until the time is right?"

Cari bit the inside of her cheek to suppress a shiver. "*Is* that what happened?"

Holly closed her eyes as a dark liquid dribbled down the wall behind her head. "If it did, then the best case for Mommy is becoming our new roommate."

The blood-slathered smile widened. "Actually, that's not true. Her best case is to die."

"I don't believe you," Cari spat.

"Don't you?" Her eyes slipped halfway open. "She's still in here, you know. Your little boss lady."

The shock of the words froze Cari to the core. "She is?"

"Oh, yes. She resisted at first, but eventually she saw it was the only way." She tilted her head, her face a mask of innocent curiosity. "Would you like to know if she wishes you had killed her?"

Cari's body trembled as cold fear battled hot rage. Holly hadn't been a good boss, or even a particularly nice person, but she hadn't been all bad—definitely not bad enough to justify this. She wanted to strangle whatever it was that now wore her skin. Instead, she bolted, dashing past the lockers and up the stairs to the main floor.

She would not give it the satisfaction of seeing her cry.

Chapter Five

Grace shifted her weight from foot to foot as a bead of sweat trickled down her spine. The cramped little room had grown hot, humid, and was starting to stink. She'd been standing at the foot of the bed for what felt like years, observing as A.J. plied Nelson with questions about his relationship with Libby. But Nelson just grunted and shook his head, his mouth a tense, uncooperative line.

Then A.J. switched topics, and asked Nelson about the bank, and that horrible November morning when everyone discovered the mine had fallen. Nelson's face looked as if the bone below his milk-white skin had turned to jelly. His mouth sagged open, but no answers came out. Instead, he wailed and thrashed like a chained bull, spitting profanities and gray mucus and threats of what he would do to them as soon as he got free. The tantrum was no more productive than the silence, but at least grabbing Nelson's bound ankles while A.J. shoved the dishrag back in his mouth was something to do.

"Fine, then." A.J. huffed. Returning to the dresser, he picked up the syringe and stuck the needle into the green painkiller bottle, then the purple source of truth. "A little Good Cop, Sneaky Cop it is."

He plunged the needle into Nelson's neck, eliciting another shriek, albeit a stifled one.

"About damn time." Grace sighed with relief as Nelson's eyelids drooped and his frustrated noises turned soupy.

"There we go," A.J. cooed, removing the gag once again. "That's better, isn't it, Mr. Baines?"

Nelson's eyes twitched from A.J. to her. She stiffened, fighting the urge to recoil. Those bottomless eyes both disgusted and fascinated her, like twin voids she could get lost in.

"Let's start at the beginning." A.J. leaned back against the dresser. "Tell me about the bank."

Nelson uttered a noise like a rooting pig. His wrists flopped in their restraints.

"You were there the morning the mine fell, weren't you? What happened?"

Another deep-throated grunt, then silence.

A.J. sighed mournfully and retrieved the blackjack from the dresser. Her heart raced; finally, something she could help with.

"You need to cooperate with us, Mr. Baines," she chimed in. "It's for your own good."

Nelson turned his infinite stare back on her. "Fuck you, bitch."

A.J. brought the blackjack down hard on Nelson's left shin. The resulting crack suggested something had broken, and yet Nelson barely whimpered.

"Dammit," she said. "You gave him too much. How are we supposed to get answers if he can't feel anything?"

"Better than screaming loud enough to wake up the entire city. Besides, you're forgetting about the second part of that little cocktail." He resumed his stance by the dresser, slapping his palm with the business end of the baton. "Keep going."

She shrugged. This was A.J.'s circus. She was just one of his freaks.

"We know that there were at least ten people in the bank when the riot broke out, because that's how many were killed. Ten dead citizens, none of them you." She pressed both hands into the soiled mattress and leaned toward Nelson. "How did you escape?"

More snarling, but still no answers.

"Did someone help you, Mr. Baines? Did you have an accomplice? A partner?"

He bucked violently, as if her words were red-hot whips, sucking in breath through clenched teeth. He'd wrenched so hard against his cuffs that black blood had begun to seep from his wrists, soaking the fuzzy pink marabou lining the handcuffs. She grinned. They had him, like a bug under glass, A.J.'s truth serum the pin keeping him in place. He could rip himself to pieces trying to resist, but there would be no wriggling away from this one.

"Who was it, Mr. Baines? Who helped you get out of the bank?"

His jaw popped in defiance as his clenched teeth parted, and the words he had tried so hard to contain spewed forth:

The Story does begin anew
When the Storykeeper dies
In the rosy dawn that follows
That unfortunate demise.

When the Primal Seal is opened
And the flowered sprite received,
The Flooded Prophet takes the throne
To avenge the much deceived.

He slumped back and let out a snotty sob of defeat.

A.J. cleared his throat. His face was stoic, playing it cool. But his eyes were a little too round, the knuckles of his hand clenching the blackjack a little too white. "That mean anything to you?"

"Not all of it," she muttered back. "Storykeeper was the Courier's name for Ray. I remember he called him that on the morning of the mine fall. The Storykeeper dies...and the rosy dawn that follows...that's today. A new story starts today."

"What does that mean?"

She shook her head and turned back to Nelson. "Mr. Baines, what story are you talking about? And what about the...the Primal Seal?"

"When the Primal Seal is opened," Nelson recited, his eyes ticking in time with the rhythm, "And the flowered sprite received the Flooded Prophet takes the throne to avenge the much deceeeeeeived..." The words died beneath a peal of wild laughter.

"Mr. Baines!" she shouted. "Stop that! Mr. Baines, can you hear me?"

The laughter escalated, creating a rubbery wall of noise that filled the room and pressed into her ears, threatening to break in and leech its poisoned madness into her brain.

Staggering back a step, she pointed at A.J. He leapt from the dresser and bashed Nelson twice across the mouth. The noise stopped immediately.

"Okay," she said, taking a breath to steady herself. "Let's try that again. When you said—"

He snapped his head up to look at her. "Have you ever been to hell?"

She couldn't do anything but stare at him in surprise. For a guy who'd been hit in the face twice, he seemed remarkably sharp. Now it was her turn to play it cool.

"Hell?" she mused, hooking her thumbs into the belt loops of her coveralls. "Yeah. Every damn night."

He giggled and dropped his head back to the mattress. "You think that puppet show is hell? Hardly. What you've seen is shadows on a wall. But all that is going to change. The Prophet has awakened. He will open the Primal Seal, and then...then you'll know the ultimate truth."

"And what is that?"

He shook his head. "You're not ready."

"Try me."

He tucked his chin and gave her another maggoty once-over. "Mankind has outlived its usefulness. We tell ourselves these grand myths about being created in God's likeness, but we're the cosmic equivalent of cockroaches. We foul everything we touch with our self-indulgence and greed."

Grace raised her eyes to the ceiling. "Oh, right. We're the disease, and you're the cure. But I'm curious—have you looked in a mirror lately? Because from where I'm sitting, you look a lot more plague-like than I do."

He scoffed as if in a world full of idiots, she was the Idiot Supreme. "I knew you wouldn't understand."

"You got me there. Who fed you this garbage? Was it this Prophet guy?"

He averted his eyes and studied A.J.'s arsenal. "No one needed to tell me. It's as plain as dirt."

She smirked. "Oh, I see. You've never met the Prophet, have you?"

"No," he sighed, his voice full of regret and longing. "But I will. Soon. He's coming, and when he arrives—"

"Yeah, yeah, ultimate truth and the destruction of all humankind. We got it. I don't suppose you know where this Primal Seal is, do you?"

He gurgled into his chest like a happy baby. "Even if I did, I wouldn't tell you."

"Don't play games with us, Mr. Baines. We have methods of making you speak," A.J. said in his best Russian accent as he stuck the syringe into the red vial and drew a full dose of the pain-magnifying liquid into the chamber.

Grace flicked her hand at him dismissively. "Don't bother."

He wrinkled his forehead in confusion. She raised her eyebrows, indicating he should follow her lead. "This moron is bottom-rung. He doesn't know anything."

Nelson looked as if she'd slapped him. His cheeks flushed and his eyes bugged with wrathful tears. "That's not true!"

"Sure, it is. I mean, all you've done so far is regurgitate some lame rhetoric and recite a poem that, frankly, my six-year-old niece could've written in her sleep." She looked back at A.J. "Kill him and let's get out of here."

"You're wrong," Nelson's voice shook as A.J. picked up the stiletto. "I was chosen."

"You're a shit pile, and you're wasting our time."

Taking the cue, A.J. lowered the point of the knife toward Nelson's shriveled right eye.

"I'm a shit pile?" Nelson screamed, his voice rising to the pitch of a teen-aged boy. "I'm a *shit pile?* Then why was I in charge of raising the army?"

"Hold it." Grace said before the point could pierce its target. She extended her hand to Nelson. "Go on."

"I-I-I don't know where the Primal Seal is," he stuttered, his focus on the point hovering mere inches from his face. "Only that it's difficult to get to. The Prophet wouldn't be able to get there without reinforcements. It was my job to find them."

Cold fingers tickled the back of her neck. "That's why your prayer circle wasn't associated with any church. You were using it as a cover to farm converts. Was Libby the first?"

He snorted. "She was supposed to be, until her little brat showed up and *ruined* it."

Grace leaned forward on her hands once again. "And why her? Why did you start the affair?"

He cocked his head almost ninety degrees and grinned at her. "Because I wanted to fuck her, of course."

She didn't even try to hide her disgust. "So, this is all a coincidence? You're just some horny asshole and banging Libby didn't have anything to do with Edensgate. Or with Cari."

"Mmmmm, Cari." A deep moan reverberated from Nelson's throat as if saying her name was pleasure itself. A pit of mortal dread sunk into Grace's stomach. "What do you want with her?"

She regretted her word choice instantly.

"Wouldn't you like to know?" He thrust his crotch in the air, the tip of his mottled gray and black tongue sliding over his lower lip.

She didn't remember moving across the room or picking up Cari's blood-smeared ax where A.J. had dropped it on the mattress. But both must have happened, because the next thing Grace knew, she was pressing that ax to Nelson's throat.

"You sick bastard."

"She'd *love* it!" His eyes slid to the right, away from her.

She grabbed the back of his neck and jerked his head upward. "Look at me, motherfucker! Look at me when I'm killing you!"

"Hang on a second."

"What?" she roared, ticking her gaze toward A.J.

He smiled thoughtfully, as if the final piece of an invisible puzzle had fallen into place. "I have something I need to ask him."

"He's tapped out! All he's got left is his twisted fantasies, and I'd rather rip my ears off—or *his*—than listen to that."

"You can do all the ripping and slicing and bashing you want in a minute. But one more question first."

"Fine," she growled, recoiling temporarily to the opposite side of the bed. "*One* more."

A.J. bent low, until his mouth was level with Nelson's face, and waited until the confined man turned his dark stare on him.

"What is your middle name?"

Nelson's wide black eyes widened even more, and he bared his teeth at A.J. "Go to hell."

Sighing, A.J. dug two fingers into the seam of Nelson's not-entirely healed face wound.

"Tell me," he coaxed, as composed as a librarian over Nelson's agonized screams. The answer came out in a long rasp, as if A.J. had reached all the way down his throat and ripped it out of him. "*Aaaaarrrrthhhhur.*"

A.J. retracted his hand. "Good boy."

He patted Nelson on the forehead, leaving a big black blotch behind.

Grace gaped at him. Had she heard that right? "Arthur. As in the *Reverend* Arthur?"

A.J. pried the soiled glove off his hand. "I guess we should have let Simon take the Baines family tree all the way to the roots after all."

"Guess so. How the hell did you know?"

"There's a family resemblance. The golden hair, the fatty jawline. The *presunción arrogante*. And Simon did mention his middle initial was A. But it was when he was looking at my tools that I first noticed it. He zeroed in on the crucifix like it was a picture of an old girlfriend - a combination of nostalgia, excitement, and shame."

He picked up the wooden cross and held it in front of Nelson. His eyes widened, enthralled, and his head lifted off the pillow as if it were magnetized.

"He looked at it every time he felt insecure or threatened. When we first tied him down, when he admitted he'd never met the Prophet, and when you had the ax on him now. That last is when it finally clicked." He tossed the cross back on the dresser. Nelson flopped onto the mattress, panting with exertion. "He's a member of the Reverend's progeny. His foulness would never allow him to look at a religious tool like that otherwise."

"I'll show you a religious tool," Nelson growled through a smarmy grin.

She cocked her eyebrow at A.J. "May I?"

He shrugged. "A deal is a deal."

Grace smashed the side of the ax into Nelson's skull. Black liquid spewed from his mouth as something snapped around his right temple and his chin sagged disjointedly on his chest.

"Anyway," Grace said over Nelson's agonized gurgles, "You think the Reverend's behind this somehow?"

"A blood connection *is* significant," A.J. mused. "And the timing works out. He was free for several hours before you and John trapped him at Edensgate after the initial deal expired, during which time Nelson managed to escape a massacre without a scratch." He shrugged. "It's not rock solid, but it' the best lead we've got."

"Works for me." She pulled out her phone. "Why don't you see if you can get any more out of Dickbrain here while I give John the update?"

"Sure. Mind if I wait until he re-hinges his jaw first?"

"Whatever makes your life easier."

As she retreated to the living room, she noticed a spring in her step that had not been there earlier. Not only had they identified the likely source behind Nelson's antics, it wasn't some crazy new monster after all. And…what was the saying? The devil you know, and so on. Sure, they were nowhere on that whole Storykeeper-Primal Seal-Prophet nursery rhyme, but if there was anything left to get (other than a bunch of old pervert BS), A.J. would surely get it out of him.

She was about to dial John's number when a new nightmare emerged: three short, decisive raps on the trailer door.

Busted.

Chapter Six

The twang of a country-rock guitar roused Cooper out of his semi-conscious haze. Fortune Son. He smiled and snuggled his pillow. That was his favorite song. He liked it so much he had made it his ring tone.

Ring tone…

Was his phone ringing?

He glanced at the nightstand, taking care not to disturb the sleeping woman draped over him. The only thing glowing was the illuminated 15:13 of the digital clock. He must have left his phone in the kitchen.

"Great," he grumbled, and forced himself up.

"Don't leave me," Allie murmured, wrapping her leg around his waist.

"It's my work phone."

"You're off the clock. Let it go to voicemail."

As if it had heard her, the song cut out.

"See? Problem—"

The riff began anew. Cooper's heart rate shifted into a higher gear. Back-to-back phone calls. Never a good sign.

"I *have* to answer. They'd only be calling me if it was important."

"So, some kids spray-painted boobs on the front doors again. Is that really more important than staying here with me?"

He sighed. "Of course not. But if I don't answer, it'll be in the back of my head all day. How will I be able to give you my undivided attention?" He pressed his mouth into hers until she moaned with pleasure, then quickly pulled away, grinning. "See? I can't concentrate."

"Tease." She unwound her limbs and shoved him playfully toward the edge of the bed. "Fine, go. I hope it's worth it."

He dashed down the stairs, pulling on boxers as he went. The row of wounds that ran along the inside of his calves and thighs throbbed with every movement, but he ignored them. The pain was a mere fraction of what it had been when he'd arrived home that morning and improving by the minute. Apparently, being skewered by the feet of a giant demon centipede sounded a lot worse than it was.

He snatched the phone from the kitchen table. "O'Bannon."

"Coop? Thank God! It's about frigging time."

The voice was a little deeper and a lot rougher than last time—she must have started smoking again—but he recognized it instantly. "Lola?"

"Yeah, it's me. Sorry to call on your work phone, but it's the only number I've got for you."

"No, no, not a problem." He sat down at the table. Her voice conjured an image of Ray, smiling and congenial as always—at least, before he'd gotten sick. "I'm so sorry about your dad. How are you holding up?"

"No offense, but can we do the whole condolences thing later? I'm afraid I've got a bit of…an emergency?"

He smiled at the tablecloth. "Sure. Is there an issue with your flight? Was it delayed or something?"

"What flight?"

"Your mom told Allie that you were flying home from Honolulu today."

Silence.

"Actually, Cooper, I'm already here. Well, I'm in LA. I fly to San Francisco tonight and then I'll take a shuttle the rest of the way at first line. But I've been stateside since yesterday."

His thoughts stumbled, then righted themselves. "Oh, of course. You flew out when you heard your dad was admitted. Your mom must have gotten it mixed up."

Another long silence. *"You know that's not what happened. Though maybe it should have been. Mom's been calling me every other day for a month, telling me he was getting worse. I swear, I meant to plan a trip. But as soon as I hung up, it all sort of...faded away. And then yesterday, the whole thing hit me so hard I damn near fell out of my chair in the middle of a packed elevator. It wouldn't leave me alone after that, just kept pounding in my head like a heartbeat. Come, home. Come, home. On and on until I booked my flight. Fucking Halcyon."* She chuckled. *"But I don't need to tell you about that, do I?"*

Cooper bit the inside of his lip. Time to change the subject. "So...if it's not a problem with your flight, what is it? Whatever you need, I'm here. Allie and me both."

"Oh, yes!" she cried. *"I need to find Grace, but she's not answering her phone. Do you know where she is?"*

Cooper frowned. Had Lola ever met Grace? When would that have been? He racked his brain for memories of them together and came up blank.

"Hello?"

"I'm here. Sorry. Last I saw her she was heading home. It was...kind of a rough night. She's probably asleep."

"Cooper." The deepening of her voice on the second syllable told him to cut the BS. *"You and I both know that's a*

ridiculous statement. Now stop trying to make me feel better and help."

"Yes, ma'am." He smiled as an image of her in high school floated in front of him: long, stick-straight black hair framing her pale round face, her almond eyes and down-turned lips both smeared with black stuff that made the unamused stares she gave him even more intimidating. And while a devastating car wreck had left her body paralyzed from the waist down, the spirit he'd grown up with remained as bright and terrifying as ever. "I'll do a roll through town to see if I can find her."

"And call me as soon as you do?"

"The very minute. Don't worry. You just get here safe, okay?"

She laughed bitterly. *"Cooper my man, that's one thing I don't think I have to worry about."*

He shivered. She was probably right. What Halcyon wanted, it got. No exceptions, no substitutions, no delays.

After they said goodbye, Cooper took a shot at Grace's numbers himself. The home line rang endlessly, and while her cell phone didn't go straight to voicemail, it got there eventually. He sighed and bounded up the stairs. It seemed he was in for an afternoon of wild goose chasing—or rather, Grace-chasing.

Allie sat up as he entered the bedroom. "Who was it?"

"Lola," he said, swiping his balled-up work slacks from the floor. "She's...about to board the plane."

"Oh, good!" Allie sighed. "It'll be good for her to come home for a while. Her and Mimi both."

"Sure." He pulled on his pants, wishing he could share his wife's confidence. "Anyway, she called to ask for a favor, so I've got to run out for a while."

Her brows tightened. "Now? She's not even on the plane yet. What's the rush?"

"She needs to get a hold of Grace and can't find her. I promised I'd track her down."

"So, what? You're going to drive around town and hope you run into her?"

"I'll check her house and the mall first. Otherwise, yeah. Pretty much."

"That's insane."

"The town isn't that big. It won't take long."

"No, I mean..." Allie stared at her knees. "Look, you know I love Grace. But you're not her babysitter. If she's not answering her phone, it means exactly what it means when any adult doesn't answer their phone: she wants to be left alone."

"She might be in trouble."

"How?" Allie threw her hands up. "Has she been kidnapped by terrorists? Is she hanging off a cliff by her fingernails? No. That kind of stuff never happens here."

He pulled a maroon sweatshirt over his head and knelt to lace up his boots. Technically, it was true. *That* kind of thing never did happen.

"I'll be back as soon as I can." He stood up and dropped a kiss on top of Allie's tousled raven hair. She clutched his sleeves, holding him in place despite his attempts to pull away.

"Please. Please don't leave me."

He smiled, projecting patience. "I know you're still shook up about Ray. But Lola needs me."

"*I* need you." She pouted in that spoiled little girl way that always made him cringe. Summoning every ounce of tenderness he could, Cooper cupped her cheek in one hand.

"I know you do, sweetheart," he said, trying to keep his jaw loose and unclenched. "I'll tell her to charge her phone, then I will be right back here. It won't be more than an hour, at most."

"Promise?" she asked.

His skin crawled as her pronunciation tickled at the edge of "pwomise."

"Yes, I...*promise*."

"Okay." She tucked her chin into his palm and smiled. "I *wuv* you."

He kissed her then, as much to smother any more of that shudder-inducing baby-talk as to say goodbye.

Maybe even more so.

Chapter Seven

Nelson's head snapped up at the knock on the trailer door. He opened his mouth, but A.J. shoved the towel gag between his lips before he could utter a single screaming syllable. With the prisoner subdued, A.J. joined Grace in the hall.

"What do we do?" he whispered, pulling the bedroom door closed behind him.

Grace's mouth fell open, but no words emerged. Her brain felt like it had short-circuited. "Maybe…look and see who it is first?"

He edged passed her and peered out the small, smudged window over the sink.

"It's some lady. Blond, forties. *Terrible* jean jacket." He wrinkled his nose in disgust. "I thought we all agreed bedazzling ended in the nineties."

"Do you recognize her?"

He looked as if she'd requested that he drink from the toilet. "Bitch, do I *look* like I hang out with the Rhinestone Housewives of Storey County?"

"Bitch, it was only a question," Grace said with a giggle, as amused as she was surprised. "Think you can take the attitude down a notch?"

"*Lo siento.*" He pressed a hand to his chest. "It's that jacket. Apparently, bedazzle is a trigger for me."

"I'd say so. Let's be quiet, and maybe she'll go away."

They settled into the silence. Each knock-free second that passed buoyed Grace's spirits.

She's about to leave. Any minute now.

"*Some folks are born, silver spoon in hand…*"

They both stared in horror as Cooper's CCR ring tone belted from the phone in her hand.

"Fuck!" she hissed as she fumbled to hit Decline. *Maybe she didn't hear that. Maybe she'll think it was the radio. Maybe—*

"I know you're in there, Libby!" The thick Southern accent shivered the thin walls. "Open this door right now!"

A.J. groaned. "I don't think she's leaving."

Grace glared at him. "You don't know that for sure."

"I'm not leaving!" A flurry of knocks ensued that, if left unchecked, would probably shake the flimsy door right off its hinges.

"You were saying?"

"Fine," Grace grumbled, weighing the options. Indignance wouldn't work. Whoever this woman was, she seemed to know who lived here and who didn't. Getting aggressive would only make her suspicious—or worse, provoke her into calling the cops. But it didn't sound like she was in the mood to be soothed either. Which left only one option. A risky one, but the best they had.

"Okay, I got this." Grace ripped the handkerchief off her head and dug her fingers into her thick black curls, making them look as unkempt as she could. Then she unzipped her coveralls.

"Are you planning to…seduce her?" A.J. asked, his eyebrow arching higher with each movement.

"Not exactly." She knotted the sleeves at her waist. Her dingy white tank top looked bright against her sienna skin.

"You hide behind the door. If anything goes wrong, I'll signal for help."

"How?"

"I'll say 'bedazzle.' Then you jump in and scratch her eyes out. Sound good?"

He eyed her viciously. "*Eres la peor, mi amiga.*"

She winked at him as he tucked himself between the jamb and the counter. With one more bracing breath, she plastered on a Miss America smile and flung the door open.

"Well, hi there!" she effused in an accent even thicker than the stranger's own.

The woman recoiled. She was about Grace's height, but so thin and delicate Grace thought she could probably carry her on one shoulder. Her bleached hair fell to her shoulders in feathered waves. And the jacket...it wasn't just bedazzled, it was be*crusted*. How A.J. knew there was jean under all those blue, pink and gold sequins, Grace had no idea.

The woman scanned Grace's hair, face and body with increasing concern. "Who in Hades are you?"

Grace popped out her hip and raised her chin in a still-cordial-but-slightly-affronted pose. "I don't reckon that's any of your business, ma'am."

"My name is Leann Baines. I'm looking for—"

"Oh, my word!" She slapped her knee in fake exuberance. "You're Nelson's wife! Oh, Libby is always goin' on and on about what a blessin' he's been. I don't know if you know this, but my sister is afflicted with a bit of a...temperance problem. Your husband has been an absolute angel, helpin' her like he has."

"Uh...oh, I see," Leann said through an uncomfortable frown. "So, your Libby's—"

"Sister. Yes, ma'am, as I said. Well, half-sister." She patted her hair. "Clearly."

Leann gulped, her cheeks flushing. "Uh...yes. Of course."

"Anyway, I'm afraid Libby's not here." Grace nodded at the tire tracks gouged in the dirt near the main drive. "She took the car into town a while ago. But you're more'n welcome to wait here if you'd like."

From behind the door, A.J. flashed her a look of alarm. But Leann already backed up another half step, her palms out as if the invitation were a raised fist. "No! No, that's not necessary. I was looking for Nelson, but I guess...maybe he's made his way back home by now."

"I reckon that's probably it, though I'm awful sorry to say it. I'd *love* to thank him for all he's done." Grace widened her smile. "Matter a' fact, would you mind tellin' him that when you see him? If it's not too much trouble, I mean?"

"Of course, I will." Leann stumbled backward down the steps and landed awkwardly on the ground. "Uh, thank you."

"No trouble at all. Y'all have a good day now!"

She watched Leann disappear around the back of the trailer before slamming the door.

A.J. smirked at her. "That was some accent. Dolly Parton would be proud."

"Thanks. West Virginia, born and raised."

"How did you know she wouldn't want to come inside?"

"Oh, you know. Women like that would rather peel their own skin off than share close quarters with...someone like me."

"Ah." He frowned. "Not exactly PC."

"Not exactly my fault." She smirked as she zipped up her coveralls. "Besides, it got rid of her, didn't it?"

He shrugged and smiled. "*Touché.*"

"Thank you." She lifted the blind on the window over the dining table, watching Leann as she tottered over the uneven ground toward the rear of the park and, Grace presumed, the big trailer with the river view. When the glint of the gaudy jacket faded behind the trees, she made her way back toward the bedroom. "Come on, let's snuff this candle before—"

Her voice fled the moment she opened the door.

Blood. So much blood, black and thick, soaking the blue satin mattress.

And...

"Where the fuck *is* he?"

She turned to A.J. His face had gone as pale as milk.

"It's...not possible." He shuffled toward the head of the vacant bed and poked at the handcuff with the tip of the blackjack, stooping to examine the blood-drenched metal-and-fur mechanism. "Locked. A little bent, maybe, but still, there's no way..."

Her body quaked with dread. *Of course, there was.*

She dove forward, but it was too late. Nelson's dismembered left hand leapt from its hiding spot behind the headboard and wrapped itself around A.J.'s throat. He stumbled backwards into the dresser, his mouth widening with a silent scream as he tried to pry the slick fingers from around his neck.

"Son of a bitch!" She dove for the arsenal laid out on the dresser, grabbing the first thing she saw: a pair of metal pliers. Yanking them wide open, she clamped down on the stumpy, tattered wrist and tugged as hard as she could. The deteriorating flesh tore instantly, spilling something like gray-green pudding down the front of A.J.'s chest. The stench of curdled milk and dirty diaper made her gag. But she held on, squeezing and ripping as more and more putrid ooze wept from the stump.

"It's…working," A.J. wheezed around the thing's weakening grip. "Don't…stop."

She nodded, wrenching as more and more of its insides plopped out.

Silver glinted to her right. She turned to see Nelson's other hand scurry down the front of the dresser, holding the scalpel between its index and middle finger like a cigarette.

"Fuck!" she screamed as the bladed appendage raced across the floor with spider-like speed. She barely managed to scramble onto the bed before it could take a swipe at her ankle.

"Grace…" A.J. coughed, sinking to his knees as Lefty renewed its hold around his neck. Even at this distance she could see the fingers begin to re-plump.

Fucking regeneration.

A rustle off the edge of the mattress drew her attention. Another surprise attack? Not very creative. Then again, brainless disembodied limbs weren't really known for their imagination.

Either way, two could play at that game.

"Hold on! I'm coming!" she yelled as loudly as she could (in case the thing has sprouted ears too) and launched forward.

The tiny assassin sprung upward as she crossed the edge of the bed. Just as she expected. Twisting her body away from the blow, she plucked the hand out of the air as easily as she would an apple from a branch.

"Hi there, little fella," she murmured, then turned her wrist and drove its scalpel into its brother's back. Lefty's fingers snapped open, relinquishing A.J.'s neck like a leech that had been doused in salt. A.J. gulped in air as his attacker fell to the ground, weak and impaled. Its custardy flesh ran out of the wound in a thick, ceaseless river.

Grace slammed Righty onto the dresser, picked up one of the remaining blades, and drove down, penetrating flesh and bone and particle board as she pinned the horrid creature to the veneer. It shuddered for a moment, then lay still.

A.J. looked down at the stinking gray smear on his shirt. He sneered down at the flaccid, trembling thing. "This was Ralph Lauren, you *cabrón*."

He dropped the heel of his boot onto the delicate knife and rubbery flesh, grinding and stamping until there was nothing left but a mold-colored smear in the worn carpet. Panting, he collapsed onto the bed, his hands pressed to his forehead.

"Well, that was fun," Grace said, slightly winded herself. "But we still don't know where Nelson is."

"Yes, we do." A.J. pointed to the ceiling.

She raised her eyes, and her stomach dropped. The emergency hatch above the bed was closed, but the black smears at the edges were unmistakable. It looked as if it had been pushed open by someone with two bloody, handless stumps.

She picked up the last unused blade and raced out the door.

"Stay here," she called back to her woozy companion. "I'll find him."

Chapter Eight

The mall was even more desolate than usual, due in part to the mountainous briar patch choking the East Hallway, a testament to the previous night's trial. It had been half a day since they had killed the witch, but the brambles she'd created remained, now covered in mottled gray and black spots and leeching a wet, dirty-shower smell into the closed space. Cari quickened her pace as she passed through the thicket toward the low arch that led into the rotunda. Harmless or not, they still stank.

She wandered from one end of the mall to the other, exploring far-off nooks and crannies she hadn't seen in forever. Then again, "forever" was a kind of relative. Had it only been ten days since she and Rex had sat in the movie theater lobby, scarfing down nachos and playing *Splatterfield 3*? Ten days since her biggest problem was being laid off and knowing she'd have to spend all her time at home with her mom? She nearly choked on the lump that thought brought to her throat. Her mother was a mean drunk with terrible taste in men, and that was putting it nicely.

But she didn't deserve this.

Cari sat down on the edge of the Atlas fountain. The soft splash of water trickling down his shoulders and into the basin did nothing to ease her despair. Instead, it brought back memories. Or rather, part of a memory. The only good one she had of her mom. Sunshine and lapping water. The smell of charcoal and grilling meat. Her mother with her hands around Cari's wrists, spinning faster and faster until Cari's feet left the ground. She closed her eyes and smiled. For a few seconds, it felt like she was flying.

She wished she could go back in time and take back all the terrible thoughts. She wished she had never pleaded with God or fate or whatever to help her escape. She wished...

She wished she'd just gone home that night with the beer and the cigarettes, and never started any of this at all.

The water splashed louder, bringing her back to the ground and reality. Pain wrapped itself around her chest and the tears flowed hot enough to sting and burn.

"It's not fair," she screamed at the pink glass dome above her. "It's not fucking *fair*!"

"What's not fair?"

"Shit!" She recoiled and almost fell backward, grabbing the lip of the bench in time to stop herself from falling into the fountain. She swiped her hands over her eyes as Cooper emerged from the shadows below the bridge. "You shouldn't sneak up on people like that!"

"Sorry," he said, his hands stuffed in the pockets of his slacks. "I only wanted to...are you okay?"

"I'm fine!" she snapped. "What are you even doing here anyway? I thought you were still on restricted duty."

He scowled. "That's not necessary. I don't know why I have to keep repeating that, seeing how I saved the day last night."

Cari arched an eyebrow. "As I recall, you weren't the only one who did some day-saving, thank you very much."

"Point taken. Anyway, I'm not really here. I'm trying to find Grace. She's not at home and she's not answering her cell phone. Do you know if she's around?"

Cari's stomach clenched. To answer that question meant telling him about her mother, and Nelson, and what she herself had done, or almost did. It would make him worry—or worse, it would make him sympathize. She already had one guy trying desperately to make everything normal. She didn't need another one.

But Grace isn't answering her phone.

Given what Cari knew that Cooper didn't, she had even more reason to find that concerning.

"She's at my house. Four Winds Trailer Park. Number Three."

His frown intensified. "Oh?"

She sensed the inherent question in the word but held steadfast to her silence.

"Okay, then," he said at last. "I guess I'll head over there. Thanks."

"Sure." She hesitated for a moment. "Although…you might want to take your gun."

His gaze darkened as his eyebrows drew together. This time, the question would not remain unspoken. "Cari, what the hell is going on?"

"It's a long story." She lowered her eyes to the ground as she dragged herself to her feet. "Come on, I'll walk you downstairs."

She accompanied Cooper as far as the hallway at the bottom of the stairs, getting out as much of the story as she could before she left him standing in front of his locker with a dumbfounded look on his face. As she approached the sofa, she heard whispers coming from his direction. She shot a look behind her and scowled as John, having

349

emerged from his ICU ivory tower, spoke to Cooper in a subdued tone.

Of course, she thought, balling her fingers around the cuffs of her sweatshirt. Why not? Cooper was an adult. John *would* share information with *him*. But her? *Noooo.* She was just a stupid kid. She couldn't possibly be trusted to know the truth about her own family.

She fumed until she reached the couch. The 8-bit jubilance of the video game score felt like a dozen tiny drills in her skull. With Rex's attention consumed by the faux melee, Cari slipped out of the common area and down the hall to the bunk room. Eight bunk beds ran along the perimeter of the forest green windowless box, with six single cots filling the space in the middle.

She flopped into the nearest low bunk, turned her back to the room, and wished desperately for sleep. Nightly rest was no longer a necessity—one of the perks of her new role in life, apparently—and on the occasions she'd tried it anyway, all she'd managed was a browned-out half-slumber that left her feeling groggy and a little hungover. But she would gladly take dreamless fog over the out-and-out nightmare that reality had become. Breathing deep, her eyelids heavy, she neared the edge of that semi-sweet escape when the rapid shuffle of approaching footsteps drove her conscious once again.

"Cari? Can I speak to you for a moment?"

John's overly downy voice made her ears itch. She kicked the wall, then rolled up to sit. "What do *you* want?"

He dropped down on the bed across from her and clasped his hands between his knees. He looked so composed, his glasses polished and clean, every one of his gray hairs perfectly arranged. It made her furious. This man said he was doing everything he could to save her mother, and yet he looked like he was ready for a board meeting.

"I'll be straight with you," he said. "Your mother has been fully infected with the conversion agent. Now, normally, after this much time has passed, we would be seeing a rapid decline in mental and physical stability that would necessitate a swift and merciful dispatch. However, the trajectory of your mother's conversion is not following that path. Instead, it seems to be more aligned with Holly's path. Slower, and not as all-consuming. Which means she will likely remain viable for significantly longer."

Cari's nails drove into her palms as snippets of a previous conversation floated through her mind. She knew what was coming. Still, she really, *really* hoped she was wrong.

"The bottom line is, though I can't cure her, there might still be hope. The best course now is to keep her confined and under observation and see how things progress from here."

Cari looked down at her hands. Her palms were filled with tiny red half-moons. "Like Holly."

"Precisely," John said. "In a way, it's fortunate that we had her here first. Holly's presence has allowed me to test numerous potential antidotes already. Now that there's two of them, I'm confident we will be able to recover them both eventually."

"How long?" she whispered.

"I beg your pardon?"

"You heard me. How. Long. How long before you'll have an antidote?"

"Cari, this is unexplored territory. There's no way to predict—"

Her head snapped up. "So, let me make sure I understand. You want to lock my mother in a cell and use her as a guinea pig until whenever, while you look for a cure that might not exist. Right?"

He frowned, his eyes widening slightly with surprise. "I'm sorry I can't give you a better timeline, but...Cari, this is good news. She could *survive* this." He reached for her hands. "I thought you would be happy."

"*Happy?*" Her body drained of all feeling as she leapt to her feet. Though she wasn't quite tall enough to tower over him, seeing him shrink back filled her with spiteful joy. "Bullshit. I know what's really going on. You *told* me you wanted to use Holly to try to communicate with these monsters. Now, you think you'll double your chances of catching one of them at home if you have two. You want to turn my mother into a two-way radio, and that's supposed to make me *happy?* Fuck you!"

She tore out of the room—or rather, her body tore out. Her thoughts floated a few feet behind. Her vision blurred as if she were riding in a rocket ship, and when it cleared, she stood outside the barred door to her mother's cell. Four leather straps fastened Libby to the cot. An IV stuck out of her arm connected to a bag filled with a chartreuse liquid that reminded Cari of antifreeze.

"Cari, wait! Can we please discuss this rationally?"

John's voice snaked up behind her, doubling her rage. She wanted to punch him right in the mouth. Instead, she dropped a hand to her holster.

"Don't come any closer!" she screamed, whipping toward John, ax wound up and ready to throw.

"Okay!" He ground to a halt, hands up at chin level. "I'll stay right here, I promise."

"Good." She tilted her head toward the bars. "Let me see her."

"That's not going to help."

"You could fix her if you wanted to!" Cari screamed, her voice shaking. Behind John, she saw a flash of black hair as Rex peeked around the corner, spotted the ax, and ducked away.

"I swear, I've done everything I can do for her," John whispered. "Maybe I didn't do a good job of explaining it before. Will you please let me try—"

"There's nothing else to say." She pulled her arm back further. "I've asked to see her a hundred times. I'm not asking anymore. Let me see her *right fucking now*!"

"Dude, read the room!" Rex shouted at John from his cover spot. "In case you didn't notice, you do *not* have the high ground here."

"Thank you, Mr. Ranganathan." John raised his stony eyes to the ceiling. "Mr. Mackie, please open Holding Cell Two."

"You sure, Boss?" Simon's wary voice fluttered down from the overhead speaker.

He met Cari's eyes. The pity in his face made her even more furious. "I'm sure. Open it."

The pause that followed ended in a heavy metal *chunk!* as the locks released. Her attention still on John, Cari slipped inside and hauled the door shut behind her.

"If you're not going to help her," she spat at him, "then I'll figure it out myself."

Chapter Nine

Grace flew off the stoop and dashed toward the back of the trailer. The sun had dipped behind the clouds huddling around the peaks of the western mountains, giving her at least some hope of cover. Good thing too—between her disheveled appearance and the knife, people might think she was trying to kill someone.

Well, some *human*, anyway.

A trail of oily sludge stained the back wall of the house. *That must be where he jumped down.* She scanned the ground and found more blood splashed over the packed dirt, splotchy lily pads that led to the woods. She squinted into the leafy murk, perplexed. Nelson lived in the park. He knew there was nothing beyond the trees except mountains and desert. Was he really trying to run for the wilderness? *Now?* She didn't know much about regeneration, but something as physiologically complex as a hand...that would probably take a while. And he was missing both. With no way to defend himself, he'd be easy pickings for a wolf or a bear. If something like that decided to make a meal of Nelson's corrupt, infectious flesh...what the hell kind of monster would they be dealing with then?

She didn't want to find out.

Holding the knife like a sword, she pushed forward, batting away the dense, slender branches as she followed the black streaks marring the underbrush. They got thinner the further she went, with more clean landscape between sightings. Still, she pressed on, scanning the woods for broken twigs, trodden leaves, and any other signs of disruption. She couldn't let Nelson infect anything else. Or worse, what if he somehow survived the rugged terrain and found a new town? He had fooled everyone in Halcyon for years. He could do it again, only this time there would be no one to stop him.

Leaves and branches lashed her cheeks as she broke into a jog. She had to find him. She had to end him. She had…

…lost the trail?

Her heart sank and her eyes searched the ground. How long had the splotches been missing? A few minutes? The last one she remembered had been barely more than a dribble, but maybe if she retraced her steps—

A thick appendage wrapped itself around her waist. Her hands flew up to try and defend herself, but it was too late—it pinned her arms to her side, jostling the knife from her grip as it did so.

"Fuck!" she gasped, her heart racing as a second sinewy thing hooked itself under her chin and squeezed her throat.

"I knew you'd come." The voice slithered into her left ear. "And just in time for group."

Her brain did a somersault. The prayer group. The army. He was doing the conversion tonight. That must have been why he'd turned Libby first, so he'd have some help. But he was a resourceful son of a bitch. No reason to think he couldn't do it alone.

She snapped her neck to the left, hoping to connect with his jaw, or maybe teeth.

He must have felt her muscles tense because he pulled back at the last moment, and she hit nothing but air.

"Now, now," he murmured, tightening his grip, "there's no need to be nervous. They're going to love you. Who doesn't love *snacks*?"

Grace opened her mouth to scream. With the speed of a cobra, his arm unfurled from her neck and coiled over her jaw instead. Cold, swollen flesh lodged itself between her lips, smothering her cries before they happened. Her tongue recoiled as the rancid stench of his skin invaded her nose. In the corner of her vision, three pill-sized white protuberances emerged from the tattered stump where he'd ripped his own hand off. Except for the translucent sliver of fingernail on the tip of each one, they reminded her of maggots trying to wriggle free of a corpse.

He yanked her backward. She raged against his hold the entire way to the tree line, snapping her neck and kicking her legs, all to no avail. She sucked air through her nose to stave off the panic as her thoughts turned desperate. Would A.J. come for her? He'd seemed pretty punch drunk when she'd left him. If not that, then…someone else?

But who would that be?

The forest around her began to glow, reflecting a light source she couldn't see. Her heartrate spiked. They were nearly at the park. Soon they'd be at his house, with his disciples. And Leann. Maybe even his two girls. If he made it back, they were *all* screwed.

She grazed her teeth over the flesh lodged in her mouth. It felt delicate and mushy, like an overripe strawberry. It wouldn't take much, and she knew he would feel the pain. Sure, it would mean horrible things for *her*. Infection, eventually death, but also escape. And the chance to save a hell of a lot more people.

She looked at the ground. The large black smears were barely discernible from the rest of the darkness. Another step, and they emerged from the woods.

Now or never.

She opened her jaw as wide as she could, aimed for the fleshiest part of his arm, and steeled her gag reflex as she prepared to bite.

An explosion rocketed past her head and knocked them both off their feet. Nelson's grip loosened as he fell to his knees. She threw herself out of his reach, her vision blurry and her skull ringing like the inside of a belfry.

"What the *hell?*" Nelson spluttered. His disoriented gaze wandered from the ground to the woods, and then to her. "You…"

She screamed as the second blast ripped through Nelson's chest. Darkness sprayed the tree trunks and saplings in front of him.

"Son of a bitch," he managed to slur around the glut of blood in his mouth before pitching forward into the dirt.

Grace stared at the perforated body, watching for movement, and waiting for the ringing in her head to subside. When it finally did, she lifted her eyes toward the trailer park, the smoking barrel, and the man standing behind it.

"You good?" Cooper asked, his voice tight as he lowered the shotgun to his side.

Her body trembled with joy and relief and anger. He was here. He was injured. He should have been here helping from the beginning. He should be at home recovering. He had saved her life. She wanted to hug him—and wring his neck a little. But most of all she wanted to tell him that she was *never* going to agree to do anything like this again unless he was along for the ride.

"Grace?"

She wiped an inky smear from her cheek and pointed at his gun. "I don't care what A.J. says. Best. Weapon. Ever."

"What's all that racket?" In the trailer next to Cari's, a shadowy outline of a man appeared in the window, hunkered down as if trying to see through the darkness.

"Sorry 'bout that!" Cooper shouted back. "Damn raccoons were getting into the trash cans again. Nothing to worry about."

The figure shook his head, mumbled something about "black eyed demons," and disappeared from view.

"Nice cover." Grace hauled herself to her feet and grabbed Nelson by his partially regenerated stumps. "Let's get this bastard inside before he wakes up."

"He took an AA-12 blast through the chest. He's *done*." Cooper narrowed his eyes at her. "Isn't he?"

"Not even a little."

"Ah." He smirked and shook his head. "You see? This is what happens when I take a day off."

***

A.J. greeted them at the door. They scuttled into the trailer with Nelson's undead weight sagging between them like a sack of potatoes.

"There." A.J. pointed at the bed. Additional lengths of rope lay across the mattress, along with a pile of wrinkled pants and shirts.

"I see you've been busy," Grace grunted as she hefted Nelson on the bouncy surface.

A.J. picked up one of the thick twine cords, his face stony. "We're not taking any chances this time."

He wrapped Nelson from neck to ankles in the clothing until he looked like the world's most disgusting burrito before strapping him down. He had nearly finished when

Nelson flopped his head to the side and slid one eyelid open.

"Where am I?" he moaned.

"Purgatory, you dick," Grace shot back. "Now shut your mouth and let the grownups talk."

A.J. gagged him with the dishrag and the three of them retreated to the main room.

"Now," Cooper said softly, keeping one eye on Nelson through the cracked door, "can someone please tell me what the fuck is going on?"

"If we're going to go through the whole thing, we might as well tell everyone." Grace retrieved her phone and dialed John's cell.

"Speaking of explaining things," she asked Cooper over the speakerphone ringing, "what the hell are you doing here anyway?"

"Right!" He tore his vigilant gaze away from Nelson. "I almost forgot. Lola called me. She's been trying to reach you all day. Which is funny, since I don't seem to recall you two ever even meeting each other."

"Oh?" she asked, trying to sound casual. Not easy, seeing as her tongue had gone as dry as a dune. "Yeah, we've met. But I haven't seen her in a few years now. Did she tell you what she wanted to talk to me about?"

"No, and I didn't think it was my place to ask. But it sounded important, and she's not the type of person who blows things out of proportion."

Grace nodded as sepia-colored snapshot of her last interaction with Lola flickered at the edge of her consciousness, fuzzy at first, but rapidly becoming clearer. She gripped the phone tighter and snuffed out the memory before it could fully manifest. That was not something she needed to relive. Especially not today.

Cooper's gaze fell across her, heavy with suspicion. She shrugged, as if her dread was nothing more than absent-minded reminiscing. "I'll call her after we finish up with...um, has it been ringing this whole time?"

They stared at the small brick of blue light in her hand. John never let it ring this long. A sinkhole formed in her gut.

Something wasn't right.

"Do we have anyone else's number?"

"Yeah." Cooper pulled out his cell and tapped the screen. "I think I've got Rex in here somewhere."

This time, it only rang twice.

"Whoever this is, I can't talk right now."

"Don't hang up!" Grace shouted. Her nerves, soothed by the fact he had answered, tensed back up as soon as she tagged the panic in his voice. "It's us. Me and A.J. and Cooper. What's going on?"

"I...I don't really know what's happening, but we've got a situation here. With Cari. And her mom."

Muffled shouting muddled the background of the call. She couldn't decipher the words, but she knew the voice as John's.

And he sounded terrified.

"Put us on speaker," Grace instructed, making her voice as stern and solid as she could. "If you can't explain it, then at least we can hear for ourselves."

Chapter Ten

Libby lay on the bed, as fragile and immobile as a bundle of twigs. Despite her eagerness and the adrenaline coursing down her limbs, Cari forced herself to move slowly, the way she had when her mother was in the middle of a drunken tear. She approached with soft, deliberate steps, careful not to jump or jerk. The closer she got to her mother's bedside, the more her stomach revved with uncertainty. She meant it when she said she wanted to help. But what the hell did help even *look* like?

A soft moan slipped from between Libby's pale lips, halting Cari next to her mother's elbow. She examined the vicious IV sinking into the waxy, yellowing flesh.

What can I do? What...

Her eyes slid from the bed to the ax in her hand.

It had worked for Rex. Maybe it would work here.

She adjusted her grip to hold the ax by the back of its metal head and brought the corner of the blade down to the inside of her mother's fish-belly forearm, right below the tape holding the needle in place.

"It's not going to work."

She flicked her eyes toward the bars. John stood on the other side, hands in his pockets, while Rex lurked behind him. Her grip tightened. She wasn't stupid. He could come in if he wanted to. One word to Simon and that cage door would slide right open. Instead, he stood there, watching her, his face all scrunched up in pity.

Useless.

Scowling in defiance, she turned back to her mother and lowered the blade. A trickle of black-and-green liquid bloomed from the cut. Libby whimpered, her closed eyes screwing up in pain. Cari pressed harder, drawing the blade further down her arm. Once the cut reached six inches in length she withdrew, watching the wound bleed. And bleed.

And bleed.

Her eyeballs throbbed as her heart spun up into a panic. Libby's lips and eyelids had turned the color of frosted blueberries, and still the blood remained the color of nightshade.

She shook her head in refusal. It had to turn. It had to. Maybe if she did the other arm...

Stealth no longer a priority, she tore around the head of the bed and pressed her blade to Libby's right arm.

"Cari, please. You don't want to do this."

She paused, ax hovering an inch from flesh. The heat of her anger surged through her fingers, compelling her to let the blade bite.

"Why not?" she spat back at John.

"Because it will kill her," he said. "The infection burrows too far below the surface. You could bleed her dry and it wouldn't help."

"Did you try it?" Her voice shook almost as much as her hand.

"We've tried it before. Many times, and every one of them—"

"I'm not talking about other people!" Cari shrieked, her voice nearly breaking. "Did you try it on *her?*"

He sighed. "No, I did not try it on her."

"Then how do you know it won't work?"

"Because…" He wiped a hand over his face as if that could start things fresh. "If you let her live, we might be able to cure her eventually. If you kill her now, then that's it. You'll lose her forever."

She shook her head. The blade in her hand zigged, nicking the soft skin. A single drop of blood appeared, as black as a starless night. "I've already lost her."

"She's right, John."

Cari's body stiffened as a female voice, slightly Southern and honey-sweet, wandered into range.

John shot a furious glare in the direction of Cell One. "*You* stay out of this."

"Who is that?" Cari shouted. "Is that Holly?"

"Technically?" Rex leaned back to see around the dividing wall. "Doesn't sound like any voice I've ever heard her use though."

"It's Mary."

She jumped at Cooper's buzzy, disembodied words. *Where the hell was that coming from?* Then she spotted the phone in Rex's hand. "Who?" she demanded.

"Mary Fludd. The Reverend's wife."

"That's right," the voice called Mary confirmed, its warmth and kindness making Cari shiver. "And I swear, I come as a friend. I'm sorry, little one, but your mother has one foot across the threshold and the other isn't far behind. You can't stop her from going, and neither can the good doctor over there. But there is a way you can see her one last time. I can tell you how."

"Stay out of this!" John shouted. He whipped his eyes toward Cari. "Don't listen to her. You know she can't be trusted."

"She needs something familiar," Mary continued "Something that appeals to her senses. Her favorite perfume, a special song. Something that reminds her what it was like to be human. *Her* version of human."

Cari's head ached, and every muscle in her body screamed with exhaustion. The settlers were monsters. How could she trust this one?

Because if I don't, then I might as well slit my mother's throat right now.

She opened her eyes and scanned the cell. Not much there. The bed, her mom, herself, and a small table crammed with pills, tonics, and sterilization tools.

Including rubbing alcohol.

The ax clattered on the concrete floor as Cari grabbed the bottle and tore off the cap. The astringent scent stung her nose. Holding her breath, she poured the contents into her mother's open mouth. Libby's eyes flew open as she wretched against the onslaught.

"No!" John shouted. "Mr. Mackie, the door!"

The metal gears groaned alive behind her. Cari ignored them. Instead, she grasped her mother by the forehead and jaw and clamped her mouth shut. Libby bucked and squealed, shooting some of the burning liquid out of her closed lips and nostrils. Still, Cari held on, and didn't let go until John grabbed her shoulders and yanked her away.

"Have you lost your mind?" He spun her around to face him. "You know those things have their own agenda. You might have created some kind of super solider, or a spawning point for an army of creatures, or—"

"Cari?"

Her skin turned to ice. She knew that voice, yet it had become so much softer and more delicate it seemed like something out of dream.

Or a memory.

Struggling against John's grip, she craned her neck to look behind her. From the bed blinked the blue eyes of

Libby Hembert, confused but as clear as sapphires. "Cari…what…what's going on?"

Her legs became liquid, and she went limp. Her jaw flapped numbly as she struggled to form words. At last, she managed to get out the one that mattered. "Mom?"

John's fingers dug into her arms. "I don't believe it," he sighed, but the bewilderment in his voice suggested otherwise. "It must be a…trick, or something."

Cari wriggled out of his hands and dove for her mother's bedside.

"Mom, I'm here," she said, entwining her mother's slick, black-stained fingers with her own. John made no move to stop her, but she could feel his presence hovering at her side.

"Cari…" Libby tried to sit up, but the restraints wouldn't allow her to do much more than lift her head. "Why can't I move?"

"Because…you're sick, Mom. Really sick. It's for all of our protection. Yours and ours."

"Sick? But I don't…" Her eyes widened with horrified clarity. "It was Nelson, wasn't it?"

Cari bit her lip and nodded.

"Jesus." Libby fell back and squeezed her eyes shut. "I remember. His wife and girls had gone to visit her mother, and he came over, like he always did when they went to Grandma's. But this time he was acting funny. He made me drink. Even more than normal, until I couldn't stand, and then his face went all rubbery and…and his eyes…" She whimpered and peered up at her daughter. "I don't have much time, do I?"

The words crashed into Cari like a wrecking ball. She tried to answer, but the words stuck in her throat. All she could do was bow her head and clasp her mother's hand even tighter.

Libby exhaled sharply. The tears in her eyes broke free, streaming down her temples to pool next to her ears. "I'm sorry, sweetie. I'm so sorry for bringing that man into our lives, and for all my mistakes and for...all of it."

Cari nodded as guilt and anger waged burning war inside her heart. She had so many things she wanted to say (or cry, or scream), but the pain had stolen the moisture from her tongue. If she tried to speak, she feared she would crumble to dust.

Libby cocked her head toward John. "Who are you?"

He cleared his throat. "Doctor John Virgil, ma'am. I'm her...supervisor."

"Good." Libby sat up as high as she could. "You look after my girl, you understand? You do what I can't...what I never could."

John swallowed hard. "I will, ma'am. I promise."

Libby nodded, satisfied. Her head fell back once more, and she returned her attention to Cari. Despite the restraints and Cari's own iron grip, she could feel her mother's fingers tighten around her own. "My little girl. Everything is going to be okay now. You're so much stronger and smarter than I ever was, even at my best. You're going to do great things, I know it. Wherever I go next, I hope I'll be able to see you do them."

Her eyes fluttered, and she groaned in pain. "But I don't think that's a wish I will be getting."

Her grip turned to jelly.

Cari's heart pounded. "Mom?"

Libby didn't answer. She shook her mother's hand. It was as limp and cold as raw chicken. "No," she spluttered. "Not yet. Mom! Can you hear me?"

Libby's chest rose. Cari's breath caught in her throat as her mother let go with one long, rasping breath.

"I love you."

In the sixteen years she'd spent on the planet, Cari couldn't remember her mother ever saying that to her before. Now she would never, ever forget it.

"I love you too."

She released her mom and sank to her knees. Sobs thrashed her like a tree in a storm. Her breath grew shallow as she tried to contain the sloshing and quaking in her stomach. For as long as she could recall, she had always *felt* like she was alone in the world. But that was nothing compared to the full-body assault of *knowing* she was.

I'm an orphan. She wrapped her arms around herself and pressed her forehead to the cold, rough concrete as brown shadows danced in front of her tunneling vision. *What's going to happen to me now?*

The last thing she remembered was the warm strength of John's arms, gathering her up and lifting her into…

Nothing.

Chapter Eleven

Cooper hit the Mute button and cleared his throat. "Well, that was..."

"Difficult," Grace supplied, swiping at the tears that had collected on her eyelashes. On the other side of the trailer A.J. stood facing away from them, one hand braced on his hip and the other raised to his down-turned face. If he heard them speaking, he didn't acknowledge it.

"Yes." Cooper nodded. "It was difficult. But..."

"But we still have work to do." Grace pivoted toward the bed. A man, bound and half-mutilated, but improving by the second. A woman, dead, or close enough. Add them together and what did they have?

One giant fucking mess.

She pressed a hand to her forehead. "How the hell are we ever going to clean up this one?"

"Good question," Cooper mused, rubbing his chin. "We can't keep him alive, that's for sure. He's too dangerous, especially with the regeneration."

"Right, but we can't make him disappear either. He was only gone a few hours before his wife came looking for him. She didn't strike me as the type who would let a man run out on her without having something to say about it. And as far as leaving his body in a ditch..." She gestured widely at his half-formed hands and the soaked, caved-in dark spot on his chest. "One look at him and even the Dudley Do-Nothings at Halcyon PD will know something's up. Not to mention that, if we don't kill him perfectly, he'll get right back up again."

He frowned. "And by 'perfectly,' you mean…?"

She paused, searching for the best words to describe what she was picturing before answering.

"Bits and pieces. No more, no less."

"That's what I thought." He looked from Nelson to the stove, then back again, his eyes growing both resolute and apprehensive.

"I may have an idea," he said at last. "One that should account for everything."

Grace arched her eyebrow. "Sounds great. What's the catch?"

He tilted his head sheepishly and told them.

"Jesus," A.J. muttered, wiping his face with both hands.

She sneered at Cooper in disgust. "I take it back. It's not great. It's the worst idea I've ever heard."

"I'm not arguing that," Cooper said, his eyes on the floor. "But unless either of you have a better one…"

She didn't, and they both knew it. Even so, she pretended to consider it for a full minute out of spite.

"Fine," she relented.

"Okay." Cooper pressed Unmute. "Rex, you still there?"

A startled rustle followed. *"10-4, buddy. I'm still here."*

"Good. Can you take us off speaker?"

"Sure." He disappeared for a second before returning, this time louder and much less tinny. *"Go ahead."*

"I think we've got a plan to deal with Nelson. You'll need to meet us at the trailer."

"Really?" Rex sounded stunned. *"You're tapping me in. Me?"*

Cooper smiled. "Yes, man. I'm tapping you in."

"Well, it's about time! I'll grab my stuff and be right there."

"Hold on a second, Dynamite. There's one more thing." He took a deep breath. "Can you put Cari on the phone? We need to, ah, run something by her first."

"Um, I don't know if that's such a good idea. She's, you know...pretty out of it."

"I know, but this is really important. We can't do anything without her sign-off."

Silence took the line as Rex thought it over. *"Okay. But if anything you say freaks her out, I'm cutting you off.* Capisce?"

"Capisce."

Grace pinned her gaze to the phone. She didn't want Cooper to see how Rex's loyalty made her smile. More silence followed, then some incoherent mumbling, and finally Cari's voice.

"Yeah...?"

Grace's heart broke at how fragile the word sounded.

"Hey, Cari." Cooper's cheeks had turned red with the shame of what he was about to say, but he pressed forward. "Listen, I know you've been through a lot today, and I don't even want to bring this up, but...we've still got to take care of Nelson. There's a way to do it, but..."

Heavy thumps drew Grace's attention as A.J. retreated away from the conversation toward the bathroom, unable to listen. She couldn't say she blamed him.

"...awful thing to ask, but it's our only option." Cooper inhaled deeply. His cheeks had turned the color of tomato sauce, as if he hadn't taken a breath since he started talking.

The pause on the other end of the line was so full and complete Grace briefly wondered if she had hung up on them, or possibly passed out from the shock.

"You're sure *it's the only way?"* Cari ventured.

Cooper smiled sadly. "It's the only way to guarantee this all ends tonight."

"And Nelson will be dead?"

"Yes, honey," Grace said, her voice as sweet and smooth as frosting. "He's gonna be real dead."

Another long silence. When her voice returned, it sounded about as fragile as braided steel.

"Do it."

Grace and Cooper prepped the bedroom as best they could while A.J. ran to town for extra supplies. The three of them had almost finished situating things by the time John pulled up in Libby's half-wrecked Prelude. The muscles between Grace's shoulders loosened as she watched Rex climb out of the passenger's side, messenger bag slung across his shoulder. She never would have thought the sight of that goofy kid would come as such a massive relief.

Then he tipped the seat forward, and Cari crawled out from the backseat.

"Goddammit," Grace snarled as her muscles seized up again. She stormed out the door and grabbed Rex by the sleeve.

"What were you thinking?" she demanded once she'd dragged him out of Cari's earshot. "Hasn't she been through enough without seeing this?"

The defensive fury in his glare made her delay further ranting.

"She'll never be able to come back here," he said, throwing her hand off him. "I *thought* she deserved the chance to grab some stuff. Little things, you know, like her phone charger, and toothbrush, and *everything she owns in the world."*

Grace took a step back, stunned and ashamed. She'd been so focused on the plan it had completely slipped her mind that, at least for the next few minutes, this was someone's home.

"You're right. I'm sorry. Just…give me one second."

She ducked her head inside to make sure the bedroom door was closed, then motioned for Rex. He let Cari lead the way up the stoop and into the trailer.

"Hey," Grace said, the syllable ragged and uneasy at the sight of Cari's lopsided ponytail, folded-over slouch and dull, sunken eyes. "I'm, uh…"

She wasn't sure how to finish the sentence. Regardless, Cari shrugged and bobbled her head in a vague gesture of acceptance.

Rex slipped a hand over her shoulder and squeezed. "Which way?"

She tipped her head to her left and trudged down the narrow center hallway toward the small door in the back. When she flipped on the light, Grace spotted the outline of a twin bed jammed in a crawlspace so tight that Rex could barely close the door. It didn't look big enough to house a hamster, let alone a teenager.

With the kids otherwise occupied, she tapped her knuckles on the bedroom door. It opened a crack, revealing a single blue eye.

"What's the password?"

"Move, Cooper."

"Wow, first try." The door swung open the rest of the way.

She slipped inside and closed it behind her. "Where are we?"

A.J. wrapped a hand over the wrought iron headboard and gestured toward the room with the other. "Last looks."

She took the visual tour. The semi-conscious Nelson was once again hooked to the headboard with the handcuffs, the restraints reinforced with six sets of snagged pantyhose. Thick ropes looped over the mattress, strapping him down so tight that the skin below the rough twine had already started to chafe. The sundry items from the dresser and vanity had been knocked onto the floor to make room for the dozens of candles A.J. had brought from town, supplementing the four or five half-melted ones already oozing across the cheap furniture. The candles on the right side of the room glowed like two dozen tiny suns. The ones on the left were dark.

"Not bad," she said.

A soft rap at the door made her turn. "We're done." Rex's strained voice struggled to make its way into the room. "I'm taking her outside. Let me know when you want me to...uh, when you're ready."

"Thanks," she mumbled back. It pained her to hear him sound so sad. "A.J., why don't you drive her back to Edensgate. She doesn't need to be here for the rest."

A.J. tipped a solemn finger to his forehead.

"I'll walk you out," Cooper said. "John's probably gonna need some help." He handed the box of matches to Grace. "Will you be okay by yourself?"

She took the box and nodded. Only when the door had closed behind the two men, and she stood alone in the room did she allow her shoulders to sag. She hated this day. She hated everything that had happened so far and everything that was about to happen. She hated this plan, and that Cooper had been the one to think of it, and that she was too stupid to come up with a better one.

But even if she could stop this train now, she wouldn't. It was the best solution. And she hated *that* too.

She struck a match and kissed the flame to the first unlit wick. Some days, fighting an inter-dimensional war on evil could be a real bitch.

A low, insidious rumble brought a tremor to her hand. She glanced over her shoulder at the bed. Nelson gazed up at her, eyes shining, and lips stretched in a tight smile. When he caught her looking, the rumble became a wet chuckle.

"Laugh while you can," she spat. "Won't be long now."

"Killing me won't change anything," he said around his laughter. "The Prophet approaches. He will open the Primal Seal with or without me."

"Without. If it makes no difference, let's go with that."

He dropped his head back onto the mattress, his deep laughter steady and thoroughly unsettling. She turned back to the wax army on the dresser.

"Aren't you going to ask me what's so funny?"

"Nope." Her hand swept from wick to wick, eager to get this over with.

"It's funny because, deep down, you know what I'm saying is the truth. You see what's really going on in this town. The abdication of responsibility. The selfishness, and the cruelty. You can rip yourself to pieces fighting the enemy at the gate, but the castle is already rotting from inside. And there's not a thing you can do about that."

She wanted to punch him in his cavernous chest wound. Instead, she lit another match. "You're so right. Life is hard and people suck. I should stand aside and let the hordes of hell take over."

"You can call it that if you want to. Or you can call it what it is: a new start. An era without the cowardice, hatred and greed that has been humanity's legacy on this planet."

The droplet of flame crept down the matchstick, coming dangerously close to her fingertips. She shook it out, the vigorous movement a perfect disguise for her shaking limbs, and turned around to look at him one last time.

"I don't believe you."

"You don't have to." He closed his eyes. His smile no longer looked menacing, but serene. "You'll see it for yourself. Someday."

She shivered. He didn't sound like a possessed maniac anymore. Instead, he sounded sad, and exhausted, like a reasonable human being that had seen too much.

Who couldn't relate to that?

The thought squirmed in her brain like a snake, its fangs exposed and ready to bite. She shook her head, trying to smash it against the inside of her skull. But more words wormed their way in.

You can't protect her. Her flesh is marked for us. She is ours.

Grace froze. *What the fuck does that mean?*

She ventured one last look at Nelson. His eyes rolled in their sockets as he bared his slick, drool-covered teeth. He craned his face toward the ceiling and crowed with laughter, savoring her distress. He was dying, but he was winning. She couldn't let that happen. She searched the room, the bed, the dresser…and there, in a shadowy corner near where A.J.'s arsenal had been, she spotted something interesting. Something A.J. must have missed when he was packing up.

She grabbed the syringe filled with venom and plunged it into Nelson's neck. Laughter morphed into a scream, which she stifled with the first thing she could find—a pair of lime green panties.

"I don't know what's gonna happen down the road," she whispered to his lolling eyeballs. "No one does. But here's something I do know: you're going to get what you deserve, and you're going to feel it. Every. Fucking. Second."

She ripped the needle from his flesh. The last thing she saw before turning her back on him was the geyser of black blood splashing across the mattress.

"Enjoy oblivion, asshole."

She slammed out the door. The night had gone frigid, and she paused to gulp down a couple mouthfuls of frosty air before descending from the stoop.

"All set?" Cooper asked as he and John approached the trailer, carrying a semi-conscious Libby suspended between them. A thick patch of medical tape covered her mouth, but it seemed unnecessary. In her current state, she looked about as threatening as a bag of cooked spaghetti. Behind them, Rex sulked next to the open trunk, fiddling with the strap of his bag, his eyes trained on a rock near his feet. She didn't see Cari or A.J. anywhere.

"Yeah," Grace murmured, her attention drawn to Libby. She wanted to say something to the woman. Apologize, or something, even though she didn't know what for. But Libby's eyes never opened more than halfway. "You've sedated her."

"Heavily," John said as he led the way up the steps. "She won't feel a thing."

Grace watched with a heavy heart as they took her into the house. Sedation was the right call.

Anything she would have said would've probably sounded dumb anyway.

She shuffled over to Rex. "You ready?"

"Yeah," he said sulkily. "I still don't like it though."

"Can't say I blame you. She's your girlfriend's mom, after all."

Rex threw up his hands. "For the last time, Cari is *not* my girlfriend. *GOD!*"

"First of all, *shhh!*" Grace scanned the area, making sure the mostly abandoned section of the park had stayed that way before continuing. "And second of all…are you absolutely sure about that?"

"Yes!" Rex shouted, then ducked at the sound of his own voice. "She's not…we're…yes, I'm sure."

"Fine. Whatever you say." She leaned back against the trunk next to him.

"Why, did she say something about me?"

Grace shook her head. Thank God she didn't have to be sixteen ever again.

Moments later, John and Cooper emerged from the house, Libby no longer draped between them.

"That's your cue, kid." Grace nudged Rex with her elbow. He sighed and peeled himself off the car.

Cooper stood guard next to the door when Rex went inside, weapon at the ready. Five minutes later Rex emerged, tucking something back under the flap of his messenger bag.

"Done."

"And it'll look like an accident?" Grace confirmed.

"Yeah. Enough to fool the geniuses at Halcyon PD, anyway." He smiled reluctantly. "It's actually pretty cool, how it works. All you gotta do is—"

"Let's hold off on the incendiary lessons, shall we?" Grace said. "You and Cooper can head back. John and I will stand watch to make sure nothing goes wrong."

"Or escapes," John supplemented.

"That too," she said. "Besides, we have a lot of catching up to do."

Grace crouched behind a thick tree trunk, waiting in silence as John processed the rundown she'd given him regarding the day's events. Across the clearing, the windows of the trailer pulsed with the soft orange glow of the candlelight. She could see no other movement, hear no other sound. Under the not-quite-full moon, the night was crystalline and deathly quiet.

"This isn't right."

She jumped at the sound of her own voice, thunderous in the pristine stillness. She hadn't expected to say it out loud so abruptly, though it had been on her mind ever since Cooper had come up with this horror show. Tying up Nelson's loose end would make sure no spotlights came their way. It wasn't perfect, but it *was* necessary. Still, it didn't change the fact that, in the course of twenty-four hours, a sixteen-year-old girl had lost everything. "We need to do something for her, John. Make sure she's taken care of."

Sticks and dried leaves crackled behind the tree to her left.

"She will be," John whispered, his voice a down quilt in the cold. "I promised her mother I'd look out for her, and that's exactly what I'm going to do."

Her eyes slipped closed in relief. Across the park, the light inside the trailer glowed even brighter.

"So, Nelson is an acolyte of the Reverend?" John mused.

"Seems that way," she affirmed.

"Did he infect anyone else?"

"I don't think so. He was planning to at his prayer circle tonight, but obviously he never made it."

"Thank God for that." John paused. "Still, it might be prudent to check on everyone in the group. And Nelson's family too."

"Copy that." She thought back to Simon's comment about the group's purported anonymity. "Might take a little time to track them all down, you know."

"That's fine, as long as it gets done." He drew in a long breath. She winced as the atmosphere between them tensed. *Here it comes…*

"Will there be more like him?"

And there it was. The question she'd been dreading all day.

"It's hard to know," she said as she fidgeted with her cell phone. "If this sort of conversion is limited to the Reverend's direct descendants, then probably not. Otherwise…"

She lowered her head, digging at a piece of bark with the tip of her fingernail to try to distract herself from what she had to say. "John, he walked around with a monster in his head for the better part of a decade. That's some messed up, *Manchurian Candidate*-type shit. If there's no genetic limitation, then all bets are off. Literally *anyone* in Halcyon could be infected, and we'd never know. And…if we assume there's even a *chance* that Nelson's little nursery rhyme is true…at least one more person must be."

"Indeed." John tipped his head toward her, his lens reflecting the moonlight. "Which means Edensgate is not our only responsibility anymore."

The statement dropped sixty pounds of lead square on her shoulders. Securing a building was one thing. How were the handful of them supposed to police a whole *town*? She opened her mouth to ask when she heard a hiss, then a pop. She turned back to the park as the trailer exploded in a firework of metal and glass. A wave of thunder slammed into her chest, stealing her breath and almost knocking her over.

"Christ," John muttered as the trailer shell dropped to the ground with a bang and settled into a steady, rapid blaze.

"Amen." Her shell-shocked fingers moved like uncooperative hot dogs over her phone, but at last she managed to press the right button.

"911, what is your emergency?" She could barely hear around the ringing in her ears.

"Oh my God!" she gasped. "A trailer just exploded at Four Winds! You need to get the fire department out here right now! Hurry!"

"Certainly ma'am. And can I please get your—?"

Grace hung up. "That ought to do it. We'll wait until they get here, see if anything tries to rip their faces off, then head out."

"Agreed."

They watched in silence for a moment as the tongues of fire stretched long, their light lapping at the navy sky.

"You know," Grace said, "if we are going to start patrolling the whole town, we're going to need more help."

John's chuckle was so dry it nearly disintegrated in midair.

"Don't we always?"

Chapter Twelve

Cari lost track of A.J. the moment he settled her on the couch. She sort of remembered him asking if she needed anything, and maybe something about going out on rotation. He hadn't seemed uncomfortable, or like he wanted to get away from her. Instead, he seemed to understand that hovering over her like a fussy mama pigeon would not be useful for either of them.

Finally, *someone* got it.

On the coffee table in front of her sat a cardboard box, its flaps origami-folded to keep them shut. The trip to the trailer floated through her mind in a barely retained fog of hastily grabbed items. Framed photos. Jewelry and makeup. A few treasured pieces of clothing. It had been one of those rare times when having almost no personal stuff had worked to her advantage. Even so, she didn't want to look inside the box. She didn't want to know what she'd left behind. What she would never see again.

Something moved behind her, slow and deliberate. Then came the voices. Cooper's first, followed by John's, both of them hushed and tenuous, as if the walls might collapse if they spoke any louder than a stage whisper. She registered a few scraps ("a week or two," "best option," "better solution later,"), and she definitely heard her name at least once. Everything else was a fat hum. Her brain had OD'd on emotion and information. She listened until the voice-noise faded, and silence reigned again. The loneliness pressed into her, choking and cutting at the same time, like a skeleton's hand around her heart.

"Cari?"

Startled, she looked up. Rex leaned over the back of the couch, peering down at her with weary, timid eyes.

"Hey," she said, the muscles of her face twitching into something that might have been a smile.

"Hey." He vaulted over the back of the couch and sat down next to her, rubbing his hands over his knees. "I, uh...huh. I guess I don't know what to say."

"That's okay," she sighed. "I don't feel much like talking anyway."

"Is there anything I *can* do to help?"

"Not really. Though..." She smiled weakly. "If it's not too much trouble...could you go back to playing your video game? I just want to watch."

"Really?" He stared at the controller on the table as if it were a week-old burrito. "I mean, don't you want to...cry, or yell, or...or maybe drink some tea? I'm not great at coffee, as you know, but I'm pretty good at tea."

At first, she could only stare at him. Then she exploded, all the anger and sorrow ripping through her numbness like a knife through paper. "Are you *kidding* me? You've done nothing all day except try to make everything seem normal, but as soon as I ask you to do exactly that, *now* you want to talk about feelings? Are you *serious*? Are...you...fucking...serious..."

She stopped yelling. Not because she wasn't still angry, but because she couldn't breathe. Stupid Rex, she thought, clenching her fists together as she gasped for air. Stupid Nelson. Stupid fucking world.

"It's okay." Rex slid his arm over her shoulders. "It's…going to be okay."

"No…it's…not," she wheezed, tears streaming down her cheeks. "My mom is *dead*. My house is *destroyed*. Everything is so completely *fucked up*." She kicked the cardboard box. "All I have left is this stupid pile of crap."

"And me." He wrapped his free hand around one of hers. "I'm still here."

She turned to face him. He tried to meet her gaze but seemed to be struggling to lift his eyes any higher than her chin. She frowned as she watched his lips twitch like a nervous rabbit. She'd seen him act strange plenty of times, but never like this. Never like—

Her heart started to race.

"Rex…you're not going to try to kiss me right now, are you?"

"What? No!" He recoiled as if her skin had sprouted thorns. "No, of course not. I would never do that. That would be so—"

She leaned forward and pressed her mouth to his.

He stiffened, probably as surprised as she was by her boldness. But the boy did protest too much, and this seemed like the quickest way to stop his flustering.

It worked. After a moment, she felt him relax. His lips parted, enveloping hers as he kissed her back. A spark of excitement glimmered through her. Now it was her turn to freeze.

She hadn't expected that.

Breaking the kiss, she leaned back a little so she could look at him. His eyes were still closed, and a goofy smile hung on his face.

"—so gross," he murmured dreamily.

She giggled. "Gross?"

"Yeah, super…disgusting…"

He reached for her again.

"Hey!"

The voice sent them shooting away from each other like opposing magnets. Heat flooded Cari's face as she turned to look over the back of the couch. Grace stood in the entryway outside the lockers, hands on her hips, and a mischievous grin lighting up her face. Next to her stood a tall man in the standard Virgil Security & Maintenance coveralls. He seemed slightly younger than Grace, with short black hair, dark brown skin, and twinkling brown eyes.

Or rather, his right eye twinkled. His left was obscured by a black leather patch.

"Sorry to bother you two," Grace said, her voice on the edge of a giggle. "We were just passing through this *very public area*, and I figured I'd take the opportunity to introduce you to Charlie. Charlie, this is Cari and Rex."

"Hi," Cari mumbled, waving her hand to draw attention from her presumably crimson cheeks. "Sorry, I…sorry. It's been a…rough night."

"Not a problem." He pointed to his left eye. "As you can see, I've had plenty of those myself. It's nice to meet you both."

"You too." A mosquito bite of a question itched the back of her mind. She frowned until it clicked. "Oh, Charlie! You're the guy that fell into the fountain last week, right?"

"Oh, yeah!" Rex's face lit up in recognition, and he pointed at Charlie with both index fingers. "Fountain Guy!"

Charlie turned to Grace. "Is that going to be a thing now?"

Grace shrugged. "We could call you Patchy instead. Up to you. Now come on, John wants to look you over before he signs off on your return." She arched an eyebrow at Rex as they headed for the med station. "Enjoy your totally platonic conversation."

Rex scowled after her, his face beet red.

"What was that all about?" Cari asked.

"Oh, you know." He flopped a dismissive hand toward the med station. "She keeps saying that we're...that you're my...anyway, don't worry about it. She's...crazy."

"Oh." Her heart crashed through the floor. "You're right. It would be crazy."

"No! I didn't mean it like that. I...uh..."

He trailed off. She couldn't believe it. The one time she needed him to say something, and he was at a loss for words. They both stared at the cushion's worth of space between them. She could feel the moment slipping away; it surprised her how desperate she was to cling to it. She'd never thought of Rex that way before. Okay, maybe not *never*. But never seriously. Never like...this. She cast around for something to say, something that would close the chasm that Grace's interruption had caused. Something...

"So, are you going to play your game?"

...besides that.

Rex smiled at his feet. "Sure, Mayhem. Whatever you want."

She wanted to believe she heard regret in his voice. Or was it relief? And how was she supposed to know the difference?

Ultimately, it didn't matter. Before she could dream up the perfect way to salvage the moment, Rex picked up the controller, turned away from her, and started the game.

Sunshine peeped above the trees, warming Cari's face through the truck's passenger window. To say it had been a slow night would have been an understatement bordering on felonious. At one point, when Grace had dropped by to check on them, she had mentioned that the night after a long moon was often slow. Cari kept her ears up anyway, waiting—and then wishing— for something to happen. But nothing did. She spent the whole night on the couch, watching Rex run through hundreds of 8-bit sparring matches and trying to pretend the silence between them was natural. By the time the doors opened in the morning, the elephant in the room had grown so massive they'd retreated to opposite sides of the couch to make room for it. He didn't even look up when Cooper asked to speak to her in private. He just turned his head slightly and saluted her knees.

Even now, miles away, the remembered awkwardness made her want to bury her head in her hands. As if enough of her life hadn't been literally blown to pieces today. Why did she have to go and kiss her best friend on top of it?

She pressed a hand to her forehead and tried not to think about it, concentrating on the scenery out her window instead. The town flowed by in a monotonous, gray-brown blur. On any other day she would be on the bus right now, rumbling down the country highway to the T-intersection outside the city limits, then onto the dirt road heading out to Four Winds. Instead, she was in this truck, her single box of possessions at her feet, turning right onto an asphalt one-way street that ran parallel to Halcyon's main drag. The incline sharpened as the road approached the base of a wide mountain. Black dots pitted the looming rockface, remains of the original 19th century mineral claims that had been abandoned after they sunk the main shaft on the opposite side of the peak. She'd never liked those holes, even before the history lessons Grace had given them illuminating the mine's nefarious origins. The idea of sleeping so close to them made her skin crawl. But she wasn't in any position to complain.

The truck turned onto a quiet cul-de-sac, then eased into the third driveway on the left in front of a two-story townhouse.

"Here we are," Cooper said, killing the engine. "It's not much, but we'll do our best to make you feel at home until we can find you a more permanent situation."

Cari nodded. The house was old and narrow, with barely a foot of dirt separating it from its neighbors. Still, the front porch didn't sag, and the mocha paint job looked relatively fresh. Compared to the rest of the houses on the block, it was one of the nicest.

"It's lovely," she said.

"Thanks." He unbuckled his seatbelt, then paused. "There is one more thing. My wife doesn't know about what we do, or what specifically killed your mom. So, while you live here, you *will* have to do...you know, normal kid stuff, once you're ready. School, and homework...and cut back on work hours for a while. Okay?"

She sucked in her breath. The thought of going back to school excited her. The thought of homework excited her much less. And the thought of taking a hiatus from Edensgate...

"I get it," she said softly. "Not sure I like it, but you're right. It's probably for the best."

Cooper nodded stiffly. He grabbed the box at her feet and exited the cab.

She followed him up the creaky porch steps to the front door. As she entered the dimly lit foyer, a dark-haired woman in sweats and a red thermal top swooped out of the kitchen doorway with her arms out.

"Hi! You must be Cari."

Cari skidded to a halt with a started cry, her hands shooting up to block the advance.

"Ally," Cooper whispered, a gentle warning in his tone.

The woman stopped. A look of horrified embarrassment turned her face as red as her shirt, and she yanked her arms back. "Oh my God, I'm so sorry. I didn't mean to scare you. I was just, um…"

Hug. Cari dropped her hands. *She was going to hug me.*

"Anyway," Ally said, trying to reclaim her composure. "Cooper told me about the…accident, at your house. If there's anything you need, anything at all…"

She let the sentence fade beneath a half-smile that shone like a beacon of warmth and kindness. Cari wanted to accept it and respond in kind, but she couldn't quite manage through the icy numbness that surrounded her. All she could offer was a stiff "Thanks."

"You're welcome." Ally gestured to the staircase. "The guest room is all ready for you. I'm sure you must be exhausted. Up the stairs, take a right, and it's the first door across the hall. Or—would you like me to show you?"

"That's okay," Cari said, taking the box from Cooper. "I'll find it."

She took the steps two at a time. No offense to Ally, but she'd had enough human interaction for one day in general—and, it seemed, way too much with one person in particular.

Ascending from the warmth and light of the first floor to the cool, peaceful dimness of the second felt like walking into a dream. Unlike the bouncy, carpeted metal floor of the trailer, the wood planks of the second story landing felt solid and steady beneath Cari's feet.

The door to the guest room—her room—stood slightly ajar. She used the corner of the box to nudge it the rest of the way. The scent of vanilla and lilac enveloped her immediately. Across from her, a full wall of windows overlooked a small rear garden. To her right was a walk-in closet; to the left, a wrought-iron bed that was easily the size of her entire old room. Nudging the door shut, she set her box on top of a tall chest of drawers and sat down on the puffy white duvet. It practically swallowed her.

She'd never seen a more beautiful bedroom. It was so cozy, so welcoming. So…

Not her.

She curled her fingers into the duvet as her breath turned to shallow gasps and black splotches bloomed in front of her. With all the strength she could summon, she burst upward, ripping the blanket off the bed as she did so. Grabbing her box of stuff, she dashed into the walk-in closet and slammed the door behind her.

"Thank you for agreeing to this," Cooper murmured toward Ally as Cari disappeared upstairs. "I promise, it'll only be a couple of weeks. Just until—"

"Don't worry about it."

He frowned. He had been prepared to defend his position, citing Grace's miniscule one-room hut and the fact that John's house had suffered so much neglect over the years that the last dusting of snow had almost caused the roof to cave in. But when he'd called to tell Ally about the situation, she'd agreed to help without hesitation. In fact, he'd barely even gotten the question out before she jumped on it. And now she wasn't concerned about the time frame? Something was up.

He turned to look at his wife. Her smile had collapsed, the welcoming warmth she'd shown Cari now buried under stony suspicion. Cooper shuddered as the temperature in the room dropped twenty degrees.

"An hour at most, Cooper," she said, her voice low. "That's what you told me. That's what you *promised*."

He sucked in his breath, giving himself a moment before answering. "Something came up at work. They needed me."

Her face constricted, not in a scowl or a pout, but in defeat. "They? Or *she*?"

The word backhanded him across the face. Anger seared through him as he took a calculated step toward her. "Cari's not the only person that lost someone today, you know. Lola asked me to help, so I helped."

She spat out a bitter chuckle. "It's not *Lola* I'm talking about, and you damn well know it."

His jaw dropped as indignant heat crept over his face and neck. He took deep breaths, trying desperately to diffuse the feeling. A barrage of thoughts cascaded through his mind that, though numerous, mostly fell along one of two lines.

"What is that supposed to mean?" was the one he chose to vocalize.

Ally wrapped her arms around her chest and mounted the stairs. "Forget it. I've got to get ready for work. Just…*call* next time, okay?"

She disappeared into the dark, ending the conversation, at least for the moment. He looked up after her as his second line of thinking, the one he couldn't say, would *never* say, continued to run.

How the hell did she know?

Chapter Thirteen

Grace tossed her bag on the dilapidated futon that took up most of her living room and headed for the kitchenette. Her stomach growled as she grabbed a jar of peanut butter, shoveled two fingers-worth into her mouth, and stared absently out her kitchen window at the neighboring backyard. That house had been abandoned for years, as had most of the houses on the block, and the small patch of grass was completely overrun with weeds. When she'd first moved in, she had imagined that someday she would annex the dwelling as storage space for all the stuff that didn't fit in her own tiny house. Eight years later, and that day had not yet come to pass. Turns out she didn't need nearly as much as she once thought she did.

Brrrring!

She stiffened as the jangle of her kitchen phone shattered the morning stillness.

"Nuh aguhn," she groaned around the sticky sweet paste coating on her tongue. She wished she could let it ring itself to death. But if something had gone wrong with Cari (or Nelson, or any one of a dozen other things), she'd rather know about it.

"What's wrong?" she answered, licking the last of the peanut butter from her index finger.

"Why don't you tell me?"

The deep, sultry voice on the other end of the line made her insides quake.

"Lola." She wiped her hand on the front of her coveralls. "Uh, hi. How…how are you?"

"Oh, I'm super," Lola shot back. *"I love riding ten hours through the desert in a para-shuttle. It's a dream come true."*

"Uh, yeah." Grace bit the inside of her cheek as memories gathered in the back of her mind, looming like pregnant storm clouds. "Cooper told me you called. Sorry I didn't have the chance to call you back yet. I was working, and, well…"

"Yeah, I know. Believe me, I don't want to be talking to you either. But…" She sighed heavily. *"Look, I'm not going to pretend to know much about that fucked up town, or what kind of weird shit my dad was involved with. But I know enough that when some random wild thought stabs me in the brain over and over again, I'm gonna do whatever it tells me. So here goes. And I'm only going to say this once, so write it down."*

"Okay. Hang on a sec." Grace rifled through the dirty dishes sprawled across the counter until she found a Sharpie and a takeout menu from a long-defunct Indian restaurant. "Go ahead."

"First National Bank of Halcyon. Employee Picnic. 2008." She spat the words into the phone like they were poison. *"There, responsibility over. And Grace?"*

"Yeah?"

"Do not come to the funeral."

The line went dead.

Grace stared down at the receiver in her shaking hand. The mental thunderhead split open, unleashing a torrent of images. Torn flesh. Broken bones. Lola crying. And her hammer.

In her own hand.

"It wasn't my idea," she whispered to no one. "It wasn't…"

She pitched into the counter, her chest tight and her breathing thin. The visions pulsed, stronger and stronger, as if trying to pull her back, body and soul, into one of the most horrible moments of her life. Her panicked eyes dragged the room for anything to keep her in the present. They landed on the counter and found Lola's words scrawled in black across the menu.

First National Bank of Halcyon. Employee Picnic. 2008.

She repeated them in her head, over and over like a mantra, until the panic receded, and her mind settled itself back into a normal rhythm. *First National Bank.* That's where Nelson had worked. *Employee Picnic. 2008*

What the hell did *that* mean?

She tested her legs and found herself stable enough to walk. Grabbing the menu and the peanut butter jar, she sat down at the small table nestled between the kitchenette and the living room and typed the words into her cell phone browser. "First National Bank of Halcyon" came up with a number of hits, but none of them included the word "picnic." She scrolled through the results with one hand while dipping peanut butter out of the jar with the other. Not exactly a well-balanced breakfast, but after that little death march down memory lane, it made her feel a lot better. She slogged through three pages of search results, clicking on the links that seemed most promising—and coming up empty. She slammed her phone on the table. How did Simon do it day after day after day? At least he had the advantage of knowing what he was looking for. This would take forever, with what little she had to go on.

What little Lola had given her.

She sighed and rubbed her eyes. Even if she could set aside everything that had transpired between them, Lola had just lost her father. If her one request was that Grace spending a day googling some weird phrase, how could she say no?

She retrieved the phone—and the hairs on the back of her neck prickled. When she slammed it on the table, she must have accidentally hit the Image Results button. A young Libby Hembert filled the screen, toasting the camera with a bottle of Perrier.

"Son of a bitch," Grace whispered, cradling the phone as if it had turned to pure gold. She couldn't believe how healthy Libby looked, grinning at the camera, her cheeks flushed and teeth brilliant white. Her free arm hung across the shoulders of a bearded strawberry blond man, presumably her husband. He held her by the waist with one hand while pumping a spatula in the air like a trophy with the other. They wore matching white baseball caps and red T-shirts with "Getting Things Cooking at the FNB 2008 Friends and Family Picnic" printed across the chest.

So what?

Grace returned their smiles with a scowl. So, Libby worked at the bank too. Big deal. Sure, it was kind of a surreal picture under the circumstances, but what did that have to do with—

Her eyes snagged on something over Libby's right shoulder that stopped her cold. She reverse-pinched the screen, zooming in to make sure she had seen it right.

She had. Nelson's hair was thicker and his gut significantly less pronounced, but it was definitely him. He wore the same red shirt as the couple—and so did the little girl standing in front of him. A tiny thing with blond pigtails and giant blue eyes, Cari was practically drowning in the red fabric as she reached up with both hands to accept the popsicle Nelson offered to her.

She must not have seen the thing hovering just behind him.

The image trembled as Grace's hand started to shake. Perhaps it had only appeared after the fact, isolated by the click of the camera. Or maybe Cari had mistaken it for a shadow. Which Grace might have done as well, if not for the egg-white eyes and ragged smile. Heart pounding, she traced its feathery limbs down Nelson's arms to where they sunk like tattoos into his hands.

And Cari's.

Grace collapsed backward with such force it sent her chair rocking on its rear legs. She gulped at the air, trying to stave off panic, as her own words blared in her ears like a siren.

Anyone could be infected.
And we'd never know.

Try as he might, it still refused to give up its secrets.

PREQUEL: AN ORIGINAL SIN

Chapter One

November 11ᵗʰ, 2011

Good morning honored guests, distinguished faculty, longtime colleagues and friends. As this year's recipient of the Arthur Jannish Civil Leadership Award, it is my duty and pleasure to welcome you to the twenty-third annual Small Town Fellowship Convention, held once again in beautiful Las Vegas. When I first learned I would be receiving the prestigious Jannish award, I felt so...

So...

So what?

John tapped the butt of his pen against his cheek. This was how the speech always began, every year, on the first morning of every convention. It was practically sacred. And he was going to make a mess of it.

For one thing, he hated the Small Town Fellowship Convention. It masqueraded as a networking event for civic leaders when in reality, it was an excuse for a bunch of rich old white men to misbehave in Sin City for a weekend. While he couldn't help sharing many of their surface traits—white, older, and fairly well off—he found their behavior disgraceful, and more than a little pathetic. The only reason he was going this year was to accept the Jannish.

And that was the real problem. Everyone knew the Jannish award rotated between sitting mayors that had been in office for more than two terms. It had nothing to do with his work or worthiness. It was just his time, that's all. Chuckling bitterly, he wrote in round, looping cursive:

It felt so inevitable.

"Mr. Virgil?" The voice of his part-time twenty-nothing assistant twittered from the intercom. He stifled an irritated groan and pressed the answer button.

"Not now, Ms. Larkin. I'm working on my speech for tomorrow."

"I know, sir, and I am very sorry to bother you. But there is a...man out here in the waiting room that wants to speak with you."

"Tell him I'm busy and that he can schedule an appointment for next week."

"Um..." A rustle of fabric clouded the line before her voice returned in a tremulous whisper. *"I tried that. I told him that you were getting ready to leave town and you weren't taking any meetings today. But he won't listen. And...there's something else."*

"What else?"

"I don't know. Something in his voice. His face. Something..."

Her words melted into a pained whimper.

He stifled a sigh and cursed his soft heart. She wasn't the brightest bulb on the Christmas tree by a mile, but she was a sweet kid at heart. Besides, her parents had been angel-level donors in both of his re-elections campaigns and had been adamant that helping their youngest daughter find a decent way to spend her time was really the least he could do.

He tossed his pen on the desk. "Fine. Send him in."

The door swept open so immediately it made him rock back a little in his chair. It was as if the gentleman had been standing on the other side with his hand on the knob, his right to entry already a forgone conclusion. John didn't like *that* at all. And once he had the chance to examine the gentleman's appearance, he found he liked *him* even less.

The man was round but not tall, with a shining cue ball head deep set between rounded shoulders. His dark eyes pooled like massive sinkholes in the middle of his face. His bushy mustache curled down and obscured the corners of this thin lips. His orange-and-brown checkered suit was so impeccably tailored it looked painted on, and his brown shoes were as shiny as lacquer.

"Thank you for seeing me, Mr. Mayor." His voice was a high-pitched rasp, with a hint of an accent. European, or maybe South African. John couldn't quite tell.

"Mmph," he grunted, hoping to communicate his irritation. "What can I do for you, Mr.—"

"Oh no." The gentleman waddled up to the desk. He lifted his arm to show off a small briefcase that matched his shoes in both color and sheen. "It's not what you can do for me, Mr. Mayor. It is what *I* can do for *you*."

"Of course," John sighed. He gestured to the armchair in front of the desk. "Please sit."

The man nestled in, his shoulders hunched, and his torso bent forward. Balancing his briefcase on his knees, he peered at John from below bushy black brows. "Things have gone exceedingly well for you during your two terms in office, haven't they Mr. Mayor? Yields at the mine are up! The financial district is expanding so rapidly there aren't any buildings left on Main Street to accommodate it. People are rich and healthy and happy. Yes?"

John shrugged. "Halcyon has always been a prosperous city."

"But more so lately, right? It's as if someone lit a fire under the earth, and the ground is positively *bleeding* gold. Yes?"

"Yes," John said, almost as a reflex. The man's eyes pulsed and expanded like black holes, drawing him in.

"Yessss," he sighed in sibilant satisfaction. "And people thank *you* for it. You don't create the gold, but still you benefit. You're even getting an award, aren't you?"

"Yes," John muttered again, his head swimming. Ms. Larkin must have told him about the award. She must have.

Right?

"Yes." The gentleman grinned. "But things can change, can't they? They can change fast, and hard, and without warning. You said it yourself—Halcyon has always been prosperous. And it would be a shame, wouldn't it, for a hard and fast change to befall this city during your time at the helm. That's where I come in."

His hands slid around to the front of his briefcase.

"You're a smart man, Mr. Virgil. That's why you've been elected, and re-elected, and re-elected once again. The people of Halcyon know you would never lead them into ruin. Right?"

John nodded. His brain felt wobbly, like a Jell-O mold bumping the inside of his skull.

"You want to protect this town's future?" He manipulated the triple rolling locks. "And you want to gild your legacy?"

Nodding again, John picked up his pen and scrawled the phrase "gilded legacy" onto the corner of the legal pad. He would have to work that into his speech somehow.

The gentleman's grin widened so much John could see his molars, as shriveled and brown as raisins. He flicked his fingers to release the locks. The room shook with the resulting crack.

"You're going to need that pen."

"Okay." The syllables clacked against John's tongue. He didn't feel his forearm slide over the legal pad, crumpling the page with his speech all the way up to the top spine. He was too focused on the seam where the shiny brown case split in half. It wasn't doing anything as ridiculous as glowing or smoking, but still he was drawn to it, and not just because he wanted to know what was inside. He wanted to experience it.

He wanted to *be* there.

The man's hands curled around the lid. The seam yawned, wider...and wider...

"Mr. Virgil, your wife is on line two."

John shook his head. The seismic slam of case falling shut almost made him scream.

"Uh...my apologies," he stammered, snatching up the phone. "I am in a *meeting*, Ms. Larkin. How many times do I have to tell you not to disturb—"

"I know," she interjected in another parry of artless unprofessionalism. *"And I'm sorry. But she said you were supposed to meet her at the clinic before your flight, and I told her you were in a meeting, but then she said it was urgent, so I figured it's okay to interrupt a meeting you're in if it's about another meeting that you're currently late for and—"*

"All right!" John bellowed. He checked at his watch. Almost 1:15.

He blinked. Had he really been talking to this man for forty-five minutes? But they'd barely said anything at all.

He looked up. The gentleman's hands were still wrapped around the closed briefcase as he glowered at John from below his heavy brow. John frowned back. This fellow looked more pissed off than any salesman had the right to look. Especially if he was hoping to make a sale.

"Tell her I'm on my way," John muttered into the receiver, then hung up and rose from his seat. "We will have to continue this, uh, discussion another time. I'm quite late for another appointment."

The gentleman's expression shifted from one of fury to one of fear. "But there *is* no other time. It *must* be today!"

"That is unfortunate." *For you.* John smirked to himself as he rolled down the sleeves of his crisp white dress shirt and buttoned the cuffs. Nothing gave him more pleasure than evading a hard sell. "If you change your mind, feel free to make an appointment on your way out. If not, then I'm afraid the answer is no."

He crossed to the door and retrieved his suit jacket from the coat tree. As he slipped his arm through one sleeve, he heard the man utter a phlegmy grunt. Out the corner of his eye, he saw the man's skin and clothes turned gray and fuzzy like a rabbit-eared TV with bad reception. His silhouette popped and bowed like he was having a seizure. Or was about to explode.

"What the—?" John whipped around to get a better look. The gentleman leered up at him, the same beetle-cum-insurance salesman he'd always been. And once again, he was smiling.

"As you please, Mr. Mayor." He hauled himself out of the chair. "Though for your sake I do wish we could have come to a straightforward agreement."

"Uh, right." John hoisted the strap of his overnight bag onto his shoulder and made a hasty dive for the door. "Maybe next time."

"Oh, yes. There's always next time. Yes, indeed."

The gentleman's chuckle swarmed across John's back like an intrusion of cockroaches. The hand wrapped around the doorknob trembled as a bone-deep desire to turn back wrapped itself around his left bicep and tugged. He sucked in air. Somewhere in the back of his mind he heard people singing. A hymn?

No. A dirge, full of pain and death and regret.

Gripping and twisting, he flung the door wide and lurched out of his office.

Ms. Larkin looked up from her nails as he entered the lobby. She grinned at him, long lashes fluttering over glassy blue eyes.

"Bye Mr. Virgil!" she chirped, waving her nail file at him as he fled past her desk. "Have a good trip! See you next week!"

He slammed out of the front doors without reply. She might have been a sweetheart, but damned if he
didn't need a new assistant.

Chapter Two

John sneered at the steering wheel as he whipped his Honda down yet another parking lane outside the south entrance. He'd never seen the lot this crowded except for Black Friday, and that was still weeks away. Unless there was some Veteran's Day sale he wasn't aware of (which in fairness *was* entirely possible), the overflow of cars was only there to piss him off. After several futile circles, he finally wedged the sedan into a small spot on the opposite side of the building from his destination. The pink glass dome glowed rosily against the gray autumn sky as he hustled through the crammed lot. He scowled at Corinthian columns that waited for him on either side of the east entrance. He'd always hated the fake Roman theme that had, for some reason, been the cutting edge of architecture back in the nineties. At least he wouldn't have to see it again after today. Unless he wanted to—and that seemed pretty unlikely.

The doors slid open with a metallic screech that made him cringe. Ice cold air conditioning blasted his cheeks as he pressed through the revolving door into the wide cobblestone hallway. Inside it was spangled jeans and polo shirts and gel-crisped frosted tips as far as the eye could see, a teenaged swarm circling the kiosks hawking cellphone covers and LED t-shirts and other sundry nonsense. The elevator version of some early-millennium pop song John barely recognized underscored the incessant chirp and drone of conversation, and the scent of a hundred different sugar and Old Spice body sprays made his eyes water.

Christ, he hated the mall.

"Mr. Mayor!"

A smile ripped across John's face, a Pavlovian response to hearing his formal moniker. Glancing to his right, he spotted the source of the summons. Inside the Guest Relations booth, a portly salt-and-pepper Asian man in a bespoke navy suit and bright pink shirt waved at him. Gritting his teeth to preserve his smile, John extended his hand.

"Ray. How's business?"

Beaming, Ray accepted the handshake in both of his. "Good, sir. Very good."

"I'll say. What's the occasion? You got Britney Spears signing CDs or something today?"

"Not that I know of." He assessed the crowd, grey eyes darkening in thought. "To be honest, it is a *little* weird. We haven't had any kids in here all week, and then today— bam! Here they all are. You'd think we were having a building-wide fire sale. Everything must go." His shoulders rose and fell in a jovial shrug. "Kids, right?"

John felt his rubbery, knee-jerk smile grow more genuine.

"Anyway, it's good to see you," Ray continued. "Though I'm a little surprised. I would have thought you'd be scarce around here since the, uh…dissolution."

"Yes, well." John ran his palms over the smooth marble counter. "Turns out I missed a couple of I's and T's. You know how those contracts can be."

"Of course." Ray bowed his head contritely. John shook his, and Ray straightened. Of all the people who needed to be sorry, Ray was not one of them.

"Anyway!" Ray clapped his hands and rubbed them together in an effort to break the somber mood. "What's the news from downtown? Any update on my grant application?"

John chuckled. Ray had been the mall's general manager since it opened, and in all that time, John had never known him to go more than three minutes without bringing up work. Most people found it annoying. John thought it was great. If pressed, he might even admit that he was a little jealous. It must be nice to have something in your life where you could feel like your work made a difference. Even if it was a mall.

"Ray, you know the budget committee is unlikely to fund facade improvements for businesses outside of the downtown. And of course, they will want to know why you can't secure funding from your corporate entity."

"The corporate partners are securing the loan for the security system and break room upgrades." He gestured behind him at a line of closed-circuit televisions, half of which contained nothing more than gray squiggles. To the left of that was a plain white door with a brown placard that read Break Room. "But the four bas reliefs above our entrances need to be restored as well. How can you possibly compare *that* to adding a new awning to the barber shop? After all, Edensgate is *the* place for high-end luxury shopping and entertainment on this side of the Cal-Neva state line. The more appealing it looks on the outside, the bigger the crowds on the inside...and the more people who show up at the ballot box and put their pens down next to your name. Right?" He waggled his eyebrows.

"Right." John shoved his hands into his pockets. Why did it always have to come back to that? "I'll see what I can do. Look, Bea is waiting for me, and I'm running late as it is so—"

"Oh! Yes, of course." Ray nodded down at his hands. "Well, take care, and I'm sure I'll see you…uh, soon."

"Right." John coughed around the sudden lump in his throat. "I'll, uh, let you know what I hear about the grant. Next week. Week after at the latest."

"Okay, great." His gaze flitted up long enough for their eyes to meet, then returned to the ground. "Take care, John."

"You too." John fled into the bubbly flash mob before Ray could see the effect the moment had had on him. It felt ridiculous, getting all emotional about something like this. It's not like he and Ray had been friends. They'd had a business relationship. That's all. So why did it feel so much more than that now that it was ending?

Why—and he was fully aware of how maudlin it sounded—why did it feel like one of them was dying?

Chapter Three

John closed the distance between the east and south hallways at a sprint, dodging knots of oblivious teens, middle-aged mall-walkers and one petition-wielding hippie on a mission. Snippets of conversations tickled his ears as he motored past:

"—waiting until the 4S came out before I upgraded, so now—"

"—like I'm between an A and B cup—"

"—indigenous wildlife is being eradicated as we speak—"

"—told him at least fifty times I absolutely cannot drink straight whiskey—"

"—by signing this petition—"

He flew passed Hunter's Paradise Ammo and Camo and stumbled into the brilliant white sterility of Virgil Cosmetics and Medispa. The patter of mall noise disappeared beneath the swell of soothing harps and strings. He wasn't in bad shape for a guy in his fifties—hell, compared to some of the guys he saw rolling around the Golden Springs Country Club in their golf carts, he was practically Mr. Universe. Still, the impromptu jog had taken its toll. His face pulsed with exertion and he could feel the beads of sweat slithering down his spine. More than that, his shambling arrival had drawn angry glares from the exclusively blond female population of the waiting room. He watched with satisfaction as a wave of recognition overcame their scowls. This wasn't a random blustering fool come to bother them. It was the mayor, and the man that had built this house, not to mention each one of their noses, which were all quickly buried back in their magazines advertising Better Orgasms Guaranteed and Ten Ways to Look Like a Teenager Again. It briefly occurred to him that maybe he should have been embarrassed at startling his patrons with his uncouth entrance.

Then his eyes found Bea, leaning against the check-in desk studying a clipboard, and everyone else turned to furniture. Her dark hair was piled on her head and secured with a pencil, and she had to keep pushing her horn-rimmed glasses up her (all-natural) pixie-shaped nose to keep them from falling off.

But it was the dress that really did him in. A long-sleeved, high-necked burgundy number that was the pinnacle of professionalism, yet the way it hugged her slim figure had always driven him crazy. He must have told her that a hundred times.

And she was wearing it today. Of all goddamned days.

John gulped in the cool minty air and released it in a loud cough that sounded as if he were trying to dislodge a chicken bone from his throat. The rude noise shattered the serenity of the pristine room and made every member of the blonde brigade jump and clutch her ample chest. Bea, on the other hand, raised her head as if she were moving through water.

"You're late," she said with a lethargic dip of her eyelashes. Her voice was even, almost monotone. She slipped off her glasses, letting them dangle from the gold chain around her neck as she tossed the clipboard at the receptionist. "Hold my calls."

She pivoted on her spiky black heels and disappeared into the narrow hall that led to the back offices.

He rolled his eyes. "Nice to see you too, dear."

Bea led the way while he did his best to keep his eyes off her gently swaying hips. As he was about to break right and continue on toward her office, Bea swiveled in the opposite direction and entered an all-too-familiar doorway.

"What are you doing? This is—" He cut himself off when he spotted the new placard affixed to the glass door.

Ms. Beatrice Cieca, CEO.

His guts tightened. That was his old office, his old title.

And her maiden name.

"John?" Bea poked her head back into the hall. "Is something wrong?"

He glared at her, unsure of what to say. This was the last time he would set foot in this place, and she knew it. She couldn't have waited one more day?

She blinked at him, her brown eyes as placid and innocent as a doe. It didn't fool him for a second. After twenty-odd years together, he knew exactly what she was thinking. She *wanted* something to be wrong. She wanted him to be angry. He could ask why, but it would be pointless, and he didn't have time for head games.

"Let's get this over with," he grumbled and brushed past her into *her* office.

It was exactly as he had left it. Same turquoise blue armchairs, same executive desk topped with shiny black lacquer, same teak sideboard with the Swarovski crystal wine glasses they'd gotten for their wedding. The only thing she had touched (other than the door) was the photo of them from their honeymoon in Roman that he'd kept on his desk. The silver frame now held a picture of a tiny black cat sitting on the arm of a red velvet couch. The couch he recognized. The cat he didn't.

That was a stranger's cat.

She pulled a thick stack of papers from one of the side drawers and dropped it onto the desk. "It's marked with a yellow sticker."

He grunted and flipped through the pages. His eyes caught on the familiar scrawl of his own signature, and the equally familiar loops of hers. Astonishing, how many times one had to sign his name just to destroy something.

"I don't see it."

"Fine." Her slim hands clamped down on either side of the stack. "I'll do it *for* you."

"No!" He slammed his fist onto the paper so hard it left an impression. "I can do it. You didn't give me a whole lot to go on, that's all."

She rolled her eyes. "Can we please not turn this into another opera about your feelings of inadequacy? I've got a ton of work to do and I don't have all day to stand around and watch you drag this out."

"*I'm* dragging this out? It was *your* lawyer that missed it in the first place."

"My point exactly. *I* know where it is. It will be faster if *I* do it."

He glared at her. The serene veneer over her eyes had cracked, revealing the smoldering passion below. His sneering lips trembled as a bolt of excitement sizzled through his body. She was so gorgeous when she was angry. Swallowing hard, he lifted his fist from the paper. "Bea, what are we doing?"

Her body stiffened visibly. "*We* aren't doing anything," she growled. "*I'm* taking control of the one part of my life you're not holding hostage." She ripped the papers away and fanned the pages with her thumbs. In the homogenous white blur, the bright yellow sticker revealed itself almost immediately.

"There, see?" She slammed the document back on the table. "Now sign it and get the hell out of here."

"Bea, please—"

"No, John. You may be the doctor, but I'm the one that made this place what it is. You will not be able to keep it going on your own. That's just *true*."

He sighed, and looked down at the single, blank line. She was right, of course—she *had* been the one who had spent the last ten years gaining and maintaining their client base, building their brand and convincing people that operating a medical spa and cosmetic surgery suite in a shopping mall was not only *not* crazy, but profitable as well. It was only fair that she be rewarded for all that work.

But that didn't mean he couldn't be pissed off about it.

"Fine," he said, gouging the page with his fountain pen like he was trying to make it bleed. "Anything else?"

Bea looked up at him, her furious eyes rimmed with hope. "Yes. A divorce."

He closed his eyes, chagrined. "Anything but that."

She huffed in disgust. Dropping into her chair, she slipped on her headphones and swiveled towards her laptop.

He didn't need any kind of marital telepathy to figure out what that meant.

He made for the exit. As he got close, his steps became slower and slower until bringing him to a lingering stop in the doorway. Their professional partnership was dissolved, and their marriage was fraught, to say the least. They were, for all intents and purposes, over. She had made that abundantly clear. And yet for some reason he couldn't bring himself to leave without casting one more look over his shoulder.

His breath stuck in his throat. She was watching him. More than that, she was smiling. Small, soft, with a hint of pain. Of all her expressions, the meaning behind that strange little smile was the one he had never been able to decipher. It didn't show up often—only at the end of arguments, and only when he was about to lose.

"Goodbye, John."

She turned back to her computer. The rapid-fire clack of keys struck him as hard as any bullets ever could. There was nothing left for him here. Nothing but the door without his name on it.

"Goodbye," he whispered, and saw himself out.

"Support animal rights, Mr. Mayor?"

"Huh?" John wheeled around. He had been so lost in thought he barely noticed that he'd left the clinic, let alone come back within reach of the wheedling environmentalist.

"Native animals are in danger, Mr. Mayor." He was maybe twenty-five, with ginger hair tied back in ratted twin ponytails, a scruff of orange stubble covered his chin, and a cloud of patchouli stink emanating from his freckled skin. "If we don't do something, their way of life will be destroyed."

"Oh?" John groaned inwardly. He would have much preferred the mall-walker with an aversion to straight whiskey.

"Yes, sir," The kid replied. "But you can save them. Just sign here." He extended the clipboard to John along with a toothy, tobacco-stained grin.

John averted his eyes from the unpleasant smile to the clipboard—and frowned. "You don't have any signatures there, son."

"No, sir, we don't. But a name like yours carries a lot of water. It would go a long way toward convincing others."

He held out a pen. "Please, Mr. Mayor. Won't you do your part?"

John began to raise his hand when a sharp tickle along his spine made him hesitate. This felt…familiar, but not comfortable. Like déjà vu at a murder scene, or like someone had walked over his grave—for the second time.

"Sorry," he mumbled, clutching his lapels as he backed away, "I'm afraid I'm late for a flight."

"Of course, Mr. Mayor." The reply floated after him as he jogged back toward the east entrance. "Don't worry. There's always next time!"

Chapter Four

The party was long over by the time John arrived outside Rio Ballroom D. Through a crack in the door, he could see the hotel staff clearing out the cocktail tables while a second contingent set up the shallow stage for tomorrow's opening ceremony. The sight of it made his palms dampen. After a nail-biting dash through the Reno-Tahoe Regional Airport, he'd been informed by an arch-eyed gate attendant that the jetway door could not be opened once it was closed, and that in the future he needed to arrive at the airport ninety minutes before all domestic departures. John spent the better part of the next two hours on the phone, arguing (unsuccessfully) for a refund and leaving some choice comments regarding the attendant's approach to customer service. By the time he had finally taken his seat on the next available flight, he was so tired and frustrated that he could barely focus on buckling his seatbelt, let alone writing that damned speech.

The kid behind the check-in desk (Danny, according to his name tag) was packing up the last of the registration materials as John approached. He may have been a fresh-faced college kid at the outset, but John knew from personal experience that hours spent trapped in conversation with hundreds of self-congratulating small-town politicians could strip the shine from even the freshest of apples. He recognized the signs well—Danny's eyes were bloodshot behind his smudged glasses and he was shoving fistfuls of Sharpies into a plastic bin with unabashed disgust. When he spotted John, his slim body tensed as if he were expecting an impact.

"Help you." It was more of a challenge than a question.

"I hope so." John set his bag on the floor and rifled through his pockets for his wallet. "My name is John Virgil, MD, from Halcyon, Nevada. I'm sorry to bother you so late, but I'm accepting the Jannish Award tomorrow and I don't know if I'll have time to register in the morning, so I was hoping maybe I could—"

"Oh, you're *him*." Danny's lips pressed into a smug, piteous smile. "Someone already grabbed your tag."

John hesitated, his license hovering near his chest. "Are you sure?"

"One hundred percent." Danny ripped the tablecloth off the desk and shoved it into the bin. "He was *very* insistent, even after I told him I needed your ID. He said you were both, and I quote, the Mining Mayors of the STFC."

A thousand volts of icy dread ran through John from head to toe. He knew exactly who that was. As if on cue, a loud guffaw came rolling out of the ballroom. The double doors slammed open, eliciting a combination yelp-groan from Danny.

"Hey! There's the hero of the weekend!"

Gritting his teeth, John turned and faced the inevitable. Standing in the middle of the doorway was the broad-shouldered frame of Tommy Concannon, six-term mayor of Steelflat, Wisconsin and undisputed king of the Small Town Fellowship's Iron Belt contingent.

"Dr. Mayor." Tommy touched a finger to his forehead, then let out another bellow of laughter that turned his sweaty face as red as a cranberry. He lurched forward, and before John could think to duck, Tommy had caught him around the neck in a combination headlock-hug.

"Hello, Tommy," John wheezed, keeping his breath shallow to avoid the smell of the large man's woodsy aftershave. "How are you?"

"Fit as a fiddle and twice as fun." Tommy lifted a tumbler the size of a softball to his lips and sucked down half the cinnamon-tinted liquid inside. He wiped his mouth and lowered his voice into a conspiratorial whisper. "I gotta tell ya, Doc, it's a damn relief to see you. I've had to go double-time on the Scotch just to make these two seem any kinda interesting."

He sloshed his glass toward the ballroom door. Stumbling out of the void Tommy had left were two men in nearly identical gray suits, one fair-haired and bespectacled with a vaguely rodent-like face, the other brunette and short with smushed, piggish features. John recognized them as the mayors of Colton, Michigan and Jasper, Minnesota respectively, but their actual names escaped him. Their hanging heads swung back and forth as they both stared at the floor, too intent on staying upright to notice that their party had gained another attendee. The sight turned John's stomach. Between their matching clothes and the oblivious shambling, they looked a little too much like zombies for his taste.

"But that doesn't matter!" Tommy thrust the tumbler into John's hands. He dug through his pockets and extracted a bent name tag that he also handed to John. "You're here now, thank the sweet Lord. So, what's the plan?"

"Um." John glanced down at his overnight bag. "To be honest, it's been a long day. I have to be up early for the speech tomorrow, and I haven't even really started to write—"

"Oh, that old thing." Tommy flapped his hand against John's neck. "Nobody ever listens to the Jannish speech. You could get up there and read the phone book for all anyone cares. We'll still give you the standing O. Won't we, boys?"

Twin jerks of the head and an incoherent grunt was the only response.

"There, see? Now let's get a move on. It's beer-o-clock somewhere, and you're way behind." Tommy tightened his arm around John's neck and dragged him down the hall toward the elevators.

"But, but…my bag…" John protested.

"Don't worry about that. Danny will call someone to take care of it. Won't you, Danny?" Tommy yelled without looking back.

"Right away, Mr. C," came the response. He sounded obsequious enough, and yet John was sure that, were he to turn around right now, he would see Danny vigorously flipping them the bird.

"Great." Tommy punched the down arrow with his free hand. "Come on, Doc, drink up. A couple shots of whiskey, maybe one or two more, and then we'll see what kind of trouble we can stir up in this town."

"But—"

"No, huh-uh. No excuses. Not this year. You're getting the Jannish award, buddy. Sure, it's meaningless, but you're *getting* it. And we're gonna celebrate."

John sighed. It would have been a nice sentiment if any part of it were true. But it was only an excuse. Tommy already knew he was taking them to the same place he always went on the first night of the convention. Only this time John couldn't muster the strength to wriggle out of it. He knocked back the rest of Tommy's leftovers in a resigned gulp. "If you insist."

"That's my boy!" Tommy jostled John's shoulders. "And I swear—no matter what happens, it'll never get back to your wife."

"I doubt she'll care," John mumbled, staring regretfully the empty glass. "We're kind of, well, separated."

The elevator arrived, but Tommy didn't get on. Instead, he grabbed John by both shoulders and turned him so they were looking each other square in the face. His eyes twinkled like emeralds against his flushed skin, and for a moment John thought he was going to do something crazy. Like sympathize.

Then Tommy cracked a grin as wide and wanton as the devil's own. "Buddy, that's even better."

Chapter Five

John blinked. His eyes felt like they had been dipped in hot wax and the twirling kaleidoscopic lights stabbed his retinas. His buzz had flat lined and the blood in his temples pounded slightly out of time with the throbbing music. He wanted to get some sleep, get back to the hotel, get *out* of here.

Now he if he could just remember where here was.

"And everything falls on your head. Right, Doc?"

"Hmuh?" He rolled his head to the right. On the far end of the long black leather banquette, Jasper and Colton sat with their hands on their polyester-covered thighs, gazing up at the slim, barely dressed figure undulating on the low table in front of them. The sequins on her G-string sparkled like tiny explosions, assaulting his tender eyes all over again.

"I said everything falls on your head!" Tommy shouted in John left ear. The smell of rye, cigar smoke and old meat on his breath made John's throat spasm. "Everything. All the way down to choosing the color of the goddamn Founder's Day ribbons. To this day I still have pissed-off losers writing to me about 'the Goldenrod Incident of 2006.' And that's the hell of it. When things go right, it's a team effort. Credit to the council, credit to the city planners. Even the goddamn janitors get an atta boy. But when it goes wrong, nuh uh. It was *your* decision, so it's *your* balls on the block."

Tommy knocked back another glass of whiskey. John watched the tiny rivers of sweat as they ran down his thick neck and soaked into the already damp collar of his blue dress shirt.

"I'm probably not a great person to ask for an opinion." John searched for his own glass. If he couldn't go to bed, he could at least get his buzz back. But the table in front of them was bare. "Halcyon…kind of runs itself."

"Rub it in why don't you?" Tommy snorted. "Dammit, if only it was a hundred years ago when the Iron Belt was still up and kicking. We could all be living the easy life like you, you lucky bastard. Right, boys?" Tommy flung his head toward Jasper and Colton. One of them let out a small whimper, while the other flopped his hand dismissively. As if this were some kind of signal, the woman on the table pivoted and half-fell, half-floated into a straddle over the blond one (Colton, maybe? He couldn't remember—and really, did it matter?). Her hands dug into his shoulders and her hips rolled against his in time to the music, her bare breasts hovering inches away from his pointy, rat-like nose.

"Speaking of lucky." Tommy elbowed John in the ribs and raised a hand toward the smoky murk in front of them. "Dancer here!"

John cleared his throat in protest. But the vision that emerged from the darkness drove any remaining reasonable thought from his brain.

Dark curly hair framed her face. Cool, dark eyes glittered at him from behind horn-rimmed glasses. And that shimmering burgundy corset pressed and pushed her figure in all the right ways.

"Dear God," he murmured as she came closer. There were obvious differences, of course—this woman was about five inches shorter, her skin was several shades darker, her body was more muscular, and she was, of course, *much* younger. But if someone had told him the woman standing in front of him was Bea's long-lost sister, he wouldn't have questioned it for a second.

"Hey there, darling." Tommy punched him lightly in the shoulder. "My friend here is having a tough time with his old lady. You think you can help him forget his sorrows?"

John groaned. He could have strangled the bastard with his own sweat-stained shirt. But the smell of lilacs stole his attention. The dancer stood over him, her rosy lips pursed in a seductive pout. "I'll do my best."

"Oh, that's okay. I'm—"

Before he could resist any further, the second coming of his wife fell into his lap.

"Hi," she said, sliding her hands up his chest to loop around his neck. "I'm Trixy."

"Uh, hello," he said as her smooth, bare legs came to rest across his thighs. "I'm John."

"John," she whispered in his ear. "That's my favorite name."

Her breath was warm and soft against his neck. Suddenly his head felt like it was floating, and he had no idea what to do with his hands. After a few moments of awkward flapping he found a spot for them stretched across the back of the banquette. Apparently, this was the right decision; clinging to him tighter, Trixy shifted herself to settle more completely into his lap.

"What can I do for you…John?"

He bit his lip to stifle a moan. Would it be too weird to ask her to just keep saying his name like that?

"Ow! What the *fuck*?"

John froze. Down the bench, the bedazzled dancer wrenched herself away from the gray-suited duo, clutching her right breast protectively with both hands.

Trixy whipped her head toward the commotion. John supervised his arms as they wrapped around her waist—only to make sure she didn't fall, of course. "Jasmine? You okay?"

"Hell no, I'm not okay! This pervert bit me!"

Trixy's sexy demeanor turned to iron, and John found his lap suddenly vacant.

"Who?" she demanded as she flew to the girl's side. "Which one?"

"Him." Jasmine pointed at maybe-Colton. He stared back at her like a moth contemplating a flame. "He bit me. Sick fuck."

Trixy shoved her face into Colton's until he had no choice but to look at her. Dazed pleasure quickly morphed into utter confusion. "Assaulting a dancer is a violation, asshole. You got three *seconds* to get out of here before—"

"Hold on a minute, honey." Tommy groaned as he pulled himself up off the bench. "Before you go getting all upset, let's see what really happened here." He fixed Jasmine with a stony stare. She lowered her gaze to the floor. "I'm sure my friend didn't mean to hurt you. He just got a little caught up in the moment. Isn't that right?"

He dropped a meaty hand onto Colton's shoulder and squeezed. Colton's lips split an idiotic grin, the tips of his front teeth glinting in the reddish light. To John, it looked a little like they were tinged with blood.

At least, he hoped it was the light.

Trixy narrowed her eyes. He could practically see the calculations running in her head. Rich plus Drunk plus Well-Connected equals Problem. But Tommy could do the math too. Before she could call for security, he pulled out his wallet.

"We're all adults here, right?" He flapped a wad of bills at the injured girl. "What do you say, sweetie? A little something for your trouble, and we'll call it a wash."

Chewing her lip, Jasmine cast a doubtful glance at Trixy, who shrugged and shook her head. She couldn't tell the girl what to do any more than John could—but they both knew how this was going to end.

Jasmine's hands dropped away from her chest as she reached for the money, revealing a perfect circle of teeth-patterned bruises marring the top swell of her perfect, palm breast.

"Jesus," John muttered, turning his disbelief on Colton. What the hell was *wrong* with that guy?

He wasn't the only one who noticed the mark. Arms stiff and fingers curled into tight little balls, Trixy turned back on Tommy with renewed fury. "That cash bought you fifteen minutes. I see you around here at minute sixteen, and you're getting the hard goodbye."

Tommy flashed her his full complement of teeth. "Is that right?"

She arched an eyebrow. "You know it is, Mayor Concannon."

His smile-sneer deflated so fast that John nearly choked on his laughter. Everyone knew that Tommy was no angel, but even he didn't need the notoriety of being caught up in a strip club assault scandal.

"Fifteen minutes. Loud and clear." He tipped his imaginary brim at her. It was not lost on any of them which finger he used.

John expected her to leave then, maybe head to the bar on the other side of the room so she could keep a watchful eye on their exit. Instead, she turned her attention back to him. His heart raced as she looked him over with that calculating stare. What her moral mathematics would deduce about him, he could only guess. He hadn't committed any direct indiscretions, but the company he kept had to be at least one mark in the minus column. After about a hundred years, she blinked, releasing him from his torture, and spoke:

"You look like you could use a drink."

His core temperature spiked, and he dug his fingers into the slick upholstery to keep from fidgeting. In the real world, an invitation like that could only mean one thing. But did it mean the same thing in here? He doubted it. But what if did? Could he...? And with her...?

"I, uh, thank you, but...I think I've had enough."

"Well, I haven't. And I do so hate to drink alone."

She rolled her eyes and grimaced, as if she couldn't believe what she had said. Despite his nerves, he found felt himself smile. She bit her lip and smiled back. It couldn't have been further from the seductive pout she'd given him earlier. This was friendly, guileless, and meant just for him.

"Is that a yes?" she asked, almost shyly.

He couldn't believe it, but he nodded. "That's a yes."

"Great." She cocked her head toward the back of the club. "Let's go."

"Oh, come on!" Tommy bellowed as John stood, somewhat unsteadily, and followed her. "We get booted and you get a private show. I know you're a lucky bastard, but this is—"

John was out of earshot before he could catch the end of Tommy's sentence. Trixy wove between the tables scattered across the floor until she reached an unmarked black door between the edge of the main stage and the end of the bar. She had been moving so fast that he only now managed to get himself back within speaking distance.

"Hey, Trixy?"

"Yes, John?" She eyed him over her bare shoulder.

"Uh, well…" He ran a hand through his hair, suddenly very aware of how gray and thin it was. "I just wanted to say…thank you, for not lumping me in with those guys."

She smiled and shrugged. "It wasn't exactly a tough call. You look like you're even more sick of those assholes than I am."

He rolled his eyes. "You have no idea."

"Well, in any case, you're welcome." She produced a key from somewhere John was too polite to look and unlocked the door. "And please—call me Grace."

Chapter Six

They entered into a narrow hallway, unlit except for a shaft of greenish light spilling from an open door at the other end. Shadows danced in the glow, and the scent of strawberries and hand sanitizer wafted toward him, along with the murmur of female voices and the occasional peal of laughter. Dressing room, he figured. Had to be. His pulse quickened at the thought of the scene playing out not five yards from where he stood.

"Uh, I don't think I should—" he began. But instead of continuing toward the light, Grace turned right and heading into a stubby alcove that contained a solitary wood-paneled door.

"What's that?" she asked, using the same key to unlock this door as she did the first.

"Nothing," John said as she flipped on the light. The room was a square, windowless box, barely big enough to hold its contents: a bar with two cracked brown leather stools, a scratched-up coffee table covered with papers, writing implements and various hand tools, and a wide leather couch. The yellowed light filtering down from the stained-glass Budweiser lampshade gave the whole thing a patina of 1970s Playboy spread.

"Welcome to the Champagne Room." Grace tossed the keys on the coffee table. "Close the door behind you, please?"

John did as instructed, then took a seat on one of the tall stools while she dug around behind the bar, eventually emerging with a decanter of brick-colored liquid.

He held up his hand. "Thanks, but I really have had quite enough."

"Don't worry, it's tea." She plucked two smudged Ball jars from the shelf on the wall and began to pour. "Raspberry ginger."

"I'm not much of a tea drinker."

"Neither am I, but this is good stuff." Winking, she slid him a glass. "Especially when you think you may have had too much bad stuff."

He studied the drink carefully. The dim light barely cut through the deep cherry color.

What the heck? He brought the glass to his lips. The tart, biting heat stunned his taste buds and blazed a trail of acid through his sinuses. But she was right—no sooner had he swallowed his first mouthful than the throbbing in his head faded into sweet, soft numbness.

"Not bad," he said, taking a second, more judicious sip.

"Told you," she cooed triumphantly as she sauntered over and dropped down on the couch. Crossing one leg over the other, she tipped her head back and took a long swallow. The edge of her glass caught the light, drawing his attention to the smooth curve of her cheek. He followed the shape down her neck, along her collarbone, down...

The liquid in his glass trembled. He lowered it to the bar and gripped the worn, rounded edge of the counter with both hands.

"Look," he managed around his suddenly parched throat. "I appreciate the drink, and you are…quite lovely. But this…I'm…"

"Hm?" She looked at him as if she'd forgotten he was even there. Her eyes widened with alarm, then humor. "Oh, did you think--? Oh God, I'm sorry. I totally was joking about the Champagne Room thing." She gestured at their shabby surroundings. "Obviously."

"Oh, good!" He heaved a breath, and chuckled. "I did think this was the weirdest Champagne Room I'd ever seen. Not that I've seen that many, of course."

"Of course." She winked at him again. "No, this is the manager's lounge. He never uses it, so I come here to get a break from the chaos."

"I see. In that case, I suppose I'll make myself at home." Retrieving his drink, he took a seat on the other end of the couch. His bones creaked as he slouched into the puffy, cracked leather. He stretched his feet out on the table, kicking a tack hammer out of the way as he did so, and took another sip of the spicy tea. It no longer seemed bitter to him at all, and his headache, along with that floaty, achy drunkenness, was now almost completely gone. He closed his eyes. The music was audible, but distant and muffled, like it was coming from another world. But here, in this world, it was quiet. Here it was safe. His head dipped backwards, and he might have dozed off right then if it hadn't been for the tingling sensation on his left cheek that told him she'd fixed him with another one of those evaluative stares.

"What?" he asked, reluctantly raising his head.

Smiling, she peeled off her stilettos and stretched her legs across the couch. "Did you know that 90% of men who visit strip clubs are married?"

He frowned. What did that have to do with anything? "Is that right?"

"Let's say yes. 90% of the men out there are married, and yet what do you hardly see any of?" She tapped the fourth finger on her left hand. "Wedding rings. They all take them off before they come inside. Why is that do you think?"

He shrugged into his glass. "I assume it's because they don't want anyone to know they're married."

"That's my point. *Who* are they trying to fool? Not us girls. We don't care if they're married. Only if they pay. And it's *definitely* not the men—not to sound arrogant, but they are *way* too distracted to notice another man's jewelry."

"Maybe they think that without a ring on they'll have a better chance of getting laid."

She burst out laughing.

"Oh my—I am so sorry," he stuttered, his cheeks burning. "That was indelicate."

"Don't apologize. You're right. Some of the more deluded ones might be thinking along those lines. But *most* of them know that's a fantasy. No, they take off their rings not to fool us, but themselves. They don't want to face the fact that they are *that* guy. The guy sitting in a strip club with some stranger grinding up on him while his wife is at home with the kids. But you—you're different. You're still wearing yours. Even though your marriage is on the rocks, you're wearing it."

She leaned forward over her legs and took his hand. His arm tensed all the way up to his shoulder. He knew he shouldn't be surprised by her flexibility, and yet the fact that she was able to bend almost completely in half was…impressive…

Oh, hell, what was the point of being delicate? It made him want her so bad he could hardly stand it.

He closed his eyes as she cradled his hand in both of hers. Her touch was like velvet, soft and comforting, her warmth bringing heat to his own skin. When was the last time he'd been touched this way? Sure, he shook hands with people all the time. All day, every day it seemed. But those were gestures, cold, professional, and perfunctory. This was...not that.

"This about move than love, isn't it?" she whispered. Prying his eyes open, he watched in dismay as she ran her thumb over the gold band on his finger. "You committed yourself to something, and you're going to hold yourself to it, no matter what has happened in the meantime."

Dammit. He gripped his empty glass, the sweat on his palm making it slip a little. He wanted to raise his head and look at her, to see if she was looking at him. He wanted to grab her and throw her back on the couch. He wanted to hear her scream his name.

But he stayed as immobile as a spooked deer. Because she was right. It wasn't just about love.

"When I put my name on something, I stand by it," he said, his voice coarse and strained.

"Yeah," she sighed. Maybe it was his imagination, but he thought she sounded a little sad. "That's what I thought. It's very noble. Stupid, but noble."

She let go of his hand. The kick of longing and loneliness that slammed into his chest was so powerful it made him gasp for air. At least now he could bring himself to look at her again. Her smile came as a huge relief, even if it had taken on a sardonic edge.

"You don't believe in the merit keeping one's word?" he said, setting his glass on the table.

She shrugged and crossed her arms. "My father sure didn't. He said that a contract is just ink on paper. What matters is the meeting of the hearts and minds on either side of the page. The more shit I see happen in this stupid world of ours, the more convinced that such a thing is totally impossible. Which means that every contract is basically a lie. And if every contract is a lie, then what's the point in honoring them?"

His brows tensed. "Without contracts, the world would be chaos."

She threw her head back and laughed. "Yeah, we don't want to risk all this perfect order and harmony, do we?"

"Excuse me?"

They both turned as the door slid open half an inch and a soft, smoky voice wandered in. "Are you...I mean, is it okay if I come in?"

"Yeah, come in. We're both decent." Grace giggled at his cheeks reddened once again.

The door opened. The woman that entered was at least as tall as John, though some of that height was courtesy of her chunky orange platform heels. Long, dark strands framed her sharp, equine cheekbones, and the sepia-colored mini dress she wore covered only the most essential bits of real estate. In her hands she held a black bill folder.

"I'm so sorry to interrupt," she said, "but your friends? The ones that were escorted out? They never closed their tab."

He groaned, mostly in irritation and a little from the effort of getting up from the comfy, well-worn couch. "Of course, they didn't."

"Yeah." She shifted her weight from one heel to the other. "And my shift ends at midnight, so...would you mind?"

As he came around the coffee table, John checked the dusty PBR-branded clock above the bar. She certainly had waited until the last minute, in every sense of the phrase.

S.G. Tasz

"I suppose I'll have to," he sighed. As he accepted the bill folder, he caught sight of the small plastic name tag fastened at the crook where her spaghetti strap joined her décolletage.

"Sylvia," he said. "That's a pretty name,"

"Thanks," she said shyly. "It's a family name."

"I see," he murmured, busying himself with the bill before his eyes could do any more exploring. As it turned out, that would have been far preferable—when they settled on the total due, they nearly fell out of his head. "A hundred and sixty dollars?"

"And one cent," she said, pointing at the decimal place with the tip of a long orange nail. "That's right."

"There's no way! We did not spend a hundred and sixty dollars—"

"And one cent."

"—and one cent, on drinks!"

Behind them, Grace snickered. "Man, you really don't know anything about strip clubs, do you?"

"Don't worry, Mr. Virgil," Sylvia said gently. "We've already applied the charge to Mr. Concannon's credit card. We just need someone to sign the receipt."

She extended a pen to him. The red jewel on the end of the cap sparkled like a flame in the papery yellow light. In an instant, his attention sucked down to nothing. Nothing but the dazzling red rock.

"Oh…" he murmured, swaying slightly as an all-consuming ache to possess it washed over him. Somewhere in the nebulous nothing that was the world outside the jewel, he could feel his hand started to rise.

"Good." Sylvia's lilting voice meandered through the haze. "Take it. It's yours. Scribble any old thing on there, and it will be done. You'll feel better once it's done. You'll feel lighter. You'll feel free."

435

It had been so long since he'd felt that way. The mere thought of such a thing made him want to weep. And all it would cost was a scribble on a receipt.

His signature...

His name.

He shook his head, and his hand fell like a rock. "No. I...I can't."

The PBR clock emitted a tinny ping. The pen trembled in her hand.

"*What?*" she demanded, her cajoling tone dissolving into acid fury.

"You heard me." He closed the folder and handed it back to her. "I can't sign this. It wouldn't be right."

She stepped forward, her chin low and teeth bared. "Enough is enough, John. Sign it and get it over with."

Ping. Ping. Ping...

Another step. The jewel's twinkle spasmed wildly in her furious vice-like grip. She was close enough now that he could smell her. Strawberries and hand sanitizer, of course. And something else that the other two smells couldn't quite disguise. Something of the earth.

Or something below it.

"No."

Ping. Ping. Ping...

"You're making a mistake, John. A big, big mistake."

Ping. Ping. Ping...

"I don't think so." He fixed his gaze on hers and kept it there.

Ping. Ping...

Ping.

In the silence that remained after the last chime, the sound of the pen hitting the floor was as loud as a church bell. Her head dropped forward like a rock, hair falling over her face like a curtain. She stayed that way long enough that John wondered if she had passed out on her feet.

And then she spoke.

"Without contracts, there is chaos."

Her head snapped up, eyes wide and lips stretched into a harlequin approximation of a smile. "You have no idea how true that is, John. But you're about to."

She stomped out, heels clopping like a Clydesdale, if such a beast were able to walk on two legs.

"What was that about?"

Shaking, John turned around. Grace was on her feet, hands perched on her hips as she favored him with a frown of disapproval.

"Financial dispute." John said, coming back around to the couch. "I have to say, the conduct of your bar staff leaves a lot to be desired."

"She doesn't work here."

John froze. "What are you talking about? You don't know her?"

"No, never seen her before."

"Then why on *Earth* did you let her come in?"

"What are you yelling at *me* for? *You* were the one she called by name."

The lights above them flickered, as if there were a storm. The metallic boom that followed made them both jump.

"What was *that?*" Grace asked, her hands wrapped around his bicep.

"No idea," John said, doing his best to sound unaffected. "Stay here. I'll go look."

There was no one in the unlit hallway when he emerged from the office. To his left, the door leading to the club's main room was shut tight, just as they had left it. The music, however, was about ten times louder, the thumping bass practically knocking the door off its hinges.

"What is that noise?"

John glared at Grace as she joined him in the hall. "What are you doing? I thought I told you to stay put."

He winced—that sounded way more parental than he was comfortable with, given the situation.

Luckily, Grace was too interested in the door to notice.

"It's not just the music," she said, squinting down the hall. "There's something else. Do you hear it?"

Still frowning, John closed his eyes to concentrate. She was right. In the space between the electronic pulses, he could decipher a series of thumps and crashes devoid of a meter or tempo, along with a chorus of muffled, frantic voices.

"John!"

Her scream made his skin shrivel. He wheeled around in time to see a horde of women pour out of the dressing room at the other end of the hall. There were so many of them they choked the light. A few had on scraps of neon spangled clothing. The rest were naked. Some held stiletto heels above their heads like pickaxes. Others led with their long-nailed, claw-like fingers. As they got closer, he could see their eyes had turned dark and glassy. Almost black. And their jaws seemed...stretched out. Not human. More like the snout of a dog. Or a wolf.

He shook his head. That was crazy.

Then he saw their teeth. Long, white, and deadly sharp.

Maybe it wasn't so crazy after all.

"Let's move!"

John wished he had been the one to say that, the big hero line. But it was Grace who grabbed him by the wrist, tearing him away from advancing horde and throwing him in the direction of the pulsing black door.

"Are you sure this is a good idea?" He could barely hear his own voice beneath the roar of the music.

"You have a better one?" she shouted back.

She had him there. His body tensed as they slammed through the door—and dropped into the seventh circle of hell.

Chapter Seven

Fingernails sliced through flesh like the tines of a fork through butter. The rending of clothes clashed with the sound of hair being torn from the scalp. In the booth John had left not twenty minutes earlier, Colton knelt over Jasmine, his distended jaws gnawing on the flesh of her left breast. Not to be outdone, Jasmine pecked at the top of his head with the sharp, hawkish growth that had taken the place of her mouth and nose. Her talon fingers had cut his back to ribbons. Both of them were slathered from neck to navel in thick, sticky crimson.

"Jesus," he moaned, his shock bringing him to a full stop. The thump of the approaching stampede hot on their heels filled him with terror. They were coming. Coming to join the festivities. Coming for him. Yet he couldn't seem to make himself move. He shuddered as an errant set of lime green claws ripped through his sleeve and gouged the skin of his forearm.

A sharp yank on his wrist pulled him out of his trance, away from danger. and nearly off his feet. The next thing he knew, he was on his knees in the shadowy alcove between the door and the stage with Grace hunkered down in the corner next to him.

"What are you doing?" he demanded, covering his head in preparation for the semi-human wave to collapse on top of them. But the wolfwomen rushed right past, too intoxicated by blood circus to notice them.

The music changed, and the lights cut out. For the next three seconds, he saw nothing. Then, in second number four, an all-consuming strobe light shattered the darkness and cast the room in a stiff tableau of black and white and red all over.

A naked wolfess with flaming orange hair towered over a prone, trembling man. The veins in her arms popped purple against her porcelain skin as she dragged him up across floor.

Another three seconds of darkness, and the man was on the stage, his outstretched arms pinned against the back wall by two additional women. Though his face did not seem to be as canine as the others, he did share the same beady black eyes. They roamed from semi-nude figure to the next, confused, terrified, but still…interested.

Black. Black. Black.

The redhead dropped to her knees and unzipped his pants. She smacked her lips, her long tongue rolling over a full set of pointed incisors. John's stomach clenched, but the man on stage didn't seem to have any reservations. He tilted his head back as she proceeded with her task. His jaw slackened into a pleased smile as she consumed all his attention. To either side of him, the two women kept his arms braced while, with their free hands, they each raised a long stiletto heel.

Black. Black.

Scream.

When the light flashed again, the women were gone. Only the man remained, writhing against the wall. Blood oozed from his palms, soaking the heels pinning him in place, to say nothing of the injury that John had seen coming a mile away.

"Fucking hell," Grace groaned, leaning heavily into John's shoulder as if struggling to stay on her feet.

From the resumed darkness came the crash of toppling tables and chairs as the wolfpack prowled the room for their next conquest. Back in the booth, Colton had nearly finished with his quarry, and she with him. The left side of his head was a bloody, gaping mess as he gnawed and licked at the gaping hole he'd torn in Jasmine's ribcage. But she didn't seem to mind. Her cheek rested on top of his head as she emitted a high-pitched drone through her beak that sounded like a cow on helium. Even so often she gave the exposed gray matter about his ear a languid peck that sent him into convulsions for several seconds. Their skin had become as pale as milk and their bodies had collapsed under their own weight, unlikely to rise again. They were dying, and yet neither one of them did anything to stop it.

They were enjoying it too much.

Bile burned the back of John's throat. This wasn't a massacre. It was a feast. And it wasn't going to end until every morsel in the place had been devoured.

His teeth chattered as his brain shook itself awake, dimming his emotions and galvanizing his senses. He surveyed the room again, every one of the gruesome details searing his brain in brutal clarity. This was real. This was happening. To deny or delay would only get them both killed.

"We need to get out of here," he whispered to Grace. "Now."

"I'm open to suggestions," she quipped. But the glibness of her answer couldn't disguise the tremble in her voice or the fact that her grip on his wrist was so tight it had made the tips of his fingers go numb.

"Listen," he said, covering her hand with his own. "Is there a back exit here?"

She nodded toward the opposite side of the stage. John looked out long enough to spot the red Exit sign and gauge the distance, then reoriented his gaze away from the carnival of nightmares surrounding the stage to check the rest of the room. The main entrance was on the opposite side of the building, up a shallow set of stairs and across a small foyer. More ground to cover that way, but less gory painful death as well. He liked that equation. He would like it even better, however, if they were armed.

"Are there are any weapons?"

Grace raised her hand. In it, she held the chipped and rusty tack hammer from the coffee table. He had seen flyswatters that looked more intimidating. The thought almost made him laugh, but her terror-stricken gaze kept him quiet.

"Okay, not bad. But I was thinking more along the lines of…you know, guns."

"Oh. Right. Um, I think so. There's a rumor that the bartenders keep one under the counter in case of a robbery or something."

He peered over his shoulder. The end of the bar was about ten feet from their current spot and ran the length of the main room. Rumor or not, at least it was on the way out.

Squeezing her hand one more time before peeling it off his wrist, John took her by the shoulders so he could look at her straight. She stared back at him with those strangely familiar eyes. "We're gonna move fast and quiet, and only in the dark. And we're gonna have to blend in."

She blinked, uncomprehending. He raised his bleeding arm, and her eyes widened with understanding. "Gotcha."

He winced she dragged her fingers through the red pools, then slashed at her cheeks. "How's that?"

He looked her over. Her gaze had turned to steel, and the blood on her face looking like a cross between wounds and warpaint. He nodded in approval. "Now we need to...um, act the part."

He pulled her close. Her perfume cut through the rusty stink of sweat and blood, tart and sweet and comforting.

"One. Two. Three."

The strobe flashed. Pivoting so her back was pinned to the wall, he lowered his head to her shoulder and pretended to bite. The instant the light faded, he grabbed her by the waist and swept them both along the wall.

"One. Two. Three."

Flash. The light turned her dark curls into electrified coils and glinted over her bared teeth. He grunted in surprise as her fingers curled into the back of his neck and her leg wrapped around the back of his knee.

The light disappeared, and so did her embrace.

"One. Two. Three."

He slammed her wrist into the wall above her head. "Just a few more feet," he whispered. She nodded, her hair brushing against his neck. He blinked in surprise. This flash-and-dark waltz was so disorienting, he hadn't even realized she'd turned, or that her back was now to him.

Thwap!

Grace screamed as something wet and meaty smacked into the wall next to them. Her arms wrenched against his grip. Despite his own alarm he kept his hold, pressing against her with all his strength until her instinct to flee subsided. She whimpered as a pearly pink lump slid onto the floor. To John, it looked as though it may have once been part of someone's thigh.

The light flashed out again. They should have been moving, but he couldn't bring himself to step over the recently harvested thing on the floor. All he could do was stand there, clutching the trembling girl in his arms and trying not to pass out.

A teeth-rattling scrape cut through the music as something razor sharp clawed at the wall next to his foot. His hands tightened around Grace's arms again, this time to keep himself from fleeing. When he looked back down at the floor, only the congealing red puddle remained.

"Forget stealth," he whispered. "Time to run."

They closed the last stretch at a full-out sprint. Grace slipped under the bar hatch with an elegance that made him feel like a gorilla as he lumbered in after her. Crouching low and no longer as concerned about the light, she led the way until they reached what John estimated to be the bar's halfway point. Sitting back on her heels, she pointed at a long sliding cabinet door set in the bar's lowest shelf. "If there's a gun back here, that's where it'll be."

John tugged the handle. The door bucked against the lock. He yanked harder, trying to toe the line between maximum force and minimum noise. But the door did not budge. "Do you know where the key is?"

"I have absolutely no idea—*ahh*!" She yelped as a heavy weight slammed onto the bar above them.

His stomach leapt into his throat as half his conscious mind disappeared below a flood of fear, adrenaline, and instinct. His hands shot out, grabbed Grace by her hips, pulling her to him and not stopping until he was fully on top of her.

"Scratch me," he hissed at her. "Now. As hard as you can."

A moment later, pain bit into his back and burned a warm, wet trail that pasted his shirt to his skin.

"Good," he groaned in pain, his clenched teeth grazing her collarbone. "Now scream like I'm hurting you."

The sound that ripped from her throat was so convincing it made every cell in his body scream along with her in revolt. He wanted nothing more than to throw himself as far away from her as he could. Either that or punch himself in the crotch.

The thing above them, snorted and chittered like a rabid hyena, its hot breath singing the hairs on the back of his neck. Gritting his teeth, he held on. Held tighter and listened to her scream again.

"You fucking *coward*."

The stink of the words was overpowering, like rotten eggs. He looked up to see Jasper diving toward him, black eyes glittering and pig face obscured by his protruding, stake-like teeth. He tried to get his hands up to defend himself, but it was too late. Jasper's fingers snapped taut around John's throat and threw him backward. Stars exploded in front of him as the back of his head cracked against the tile.

"You should have *signed*," Jasper croaked. "The one time you had the chance to do something of consequence, and you ran away."

The rubber band fingers tightened around John's neck. He blinked once, twice, trying to focus even as a tornado siren began whirring in his head. It wasn't working. The only thing he could see besides thick black blotches was Jasper's slick, perforating smile.

"You've had an easy life, haven't you? It's only fitting that your death will be—"

His voice died, picket-fence smile sagging as his glassy eyes bugged in silent shock. The noose around John's neck disappeared, his visioning cleared in time for him to cover his face and prevent Jasper from planting what he imagined would be a very unpleasant kiss on his cheek. He wanted to throw the son of a bitch across the room, but the veins in his arms felt like they were full of red-hot pudding and it was all he could do to wriggle out from under Jasper's weight without fainting.

It was only then, when he was sitting upright, coughing and gasping for air, that he realized he was looking at a corpse. The back of Jasper's head was a caved-in mass of bone and brain.

And standing over them both, bloodied tack hammer in hand, was Grace.

"Christ," John whispered, his eyes darting from the hammer to the body and back. "I never would have imagined…"

"Yeah." Grace sank to her knees, staring at her gore-streaked hammer as if it were a live grenade. "Me either."

"You didn't have a choice," he said softly. "It would have been me otherwise. You didn't—"

"I know that," Grace cut him off. Clenching her jaw, she turned her attention to the cabinet, and the lock. "Let's see how I do with a smaller target."

She timed her hit with the pounding bass that still poured from the speakers. After the collision with Jasper's skull, John expected the tiny hammer to snap. And yet, three whacks later, the mangled lock was barely hanging on by a thread. Defying the pain that seared his muscles, John grasped the handle and wrenched the door open.

Inside was a double-barrel shotgun.

"Thank God." Grace sighed. "Take it. I don't do guns."

The feeling of smooth wood and cold metal in his hands soothed him like a security blanket. He cracked the stock to check if it was loaded.

Only one round. He searched the recesses of the cabinet. No extra ammo, and no more guns.

The floor trembled beneath them, and the music cut out. The emergency lights flickered, accompanied by a soft moan that quickly escalated into a raspy, high-pitched warble.

"Goddammit. What now?" Grace poked her head over the counter.

He snapped the stock back into place. If one round was all he had, then he'd have to choose his shot carefully. Letting the gun lead the way, he rose just enough to see over the top of the bar.

Thanks to the return of semi-normal lighting, the one-on, three-off flip-book massacre was now presented in full-on Technicolor. Blood dripped down the walls and oozed across the floor. It was puddled around the torn booths and splashed across the broken tables and chairs. And the bodies...they were everywhere. Most were dead, and for them John was grateful. The less lucky ones wriggled toward the stage on whatever limbs they had left, their shrieks of agony creating a symphony of human suffering. It was as if they were being drawn forth by a dark, heartless gravity that they, even wretched and half-dead, were helpless to resist.

Grace exhaled. "What do we do?"

"Do you have to ask?" John drew the gun back to his chest. "We run. Same rules apply. You go, and you don't stop for anything. Understood?"

She nodded, clutching her tiny hammer with both hands in a striking pose. It would have looked ludicrous had it not been for Jasper's gaping head wound oozing onto the floor next to them.

He cocked the gun. "On three?"

"How about just—one!"

She was off before he could respond, so he simply followed, turning every few seconds to make sure nothing was on their trail. When she reached the end of the bar she vaulted the counter with stunning ease. By the time he had shimmied out from under the hatch, she was up the stairs and crossing the foyer in an all-out sprint toward the doors.

A loud crack shook the room. He gasped as she stumbled, pitching forward onto her hands and knees. But she kept moving, scrambling like a dog on ice before launching herself into the front doors. A shaft of dusty yellow light split the darkness, and she was gone. Outside. Safe.

Thank God.

"John…"

He whipped around. A sharp, orange-tinted spotlight cut a hole in the middle of the darkened stage, clearly defining the man pinned to the back wall. His struggles had ceased, and he now hung as limp and dead as a butterfly. At the edge of the light, outstretched hands clawed and beckoned from the shadows.

"John."

The voice sent a phalanx of spiders running up his spine. His trigger finger trembled as Sylvia clopped onto the stage. She still looked mostly human—except, of course, for the horns, an iron-black pair of appendages bursting out her forehead and rolling back over her hair. Twin rivers of black blood flowed from their bases, running from her temples to her collarbone and down the length of her curvy figure, not dripping so much as spreading like thick, cottony spiderwebs. The population of the room uttered a collective sigh of appreciation at the sight of her. But she was focused solely on John. Her onyx eyes traveled the length of him, sharp enough to strip the clothes off his back and slice flesh from his bones. He bit back a shudder.

"Stop." His voice was weak and brittle, but he had a feeling she would hear him anyway. "Stop it or I'll kill you."

"Dear little John," she tittered, her words soaked in condescension. "If I wanted to hurt you, I would have." She raised her outstretched palms until they were level with her shoulders. Another moan shook her audience, only this time it sounded less titillated and more...ravenous. The hands clawing at the edge of the light moved in. Grubby fingers grazing the base of her shoes, leaving trails of blood behind.

"In fact, who's to say I haven't already?"

Her hands closed into fists, and the lights snuffed out. The squeals and wet snaps that followed were all the incentive John needed. He stumbled up the steps in the general direction of the door, one hand outstretched in the pitch dark ahead of him as a guide. But he felt nothing.

A scream of pleasure erupted, then faded into a strangled gurgle. Was it his terror-stricken brain, or were those sounds getting closer? He swept his arm to either side. *Where the hell were the fucking doors?*

A glottal purr grazed his ear. He shrieked and blindly sprinted forward. His hand bent back against something smooth and unflinching. The back wall. He barely had time to curse his error before a bony hand wrapped itself around his left calf and a handful of razors pierced his flesh.

Sylvia's hideous laughter rattle in his head, louder even than his own scream.

The hand jerked backward, gouging deeper into the muscle. He clawed at the wall, searching desperately for something to keep himself upright. But it was no use. One more yank, and down he went, landing on his gut so hard he couldn't breathe. The spikes in his leg retracted, and something equally strong squeezed him around the ribs and lifted him off the ground. He hovered for a moment, only to land hard once again, on his back this time. He tried to sit up when the iron grip of his captor clamped around both his arms and pressed him back into the floor. The hand holding the gun bucked against the restraint, but it was no use. He groaned as the full weight of his captor settled onto his chest.

"Mmm…baby, you smell good."

A slippery tongue slithered like a slug down his cheek. He squeezed his eyes shut, preparing for the pain that would fill the final minutes or hours of his life.

Light sliced through the darkness, followed by a blast of hot, dry air. The thing on top of him recoiled with a shriek. In the sudden light, her orange hair lit up like a birthday candle. Her blood-streaked teeth glimmered like the most perverse toothpaste ad in history.

"Oh, fuck no!" John yelled, swinging the gun until it connected with her skull. She flew off him, blood spurting from the gash in her temple, and landed in a heap on the floor.

"John!"

Grace's voice rang out over the wailing and gnashing of teeth. Strong arms hooked under his own and started dragging him toward the light. He looked up, expecting to see her. Instead, he found a different face. Different, but no less familiar.

"Tommy?"

"You betcha, Doc." He offered a grimacing half-smile. "Think you could help me out a little here?"

Shaking off his surprise, John scrambled to his feet. His clawed calf screamed in protest, and he would have fallen again if Tommy hadn't grabbed him by the elbow and flung him toward the exit. They burst into the sweltering desert night. Grace slammed the doors, sealing the nightmares inside.

"I think it's safe to say I'm never coming back to this place again." Tommy paused to wipe the sweat from his eyes. It was then John noticed that Tommy exposed undershirt—and the knot of long, red claw marks covering it.

"Tommy," he exhaled in horror. "What the hell did they do to you?"

"No!" Tommy's head jiggled rapidly from side to side, his eyes screwed shut as his whole body went stiff. A moment later he was fine, grinning at John as if nothing had happened. "Not the time, Doc. Not before we make like a hooker and blow."

John nodded, frowning. He wasn't a psychiatrist, but that reaction...it didn't seem look good.

Taking John's arm and placing it gingerly across his shoulders, Tommy guided him toward the car. "You know, you're bleeding pretty bad yourself here, Doc."

"Actually," Grace called as she finished wedging a patio chair against the door handles. "The scratches on his back were from me."

"Oh?" Tommy waggled his eyebrows at John. "You dog."

"It's not like that." John sighed. Apparently not even the trauma associated with an apocalypse-level cannibal orgy could suppress Tommy's ability to be absolutely disgusting.

"Yeah, right." Tommy pressed his key fob. The rented sedan chirped in response. "Anyway, what say the three of us continue this little catch-up session at the hospital? I want details."

"No!" John shouted. "I need to get back to Halcyon immediately."

Tommy frowned. "Why?"

"Sylvia. That...creature that kicked it all off. She said she knew how to hurt me." John winced as he lowered himself into the front passenger seat. "Which means she knows about Bea."

Tommy snorted. "So what?"

Grace rolled her eyes. "Well, that figures."

He turned to her, hands on hips. "And what's that supposed to mean?"

"Nothing. It just doesn't surprise me that you would think any woman who isn't falling all over herself to please a man isn't worth caring about."

He grinned snidely. "That's pretty ironic, coming from a stripper."

She glared at him. "You shut your mouth."

"Why don't you come over here and *make me*?"

"Stop!" John pounded his fist against the dashboard. "I don't give a shit! Bea is my wife. Issues or not, I care about her, and right now she may be injured, or worse." He held out his hand to Tommy. "You want to stay here and bicker? Fine. Give me the keys and I'll go by myself."

Tommy glanced sullenly at Grace, then at the ground. "Okay, Doc. Sorry." He climbed into the driver's seat.

"Good." John slammed the door closed. "I'm also going to need your Blackberry."

"What for?"

"I'm starving and I was gonna order a pizza." John snarled. "What do you think it's for? I need to call Bea and my phone is back at the hotel with my luggage because *someone* had to get his T and A fix tonight."

Tommy's cheeks reddened. Shimmying in his seat, he freed the device from his back pocket and handed it over. John's fingers shook as he struggled with the tiny keys. Good thing he still knew Bea's number by heart. He was about to press the call button when he heard the rear door click open.

"What do you think you're doing?" he demanded as Grace slid into the seat behind him.

"What does it look like? I'm going with you."

"Absolutely not. This could be dangerous, and I don't want you to—"

"Don't. Even. Think about it." She fastened her seatbelt with an adamant click. "I'll find us the route. You concentrate on finding your wife. You said Halcyon, right?"

Dull pressure rolled against his lower back as she dug through the seat pocket for the map. He closed his mouth. To his surprise, his rejoined lips formed a smile. After all, good help was so hard to find.

"Ready?" Tommy asked.

John nodded and pressed the phone to his ear. "Drive."

Chapter Eight

November 12th, 2011

John drummed his fingers on the dashboard as they sped past the sign welcoming visitors to Halcyon, City of Fortune, at seventy miles per hour. Such bold-faced disregard for the posted speed limit of thirty would normally make his teeth ache, but at the moment it barely registered. The past seven hours had been the longest in his life. He'd tried calling Bea every ten minutes since they'd left Vegas, pausing only during the patches of no service, several of which had been distressingly large. But every call had dead-ended in the same robotic voicemail greeting. He'd left messages begging her to call him back on Tommy's number. Still—nothing but silence.

The first slivers of sun sliced into the horizon as they passed the Main Street, raced up the hill and made their way toward the other side of town where Bea rented a two-bedroom condo in one of Halcyon's newer developments. His drumming increased. If only her outgoing had been personalized. Hearing her voice would have calmed him down, even if it was just a recording. At least then he would know that some small part of her was still alive. Even if the rest of her—

He yelped as strong, slim arms wrapped around his chest and pulled him back against his seat, yanking his pattering hands away from the dashboard.

"Relax," Grace whispered, her chin resting on the edge of the seatback near his left shoulder. "You don't know that anything has happened to her. You've got to stay calm."

"She hasn't answered," he said, rubbing his palms along his thighs. His pants were stiff with dried blood and whatever other grime they had collected from the strip club floor. "I've called and called, and still..."

"I know." She ran her hands over his upper arms. "But it was the middle of the night for a lot of those. Maybe she was asleep. Or maybe she changed her number. Or maybe she's one of those people who doesn't answer calls from numbers she doesn't recognize." Grace tipped her head in Tommy's direction. "Any reason she would have *your* number in her phone?"

Tommy blew out his lips. "Of course not! And I resent the implication that I would go behind a friend's back and make a play for his wife."

"Hey, if it walks like a creepy, lecherous duck—whoa! John, are you okay? You're shaking."

He could only answer with a shuddering moan. He had been overcome with a frigid sense of foreboding the moment the rose-tinted dome of Edensgate had come into view. The feeling only grew deeper as the rest of the building and the surrounding land came into view. The parking lot was mostly empty except for a luxury SUV, a couple of mall utility vehicles...and one powder blue Volkswagen convertible that he would recognize anywhere.

"She's there." He wriggled Grace's hands away. "Take the next exit. Go to the south entrance, and park as close to the door as you can.

"You got it." Tommy swung the car off the highway, rocketed through the parking lot and jumped the sedan onto the curb next to the east entrance. "How's that?"

"Perfect," John said as he fumbled with his seatbelt. Despite the panic and fear stoking his adrenaline, his injuries had him moving much slower than his cohorts. By the time he'd gotten his door open Grace was already there, waiting to help him out.

"How's this?" she asked after she'd situated herself under his left arm.

John tried putting weight on his injured leg. The bleeding had stopped some time ago thanks to the makeshift tourniquet he'd manufactured from a ripped-up bit of his jacket, but the muscles still pleaded for rest. He could walk, provided he had help, but it was about it.

"Anything I can do?"

John looked at Tommy where he stood to one side, hands jammed in his pockets, watching the scene with growing unease. He seemed so isolated and fearful, John very nearly felt sorry for him.

"Actually, yes. There is." Reaching back into the car, he retrieved the shotgun from where he had wedged it between the center console and his seat. Tommy's lips parted in surprise as John handed it over. "Doc, are you sure?"

"Yeah, I don't know about that," Grace added, eying Tommy warily. "I mean, there might be nothing in there. Do we really need to go full metal?"

"It's precisely because we *don't* know what's in there that this is necessary," John said, slamming the door. "Besides, my stance is compromised. I'm the last one that should be holding it."

He jiggled the weapon it at Tommy, who accepted it as if it were the shroud of Turin.

"So you know, there's only one round in there. If you shoot something, try not to miss."

"What?" Tommy's eyes widened, his reverence rapidly curdling into annoyance. "Why the hell didn't we stop and buy more ammo?"

"Uh, John?" Grace pointed down the sidewalk toward the mall entrance. The automatic doors had opened, but no one was coming out. The doors closed and opened again.

"Hm," John said. "That's strange."

They shuffled toward the entrance, Tommy a couple paces ahead with the gun at the ready. As they got closer, they could hear the grind of the motor and the screech of under-greased doors as they slid back and forth. It sounded like an animal's warning growl. When the trio reached the rubber mat in front of the entrance, the motion sensors commanded the doors to stay open.

But growling continued.

John turned to Grace. "That look like nothing to you?"

She tilted her head complacently. "I stand corrected."

They passed through the entrance as fast as his hobbled leg would allow.

Only half of the overhead lights were on in the east hallway. The alternating pools of light and shadow made the cobbled floor look like the scaly back of a monochromatic snake. As they proceeded to the south side of the building, past storefront after locked and caged storefront, John couldn't help feeling like they weren't in a mall, but a zoo.

"Bea!" The word bounced against the high walls, drowning out five normal footsteps and the pathetic scrape of his useless foot. "Bea? Can you hear me?"

They stopped in their tracks as the floor trembled beneath them.

"Maybe you should take it easy with the yelling," Tommy said, his head ticking to either side. "Like you said—we don't know what else might be in here with us."

"I swear, I'm gonna kill him."

They all jumped at the disembodied voice. Tommy raised the gun to his shoulder, then dropped it instantly as two blonde, heavier women in velvet track-suits—one pink, one purple—appeared in a far-off pool of light.

"I told him, straight whiskey gives me a headache," railed the woman in purple. "How many times have I told him, Della?"

"At least fifty," replied the woman in pink.

"At least fifty, right. But he keeps on insisting I shoot it. No water, no ice, just right down the gullet. Can you imagine? But he wants what he wants, and everyone else has to accommodate."

"I know exactly what you mean." Della wiped her sweat-banded forehead with the back of her hand. "It's like, when we were in Chianti, all Ralph wanted to drink was Burgundy. But then when we were in Burgundy—"

She stopped in mid-sentence when she spotted the trio. John wondered which part of this image the women found the most disturbing—his injuries, the half-naked woman holding him up, or the guy with the gun.

"Mayor Virgil? Is that you?"

"Uh, yes." John stood as straight as he could without provoking the pain in his leg. "Good morning, ladies. I'm sorry to do this, but I'm going to have to ask you to leave. Official business."

"Oh dear, is something wrong?"

The women in purple glared at her. "Stuff it, Dell. He doesn't need to explain."

Della's head drooped. "Right, Vickie. Sorry, Mr. Mayor."

"Oh, that's okay," John insisted. "No, nothing is wrong. Routine safety inspection, that's all."

"Of course." Vickie bobbed her head eagerly. "We understand. Thank you, Mr. Mayor. Take care." She grabbed Della by the arm and speed-walked away, careful to avoid looking at both Tommy and Grace as they went.

"That was…easy." Grace frowned after them.

"Sure was!" Tommy clapped John on the shoulder. "Nice job, Doc. Way to think on your feet."

Grace shook her head. "No, that story was ridiculous. They never should have believed it."

"But they did, so who cares?" Tommy released John and re-situated the gun. "Now let's go find your woman and get the hell out of here."

John looked at Grace for confirmation. After another second of staring after the women with that analytical gaze of hers, she repositioned herself more resolutely under his arm. "Fine, let's do it. And…I can't believe I'm saying this, but I agree with Tommy. At this point, stealth is probably the better option."

Chapter Nine

Unlike the rest of the storefronts, the metal security gate at Virgil Cosmetics and Medispa stood open. Icy shivers rattled John's bones once again as they crossed the threshold.

"Sh-sh-she's gotta be here." John pointed to the hallway that led to the back rooms. "That w-w-way."

Nodding, Tommy took the lead while John and Grace fell in step behind him.

He had hoped to find her at her desk, safe and sound. But the frosted glass surrounding her newly etched name was as dark as a tomb.

"Doesn't look like she's here, buddy," Tommy said.

"Sh-sh-she has to be," John chattered. "I f-f-feel it."

"Maybe she's in another store," Grace said, pulling him closer to keep his shaking body upright. "This place is massive. We could check the bathrooms, the food court—"

"Bea!" John wailed. He grunted as Grace elbowed him in the ribs.

"Shhhh! What did we just say? Be *stealth*."

"She's right," Tommy added. "You want those lady mall-walkers to hear you?"

"I was more concerned with any flesh-eating demon monster that may or may not be out there. But sure, the mall-walkers too."

"I don't care," John said, slumping more fully into her strength. "I need her."

He opened his mouth.

"Oh no you don't!" Grace clamped her hand over his face before he could get it out.

"Buh!" he screamed against her palm, whipping his head back and forth like a bridled horse. "Buh! *Buh!*"

"John?"

He froze as the familiar figure of his wife stepped out from around the corner that led all the way to the back offices.

"Bea!" He slid out of Grace arms and limped down the hall as fast as his injured leg and jackhammering heart would let him. "You're here. You're okay."

Her eyebrows squeezed together with concern, but she held her ground. She didn't even shrink away when he wrapped her in his arms and pressed his forehead to her shoulder. She'd been in a different office. Her old office. In his relief-induced euphoria, he found himself wondering if it still had her old name etched on that door. The thought made him hold her even tighter.

When he felt her delicate arms wrap themselves tentatively around his waist and hug him back, he nearly started to cry.

"Of course, I'm okay," she said. "I came in earlier to get a jump on today's paperwork. *I* am fine." She pulled away and looked him over. Her face contorted in alarm. "What on earth happened to your leg? And what is all this...*stuff* on your clothes? If I didn't know better, I'd say it looked a lot like—"

The room around them quaked, harder and longer than before. The florescent light above them swung on its mount and John pitched off his already unstable feet. As he careened into the wall, he felt Bea's hands press into his sides to try and keep him from falling completely. They stayed that way until the shaking stopped.

"What was that?" Bea asked.

"I'll explain later," he said. "Right now, we need to get out of here, and as far out of town as possible." Taking her by the hand, he led her over to Tommy. "Stay with him. He'll protect you."

Bea looked Tommy up and down. "John, who is the man? And why does he have a gun? And what—?"

The question died in her mouth when she spotted the stained tack hammer dangling from Grace's garter belt, not to mention the stained corset, ripped stockings, and bare feet.

"Uh, hello," Bea mumbled before abruptly turning back to John. Her eyebrows arched halfway up her forehead.

Who the hell is this whore?

Their marital telepathy hit him as hard as it always had. Her displeasure should have made him cringe, and it did...but he couldn't help chuckling a little in satisfaction. It had been a long time since he'd seen Bea get jealous of anything, let alone because of him.

Grace must have gotten a sense of it as well. She raised her hand at Bea in half-wave, half-surrender. "Hi. I'm Grace. Grace Henry. It's a pleasure to meet you. John has told me such wonderful things."

"Really?" Bea said, the surprise in her voice as palpable as it was rare. "And how do you two...*know* each other?"

He groaned. "Look, we really don't have time—"

"We work together," Grace said smoothly. "I'm his new assistant."

"Oh?" Another arched brow in his direction.

You expect me to believe that?

He shrugged and flashed his sincerest smile. "She started yesterday."

"I see." Bea gave Grace another once-over. "That's good, I suppose. He's been complaining about the last one for ages." Back straight and elbows tight, Bea held out her hand. "Pleasure."

Grace accepted. "Likewise."

A seismic blast that knocked them all sideways. Grace grunted as she slammed back against the wall, then cried out again as Bea fell into her. Both of them narrowly avoided the florescent bulbs that, having decided they'd taken enough punishment for one day, threw themselves to the floor in an explosion of sugary glass.

"Come on!" John grabbed Bea by the elbow and thrust her in front of him. He gestured for Tommy to go next.

"Promise me," John said as he looped his arm over Grace's shoulder once again. "If something happens, you'll stay with her. Leave me and get her out."

Grace scoffed. "I didn't listen to you when you said that last time. Why would I do it now?"

He shot her a pained smile. "Because last time you weren't my assistant, *Ms.* Henry."

She rolled her eyes. "In that case, you should probably know that I'm not super great at taking directions. *Boss.*"

The patches of light shimmied over the black cobblestones as they raced down the hall. Hobbling past one of many women's clothing stores, John swore he saw the mannequins' chic bald heads swivel on their necks, blank faces marking his progress. Frigid air crashed into him like waves of icicles until his teeth throbbed and his extremities lost all feeling. His toes bashed against the uneven ground so often that by the time they came in sight of the entrance, Grace was practically carrying him. The grating growl had stopped, and the doors gaped open. As they got closer, John expected the glass panels to slam shut in their faces.

Instead, a large figure lumbered in and blocked their path.

"Ray?" John asked as they slowed to halt. Around them, the walls downgraded their convulsions to a low buzz.

"John! Thank God!" Ray braced himself on his knees so he could catch his breath. The unbuttoned jacket of his bespoke suit flapped against his thighs. "It's gone, John. It's all gone."

"What, Ray? What's all gone?"

"The mine!" Ray wailed. "The Halcyon gold mine. It's gone. And I don't mean caved in or tapped out. It's like it was never there. Which makes sense, I suppose—technically speaking, it never really was."

Dread and exhaustion clashed in his chest. He felt as if his heart had been trapped in an iron maiden that had been set on fire. "She said she knew how to hurt me," he moaned. "This is what she meant."

"It's not too late," Ray said. "You can fix this, John. And you have to fix it. Call the Courier. Tell him you'll make a deal. Tell him you'll sign."

"Sign?" John and Grace said in near-perfect unison.

"Yes!" Ray shouted back. "Halcyon only exists because of a deal our founder made with the Courier. Duration, benefit, signature; that's how it works. And now the duration has run out, and the benefit...has ended."

"Whoa, hey, slow your roll there, pal." Grace rubbed her eyes. "Before you keep rambling, I have a couple of questions. Specifically—who the hell are you and what the hell are you talking about?"

At last, it seemed Ray had found a compelling reason to stand up straight. "I am Ray Lei Wan," he said, smoothing the front of his rumpled shirt. "I am the manager of this mall. More importantly, my family has been in the region since Halcyon began My great grandfather worked as a foreman on the V&T Railroad."

John raised his brows. "I didn't know that."

"You never asked. The founders may have been a group of twelve middle-class missionaries from Louisiana, but people like my great-grandparents built this town. On a foundation of sand, as it turned out." He shook his head. "I'm so sorry, John. This never should have fallen on you. The original signature came from a selfish, greedy man who put his own interests over the well-being of others every chance he got. The second signature should come from a similar hand. But...here we are."

Grace frowned. "Call me crazy, but it really seems like you're asking him to sign away his soul."

"No, no. You're not crazy at all. In fact, that's pretty much spot on."

His words hung heavy in the stunned silence that followed.

"I can't believe this," John whispered. "I mean, I won't mince words—today has been a complete debacle. But...even if the mine is gone, my *immortal soul* seems a pretty high price to bring it back."

"It's not just about the mine," Ray pleaded. "Halcyon has only ever been a certain way. Prosperous, orderly, and wanting for nothing. The people here have gotten used to that. It's all they know; all they can possibly conceive. If you rip that away and turn their neat lives into chaos...there's no telling what they will do."

John's skin rippled with gooseflesh. He surveyed the hall, taking in the posh storefronts, lush frescoes, and the Roman-inspired architectural touches.

Then he pictured the riots. The windows smashed and the displays ripped apart. The beautiful frescoes scratched up and smeared with all manner of filth. The fires blazing in the faux marble trash cans.

The mall-walkers in their monochromatic sweat suits, trampled and bleeding on the ground.

He jumped as Ray dropped a hand onto his shoulder. "It isn't fair. God knows isn't. And when you're on the other side of this, I will do whatever I can to help. But you're the mayor. It's your responsibility now."

His gray eyes shone so intensely that John had to look away, his gaze traveling from Grace to Tommy, and finally to Bea. At first, she seemed as detached and unconcerned as always. But upon closer inspection, he saw her lower lip tremble and a thin line of worry crease the smooth skin between her eyebrows. His heart panged. To betray that much emotion meant that she must be terrified. He closed his eyes as exhaustion sliced all the way to his bones. She didn't deserve this. None of them did.

Ray was right. This was his responsibility. If he didn't fix it, then who would?

"Okay," he said at last. "I'll do it. I'll sign."

Chapter Ten

The tremors in the walls intensified once again. Everyone jumped as the sliding doors snapped closed.

A burbling noise drew his attention. A few yards down the hall, thick black goo oozed up from between the cobblestones. He moaned as the cold overwhelmed him and he sank to his knees, his breath coming in short, frosty puffs.

"John?" Bea's voice, full of concern.

"I'm okay," he managed. "Stay where you are. It's all going to be..."

His trailed off. Wisps of black smoke wafted up from the ooze, shifting and twisting until they formed the outline of a semi-human form. Its body was round but not flabby, like a balloon covered in short black bristles. Black soot fell from its steely horns like infernal dandruff as it stamped its hoof against the cobblestones.

"Greetings, Storykeeper." It nodded at Ray. "The Courier has come."

"Greetings." Ray spread his arms but stopped short of bowing. "Thank you for your attention."

"It's our pleasure. Besides, we can smell a deal a mile away." It snapped its hairy, humanoid fingers. A plate of red light blinked into existence in front of its chest. Out of it rose a book, as big as a washboard and four times as thick, bound in black leather and banded with slates of iron. "What is your request?"

"The future of Halcyon." Strong fingers tugged at John's arm as Ray helped him to his feet. "This custodian is a good man, and in exchange for another eight score and one day, he has agreed to enter his name in your book."

The Courier regarded John with its smoldering ember eyes. "Is that true, Custodian? Will you give us your name?"

John took a breath and nodded. "I will."

"Interesting." It looked down at the book's cover for a moment, then back at John. "Your request has been considered and rejected."

"What?" John glanced at Ray, whose face had drained of all color.

"You can't do that," Ray spluttered. "Those were the terms set forth by—"

"You speak of the Reverend's terms. But that deal ended last midnight. This is a new contract, and the conditions have changed." It passed a hand over the book. The cover flopped opened and the pages fluttered until stopping halfway through the volume. "See here, Storykeeper. There is not one name on Halcyon's ledger, but twelve."

Ray studied the page. The color in his cheeks shifted again, fading from lily white to puke green. "The twelve missionaries. The founders. You have them all."

"It wasn't hard. A young town in wild country is a desperate place. Needs spring up like Jimson weed. All we had to do was find the right blade for the harvest." Its bovine nose snuffled over the pages as if they were pies fresh from the oven. "Yes…all that misery in those names. All that fear and greed and hate. With the power those names hold, we can spread our will much further than Halcyon. That settlement to the south, for example. The one with the lights and the whores."

Its dark eyes flickered like an old movie. In them, John saw the strip club stage—and the man that had been crucified, dismembered, and left to die.

The Courier grinned. "Yes, that was fun. We will go back there next. And then on. And on."

John heard. Tommy grunt like he'd been punched.

"What do you want?" John demanded.

Rotten teeth and blood red gums flashed between cracked black lips. "The Storykeeper does not lie, Custodian. You are a good man with a good heart. That will make a fine trophy."

It flicked its wrist. Another, smaller disc of light appeared, in front of John this time, and a dull black scimitar with a ruby handle fell from the bottom. It landed on the stones with tinny smack.

"First, your name. Then, your heart. Or watch us tear your world apart." It emitted a maniacal giggle of delight at its own whimsy.

"This is outrageous!" Ray fumed. "His life was never part of the deal."

"It is now."

"You can't—"

"We can, we do, and we will." The Courier snapped his fingers, and Ray collapsed.

"Jesus!" John dropped to the floor, pawing at Ray's neck in search of a pulse.

"Invoke whatever god you like," The Courier snickered. "All the denizens of Olympus itself could not save you now. This is the agreement, and it is the only one we will offer. Make your choice."

"Hell no."

John clenched his jaw as Grace stormed to his side. "Ms. Henry, please—"

"Absolutely not," she cut him off. "Look, I get it, okay? I know you want to do the right thing. But if you think I'm gonna stand aside and watch you cut out your own heart—I mean, all due respect, but fuck that. *No*. We will figure something else out."

John shook his head as he struggled to his feet. "There's no figuring your way out of the apocalypse."

"Amen." The Courier winced and spat, its saliva sizzling as it burned a hole through the cobblestones.

"Fine." Sneering, she slipped the hammer out from her garter belt. "Then I guess we'll do the apocalypse."

She kicked the scimitar with her bare heel. It skittered across the lumpy floor and knocked into the Courier's left hoof. It regarded the weapon for a moment before leveling a furious gaze at her. "He will not sign?"

She raised the hammer above her head. "No, he won't."

Click-click.

"Yes, he will."

John stiffened. Moving cautiously so as not to provoke any rash action, he turned to look down the barrel of the shotgun.

"Tommy, what are you doing?"

"I'm sorry, John," Tommy said, his voice brittle and his forehead pinched with terror. "I can't do it. I can't go back to that hell pit we were in last night. You're gonna sign that book. And then...you're gonna give him your heart."

The Courier chuckled. "Finally, a reasonable man."

"Come on, Tom, think about this," John pleaded. "If I don't sign my name, and you shoot me, then I'll *never* be able to sign. No signature, no deal. No deal...well, you know."

Tommy's eyes darted side to side in a panic. "That's true…"

"Exactly. So why don't you put the gun down and we can—"

Swinging to his right, Tommy pointed the gun at Bea.

"No!" John cried as her hands shot up, her eyes and mouth widening into three perfect circles. "Tommy, you don't need to do that."

"Sign the fucking book!" Tommy screamed, spit flying from his mouth and desperate tears rolling down his sweat-filmed cheeks. "Sign it or I swear to God I will blow her head off!"

"Okay!" Shaking, John turned back to Grace, hoping against hope that she might have another idea.

But she just stared back at him, face ashy and lower lip trembling. Her fear confirmed his own.

There was no out. Only through.

Head bowed, he turned to face the Courier. "Do you have a pen?"

It smiled so wide its lower lip started to bleed. A lift of its left hand brought the scimitar floating up to elbow height. With its right, it pushed the book through the air until it was positioned between John and Grace. A twist of the wrist, and the scimitar flipped so the blade was facing up. It waggled an index finger at him.

"Your pen, Custodian."

Grace whimpered. John wanted to give her some indication that it was okay, but the thought of seeing her cry was almost enough to make him break down himself. Holding his finger above the blade, he glared at Tommy instead. Tommy stared back at him, resolute but miserable. Good. John hoped Tommy would be miserable for the rest of his disgusting, pathetic life.

Taking one more fortifying breath, he turned his attention, at last, to Bea. She had acclimated to having a gun pointed at her surprisingly well. In fact, she barely seemed to notice. Her face was the stoniest he had ever seen it, even during the worst of their arguments. Her opaque gaze flicked from him to Tommy and back again.

What was she thinking?

He frowned. His marital telepathy was failing him. Why? What didn't she want him to know?

By the time it dawned on him, Bea had already thrown herself at the gun.

"Get down!" John grabbed Grace by the arm and yanked. They landed in a tangle several feet away from the hovering book. He looked up to see Bea wrench the gun from Tommy's hands and slam the butt of it into his groin. He crumpled like a paper bag, pressing his hands to the offended area as he fell gracelessly to the ground.

"Thank God," John sighed as cool relief flooded his limbs.

Dropping the gun to her waist, Bea leveled the barrel at the book.

"No!" bellowed the Courier a moment before John could say it himself. He clambered to stand, but the searing burn of his mangled calf made him fall hard on his knees.

The walls trembled as the roaring bullet struck the tome dead center, embedding red hot metal in the wizened spine. The black leather rippled like a puddle of oil as a web of liquid gold spider-cracked out from the point of impact. For a moment, it appeared as though the whole thing would burst into flames.

Instead, the oil and gold repelled like liquid magnets, ripping a hole not in the book in the air above it and letting a sliver of burning red light seep out. The Courier roared as the repelled black murk soaked him up to the shoulders while the gold, retracing the path of the bullet, splashed Bea with wet, shimmering light.

"Bea!" John cried.

She turned to him, her face framed by a fiery corona and her skin glowing like the dawn. She looked so gorgeous, so horribly beautiful, he could barely bring himself to look. The chasm of red light above the book sparked and surged, following the bullet's path and fueling the golden second skin. He heard the Courier roar again. This time it ended in a squealing wretch.

"Bea…"

She smiled. That mysterious, pained little smile that he'd never been able to figure out before. Now, in this moment, he knew exactly what it meant.

Darling, I must.

His eyes watered. She was so bright it hurt. But he refused to turn away. He had to see her, all of her, until the very last second.

Diamonds burst from every pore, ripping through her chest and shooting out the ends of her hair. He collapsed, curling his arms around his head as a blast of heat buffeted his body.

She's gone.

"No." He clamped his hands over his ears, desperate to deny the words that had ferreted their way into his head. "No…"

But when the raging heat above him subsided, and he looked up, all that remained of the Courier and his wife were large smears of black and gold splashed across the walls.

She's really gone.

He squinted with his sun-burned eyes as the smears bulged and twisted across the walls. More details emerged—faces, several of which he recognized. The bloated, mustachioed insurance salesman. The long-haired hippie with the stained teeth. Sylvia, with her horrid horns and hollowed-out eyes. They roiled against the marble, slick appendages bubbling and clawing at the air, searching desperately for a way out. But there wasn't one. They were all wrapped in delicate strands of gold, and no matter how the shadows surged and raged, they could not break free.

The images began to fade. John watched through his tears as the colors grew faint and finally disappeared. He heard Grace stir behind him, then fall silent once again. They didn't speak or touch, but the fact that she was still meant more to him than he could ever explain. They stayed there until the smears faded and all that remained was an expanse of pale, cold rock.

And the book, apparently unscathed, lying open on the floor in front of them.

Epilogue

It's been seven days since the bizarre events at the Snapdragon Gentleman's Club, and Las Vegas Metro Police are still no closer to determining what happened."

From the pilled avocado green couch, Grace pointed at the image of the solemn salt and pepper anchor on the screen.

"Cut."

The anchor disappeared, replaced with stock footage of milling officers and flashing cruisers arranged around the caution-taped club entrance. She smiled to herself. She'd seen the report so many times, she'd gotten very good at calling the shots.

"*At precisely midnight on November 11th, the security system inside the club suffered a fatal error, taking the entire network of cameras offline.*"

"Cut."

A four-way split of grainy images from the club's overhead security cameras appeared. The front entrance, the main stage, the private rooms—all heavily censored, of course.

"*These are some of the last visual records we have of the Snapdragon before the system went down. The next time anyone had* time with the inside of the club was six hours later when the morning bartender arrived for his shift—and discovered a chilling mystery waiting."

"Cut."

The quadruple angles melted into footage from a first-person shaky cam. It jiggled above overturned tables and torn vinyl banquettes as it approached the main stage. If she sat close to the screen and squinted, she could make out the two holes punched in the back wall. But the mutilated body wasn't there. And neither were any others. There wasn't so much as a drop of blood in sight. It was as if the place had been power-washed.

Or licked clean.

"The interior of the property suffered significant damage. As one officer reported, quote, it looked as if it had been overrun by an assault team and a pack of wolves, unquote. Despite this, there is no indication as to what may have become of the club's patrons or employees."

"And…cut."

She leaned forward intently as the visual shifted one more time into the coup de grace: a profile picture slide show of the missing with an 800-number plastered along the bottom in bold red lettering.

"Police put the total number of people in the club at forty-one on the night of November 11th, based on available security footage, timecards, and credit card receipts."

"How's it looking?"

She craned her neck over the back of the couch as Ray descended the stairs from the security suite, paper bag in one hand and a cardboard drink caddy in the other.

"They're getting to the array now." She sneered as the boisterous, shit-eating grin of Tommy Concannon appeared. Once again, she said a little prayer that whatever desert Ray had dumped him in had collapsed into the deepest circle of hell.

The slide show transitioned from patrons to employees. Sadness rattled her as she said another silent goodbye to her former coworkers and her former life. At least she didn't have to see her own face up there—since her Facebook photo had been a cartoon dog, she was one of the few that appeared listed in name only. Apparently, the nightly news team was too busy to hunt down a picture of what was, from their perspective, just another dead stripper.

"Anyone with information pertaining to the whereabouts of any of these individuals is encouraged to call the tip line number you see on the screen." The anchor casted one more forlorn look at his desk. When he looked back at the camera, he was the picture of joy. "And speaking of mysteries, what is the story behind this heat wave? We go now to Sunny Bellows with weather."

"Still looks good." Grace swiveled around on the cushion. "As far as Metro knows, he was never there that night."

"Good." Ray handed her one of the disposable drink cups with the words PEACHY CREAM stamped along the side. Chewing on the straw, she watched him unpack the bag: three bags of single serve potato chips, three soft pretzels, a gallon of milk, and two more boxes of ammo, courtesy of Hunter's Paradise.

"God, I'd kill for a salad."

"At least the smoothies taste kind of like real food." He folded the bag in half and tucked it under the table. "If it makes you feel any better, I don't think we'll have to hold out for too much longer."

Her ears perked up. "Oh yeah?"

"Yeah. I haven't seen a single car pass on the highway all day, and it's been almost a week since anyone came close to any of the entrances. Maybe everyone is worn out from looting downtown."

"Right. That's probably it, and not, you know…" She cocked her chin toward the closed door in the middle of the back wall.

"That may also have something to do with it," Ray conceded, taking a sip of his own smoothie. "I'd still prefer to have a modern security system in addition to any metaphysical help we might be getting."

"No doubt. When are you supposed to hear back from the bank?"

"Tomorrow. I'm not worried though. With the mine closed, this mall is the only asset the town has left. We've got to protect it."

Grace laughed bitterly. "That might be the understatement of the century. What about corporate? Won't they be suspicious when they see the cost of the upgrade has gotten considerably higher?"

He waved a hand. "Leave that to me. I've been dealing with those guys for years. I know how to handle them. Point is, once we've got the new system installed, then I'll be able to breathe easy."

"Yeah, right," Grace sighed. New security system or not, she saw very little chance of any of them breathing easy ever again.

"From all of us at the eleven 'o'clock news, I'm Monty Allegro. Stay safe out there."

The brass and strings played him out. A moment later, Grace felt a soft rumble shimmy through the cushions beneath her. On the table, the milk rippled and sloshed in its plastic jug.

"Good talk as always, Ray," she said. "But it seems they're playing my song." She stood and zipped up the front of the gray maintenance jumpsuit. It was two sizes too big for her, but it was miles better than running around in a blood-soaked corset. Cup in her left hand, she swiped her tiny hammer off of the coffee table with her right. The sticky, slivered handle made her cringe.

"FYI," she said as she made her way toward the door in the back, "the *second* we can get to a real hardware store, I'm buying a bigger gun."

Knock. Knock. A pair of quick, gentle taps, and the door to the long, cylindrical room creaked open.

"John?" Grace's voice wafted like an angel through the gloomy light. Ray had told them the room had been for uniform storage.

Not anymore.

"John, it's time."

"Okay." Blinking his exhausted eyes, he turned away from his lectern and offered her a small smile. "I just need a few more minutes."

"Well, shake a leg. We've got a long night ahead." Her smile was more concerned than happy. She turned to go, then paused. "Oh, and before I forget—you need to eat something."

She handed him a plastic cup with a slightly chewed straw. He sighed but accepted it. She lingered in the doorway until he had sucked down three seconds worth of the fruit-and-sugar semi-solid before she retreated, leaving the door pitched wide open behind her.

He turned back to the lectern. The yellowed pages of the Courier's book gaped at him like a drunken, sloppy mouth. He scowled back. Try as he might, it still refused to give up its secrets.

He grunted as a curled claw of agony plunged into his aorta and dark laughter swirled in his ears.

We got you, Custodian. We got you.

"Do you?" he growled back, slapping his left palm onto the page. Golden power flowed up his arm, and the hook in his chest disappeared.

"Thanks, hon," he whispered, his teeth clamped around the straw. As loathed as he was to admit it, Ray made damn good smoothie. He stooped to retrieve his weapon, his wedding ring still humming like a tuning fork around his finger.

You're welcome.

He smiled. That telepathic voice was still there, brushing against the back of his ear, the words as clear and bright as a sunrise. "I love you."

I love you too.

He nodded and cocked the gun.

Time to go to work.

They made their way through the East Hall, keeping to the shadows as much as they could. As always, the plan was to do a full sweep. But they didn't make it more than twenty yards before the rapid squeak of gym shoes made them stop in their tracks.

"There," Grace whispered, gesturing with the head of the hammer at the mouth of the rotunda. John aimed where she pointed.

A moment later, two jewel-toned blobs hustled into view. Smears of mud and other foulness clung to the matted microfibers of their sweat suits, and wrinkled semblance of flesh hung from their jaws in wobbling green sacs. They didn't run, of course, but motored toward the entrance as fast as their lumpy forms could take them.

"Evening, ladies," Grace called out.

The pair turned in her direction. Their blank, sagging eye sockets belied no emotion, but they bared their rotting teeth in obvious fury.

"If I've told you once, I've told you fifty times," the Vickie-thing rasped. "No. More. Shots."

The shotgun blast ripped the figure in half, splattering the marble behind it with chunky black liquid. Shrieking like a terrified chihuahua, the Della-thing sped up until she was almost, but not quite, running. She may have even made it to the doors if not for the uneven jut of cobblestone that caught its toe and sent its flying across the floor.

Funny thing was, John was sure that outcropping hadn't been there a moment ago. It was almost as if it had sprung from the ground in the blink of an eye.

Or in a flash of gold.

Whatever the cause, Grace did not let the opportunity go to waste. Leaping into a crouch over the supine creature, she brought the tiny hammer down in a series of swift, well-practiced blows: right knee, left knee, base of the spine, back of the head. Each one provoked a scream of agony except, of course, the last. That one produced only silence.

"Nice hit," John said, lowering his gun as he joined her.

"You too." She wiped the head of her hammer on the front of her jumpsuit, then looked up at him with a wry smile. "You wanna know something funny?"

"What?"

"I always hated malls."

John smiled wistfully. "So did I, Miss Henry. So did I."

CHARACTER GALLERY

"I'm thinking we should go bowling."
-Rex Ranganathan-

-Cari Hembert-

"It's all the same nightmare underneath."
-Grace Henry-

"I always wanted to know what deep-fried cockroach tasted like."
-Cooper O'Bannon-

"An angelic face is the perfect disguise for steel and fire."

Acknowledgments

The *Dead Mall* series would not have been possible without the time and support of numerous people. Big thanks go out to my critique partner Jeff; my Sin City Writers Group (especially Toni, Terri, Melissa, Jason, Diana, and Kurt); my editor, Jami; and my husband, Marcin, who suffered through the early drafts so you didn't have to.

Thank you as well to William Burleson for sharing his knowledge of business things; to Scott Burtness for his insights into the world of indie publishing; and to Fran and Erica for their endless quest to purge my work of extraneous commas.

Finally, a huge thanks to Joseph Reedy, illustrator-slash-genius. Your art has really made this book come alive.

Please rate or review *The January Hours* on Amazon or Goodreads. For the latest news regarding future *Dead Mall* installments, visit www.sgtasz.com.

About the Author

S.G. Tasz is a graduate of Lawrence University in Appleton, Wisconsin. Previous writing credits include the web series *Chic*, the award-winning 48-hour Film Project "A Fairly Normal Love Story," and several pieces of short fiction. In addition to plotting the *Dead Mawl* gang's next adventure, she is also working on her debut novel, an excerpt for which was the top selection for the 2019 Writer's Bloc Anthology. She lives in Las Vegas with her husband, two cats, and a turtle.

About the Illustrator

Joseph Reedy is an artist based out of Madison, Wisconsin primarily working in the video game and music industries. He also pets lots of doggos.

www.ingramcontent.com/pod-product-compliance
Lightning Source LLC
Chambersburg PA
CBHW020228110726
47898CB00004B/1187